Harbour Falls

S.R. Grey

This is a work of fiction. Names, characters, places, and incidents are products of the author's imagination or are used fictitiously and are not considered to be real. Any resemblance to actual events, locales, organizations, or persons, living or dead, is entirely coincidental.

Harbour Falls (A Harbour Falls Mystery I)
Copyright © 2012 by S.R. Grey

All rights reserved. No part of this book may be used or reproduced in any manner whatsoever without written permission, except in the case of brief quotations embodied in critical articles and reviews.

Copy Editing by Barbara at Create Space
Cover Design by Damonza at Awesome Book Covers
Print and Ebook Formatting by Benjamin Carrancho at Awesome Book Layouts

ISBN-13: 978-0615700298
ISBN-10: 0615700292

Chapter 1

Sitting in the idling car in the deserted and rain-drenched parking lot on tiny Cove Beach in Harbour Falls, I absently turned a business card over and over in my hands. Fingertips over smooth, heavy cardstock, with raised, royal-blue printing on one side...

Harbour Falls Realtors
Northern Maine Coastal Properties
Ami Dubois-Hensley
Agent

Phone numbers and an e-mail address. And to the left of *Harbour*, a simple company logo: a lighthouse.

With an edge of a fingernail free of polish, I traced the outline of the design. It was meant to be a representation of my destination today: a mass of land out there in the churning waters bearing the ominous name of Fade Island. Heavy fogs, quite common in this tucked-away corner of northern Maine, often swallowed up the island—giving the illusion of it "fading" into the sea.

Suddenly the rain intensified without warning. Sheeting off the windshield in thick bands of water, my view of the ink-colored waves crashing along the beach blurred. I leaned forward to turn the wiper control up a notch and caught my refection in the rearview mirror. Wow, this perpetual dampness was really wreaking havoc on my long hair. I smoothed the unruly strands back into place as best as I could and noticed the California sun-kissed highlights, always so evident in my natural honey-brown shade, were already fading. Just like the island in the fog.

I'd only been back a few days, but life as I knew it felt slippery, like it could get away from me if I let my guard down. I adjusted the mirror; uncertainty warred with determination in the hazel eyes—so like my father's—staring back at me. Questions that had haunted me since I'd first decided to return home washed over me anew. *Why had I really come back to Harbour Falls? Just how dangerous could it end up being? Should I turn around and go back...before it turned out to be too late?*

But it was too late. A white SUV had just pulled to a stop and parked in the space to the right of my car. Ami Dubois—or rather Ami Dubois-*Hensley*—opened the driver's side door. As she began to fumble with one of those oversized golf umbrellas, it was clear, despite her seated position and long raincoat, that she was very pregnant. Guess she and Sean Hensley, friends of mine from the past, had decided it was finally time to start a family. Truthfully, it surprised me they'd waited this long.

Five years had passed since I'd last seen Sean and Ami, having attended their wedding in Harbour Falls. At the time we'd all been twenty-two years old and freshly graduated from college—me from Yale, and Sean and Ami from the University of Maine.

How time flew.

A twinge of sorrow tugged at my heart as I recalled how their wedding was the first major event I'd attended with Julian, a man with whom I ended up spending six years of my life. Of course we'd just been starting out back then. And now it was all over. Back in May we'd decided to go our separate ways. People change over time, sometimes drifting in different directions without ever realizing it. Until it's too late.

Ami's sudden rap on my driver's side window tore me from my ruminations. I yanked at the belt of the black trench coat I was wearing, tightening it, as the thin material of the wrap dress I wore underneath would offer little respite from the cold and rain.

I opened the car door, and Amy, stepping back, smiled

warmly and tilted the umbrella so I could slip underneath it. "Maddy, it's been too long. God, how have you been?"

"Good," I replied. "Just trying to adjust to this weather."

Her pale blue eyes scanned down my form. "Well, you look *amazing*. I was so excited when Mayor Fitch…uh, I mean, your dad called and said you were moving back."

Somehow balancing the umbrella in such a way as to keep us dry, she pulled me in for an awkward one-armed hug. Her swollen tummy pressed against my slender frame for a moment, until she drew away.

"It's great to see you too," I said. "But I'm not moving back permanently, you know. It's just for a few months." To keep the conversation from delving into exactly *why* I was back for such a specific amount of time, I motioned to her stomach. "Congratulations, by the way. My dad didn't say anything about—"

"Oh, Maddy, I am *so* excited," Ami interrupted. "Only one more month."

She rubbed her stomach, her hand gliding over the big, clear buttons on her powder-blue raincoat. Standing there—ash-blond hair cascading down her shoulders in big, bouncy curls and a smile as vibrant as ever—Ami radiated happiness.

I'd forgotten how pretty she was, and pregnancy certainly agreed with her. Truly pleased for my once dear friend, I said, "How's Sean? Thrilled, I bet."

"*Very.*"

"Do you know if you're having a boy or a girl?"

"Um, no." Ami hesitated and pressed her lips together. She took an inordinate amount of time to adjust the umbrella to block the swirling winds that were starting to kick up all around us, and added flatly, "We'd rather be surprised."

"Oh," I said slowly, "OK."

An awkward silence ensued, and we both watched as a fast-food wrapper of some sort blew by us. It adhered to the trunk of my car, and Ami reached to snatch it up. "Nice car," she murmured, crumpling the wrapper in her palm and dragging a finger through the beading raindrops. "Sean would love a BMW."

There was something in her tone, something that made me

feel self-conscious. Being a best-selling author of several novels allowed me to enjoy perks, such as my burgundy M3, back in Los Angeles. Flashy sports cars were a dime a dozen in California. But I'd forgotten, the people from this part of my life remembered me best as quiet, unassuming Madeleine Fitch— daughter of beloved and low-key widower, Mayor William V. Fitch.

"Thanks," I mumbled as I shifted away, shivering as icy raindrops began to pelt the back of my head.

Ami stuffed the crumpled wrapper in her raincoat pocket and said, "Uh, we should start over to the ferry. Jennifer is expecting us by two." And just like that, everything was back to normal.

Jennifer Weston and her cousin, Brody, owned the only two passenger ferries that operated out of Cove Beach. During the summer, in addition to the usual service, the Westons offered whale-watching excursions, usually for tourists passing through on the much less-traveled route to Canada. Or sometimes folks would venture up from Bar Harbor to explore this quiet little area, since it was relatively close. Not to mention somewhat infamous. But now that we were well into September, there'd be no whale watchers, no curiosity seekers. The ferries would be used strictly as transportation between Harbour Falls and my destination today, Fade Island.

A rocky and rugged landmass, mostly covered in thick, impenetrable forests, the island was located several miles from the mainland. While the eastern half remained untouched wilderness, the western half had seen its share of development over the years. Long ago a tiny fishing village had sprung up near the docks, and several Cotswold-style cottages were built to house the fishermen and their families.

Over time those early settlers dispersed, and the state had the cottages converted into rental properties. When I was growing up in Harbour Falls, it was not uncommon for families to spend at least a part of their summer vacation over on Fade Island. But I'd never been there. Not once. Eventually, as the residents of Harbour Falls expanded their vacation horizons, fewer and fewer people came to the island, and the cottages soon fell into disrepair.

But all that changed a few years back when the state of Maine sold the island to a private party. Almost immediately money poured in. The little fishing town was renovated, giving it a quirky, art deco uplift. The rental cottages were refurbished and made modern but in such a way as to retain their charm.

And a former resident of Harbour Falls—a man named Adam Ward—had a huge home in the style of Frank Lloyd Wright built overlooking the sea on the northern end of the island. Really it was more like a compound, complete with a private dock, a set of garages, even an airfield. It was hard to believe I'd once gone to school with the guy.

I had searched and searched to see if Adam had been the person who'd bought the island. It made sense, with the fancy home and all. But I came up empty-handed. The real estate transaction I culled from public records listed only a limited liability company with a bogus name as the owner. And the bogus name led me back to Harbour Falls Realtors but not to Adam. So the owner wished to remain anonymous. That was fine with me. I was tired of running around in circles.

One thing I knew for certain: Ami, as an agent of Harbour Falls Realtors, handled the business of renting out the cottages to a now-steady stream of wealthy summer vacationers looking for a private retreat. But Ami had no idea, in my case, she was about to rent to someone with a secret reason for wanting to stay on Fade Island.

It wasn't the peace and solitude touted in the online brochure that I sought. Nor did I have a desire to just hang out in a nicely renovated cottage. Not even that picturesque lighthouse depicted on Ami's business card, and located on the far southeastern tip of the island, held any appeal. Many a painter and photographer had traveled to the island to capture the image of the tall, imposing structure that harkened back to days past. Positioned at the end of a rocky peninsula and standing sentry in the shadow of a curved shelf of steep, jutting cliffs, the lighthouse was an artist's dream, even if it was no longer in use. But

I wasn't here for that either.

No, I was much more intrigued by something the brochure failed to mention: the huge, private estate overlooking the sea on the *other* end of the island. To be more precise, I was intrigued by the sole occupant of that estate, the former Harbour Falls resident, Adam Ward. In fact, I'd purposely chosen the cottage closest to his home as the one I wished to view.

My father told Ami I needed a quiet place to work through a bad case of writer's block. But that was far from the truth. Only he—and my agent, Katie—knew the real reason behind my wanting to spend these autumn months on a lonely, isolated island. It had *everything* to do with researching the subject matter for my next book and absolutely nothing to do with some silly, made-up case of writer's block.

And my research had begun before I'd even arrived. For example, I knew there were only four year-round residents on Fade Island, as it was not the most hospitable place once the summer faded into fall. Heavy rains and storms were common throughout most of the year, but things became particularly treacherous during the winter months.

Snowstorms and loss of power were not uncommon. And there was no reliable way to get off the island, except for the ferry. But the ferry didn't run when the weather got too crazy. Nothing did, not even the alternative means of transportation—several boats and a corporate jet—that Mr. Ward often employed. During those times Fade Island lived up to its name in another way; it was as if it faded from civilization.

The rain slowed to a fine mist as we approached the ferry, and Ami lowered the umbrella. "So who can I expect to see once we get over there?" I asked and then added, "Like, who lives out there year-round?"

Obviously I was well aware of the identities of the full-time residents. I thought I was being clever, feigning ignorance for Ami's benefit. The less she knew *I* knew, the more likely she'd not question my cover story. Right? Maybe not.

I took one look at her face and wished I'd kept my mouth shut. "You don't know? You've never heard?" She eyed me skeptically. "Surely, your father told you."

I shook my head and looked away. A slender, pale girl with dark hair was messing with some ropes aboard the ferry, so I pretended to be focused on her.

But when I tried to keep on walking, Ami stopped and grabbed my arm. I couldn't meet her gaze, certain she'd catch on to my deception. "Madeleine! You *have* to know Adam Ward lives on the island. It's no secret he moved out there after..." She lowered her voice. "Well, after what happened."

She was right; it was no secret. Back when Adam lived in Harbour Falls, he had everything, the world at his feet. A brilliant mind, he excelled in all things academic. But software engineering was his specialty. He coded and developed elaborate software systems that had every college and university with a computer engineering program vying for his commitment to study at their institution. And since his academic abilities were rivaled only by his athletic prowess, those schools with a football program offered Adam everything they could without attracting the attention of the NCAA. In the end, though, he gave up football and enrolled at MIT.

All those things were impressive, but what had caught my attention back then were his striking good looks. He was tall and had an amazing body, gorgeous jet-black hair, and stunning blue eyes. Yeah, it had been hard not to notice him. And notice him I did. But, sadly, he never seemed to look my way.

"Maddyyyy! Earth to Maddy." Ami waved her hand in front of my face.

"Oh, sorry. I was just...I was just remembering," I stammered, "um, high school."

Ami had once been one of my best friends, and surely she recalled my unrequited interest in Mr. Ward. As if on cue, she smiled knowingly and said, "In case you were maybe wondering, he *is* still single."

I barked out a nervous laugh. "We're not in high school, Ami. I think my crushing days are behind me. Besides..." I trailed off.

She knew why. After all, everyone had heard the rumors.

"They're just unfounded accusations and idle gossip," Ami said in a hushed voice, her defense of Adam surprisingly fervent. "You know that, right?"

"It's really not that." And it wasn't, but I didn't want to explain myself to Ami. "It's just…" I fumbled for an explanation. "I didn't come here to start something with Adam Ward, OK?" *Small lie.*

Ami cast a doubtful glance my way, but before she could persist in her matchmaking attempt, I pointed to the ferry and said, "It's after two. We'd better get going."

The half-hour ride through the choppy waters to Fade Island was mostly silent, Ami and I lost in our own thoughts. Jennifer Weston, the slender, pale girl who'd been messing with the ropes, didn't say anything more to us than she absolutely had to. A number of times when I glanced over at the ferry pilot's house, I caught her glaring at me. But I had no idea why.

Before today I'd never had contact with her. She'd gone to school at Harbour Falls High but graduated a few years before me. Still, I knew who she was. How could I not? Jennifer had been married for two years to my other best friend back in high school, J.T. O'Brien. I hadn't kept in touch with J.T. after leaving Harbour Falls, but I heard a lot about him from my dad. And what he told me wasn't good.

A few years back, J.T. had gotten into trouble with the law—some kind of drug and alcohol charge. After a stint in rehab, he surprised everyone by marrying Jennifer. She'd always had a thing for J.T., but he'd never shown any interest in her. So when they ran off to Vegas for a quickie wedding, nobody could figure out why. My father said there was speculation that she'd gotten knocked up. But nine months came…and went…with no baby.

All of this occurred during the spring and summer before my final year at Yale. At the time I was interning at a publishing house in New York, so I didn't pay too much attention to the updates from home. When I returned to college that fall, I met Julian. And once we were together, I hardly kept up with the Harbour Falls gossip. Following a quick visit back for Ami and Sean's wedding the following summer, Julian and I moved to Los Angeles. I embarked on my writing career, and soon my life was too busy to worry about people from my past. Except for the occasional, short holiday visit home, this whole area had fallen off my radar completely.

Well, maybe not *completely*.

There was one huge Harbour Falls Mystery—as the press had dubbed it—I could not avoid hearing about. The story even dominated the national news for a time. And inevitably, mostly on book tours and during interviews, I was asked for *my* thoughts regarding the case. I imagined people were curious for two reasons. One, I was from Harbour Falls, a primary location involved in the mystery. And two, I was a crime and mystery novelist, and the facts of the case mirrored the kinds of things I wrote about.

Only my cases were purely fictional, so my standard response had always been the same: *I have no interest in real-life cases*. And that had been true. But it no longer was; things were about to change.

The Harbour Falls Mystery was the real reason I was here. I had every intention of basing my next novel on the facts of the case. I was tired of fiction; I wanted to write a true crime novel. Plus there was a little part of me—the detective that lurks in all of us—that dreamed of *solving* this case.

But nobody knew that this case held more than a professional interest for me. Not because the main locale was Harbour Falls, and not because the mystery involved the disappearance of a local I'd once known. And, truth be told, had once envied. Nor was it the fact that this local, Chelsea Hannigan, had gone missing the night before her wedding. Scandalous, though it was.

What piqued my curiosity was the man Chelsea had been on the verge of marrying—Adam Ward. He was the man at the center of the mystery. He was the man whose life had been altered when Chelsea disappeared, after he was named as the number one suspect.

What role, if any, had he played in her disappearance?

Though never formally charged, many believed he was far from innocent.

Well I was here to uncover the truth. There was just one small problem. Contrary to what I'd told Ami, I *was* interested in Adam Ward. Still. Despite how ridiculous I knew it was, I couldn't wait to run into Adam. Would he even remember me? Maybe not. But I wasn't the shy girl I'd been back then.

Of course I was playing with fire. If he ever suspected I was investigating him in order to research my new novel, he'd hardly be pleased. I might even see firsthand just how supposedly dangerous he could be.

At the thought, a little shudder ran through me. Whether it was due to fear, excitement, or both, I wasn't sure. I knew I should analyze it and get my head straight before I ended up in trouble.

But I'd run out of time. Because the fog began to lift, and in the distance, Fade Island came into view.

Chapter 2

Jennifer Weston secured the ferry to an old, weatherworn dock on the southwest side of Fade Island. A lobster boat—looking a little worse for wear—bobbed in the water a few yards away. I shot a questioning look at Ami, and she shrugged, "Probably a fisherman stopping for a cup of coffee."

"Coffee?" I questioned. I'd expected the island to be mostly deserted this time of year. But before she had a chance to explain, Jennifer reappeared, holding her hand out to help Ami disembark.

The light mist of rain that had been falling since we'd left Cove Beach continued, but over here the wind was *much* fiercer. Hair lashed at my face as I stepped up the aluminum rungs to reach the dock. Jennifer waited, arms crossed. And just as she'd done on the ride over, she was glaring at me.

I didn't appreciate her uncalled-for attitude, so I rolled my eyes at her and stepped out onto the dock unassisted. Unfortunately the wood was slippery from the rain, and I nearly lost my footing. *Maybe heels weren't such a brilliant idea today.*

Jennifer's hand shot out to steady me. But instead of a light grasp, she dug her fingers into the material of my trench coat, squeezing my upper arm. I tried to twist away, but she tightened her grip in response and leaned close to my ear, hissing, "Go back to California where you belong, Fitch, before you end up getting hurt. Or worse."

What the—?

I wrenched my arm just as she let go and nearly fell, again. Walking forward without looking back, I mumbled "Bitch," to myself. I also made a mental note to find out as much as I could about Jennifer Weston. All I knew was that her parents had turned the ferry business over to her years ago, before they moved down to Florida. Maybe J.T. would talk to me about her? I hadn't seen him in years, but it was worth a try. Why had he ever married her? Little wonder they were divorced.

Ami was already way ahead, standing next to a sleek, black luxury sedan that looked remarkably similar to the car Adam Ward had once driven in high school. *Weird.* Ami had mentioned all of the cottages included an automobile for the tenant to use to travel about the island. Maybe this one, a Lexus, was going to be mine? Did that mean the cottage I was about to view—and possibly rent—was owned by Adam? Did he own *all* the cottages then? Maybe he'd just donated the car? From what I'd read, he could certainly afford such an act of generosity.

Picking up the pace, I caught up with Ami just as she was opening the car door on the driver's side. "What the hell is the Weston girl's problem with me?" I complained, still shaken by Jennifer's actions and hoping for a little compassion from my former friend. "So much for a warm welcome back."

"Try not to take it personally, Maddy. She's always like that," Ami said, her tone unusually dismissive.

Ooo-kay, I thought as we got into the car.

"By the way, this car comes with the cottage I'll be showing you today." *Guess that answers that question.* But I just could not bring myself to ask if this car was the same one Adam had once driven. I also nixed the compulsion to elaborate on the veiled threat Jennifer had whispered to me. Ami didn't seem willing to discuss it anyway. It was probably better to keep as many people out of my troubles as possible, especially my clueless, very pregnant, and once-upon-a-time best friend.

Ami pressed the gas pedal, and we surged up a steep, paved grade leading away from the blacktop parking lot. We turned left onto a neat and tidy cobblestone lane. The misty rain had abated but not the winds. A decorative brass sign with letters spelling out *Main Street* oscillated atop a fluted post on the corner. We drove by and slowly made our way along Main Street.

Colorful, two-story storefronts stood on both sides of the road: a teal-blue hardware store, a general store painted the color of a freshly unfurled spring leaf, a store selling candy—the pink exterior a perfect match to the bubble gum advertised on a placard in the window. All the businesses were closed for the season. The proprietors, who generally lived in the second-floor apartments, had gone back over to the mainland. We passed darkened building after darkened building until we reached the last one on the left.

A cute, olive-colored affair with a paned picture window and an awning big enough to shelter patrons from the rain was not closed. The scalloped front edge of the dark green awning flapped erratically in the wind, intermittently obscuring the bright white lettering that read: *Café*. The lights inside blazed. Aha, this was where the fisherman with the lobster boat would be procuring his coffee.

"Why's that one not closed for the season?" I asked Ami, pointing to a small sign in the window that was turned to the side that proclaimed it was *open*.

"Nate's wife, Helena, keeps it open year-round. She runs the place. The fishermen passing by the island appreciate a place where they can stop and grab a cup of coffee. Besides, there are always people going back and forth, even during the off-season." Ami slowed to a crawl. "The café is also where you'll pick up your mail. It comes over every weekday on the ferry. And you can order groceries through Nate and Helena. I don't know if your dad told you, but Nate's the manager of Fade Island."

I nodded absently, because I *had* already heard that from my dad. And I found it odd. Nate had been almost as adept as Adam at things like computer programming and software development. In fact, I recalled a time that together they'd hacked into the school computers and changed all the grades. So why was Nate just "managing" this island? Or was it some kind of cover?

Ami cleared her throat and, in a worried voice, asked, "You do remember Nate and Helena from high school, right?"

"Of course I remember them," I replied.

And I did. Quite well in fact. In addition to his skill with all things computer-related, Nate had been the star quarterback for the football team—big, muscular, mocha-colored skin, amiable brown eyes. Yeah, he was a good-looking guy. And one of the nicest. I remembered him always trying to make me laugh. He had a legendary sense of humor.

Back then and apparently now, based on their close proximity, Nate and Adam had been best friends. And they'd been teammates. With cheering crowds of Harbour Falls residents—myself included—Nate Jackson had thrown many a winning touchdown to his top wide receiver, Adam Ward.

Helena, who had dated Nate since sophomore year, was his perfect match—friendly and fun to be around. With her model-like looks—beautiful, long legs, blonde hair, and big, expressive blue eyes—it would have been easy to hate her. But quite the opposite was true; everyone adored her. In fact, she and Nate were voted "Most Perfect Couple" senior year.

But things were far from perfect for Helena. Following her parents' particularly unpleasant divorce, her mother met and married what seemed like the first guy who came along. Helena was just fourteen. At first her new stepdad appeared to be an average guy in almost every way: average looks, average build, average job. He even had an average name, Ron. He was the kind of guy people passed on the street and forgot about a second later.

But Ron's anger wasn't average. He had a violent temper, and before long the whole town bore witness to the bruises his rages left on Helena and her mother. After all, even the best makeup doesn't always conceal a black eye.

Thankfully, during her freshman year away at college, Helena's stepdad left her mom, taking off for places unknown with no explanation. The general sentiment was *good riddance*. At the time Helena had been attending the University of Maine with Ami. In fact, she and Ami shared not just a dorm but a room as well.

At the end of freshman year, though, Helena quit college and moved down to Massachusetts to be closer to Nate. He was attending, and playing football for, Boston College. They were married in a small, private ceremony shortly thereafter. And that was it. I'd heard nothing more. It was strange to think that they'd ended up living out here on secluded Fade Island. Something to look into, for sure.

Ami resumed her slow crawl up toward the northern boundary of Main Street, to where it turned into a paved, two-lane road twisting through the forest on the west side of the island.

Ami was pointing to an olive-colored bungalow adjacent to the café, so I focused my attention back on the here and now.

"That's Nate and Helena's house," she said.

The home was fairly large, with an elaborately landscaped front lawn. "But Helena spends most of the day at the café," Ami continued. "If you're trying to catch her, always check there before you go anywhere else. She's almost always there."

Another bungalow, this one smaller and also painted olive-green, sat directly across from Nate and Helena's. "Who lives there?" I asked.

"Max," Ami replied. "He was in the military a while back, did a few tours of duty. But now he handles security here on the island."

"Is he a police officer for Harbour Falls then?" I asked, knowing Fade Island, though privately owned, still fell under the Harbour Falls jurisdiction.

"Uh, I think so," Ami answered, picking up speed. "I don't know all the details of his qualifications or whatever. But he provides security for the island, its residents, and any visitors."

Spoken like a true real estate agent. *Uh-huh*, I thought, *sure*. It sounded more to me like "security for the island" was code for "security for Adam Ward." But I let it drop.

Thinking of Adam, I asked, "Hey, wasn't Helena friends with Chelsea at one time? Isn't that how Adam originally met her?"

The car bucked as Ami wavered on the gas. "Um, I *think* that's how they met. I'm not exactly sure." For whatever reason, she seemed irritated. "But, to be honest, I wouldn't ask too many questions about Chelsea around here." *Around here?* Did she mean on the island or the entire area in general?

"Sure," I replied, hesitant to ask for elaboration for fear this line of conversation might lead to me blowing my cover.

Besides, I remembered plenty about Chelsea Hannigan. And really who could forget? She had attended a private school in Harbourtown, a neighboring town of Harbour Falls located a few miles inland. For as beautiful as Helena was, Chelsea had her beat. No contest. If Helena could be described as a model, then Chelsea was a supermodel.

Exquisitely styled, strawberry-blonde hair; endless legs; flawless skin; high cheekbones; eyes that were the most unusual shade of green. To many, Chelsea embodied perfection. Every female dreamed of having her body, and so did all the guys. Of course, both had vastly differing definitions of what "having" meant.

To top it all off, Chelsea was rich. Well, her family was. Sometimes she would pick Adam up at school in her father's Ferrari, and Adam's younger sister, Trina, would get stuck driving his car back home all alone.

This reminded me to ask, "Whatever happened to Trina?"

"She lives in Boston." Ami glanced over, probably wondering what was with all the questions.

But I continued, "What about their parents? Do they still live in town?"

Ami nodded, and I shot off another question, "I heard Dr. Ward retired as dean at Harbour Falls U and that he and Mrs. Ward travel all the time now. Is that true?"

Ami's eyebrows knitted together as she frowned. "Maddy, are you *sure* you're not still into Adam? 'Cause you sure are asking a lot of questions that have to do with him and his family."

"Yeah, I'm sure," I replied, a little too sharply. "I'm just trying to get caught up on all I've missed."

Ami didn't need to know getting "caught up" was an integral part of doing research for my next book. To be based on what had *really* happened to Chelsea Hannigan four years ago, the night before Chelsea was supposed to marry Adam Ward.

I had little doubt Ami would have further questioned my intentions, but we'd reached the property. *Thank God.*

As she crunched along the gravel driveway that ran along the side of the property, I maneuvered in my seat so I could see more clearly through the windshield.

The cottage, constructed primarily of gray flagstone, boasted a deep-sloping slate roof with a dark green-trimmed dormer window on the right. A prominent stone chimney bisected the façade of the house. Adorable and quaint were words that came to mind. A gable, painted the same deep shade of green as the trim on the dormer window, accented the area directly above the recessed wooden front door. Truth be told, I was taken with its charm.

Placing the car in park, Ami shifted in her seat and took a deep breath. "Look, I'm sorry if I acted weird before, when you mentioned Chelsea. I know you haven't been back in Harbour Falls for more than a few days, but there are some things we just don't discuss around here. Make sense?" *Oh, we're back to that.* She sat waiting for a response, so I nodded, thinking, *sure, whatever.*

Seemingly satisfied, Ami threw open the door. With more fanfare than seemed necessary, she huffed and puffed her way out of the driver's seat. Standing, she stretched and then popped her head back in. "Now come take a look at this incredible cottage. I just know you're gonna love it."

I got out while Ami fumbled around in the backseat gathering up paperwork. Ami may have been acting strangely, but as I stood on the cobbled walkway leading to the front door, the cottage felt *right*. I knew I'd be comfortable living in a house like this for the next few months. I suddenly wanted to bake cookies, curl up by the fireplace, read a book in one of the little nooks I was sure would be found inside. It emanated the kind of homey feel that made me want to nest.

We'd reached the door, but Ami was digging around in her bag looking for the house key. My eyes wandered to a flower box beneath a window next to the door. Filled with dark, rich soil but no flowers, I started to make plans. Immediately, white chrysanthemums came to mind. An autumn bloom I'd always loved, I could already see the white blooms contrasting beautifully with the deep green shade of the window box.

Ami held up the house key victoriously and said in a relieved voice, "God, I thought I lost it."

I followed her inside with a last, wistful look at the flower box. I made a mental note to ask Ami, before we parted ways, if she knew of a place where I could buy a couple potted white mums.

The next half hour flew by. With speed and efficiency, Ami whisked me from one beautifully decorated room to the next. Gleaming hardwood floors, warm and natural color schemes, a big bed covered in a fluffy down comforter. Oh, and the artwork on the walls. The angle, the treatment of light, the brush strokes—all beautiful works of Impressionist-style painters.

And then there was the spacious cedar closet upstairs, the soaking tub, the kitchen with the state-of-the-art appliances and a window above the sink with a view of a back yard that overlooked the ocean. My mind was reeling, my senses overloaded with texture, color, beauty.

We finished the grand tour, and Ami turned to me. She asked, "So what do you think?"

"You were right," I replied, breathless. "I absolutely love it."

Signing the necessary paperwork was quick and straightforward. As I flipped through the pages—signing at each of the designated *x*'s—I kept scanning for some kind of information that would reveal the identity of the owner of the property.

The header at the top of each page was the same as the one on Ami's business card, *Harbour Falls Realtors*. That really didn't tell me much, so I asked, "Do Harbour Falls Realtors own this cottage, or are they just in charge of the lease agreements?"

Ami hesitated, and then she started gathering some papers that were spread out on the oak table in the dining room. "Uh, they own all the cottages on the island," she answered, eyes averted.

I hastily signed the last page and stacked the contract pages into a neat pile. As I held them out, I asked, "Well, *who* owns

Harbour Falls Realtors?" After signing a lease agreement that was going to cost me a pretty penny for the next three months, I wasn't about to give up so easily.

"Maddy, I'm really not at liberty to say," she said quietly as she reached to take the contract without meeting my gaze.

For as much as she could read me, I knew her tells pretty well too. "Ami, come on." I pulled the contract back. "What are you not telling me?"

She glanced up, guilt etched across her face. I knew she was going to spill. "Can you promise me you can keep it a secret?"

I nodded. "Yes, yes, of course."

"Adam. Adam Ward owns Harbour Falls Realtors," Ami said, meeting my widened eyes. "And," she continued, "he owns just about everything on this island. In fact, Adam *owns* Fade Island. Like the entire island, Maddy."

I pulled out a chair and sat down. "Wow!"

I was truly speechless. I knew the Wards were a wealthy family. What with their long-standing ties to the local private university. And, of course, Adam had accrued a great deal of wealth of his own over the past several years. Hell, he was not just a computer genius; he was a very successful entrepreneur. And that was an understatement if ever there was one.

I'd perused all the financial magazines, reading all about how Mr. Ward amassed his vast fortune by designing and implementing elaborate and sophisticated security software programs for both domestic and international organizations. Supposedly some of it was really high-intrigue stuff—rumors abounded that some of his work even involved secret government contracts.

I didn't know about that—Lord knew there were enough rumors floating around about Adam—but I did know his fledgling company had just been gaining momentum back when he and Chelsea were planning to marry. After graduating at the top of his class at MIT, he'd moved back here to be close to his family. And presumably to Chelsea, since they'd gotten engaged in the spring before his senior year. Although talk back then indicated the relationship was strained.

After her disappearance the tales grew more sordid. Chelsea cheated on Adam while he was away at college, Chelsea dabbled in drugs, Chelsea led a secret life that she kept well hidden from her fiancé. One thing for certain, separating the truths from the fabrications wasn't going to be easy.

A fact that was not in dispute was that Adam and Chelsea had been planning on building a home in Harbourtown. But after she went missing, Adam moved out to Fade Island, where he spent a great deal of time traveling for work but otherwise kept to himself.

Now it made sense. Adam *owned* the island. Why not move out here to get away from the ugly accusations flying around? Focus on work instead of a missing woman. And, according to the financial magazines, Adam had poured every ounce of energy into his company after his fiancée's disappearance. In return his company grew exponentially, so much so that he was able to buy his own corporate jet and obtain a private pilot's license in his spare time. I imagined that made all that traveling that much easier.

But in all my research, I'd found nothing disclosing Adam Ward's apparently vast real estate holdings. Well, now I knew who was behind the limited liability company, who the person was who had wished to remain anonymous.

Ami appeared to be pleased she had shocked me into silence. "Impressive, right?" she said smugly. "Are you *sure* you're still not interested?"

I refrained from answering her ridiculous question, because I didn't want her to know the truth. Of course I was interested. But she didn't need to know that.

I reminded her that we had to be at the dock soon to catch the ferry back to Cove Beach before dark. I was dreading having to deal with the ill-tempered Jennifer again, so as Ami and I approached the dock, I was pleasantly surprised when I saw there was a guy at the helm. Something struck me as familiar as I scanned over his neatly trimmed red hair and muscular build.

Leaning toward Ami, I whispered, "Is that...?"

Before I finished my question, the man turned, and I instantly recognized my one-time friend J.T. O'Brien. He reached out to help me onto the ferry, smiling, and I returned his infectious grin. "Well, if it isn't Maddy Fitch gracing us with her presence. Welcome back."

"Thanks, J.T.," I replied, taking his outstretched hand. Once I was on the ferry, though, I had to pry my hand away from his sweaty, too-tight grasp. J.T. shot me an indecipherable look. On the surface he was still the same friendly guy I'd once known, but there was a cold, hard glint in his eyes that hadn't been there in the past. Confusion washed over me as I took a seat.

I watched as J.T. helped Ami onto the ferry, but he was nothing but careful and gentle with her. In that singular moment, he was exactly the same as he'd always been. Had I imagined his disdain? *It's been a long day; maybe I'm reading too much into it.*

On the way back to Cove Beach, J.T. attempted to make conversation as he piloted the ferry. He asked things like: What was it like being a best-selling novelist? *Like anything, there were good and bad points.* Did I ever miss Maine? *Not really, but I missed my dad.* And did I have a boyfriend? *No, not anymore.*

Following the last response, he turned to me and smiled in what could only be described as a flirtatious manner. His behavior was perplexing, as we'd never been more than just friends. He proceeded to wink lazily, and I quickly averted my eyes—but not before catching the flash of anger that crossed his expression. He turned away and was silent for the rest of the ferry ride back. Shaken, I glanced over at Ami to see if she'd caught any of this bizarre exchange, but she'd dozed off.

Dusk was upon us, blue-white flashes of lightning illuminating the sky directly above Fade Island. The only sounds were the hum of the ferry motor and the sloshing of the choppy waves all around us. Damp and cold, I questioned just what in the hell I was getting myself into. In need of some kind of comfort, I leaned into Ami, like old times, and closed my eyes. But I still couldn't shake the feeling that I'd stepped into the pages of one of my own novels…and that I was quickly becoming the doomed heroine.

The next day my dad helped me pack the clothes I'd brought from Los Angeles. He then followed me out to Cove Beach. Always one to think of everything, he'd planned ahead and rented out one of the garages located next to the ferry dock. "You'll still need your car for travel over here on the mainland," he reminded me. "This way it'll be close."

One thing I was especially curious about since yesterday evening was *why* J.T. had been piloting our return ferry. I was under the impression Jennifer and J.T.'s divorce had been less than amicable. Why would he still be involved with the Westons' business?

To my surprise, my dad informed me that J.T. actually owned half of the ferry service operation, a condition of the divorce settlement. Maybe that was part of the reason why Jennifer was so unpleasant? It couldn't be easy having to work every day with a man you loved who didn't love you in return.

I may have felt a little bad for her, but I was still less than thrilled when I saw she was going to be transporting me and my father over to the island. Around the mayor, however, her demeanor was vastly different. She made small talk with my dad and even offered me a hand, albeit reluctantly, off the ferry upon reaching the dock at Fade Island.

Turning up my nose, I made a point to stare straight ahead, ignore her outstretched hand, and disembark *without* her assistance.

The black sedan from yesterday was parked at the dock, and as promised Ami had left it unlocked, the keys under the driver's side floor mat. My father and I loaded my several bags and suitcases into the trunk. Our load included a big crate of bottled water and nonperishable food (mainly lots of energy bars) that my father had insisted I bring to hold me over until I had time to figure out the grocery-ordering system. I thought it unnecessary, since Ami had left detailed instructions back at the cottage, but I kept quiet. It was kind of adorable that he acted like I was moving onto a deserted island. Fade Island was isolated, but it wasn't like it lacked civilization.

After we were buckled in, I drove up the steep grade and made the left onto Main Street. We passed the tiny enclave of businesses, as well as the two olive-green bungalows, and then traveled the paved road that snaked its way along the lushness of the west side of the island. I imagined from above it looked like a snake winding through the grass.

Unlike the day before, today the sun was shining brightly and everything glowed in the afternoon light. Bright sunlight streamed through the foliage—just beginning to change from green to gold, orange, plum—and created a kaleidoscope of light on the road. Through the breaks in the trees, the blue ocean sparkled, a jewel off in the distance.

When we reached the last cottage, my dad helped carry everything into what was to be my home for at least the next three months—or however long it took to gather the necessary research to write my next novel. Fade Island was going to be the perfect location to conduct my own little investigation. It was quiet and private. And one of the main players, if not *the* main player in the Harbour Falls Mystery, lived less than one mile north of my new residence. The logistics were perfect.

After settling in, I walked into the living room. My father stood quietly, intently studying one of the impressionist-style paintings adorning the wall. The play of light coming through the window accentuated his salt-and-pepper hair, and it saddened me to see there was more salt than pepper. My dad stayed fit, but he was getting older. It scared me because he was all I had. My mother had passed away when I was a very young girl, and my only sibling, a much older brother, had left for college not long after. Over the years he visited occasionally, but he had his own new life in Chicago. So, for a long time, it had just been my dad and me.

I didn't want to spend my first day on the island being maudlin, so I plopped down on the sofa and flipped up the cap on one of the bottled waters we'd brought from home. My father wasn't *that* interested in art, so I asked, "Dad, is there something on your mind?"

"I'm just worried." He sighed, making his way to the sofa. I scooted over, and he sat down next to me. "Just don't get into any trouble out here, OK? Are you sure you want to start poking around in a case that's been cold for more than four years?" We'd been over this topic at least a dozen times since I'd been back. He knew I wanted my next novel to be based on the Harbour Falls Mystery. But he certainly had his misgivings. Not that I could blame him.

"I have to, Dad," I tried to explain. "I need to know what really happened so I can write my book." My dad looked away, and I added, "Hey, look on the bright side, maybe I'll end up solving it."

"Maddy." His voice sounded chastising but in a half-hearted way. "Just get what you need for your research. Forget about solving this thing." His eyes met mine. "And remember, I'll do anything I can to help."

"Were you able to get a copy of the case files?" I asked in a whisper.

I hated to push the issue, but I'd been secretly hoping he could pull a few strings and obtain a copy of the official documents pertaining to the Chelsea Hannigan disappearance. The files would give me a starting point, an insight into things that hadn't been revealed to the public. Anything related to the case had been sealed to preserve the integrity of the investigation, making it nearly impossible for an individual without *some* kind of political pull to get his hands on those files.

My father, attempting to sound stern once again but failing, said, "Madeleine, I'm not kidding about you staying out of trouble. There are people here who aren't going to take kindly to you asking questions about something most would rather forget."

Recalling Ami's words of warning, I conceded, "You're right. I'll watch my step." It was looking like I'd have to forge forward without the case files. I picked up one of the throw pillows on the sofa and rolled a loose string between my fingers. I'd make do.

"Look," my dad began. "I've thought about it a lot. You

should be armed with some kind of background on this case. The fewer chains you have to rattle, the better." I stopped picking at the loose string and looked up expectantly.

My dad harrumphed and said, "Why don't you take a look inside the zippered compartment there in the front of that suitcase?" He gestured to a bag we'd not unpacked.

I reached over, unzipped the front pocket, and pulled out a thick folder stuffed with pages and pages of official-looking documents. A big "Classified" sticker was affixed to the front. "The case files," I murmured.

"They're just copies, but keep them in a safe place, Maddy," he warned. "By safe I mean *hidden*."

I placed the folder on the coffee table and threw my arms around my father. "Thank you, Dad. These are going to help so much. And everything will be fine, you'll see."

My dad tightened his arms around me. Guilt tugged at my conscience as I sensed the tension in his hold. "I love you, sweetheart. I just pray you know what you're doing."

I hoped so too, but I didn't say it out loud. Instead I said, "I love you, Dad," and clung to the one person I could always count on.

Chapter 3

After I drove my dad back to the dock—and watched the ferry disappear in the distance—a feeling of loneliness washed over me. I drove down Main Street and slowed at the café storefront. *Should I go in?* A woman with blonde hair flowing down her back was seated at a table on the other side of the picture window in front. She glanced up as I drove the Lexus by at a snail's pace, and a look of recognition crossed her face. I was certain the blonde woman was Helena, but I wasn't sure if it was me—or the car—that she recognized, so I drove on.

Even though it was fast approaching late afternoon, the air remained warm, and the island was still bathed in sunshine. My loneliness was rapidly turning to restlessness, so I hit the gas and headed back to the cottage. The surrounding landscape went by in a blur, until, at last, I reached my new home and eased into the driveway.

After dropping the car keys into a wicker bowl on the coffee table, I paced around the living room, undecided as to what I felt like doing next. I kicked off my flats and picked up the thick case file folder from the coffee table, but I was feeling much too agitated to delve into its contents. Instead I looked around the room for a good place to hide the folder.

Bookcases, packed tight with numerous volumes of hardcover books, covered most of one wall of the room. I tucked the folder between two heavy tomes and stood back.

Perfect! The folder was indistinguishable mixed in among the books. Satisfied with the hiding spot I'd chosen, I went upstairs and slipped out of the slacks and blouse I was wearing, and then stepped into a cedar closet that was big enough to serve as a small guest room.

Thankful my dad had helped me unpack some clothing before leaving, I grabbed a white cotton tank top and a pair of navy yoga pants from one of the shelves. I slipped the clothes on and then proceeded to rummage through a still-packed satchel. I mouthed a victorious "yes" when I finally located a pair of running shoes near the bottom. A hair tie had somehow ended up in one of the shoes, so I grabbed it, too, and secured my hair into a high ponytail.

I hurried back down the stairs, locked up, and went out the back door. The small lawn in the back, perched high above the sea, offered a sweeping view of the ocean below. It was magnificent, if not a little daunting when nearing the edge. Several maple saplings lined the south end of the yard, their fiery red, orange, and yellow leaves made more vivid by a palette of violet hues in the early evening sky.

I turned toward the north end of the lawn where the forest trees were no less vibrant—but much taller and imposing—than their younger counterparts across the property. There was a break in the tree line where a dirt path winded its way through the forest. It appeared to head north along the high cliffs above the sea.

I rocked back and forth on my heels, contemplating my next move. *No time like the present for a little exploring, right?*

I glanced back at the cottage, tucked my house key into a small pocket in my pants, and then started to jog along the path. I considered going back to grab my IPod but quickly squashed the idea. As I headed deeper and deeper into the woods, the sounds of birds chirping, the crashing of the waves on the rocks below, and my own footfalls lulled me into a sense of peacefulness. A sort of zone. Soon I completely lost track of time.

Darkness crept in, the birds silenced. The trees closed in on me like a crowd closing in on a guilty party. Low-hanging branches scraped at my bare arms, making me cry out. My pulse raced as my dad's words echoed in my mind: *Just don't get into any trouble out here, OK?*

Yeah, that was going well. Just as panic began to set in, I

spotted an end to the trail. Breathing a sigh of relief, I sprinted ahead to escape the blackness of the forest. *Maybe I'll come out on the main road,* I thought.

But that was asking too much. The trail dumped me out onto a luxurious, meticulously manicured piece of property that very obviously belonged to Adam Ward. And here I was, the newest resident on the island—*his island*—trespassing on his private property. *Not exactly subtle.*

A huge wood and stone contemporary home, with a low-pitched roof and endless walls of windows, stood before me. The house was nestled in the forest, but the surrounding trees were not nearly as dense as the ones I'd just traveled through. A few lights were on inside, and a black Porsche was parked outside the front entrance. *Shit, that means he's most likely home. This is definitely bad.*

The driveway curved off into another portion of the woods. I was sure it led to the main road, but I had no way of knowing how far I'd have to travel to reach it. The idea of getting caught traipsing down Adam's driveway was appalling. But so was the thought of going back into the heart of the forest. To make matters worse, the air had grown chilly now that the sun was down. I wrapped my arms around myself and bounced up and down on my toes to keep warm. I knew I couldn't stand here forever staring at Adam's house—like some kind of a crazed stalker—so I decided to make a run for the driveway, crossing my fingers that I'd not get caught.

Just as I was about to step out of the darkness of the trees, the front door of the house opened, and the man I'd hoped to avoid—Adam Ward—walked out. I took a step back and stood frozen as I watched him descend the front steps, walking—no, *striding*— to his Porsche.

Tall and still lean but definitely more muscular. A man now, no longer a boy. Dressed in faded jeans and a pale blue button-down, untucked with the sleeves casually rolled up his forearms, he made his way to his car. The soft lights emanating from his home illuminated his slightly tousled raven hair, but his face remained shadowed. He retrieved a briefcase from the passenger side of the car, and then he straightened, the light hitting him in just the right way. *Oh my.* My memory had *not* done him justice, he was much...hotter. Still as gorgeous as ever with the same strong jaw, aquiline nose, full lips, but there was something more. Something indefinable, something feral that called to my basest instincts like a siren song.

A loud, cracking noise—like a branch breaking—came from the woods behind me, and I was reminded of the situation at hand. Adam had been on his way back into the house, but now he stopped and looked in my direction. My heart pounded fiercely; I feared it could be heard. Holding my breath and squeezing my eyes shut for a beat, I desperately prayed Adam would just go back in the damn house, so I could make my escape.

The seconds crept by slowly, and finally Adam relaxed his posture. He started back up the front steps, his stride as cool and confident as ever. As he disappeared behind the closing door, I let out my breath in a big whoosh of air. *That was close.*

Then, with no warning, a large, calloused hand closed over my mouth. My scream was effectively muffled, and I promptly lost consciousness.

I woke up feeling, strangely enough, warm and comfortable. Snuggling deeper into the surface I was laying on, so buttery soft, I inhaled deeply. A spicy, masculine aroma, with just a hint of laundry detergent, filled my nose. I pulled the source of this appealing scent—some kind of fabric draped over my shoulder—to my face and drank it in.

A soft chuckle came from behind my curled-up form. My eyes flew open. I stared blankly at the pale blue material—a shirt of some sort—in my hand. *What the?*

All at once the events of the evening came back to me in a rush of jumbled images. I quickly rolled away from the back of the black leather sofa I was on and almost tumbled to the floor. Sitting up abruptly, the shirt fell to my lap.

Embarrassment tore through me as I realized the soft laughter had come from the last person I cared to see at the moment—

Adam Ward. Seated across from me in an overstuffed black leather chair, he was shirtless and smirking, his jean-clad legs propped up casually on a mahogany wood coffee table situated between us.

"W-where am I?" I stammered, glancing around a living room lit only by the warm glow of a crackling fire in a soaring stone fireplace. My feet rested on a Persian rug, pigmented in rich shades of chocolate and claret. I had no doubt it was a genuine.

I looked up, and Adam raised an eyebrow. *Pay attention, Maddy. You're obviously in the house of the person whose property you were trespassing on.*

"I mean," I hastily corrected, "what happened? How did I end up here?" A chill ran through me as I recalled the calloused hand covering my mouth before everything flashed black.

Adam raked his fingers through his messy hair. There was something insanely sensual about the way his long fingers lingered in the silky, dark strands; the way his eyes, blue but stormy, studied me. "Shouldn't I be asking *you* that question, Madeleine?"

As crazy as it was, in that moment, all I could think was: *Well, I guess he remembers me from high school.*

My fingers absently traced the collar of the blue shirt—his shirt—while I tried to think of a plausible explanation. I glanced over at Adam, his eyes taking in the lazy movement of my hand and then traveling up to my too-thin tank. Unapologetic, he met my gaze, and his mouth turned up into a wickedly suggestive smile. I stilled, suddenly feeling incredibly warm but definitely overexposed. I struggled to arrange the damn blue shirt in such a way as to cover myself, while Adam looked on with amusement.

My mind screamed danger, but my body began to feel alive in a way that had been dormant for far too long. God, the sinful thoughts this man evoked. I needed to get a grip, but no. Unable, or maybe unwilling, to stop myself, I involuntarily licked my lips and allowed my eyes to wander over the unclothed parts of his body—the curves of his biceps, the impressive breadth of his broad shoulders, the expanse of his bare chest. My gaze descended to the perfectly shaped *v* of his torso, down to his hips, and just kind of lingered there.

Adam cleared his throat. Quickly, I looked away, questioning my sanity. Had I hit my head when I fainted?

"Madeleine." Adam's voice was low and seductive, served up with maybe a hint of jest. "If you were looking for *that*, you should have just rung the doorbell."

Could this get any more embarrassing? Clearly this was all some sort of a game to him. Certainly he'd been made aware that this was my first day on the island—*his* damn island. Yet he allowed some kind of henchman of his to scare the living daylights out of me. All due to the fact I'd dared to step onto his precious property. Never mind I'd been trespassing and, really, kind of spying.

The *most* enraging part, though, was that I was so, so madly attracted to Adam—even after all these years. But sitting there so cool and calm, he was having far too much fun at my expense. So I retaliated in the only way I could think of, I balled up the blue shirt and threw it at him.

Adam began to laugh, blue eyes no longer stormy. Now they sparkled like ocean water rippling under the sun, much like this afternoon. He caught the shirt with one hand. "It was just a joke," he said. "But I am curious as to why you were out in the woods watching me."

"I got lost. I went for a run and ended up here," I explained. "It's the truth, no matter how bad it looks." And it mostly was.

I folded my arms defiantly over my chest, and Adam lowered his legs from the coffee table and leaned forward. He fluffed out the blue shirt I'd thrown and slipped it on. "Fair enough," he said.

I mumbled something about how a person couldn't even take a stroll through the woods around here without getting accosted, and Adam, apparently possessing exceptional hearing to go along with his many other fine attributes, said, "For the record, Max never intended to frighten you so badly. He was merely doing his job."

"Oh, Max, the security guy for the *island*?" I retorted sarcastically. I'd already suspected Max's top priority was keeping Mr. Ward safe, and this just proved it.

Adam didn't acknowledge my sarcasm. Instead he hesitated and then said in a quiet voice, "You know, you've changed a lot since high school."

I almost laughed. *I'd* changed? I felt like saying, *"Seriously?"* But I went with the more benign, "Haven't we all?"

I wasn't sure where *this* turn in the conversation might possibly lead, so best to tread carefully.

"Yeah, I guess that's true," Adam sighed. "Unfortunately not all of us have changed for the better." His voice now laced with bitterness, he looked away. Maybe this was the *real* Mr. Ward—bitter. It was kind of sad.

Feeling the need to lighten the mood, I quipped, "Well, you've certainly done very well for yourself." I motioned around the room like a game show hostess. *Oh God, Maddy, stop now!*

"I guess it depends on one's perspective," Adam said distractedly, while finally getting around to buttoning his shirt. "But I appreciate the sentiment nonetheless."

"It's true though," I muttered to myself.

Adam leaned back in the chair. Gone was the playful, naughty man who had made me feel so frustrated and angry. But, in all honesty, he'd also reminded me I could be desirable to someone. Maybe even desirable to him.

"We should probably get you back to the cottage," he said, waylaying my train of thought. "It's getting late."

"Yeah, probably," I agreed.

Adam drove me back to my cottage in his Porsche. And what a ride it was. Between the short distance and his lead foot, we reached the driveway in what had to be a new time for the record books.

Once I recovered from the impromptu Indy 500 experience, I said, "Well, thank you for driving me back, and I truly am sorry for trespassing on—"

"Maddy, don't be foolish. I'm the one who should be

apologizing. I knew you were moving onto the island today. I shouldn't have been so suspicious when you wandered onto my property." He paused, smiled knowingly, and then added, "After all, you were probably just taking a little stroll to get started on clearing that *writer's block*, yes?"

His eyes met mine in the eerie glow of the instrument panel, and it was impossible to discern if he was joking. Or not. "Um, yeah, exactly," I said shakily, while nodding profusely.

He didn't seem to be buying the writer's block story. I only hoped he hadn't caught on to the *real* reason I was on the island.

"Yeah...*right*," he said in a dubious tone of voice.

I prayed he wouldn't question me further, because I had the distinct impression Adam could be *very* persuasive, if need be. Thankfully he flashed me a smile. Though brief, I thought it genuine.

Relief flooded over me. I grabbed the door handle, my palm sweaty. "OK, thanks again." Adam said nothing, so I continued, "I'm sure I'll see you around. Take care." Knowing I was blabbering on like, well, like a high school girl with an unrequited crush, I opened the door and clambered out.

"Wait, I'll walk you to your door," I heard him say.

Before I could decline, Adam was out of the car. I nearly ran into him on the walkway, and he moved aside, motioning for me to go ahead of him. As we walked the short distance from his car to my front door, I felt his eyes on me. It was lunacy, but instead of being uncomfortable, I was kind of hoping he was checking me out.

The intoxicating feeling of possibly being desired by someone I felt *so* attracted to was making me feel flirtatious, and consequently, impetuous. At the door I turned to him and asked, "Do you want to come in?"

"Madeleine..." He breathed out. "I don't think that's a good idea."

"Oh God, I didn't mean *that*!" *Or did I?* I was sure my face was turning shades of red to rival the changing leaves on the trees. My only saving grace was that it was dark out.

"I'm sorry," I murmured, feeling foolish for sticking my foot in my mouth. Adam reached out and ghosted his fingertips along my jaw. "There's nothing to apologize for." I closed my eyes and relaxed into his warm touch, allowing his fingers to make a slow, silky path down the side of my neck to my shoulder. Toying with the flimsy strap of my top, he whispered, "Exquisite."

"Adam," I began.

Our eyes met, and even in the darkness, I saw conflict in his. "I better just...go," he said, dropping his hand and turning away.

Not sure what had just happened, I mumbled, "Good night," and went into the cottage. In the dark I leaned back against the inside of the door. After several minutes I turned on a lamp and pulled myself together.

One thing for sure, my first time seeing Adam Ward after all these years had not gone the way I'd ever expected. Now that I was away from him, I was able to think a bit more clearly. I sat down on the sofa and pulled my knees up to my chest.

Viewing Adam with an objective eye was going to be a challenge. I couldn't allow this attraction to him to get in the way of my reason for being here. It was going to be tough, because being around him had made me feel awake and alive. Like giddy, skin-tingling, pulse-racing *alive*. And now that I'd experienced it, I really craved that feeling.

But it was imperative to keep reminding myself that Adam Ward was more than just some heartbreakingly handsome guy. Hell, he was the primary suspect in this case. He could end up being downright dangerous. And not the sexy kind of dangerous that had excited me tonight.

No, Adam was not to be underestimated. Someone had already enlightened him to my "writer's block" story. And it was clear he wasn't buying it—at all. What would he do if he knew I planned to investigate his one-time fiancée's disappearance and, in turn, investigate *him*?

Logic dictated that the wisest course of action in this situation would be to stay away from him. Investigate from afar. I whispered to myself, "Stay away from Adam Ward, stay away from Adam Ward."

But, like whispering affirmations, some things are easier said than done.

Chapter 4

The following day, I was back on task. I had the case files to review, and I planned to drop by the café. Not only did I have to place an order for some real groceries—energy bars and water were just not cutting it—it was also time to start digging around to find out exactly why Nate and Helena had chosen to live on this island. Did it have anything at all to do with the Harbour Falls Mystery?

With a renewed sense of purpose, I threw back the thick pile of blankets and got out of bed, yelping when my bare feet hit the hardwood floor. *Brrr, cold.* I'd forgotten to turn up the heat before retiring for the night, and now it was damn nippy in here.

With a quick peek out the blinds, I was not the least bit surprised to be greeted with a steel-colored sky, winds strong enough to kick up little tornadoes of soggy—but still brightly colored—leaves, and a view of the tempestuous sea. This last muted by a dense film of fog.

Yes, it was true Fade Island weather, and I'd better get used to it. A steaming hot shower helped warm me up, but it was the oversized fisherman's knit sweater that I threw on over my long-sleeved tee and jeans ensemble that promised to keep the island's perpetual dampness at bay.

Tromping down the stairs, running a towel through hair that just refused to dry, I was startled by two heavy knocks on the front door. Who would be calling at this early hour? As foolish as it was, a part of me hoped it was Adam.

But when I peered through the peephole in the door, a fisheye, distorted image of a hulking mass of a man greeted me.

Though he wore a dark gray raincoat, the hood was down. His light brown hair was shorn close to his scalp. And, though he couldn't have been much older than thirty, his features gave him a hardened appearance. He wasn't a bad-looking guy, not at all, but he looked like he'd seen far more than he should have for his years.

There was only one person on the island who fit that description, and I guessed from the two potted, white-flowering plants that he held carefully cradled—one in each arm—that this man, Adam's security, had come to apologize.

"Maddy Fitch?" he ventured when I opened the door a crack.

I gave him a quick nod, and he continued, "I'm Max"—just as I suspected—"I hope you don't mind, but I wanted to stop by in person to apologize for scaring you last night." He shook his head regretfully. "If I'd known it was you, I wouldn't have snuck up on you like that." He offered his hand, while attempting to balance the plants in the crook of one arm.

He didn't seem like such a bad guy in the light of day, so I opened the door the rest of the way and shook his hand. He readjusted the potted plants, and I asked if he needed some help with his floral cargo. "They're actually for you," he said, lowering one plant to the doorstep and handing me the other.

"They're white mums," I mused, slowly turning the blossoming plant in my hands.

Ami sure hadn't wasted any time getting the word out that I was in the market for some white chrysanthemums. Had she mentioned it to Max, the security guy? Or to someone else? Like, maybe, Adam.

Though he had no idea I was thinking such a thing, Max confirmed my suspicions when he said, "Mr. Ward told me he'd heard you wanted this kind of flower to plant in the window box, so he suggested I give them to you as a kind of peace offering for last night."

My face warmed at the mention of Adam's name. I looked down at the snowy blossoms. *Interesting how Ami mentioned my inquiry to "Mr. Ward," and he just happened to remember the exact details.* All I said to Max, though, was a simple, "Thank you."

I handed him the plant, and he placed it gently next to the other. "I'll just leave them here, if that's OK," he said, nodding to the doorstep.

"That's fine," I said and thanked him once more.

"Well, I guess I'll see you around," Max said as he turned to leave, but then he hesitated. "Oh, one more thing." He dipped into the pocket of his rain jacket and pulled out a damp card. "Uh, Mr. Ward wanted me to give you my number, in case you ever need anything."

I took the card and gave it a glance: Max Cleary and a phone number. I thanked him, and we said our good-byes. I watched him drive away in a dark green Hummer, and then I went back in and entered his number into my cell phone contacts. Tapping the phone to my chin, I wondered why Adam would want me to have this phone number. Max was in charge of security for the island, sure, but as proven, that really equated to security for Adam. What possible trouble could Adam expect me to get into out here on the island? If the trouble happened to involve Adam himself, Max would be of no use to me.

But what if the trouble involved *someone else*? Was Adam trying to protect me from someone in particular? One of the island residents? Or someone who had access to the island?

The questions were piling up, and it was high time to start getting some answers. I tossed my cell onto the coffee table and crossed to the bookcase. I yanked the case files from their hiding spot, spread them out on the dining room table, and began to delve into the facts relating to the disappearance of Chelsea Hannigan.

The files were divided into two sections, one for the Harbourtown portion of the investigation, and one for Harbour Falls. There were reams and reams of official reports from both police departments, dozens of notes from a slew of officers and detectives who had worked on the case, and several grainy still photos taken from surveillance footage.

This is what I found in the Harbourtown section:

In July, four years ago, following a church rehearsal, a dinner was held the night before Adam Ward and Chelsea Hannigan were to marry. Having interviewed everyone in attendance, the police concluded that nothing out of the ordinary had happened at the church. However, at the dinner that was held afterward, back at the hotel—where most of the guests were staying—a number of people reported that Adam and Chelsea had gotten into a rather heated argument. What it was about? Nobody could say. But a lot of people did report that Adam took steps to avoid Chelsea for the rest of the evening.

I picked up a partial transcript from a witness, a male cousin on the Hannigan side. It read:

Police Officer: "So what did you observe at the dinner?"

Witness: "Adam didn't touch his food, which I thought was crazy because that food was incredible.

Police Officer: "Was that it?"

Witness: "No no. He got up, said something to Chelsea that she didn't look happy about, and sat down next to someone else."

There was some more unrelated conversation, so I scanned the transcript to see if any names were mentioned. And what did I find? Who'd Adam ended up sitting with? His best man, Nate Jackson. I wished there was some way to find out what *they* had talked about that evening. But paging through the interviews, I concluded the police had never asked.

I put the transcript aside, and continued with the timeline...

The dinner ended at about ten o'clock that night, and around that same time, Chelsea was seen leaving the hotel—alone—in the late-model Jaguar her parents had bought her that summer.

Shortly after ten Adam was spotted at the hotel bar, drinking with Nate and Helena. All three stayed until the bar closed, at midnight that particular night. The waitress who'd served them stated in her interview that all three were courteous and nice. And though at points they'd gotten kind of boisterous and loud, they all seemed to be in good spirits. Further evidenced by the fact that they'd left her a huge tip.

The next section I read detailed Nate and Helena's movements following their departure from the hotel bar.

They returned to their, at the time, Harbourtown apartment. As it turned out, the couple had a fairly ironclad alibi. A water line of some sort had broken that night and flooded out their floor of the building. Nate and Helena, as well as a few other occupants from that part of the complex, were relegated to spend the night in a conference room located next to the rental office on the first floor. Interviews indicated the displaced residents spent most of the night talking with one another about what had happened, until everyone finally fell off to sleep.

Interestingly, though, one of the female residents reported waking up in the middle of the night and noticing that Helena was missing. When the police questioned Helena on this, she claimed she'd just gone down the hall to use the bathroom. The Harbourtown detectives were apparently satisfied since they eliminated Nate and Helena from their list of suspects.

So Nate had an ironclad alibi. And Helena had an almost *ironclad alibi.*

I paged to the next report...

Trina, Adam's sister, and her boyfriend, a guy named Walker, were staying at the hotel where the dinner had been held. Both Trina and Walker gave statements that they'd gone up to their room after dinner, watched some television, and fallen asleep. Nobody could confirm this story.

Walker was pretty much off the hook, as he was from Boston and barely knew the missing Chelsea. Trina, however, became a suspect when one of the detectives received a lead—from an unnamed source—stating that Adam's sister despised Chelsea and desperately did not want her brother to marry her.

Strange, there were no further details on the allegation. What reason could Trina have for hating Chelsea? Whatever it was, I planned on finding out.

Dr. and Mrs. Ward, though never really suspects, were still questioned. Their alibi was solid. *Scratch them off the list of potential suspects.* And much like Adam's parents, all of Chelsea's family had solid alibis. *Scratch Chelsea's family—which was rather small anyway—off the suspect list as well.*

There was a side entry attached to this section stating that

Mr. Hannigan, Chelsea's father, following his dissatisfaction with the work of both police departments, had hired a private investigator in late July of that year. Notes from several months later, made by a Harbourtown detective, indicated the PI had run into so many dead ends and false leads that he resigned, publicly stating that Ms. Hannigan's disappearance would probably never be solved. Mr. Hannigan never hired another detective.

I knew that, sadly, he'd fallen seriously ill the following year. When, months later, he passed away, Chelsea's mother moved away from Maine. Not that I could blame her.

Reaching the final pages in this section of the files, I began to read about Chelsea's last moves in Harbourtown, following her lone departure from the hotel.

Grainy surveillance footage showed her entering a seedy-looking bar named Billy's. I'd heard of the place before; it was a rundown watering hole with a bad reputation, located somewhere down by the river docks in Harbourtown. The time stamp read 22:32. So she'd been there shortly after ten thirty. Only one photo had been lifted from the surveillance footage, as there was only one camera at Billy's, and it recorded only the comings and goings of patrons as they passed through the entrance to the bar.

I studied this shot, and though in black and white, Chelsea's flowery sundress and sky-high heels were clearly out of place with the hard atmosphere of the bar. *Why was she there?*

Detectives interviewed the bartender at the time, a man known simply as Old Carl. He hadn't coughed up much information to the police, but he did confirm Chelsea had been a regular at the bar. He recalled that on that hot July night, Chelsea had consumed a couple of wine coolers and then asked Old Carl a rather odd question.

She wanted to know why he'd never gotten married. When he replied that he'd just "never met the right one," Chelsea laughed and said something to the effect of "Neither have I, Old Carl, neither have I." Even the bartender had to admit it was a bizarre response, especially since he knew Chelsea was getting married the very next day. But who knew why people sometimes said the things they said. Chelsea left the bar at 23:30, less than an hour following her arrival there.

A number of Billy's regulars were also questioned. Nothing could be substantiated, but a scandalous picture of Chelsea began to emerge. Most of the men had "no comment" when asked, but a few of the women patrons talked.

Several claimed to have walked in on Chelsea—more than once—while she was snorting lines of cocaine from a small mirror she'd placed on the bathroom counter. A few of the women claimed they'd sometimes seen her in there doing those drugs with a good-looking, muscular guy. But they had no idea who he was. Descriptions were sketchy, but every single one said he had short-cropped red hair and brown eyes.

Oh my God, J.T.?

He'd once had a drug problem. But what would J.T. be doing at a place like Billy's *with Chelsea Hannigan*? I couldn't remember the two of them ever even acknowledging one another. There was no way this man could have been J.T., right?

Paging hastily through the files, I searched for, but could not find, any mention of J.T. O'Brien. He'd never been questioned, never been considered. And, really, why would the police suspect him? He had no known connection to Chelsea. But for some reason, I couldn't shake my first impression that the muscular man with the red hair was, in fact, J.T. O'Brien.

There was one way I could find out who the man had been: go to Billy's. If this Old Carl was still bartending—and I hoped to God he was—then I'd ask if he'd ever seen J.T. with Chelsea. Chelsea had been a regular, so he'd surely recall her. And I had plenty of old photos of J.T. from back when we were in high school.

Anxious to get started on really investigating this thing, I considered heading over to the mainland today. But it was a Saturday, and the bar would probably be too busy by the time I got there. I decided to try Monday instead, late morning or early afternoon. A time when the bar would be open but most likely not busy.

Since I'd reached the end of the Harbourtown section, I took a quick break. More energy bars and bottled water. Ugh, I couldn't wait to get some real food in the place.

I gathered up the metallic wrappers, crinkled them in my fist, and tossed them in the trash. And then I hunkered down and started on the Harbour Falls part of the case files...

Shortly after midnight Chelsea was observed in surveillance footage taken from a bank on the edge of town. She used a pay phone that had once stood in front of the establishment. She was in the phone booth for less than a minute, and then she was seen pacing around the parking lot in her high-heels, looking agitated. A few still shots from the surveillance footage were attached to the file. I flipped through the photos and surmised she'd definitely been mad about something. *Perhaps it had to do with the phone call?*

So whom had she been calling?

I scanned the next several pages, but shockingly, no one had ever thought to get the call records from the pay phone company. Even though those records were probably no longer in existence, I made a note to ask my dad if he could get ahold of them. Since the bank was in Harbour Falls, I was confident the mayor would be able to track them down. So long as they'd not been destroyed.

Chelsea's next stop was her last. Well, the last place where her movements were documented—a convenience store located a few blocks from Cove Beach.

More still photos from surveillance video...

Shortly after one in the morning Chelsea's image is captured as she enters the convenience store. The kid working the overnight shift stated that the blonde woman (Chelsea) asked if she could use the phone behind the counter. He refused when he saw her cell phone—on and clearly charged—in her hand. According to the kid, she accepted his refusal and left without incident.

Why didn't Chelsea use her cell phone?

Asking to use the store phone, the pay phone at the bank. Was she worried calls were being traced to and from her cell phone? How many other calls had she made that weren't captured on video? Most importantly, *whom* had she been calling? The person responsible for her disappearance? If the nature of their connection was so shrouded in secrecy, then it was quite possible.

I spread several still photos depicting the outside of the convenience store across the table, placing them in chronological order based on the time stamps. OK, first Chelsea stood by her car for several minutes. *Contemplating something?* She then turned and walked to the sidewalk. And then...the last image ever captured of Chelsea Hannigan showed her walking out of camera range, heading east toward the dock.

I went through the files again to highlight some pertinent details.

Chelsea's Jaguar was recovered the next day, but nothing was missing. In fact, the car was still locked. Since she'd been heading toward the water, the Coast Guard searched to see if Chelsea had drowned, but no body was recovered. Based on the tides and currents at that time, experts claimed her body would have most likely washed ashore if she'd drowned that night. So that theory was discarded.

She really had disappeared without a trace. Even her cell phone was never recovered. It was as if she'd dissolved into thin air.

Finally, I picked up the part of the files I'd purposely saved for last: The investigation of Adam Ward.

Being the primary suspect meant he'd been questioned on numerous occasions, but Adam continued to maintain his innocence of any wrongdoing. His weak alibi, however, kept him in the police—as well as the public—crosshairs.

No one could substantiate his whereabouts after he'd left the hotel bar and parted ways with Nate and Helena. Adam admitted to being intoxicated and said he'd gone up to his hotel room and fallen asleep. He was not seen again until the next morning at breakfast, at around seven o'clock. Even more damning, witnesses claimed he appeared "disheveled" and "exhausted" at breakfast.

In a quest for clues, a hotline was set up. One anonymous tipster claimed Chelsea had once complained that Adam didn't love her anymore, had quit sleeping with her, did *not* want to marry her. The tipster further hinted that Chelsea may have had something on Adam—something *really damning*—and was using it to blackmail him into marrying her. The police were unable to track down the tipster. And they didn't uncover any evidence to support the outlandish allegation. In fact, Adam's past turned out to be squeaky clean, so it seemed unlikely he'd been a target for blackmail. Reaching yet another dead end, the police finally began to let up on him.

I set the files aside. *So that's how it all went down.*

I had to admit, blackmail would be a strong motive for wanting to silence someone. But I didn't want to believe Adam had anything to do with Chelsea's disappearance. Surely, the police would have uncovered *something* if he had. *With enough money, anyone can hide anything,* a traitorous voice whispered in my head.

No, Chelsea's life had been full of secrets and lies. I was more inclined to believe someone from her tawdry past had caught up to her. But the question remained, who?

My head was starting to ache; I'd been poring over the case files for hours. I slid the folder back into the bookcase and, in preparation for my visit to the café, began to look over the instructions for ordering groceries.

Residents were to place their orders with Helena, either through an online ordering system or by taking in a hard copy to the café. Pay options were available online, or payments could be made in person. Nate would then deliver the groceries within a couple of days. A web address and several printed copies of the ordering forms were attached to the instructions. *Simple enough.* I checked off the items I wanted, wrote in a few not on the list, and left for the café.

It was raining like crazy, so, once I arrived, I parked in front, lowered my head, and made a mad dash for the door. I didn't see Nate under the huge awning that sheltered the café entrance from the rain until the last second, and I pretty much collided with him as we both reached for the door handle at the same time.

Stepping aside, I blubbered, "Oh my God, I'm sorry—"

"Maddy!" Nate interrupted, laughing and pulling me into a much-unexpected hug. "It's good to see you. We heard you were going to be staying here on the island with us for a while." He pulled back, holding me at arm's length. "Wow, you look great."

The café door opened, and Helena appeared in the doorway. "Nate," she said, clearly exasperated. "Don't make the poor girl stand out there in this weather." She propped the door open with her hip. "Come on in, Maddy. And welcome to Fade Island."

The café interior was warm and inviting. There were a few small wooden tables scattered about, a plush sofa covered in a nubby, maroon fabric off to the left, and a coffee bar in the back. A menu board hanging behind the bar held only the chalky smears from a swipe of an eraser, but nevertheless, the smell of freshly brewed coffee punctuated the air.

After a few customary niceties of the recently reacquainted, I said, "Oh, I wanted to drop off my grocery order." I pulled the folded form from my back pocket. "I'll probably order online next time, but I really wanted to stop in, see the café, and say hello of course."

Helena took the order. "I'm glad you decided to come in. I thought I saw you drive by yesterday in Adam's old Lexus."

Aha, so I was right about the car!

"Yeah, that was me," I replied, feeling somewhat foolish that I'd been noticed and had not stopped in.

"How 'bout some coffee?" Nate chimed in. "It'll warm you up before you go back out in this mess."

Helena added, "I was about to make myself a cappuccino. But I can make you whatever you like. I even have soup today since we've had a lot of fishermen stopping by lately."

"Just a cappuccino is fine," I said as I sat down at one of the tables in the middle of the café.

Just as Nate was about to sit down in the chair across from

me, the café door swung open. I fully expected it to be a fisherman or maybe Max. But no.

It was Adam who stepped in, clad in a dark brown field coat, jeans, and hiking boots. Very outdoorsy, very handsome, I noted. He looked especially good as he ran his fingers through his wet hair, and a trickle of rainwater trailed down his temple.

Adam caught me watching him and started to smile, but then Nate distracted him as he waved him over. "We were just getting caught up with Maddy," Nate said.

Adam came over to the table, and Nate motioned to the chair across from me. "Here, have a seat."

Adam glanced at the empty chair, and then, smirking, he said, "Actually Madeleine and I had a rather unexpected, but certainly not unpleasant, opportunity to get reacquainted last night. I think it's safe to say we're all *caught up*." He looked my way and added, "Isn't that right, Maddy."

Nate looked perplexed, and I tried to explain lest he think the worst from Adam's vague, innuendo-laden comment. "We sort of ran into each other yesterday evening."

Adam coughed to stifle a laugh. I shot him a pointed look, but he pretended not to notice.

Nate, surely catching all this but being too much of a gentleman to comment on it, said to Adam, "OK, well, what brings you down to the café today, then?"

"I need to discuss something with you," Adam said, suddenly serious and somber.

Helena was returning with the cappuccino, and she smiled and said "hi" to Adam.

Adam nodded to her, and Nate said, "Let's give the girls some private time. We can talk in the back room."

Helena set the steaming mug on the table and sat down. "What was that all about?"

I watched as Nate followed Adam through a door in the back of the café that I guessed led to the mysterious back room. "I don't know. Um, Adam said he wanted to talk to Nate about something."

"Hmm," she said, "I overheard your conversation. So you

ran into Adam last night, eh?"

"Uh, kind of," I muttered. My cheeks warmed; surely I was blushing.

Helena didn't ask for details, thank heavens, but her eyes did meet mine. She leaned forward and whispered conspiratorially, "You should go for it, Maddy."

"I don't think so," I replied a little too quickly.

She drummed her perfectly manicured fingernails on the table, seemingly contemplating something. "I'll tell you a secret, but you have to promise to keep it to yourself."

What is it with this island and secrets? I thought. Out loud, though, I said, "Sure, my lips are sealed."

Keeping her voice low, she said, "Bet you never knew Adam wanted to ask you out back in high school."

I almost spit out my cappuccino and then checked to make sure the back room door was definitely closed. "No way. He never even looked my way, and besides, he was dating Chelsea."

"That girl was a bitch," Helena snapped. "He would have been better off if he'd dumped her back then." Not knowing how to respond, I just sat and let her go on. "Believe what you want, Maddy, but I know for a *fact* Adam had a thing for you. And I bet he still does."

"How can you be so sure?"

She nodded to the back room. "Nate told me."

"It doesn't matter." I sighed. "That was a long time ago, and I don't get the impression he's interested now. I mean, not really."

Sure, Adam may have flirted last night, but Helena was making it sound like he'd once been *genuinely* interested in me.

She was about to say something else, but just then Adam and Nate emerged from the back room. As Adam headed toward our table, Helena got up and whispered to me, "I have your number on the order form. We'll talk more later, OK?"

I nodded, and from back at the coffee bar, Nate called out, "Hey, babe, can you give me a hand over here?"

It was like they were both conspiring to give Adam and

me alone time. Maybe they were. I took a sip of cappuccino as Adam slid into Helena's vacated seat. "Hey," he said, leaning back in his chair and throwing me off with a particularly captivating smile. "Sorry about bringing last night up in front of Nate."

I wanted to play it cool, because, really, he didn't look remorseful in the least.

But I couldn't help but break into a smile of my own. Not when he looked this damn good—hair still damp, eyes a sea of blue. So I gave up on being mad and said, "No problem."

Another dazzling smile and then he said, "It stopped raining." A vague gesture to the window. "Do you want to take a walk with me?" Adam's voice was liquid silk, his tone softly sweet but dangerously alluring.

Unable to resist, I said, "Yeah, sure."

So much for my grand plan to stay away from him. Hell, I was already caving. But after hearing Helena's revelations, I wanted to spend more time with this man. I didn't care to talk about the case, think about the case, nothing. I just wanted to enjoy this moment with a gorgeous guy who, just maybe, had a thing for me. Still.

We left the café—but not before saying our farewells to a smug-looking Helena and Nate. *Clever matchmakers,* I thought, smiling, as Adam and I walked side by side through town, passing the brightly colored buildings. "I love all the colors," I told him. "I'll have to come back next year when everything's open."

"You should," Adam replied. "It's a lot different in the summer."

"What made you choose the art deco theme?" As soon as the words were out of my mouth, I winced. I'd promised Ami I'd not say anything to anyone about knowing Adam owned the island. I was sure she'd especially meant the owner himself.

But Adam just chuckled. "Ami?" he asked, quirking an eyebrow.

We reached the top of the hill that led to the dock parking lot, and I slowed. "Please don't be mad at her. I was the one digging for information."

Maybe that wasn't the best thing to say, but I didn't want Adam to be angry with Ami. Much to my relief, he said, "It's fine, I'm not mad." And he really looked OK with it. "Come on," he added. "We just have a little further to go."

I knew we were nearing the southern edge of the island, but I had no idea what our destination was. Adam led me to a narrow, gravel pathway that cut through some low-lying scrub grass and shrubbery. We walked to the end of the pathway, to a point where the land just appeared to drop off to the sea.

Cautiously, I peered forward. A set of uneven steps, crudely cut into the cliffs, weaved their way down to a narrow peninsula. The blanket of thick fog at the base made it impossible to see more than the outlines of the rocks below. "Where are we going?" I asked, turning to face Adam, as the wind, icy cold this close to the sea, whipped hair into my face.

Adam reached out and gently smoothed the wayward strands back, the warmth of his fingers a welcome contrast to the cool air.

"You're cold, Maddy. Here, take this," he said, shucking his coat off and holding it up for me to slip on.

"Thanks." I slid my arms into the sleeves, and then Adam gently lifted my hair and secured the jacket around my shoulders.

"Better?" he asked, turning me to face him once more, while rolling the sleeves up over the bulkiness of my sweater.

"Mm-hmm," I answered, breathing in the unique scent of Adam. *I could get used to this.*

He rubbed my very cold hands between his own very warm hands. "You ready, then?"

"Are we going down *there*?" I asked, my voice raising an octave as he began to lead me to the top of the precarious-looking steps.

"Don't worry, I'll keep you safe." He squeezed my hand reassuringly. "It's actually pretty cool down there when the weather is like this. I think you'll like it."

For some crazy reason, I *did* feel safe with Adam. Besides,

I was curious to see what—besides the black, jagged edges of rocks peeking through the fog—was on the peninsula.

I stayed close to Adam as we began the steep descent, the misty air engulfing us. "What's down here anyway?" I asked, my voice muted by the ever-increasing volume of the crashing waves.

"The lighthouse," Adam replied.

Chapter 5

At the base of the steps, in the shadow of the towering cliffs, surge after surge of waves battered the sides of the rocky peninsula. Viewed through the cottony haze of fog, the landscape of oil-black rocks—some unusually large and oddly shaped—lent a mystical feel to the whole area.

"Pretty cool, eh?" Adam asked when he caught me, mouth open, ogling the place.

OK, so I was impressed. I snapped my mouth closed and playfully elbowed him for looking so smug. But then I agreed that the atmosphere down here was definitely something worth seeing.

Adam pointed to a tall, stark white structure off in the distance, and realizing what it was, I exclaimed, "The lighthouse! Can we get closer?"

"Absolutely," he said, smiling, as he led the way to what appeared to be the least treacherous route to the lighthouse.

Down here the terrain was unforgiving, especially in the fog. One wrong move could easily result in a bad fall. But I took my time, allowing Adam to help me traverse the more slippery surfaces and climb across the largest of the boulders.

At last we reached a swath of hard-packed sand. "It's mostly easy going from here," Adam said, breaking the silence that had ensued as we'd navigated our way.

Now that the most difficult part of our little journey was behind us, conversation resumed. We shared stories about our college days. Although I had a few good tales of my own, Adam surprised me with several hilarious anecdotes of his own. I laughed a lot, both at the content of his stories and the animated way in which he told them. Unlike the mercurial man I'd dealt with last night, when he spoke of these obviously happy days at school, Adam was more like the guy I'd once longed to get to know.

But that changed when I asked him about his company. Adam grew reticent, giving me short, clipped answers that sounded almost rehearsed. He finally just said he didn't want to think about work, so instead I told him about how I'd become a novelist.

"I've heard of your books," Adam said. "But I must confess I've never read any of them. I'll have to pick one up."

Thrilled that he wanted to read something I'd written, I said, "I have a bunch of extra copies at the cottage. I could just give you one."

"Only if you sign it," Adam said, his tone teasing as he lightly bumped his shoulder into mine.

We continued, closer, closer to the lighthouse, until Adam stopped abruptly. He turned to me. "You write mystery novels, right?"

His face was unreadable, so I answered with an "uh-huh," my voice cracking on the second syllable.

"And all of them are fiction?"

I nervously pushed the toe of my hiking boot into the wet sand and replied, "Yep, all fiction."

Adam looked to be contemplating my answer as he took several steps backward, beckoning for me to follow. I took a few tentative steps toward him, my eyes lowering to the squishy prints my boots were making in the wet sand. Impressions that were there for a moment and then gone as if they'd never been there.

I kept walking, watching my prints appear and disappear, but then Adam halted. To avoid stumbling headfirst into him, I thrust my hand forward, grasping the thermal material of his shirt. His chest flexed beneath my hold as he caught my elbows and steadied me. I met his gaze, and he asked softly, "Ever consider writing a book about the mystery right in front of you?"

I swallowed hard, all the while wondering if he meant himself…or the Harbour Falls Mystery. Worse yet, was he onto me? Was he trying to get me to fess up? My pulse began to race, and I searched his stormy eyes. I couldn't tell him the truth. The mystery was too intertwined with his life. Hell, the mystery *was* his life.

I glanced down at my hand, still fisted in his shirt—maybe more so, now—and did what I was learning to do best. I lied. "Um, no, I think I'll stick to fiction."

Adam was silent, but then he released his hold on my elbows and raised one hand to nudge my chin. "You sure, Maddy?"

I croaked out a shaky, "Yeah, I'm sure."

Adam's mouth turned up into what I hoped was a smile, not a grimace. "Good to hear," he said as he gently pried my hand from his shirt. Embarrassed, I ran a quick, smoothing pass over the material.

The fog had dissipated slightly, and I could now see we'd reached the base of the lighthouse. The structure itself stood perched atop layers of black rock, with no visible way up. "How to we get up there?" I asked.

"Over here." Adam led me to a hidden, sandy trail that curved like a serpent through the rocks, ending at the lighthouse door.

Thankfully, any lingering tension quickly passed as we focused on making our way up the short trail.

When we reached the looming structure, I stared straight up and, without thinking, gushed, "God, it's so much bigger up close."

Adam smirked and cocked his head to the side. My cheeks warmed, realizing how fraught with innuendo *that* statement had been. "I mean, it's bigger than it looked, uh,"—I flailed a hand to the barely visible rocky ledge from which we'd descended— "from up there."

"Yeah, that's what I figured you meant," Adam deadpanned. He was doing his best to not laugh at me, so I rolled my eyes at him. But, really, I was just happy we were back to playful banter.

I turned to the metal door on the side of the lighthouse, put my hand on the handle, and pulled, and pulled. "Hey, it's locked." *Nothing like stating the obvious there, Maddy.*

Adam pulled out a key ring from the pocket of his jeans. "Lucky for you, I have the only key," he said smugly.

"I guess so, since it's your *island*," I muttered under my breath.

Adam shot me a cocky grin, having heard me, as he unlocked the metal door. I rolled my eyes, again. Only this time it was in pretend exasperation. Chuckling, he pushed the creaky door open.

I took a few tentative steps inside and faltered when a sudden, inexplicable feeling of unease rushed over me in the cool and damp surroundings. Adam was beside me in an instant. "Are you OK?" he asked.

Though it made little sense, his proximity comforted me. I didn't know if it was my head—or more likely my heart—talking, but I wanted to believe Adam was innocent of any involvement in Chelsea's disappearance. I wanted to believe he was just another victim in this whole Harbour Falls Mystery mess.

Despite the chill in the air, my traitorous body warmed as he moved closer. "Maddy?" he asked, his voice laden with concern.

Whatever weird moment I'd had, had passed. "Yeah, I'm fine. I guess I just needed a minute."

My eyes adjusted to the dimly lit interior, and I glanced around. A winding iron staircase circled up and up. Standing in the center of the lighthouse, staring up, it had the appearance of a black snail that had attached itself to the smooth, conical interior walls. A few tiny, recessed windows along the staircase provided the only illumination, dust motes swirling in the strips of light streaming in.

"Can we go up?" I asked, nodding to the spiraling steps.

"Yeah," Adam said. "But we'll have to be careful. It's damp in here, and the steps are bound to be slippery." And many of them were, but Adam was right behind me the whole way up. Ready to catch me if I fell.

Higher and higher we ascended. I stopped counting the steps when I reached two hundred, gasping when I made the mistake of glancing down.

I felt Adam's hands come to rest above my hips. "I'm right behind you; you'll be fine," he promised. "We're almost there."

A few more steps and we reached a service room, no longer in use, of course. A small wooden ladder was attached to the wall. Adam climbed up first and then offered me a hand. "Still want to come up? Or are you backing out?" he asked. His tone was playful, and I could tell he was trying to put me at ease.

The ladder led to the lantern room, which was enclosed by large, glass storm panes. I wasn't afraid anymore, so I took his hand and said, "I made it this far, didn't I?"

"Brave girl," Adam said as he hoisted me up with ease.

We'd finally reached the very top. I walked over to the large, dusty lens of the lighthouse beacon. Reaching out to brush away a few cobwebs, I said, "Think of all the sailors this light once guided to safety."

"Or warned of the danger," Adam added, though he said it so quietly I barely heard him.

I turned away from the lens and walked over to place my hand on one of the storm panes that separated us from the harsh elements. It was like being on a viewing deck, but unfortunately the thick haze of white made it impossible to see more than a few feet beyond the structure.

"I bet the view from up here is amazing on a clear day," I said, sighing as I stared out into the dense veil of fog.

"It is." Adam's breath brushed over my hair as I felt him come up behind me. "There are hidden caves in the face of the cliffs." He pointed, but there was entirely too much fog. "You can see them best from up here. When there's no fog, of course."

"Oooh, hidden caves. Sounds spooky," I said, pretending to shudder. "You'll have to show me sometime." I leaned back into him, and he circled his arms around me, his heart a soothing tattoo of beats against my spine.

"I will. I'll bring you back up here when it's sunny."

"Promise, Adam?" I asked coyly.

He spun me around so we were face-to-face, and I leaned back against the metal handrail. He said, "Under one condition."

Oh, this is getting interesting.

I raised an inquisitive eyebrow. "Do go on, Mr. Ward."

"Let me take you to dinner next week, Ms. Fitch."

"Next week?" I asked, glancing up at him through my lashes. "Why wait?"

Adam pulled me to him. "Well, I'd say 'as soon as possible,' believe me." He brushed a stray wisp of hair from my cheek, carefully tucking it behind my ear. "But unfortunately, I have to fly out on business tomorrow, and I won't be back until Wednesday." Adam's fingertips left a heated path as he traced my earlobe. "Let me take you to dinner when I return. We can fly down to Boston."

Adam's long fingers continued a lazy path to the back of my neck, where they lingered. He traced little circles, leaving my mind as foggy as the air outside. "Will you say yes, Maddy?" His voice dropped to a seductive whisper. "Say yes," he coaxed.

"Boston," I mused dreamily as I tilted my face to his. I closed my eyes as Adam leaned down. His lips so, so close. "Yes, yes," I whispered in response.

Adam's mouth brushed over mine. There and gone, soft as a feather. His hands trailed down my back, as my own lingered at the nape of his neck. I pressed myself shamelessly to him, and his breathing quickened in response. He ghosted his lips over mine once more, a shadow of a kiss that left my body aching for much more. *Oh God, help me, I am falling for you, Adam Ward*

"Madeleine," Adam whispered against my lips. "There's something I should tell you."

Are you falling for me too? I thought. Hoped. Wished. But before he could continue, a loud buzzing sound pierced the quiet. He sighed against my lips. I let out a soft cry of frustration and dropped my forehead to his shoulder. The magic was lost. The moment passed.

"I'm sorry, Maddy," Adam whispered into my hair, while fumbling in his back pocket for his phone.

Once in his hand, Adam barked into the offending cell, "Talk. This had better be fucking important." I could hear a male voice on the other end, but I couldn't make out what the man was saying. From the caller's tone and Adam's monosyllabic responses, I gathered it was a business call. I kept my head on his shoulder while he talked. One arm remained around me, his fingers winding absently in my hair. Several more seconds elapsed, and Adam ended the call. He kissed the top of my head. "Maddy?" I glanced up to find apologetic blue eyes looking down at me. "I'm sorry, but I had to take that call."

"I understand. I guess we need to get back?"

Adam sighed. "Yeah, we should. Before it gets dark."

Despite the fog, the trip back seemed to take less time. Perhaps it was because I didn't want my time with Adam to end. He talked about the island, telling me how there had once been a keeper's house next to the lighthouse. But it had been destroyed in a particularly bad storm many years ago.

When we reached my car, Adam walked me to the driver's side door. "Be careful driving back," he said, while I reluctantly slipped his coat off.

"Like it's such a long drive," I joked, handing him his coat. "Besides, you'll be right behind me."

"No, I won't. I'm not going directly to my house." I followed his glance to the café, now dark and closed for the night. Had Nate been the one calling him down at the lighthouse?

Disappointed, I uttered, "Oh, OK."

I had to admit, I kind of liked the idea of Adam following me back. It made me feel protected. As I was getting in my car, he asked for my cell phone number. I had a sneaking suspicion he already had it, seeing that Ami had my number. But I still made a quick call to his cell from mine so he'd definitely have it ready to program in. We made plans for him to pick me up at seven on Wednesday evening, and he promised to call if anything changed.

As I drove along the lonely, dark road back to my cottage, I thought about how I was driving Adam's old Lexus. *I wonder if he has an extra set of keys for it*, I thought to myself. "Probably," I muttered aloud, sure that Adam had access to *everything* on this island.

After I reached the cottage, I put on my pajamas, settled on the sofa, and turned on the television. Thankfully, there was digital satellite service out here on the island, so I had something like four hundred channels from which to choose. I flipped through several and finally left on some kind of crime drama. It seemed apropos, all things considered.

There was an interrogation scene playing out, and it made me think about my upcoming visit to Billy's. If the same bartender, Old Carl, was still working there, would he remember if the man witnesses had seen with Chelsea was J.T.? I had lots of pictures of J.T. from when I'd lived in Harbour Falls. Most were on my laptop. I scribbled down a note to print one out before Monday, so I'd have a photo to take with me for my own little interrogation of sorts.

At last I turned the television off and went up to bed. While I tossed and turned, waiting for sleep to come, I replayed my time with Adam at the lighthouse. Keeping my plans from him—to write a nonfiction account of the Harbour Falls Mystery—was going to be tricky. What had he meant when he'd asked if I'd ever considered writing about the mystery right in front of me? If he'd been referring to the Harbour Falls Mystery—and, really, what else could it have been?—then he was evidently taking it in stride. He'd not sounded *too* upset and had, to my relief, dropped the subject rather quickly.

Much like the Harbour Falls Mystery itself, the man at the center was a puzzle. And I longed to solve him, piece by piece.

Chapter 6

The next afternoon yet another visitor darkened my doorstep. But this one was not completely unexpected. "Nate," I said in acknowledgment as I opened the door.

"Hey, Maddy," he replied as he lifted up four bags of groceries from the doorstep. "Your order was ready, so I figured I'd get it out to you."

"Wow, that was some quick service," I remarked, moving aside so Nate could come in.

"We aim to please, Maddy. We aim to please." He nodded to the back of the house. "Kitchen?"

"That'd be perfect. It's right in here."

Nate followed me into the kitchen and then placed the bags on the counter. "Oh wait," he said, grabbing some kind of letter wedged between the bananas and a box of cereal. "Here." He handed me an envelope. "You've got some mail already."

I'd been told the mail coming out to the island was first delivered in bulk to Cove Beach, sorted by the Westons, brought over on the ferry, and lastly dropped off at the café. Residents were to pick up the mail at their leisure, but if one forgot or just didn't want to bother, Nate would bring it en masse with the grocery orders.

This particular piece looked like junk mail that had been forwarded from my dad's. I thumbed open the flap on the back and pulled out a letter. "Oooh, look, I won," I joked, holding up a notice that stated someone with my initials would most assuredly find themselves a *big* winner in the coming days.

"Nice," Nate said, dragging out the *i*. "Balloons and camera crews. I always wanted to meet the prize patrol."

We both burst out laughing, and I couldn't help but remark, "And just think what a warm welcome they'll receive ferrying over with Jennifer."

"Sweet as sugar, that girl," Nate said, rolling his eyes. Apparently Jennifer's bitchiness was known by all.

Before leaving Nate urged me to stop back into the café soon. "It starts to get rather lonely around here this time of year, and I know Helena would love the company."

So I promised to visit during the week but, again, wondered why Nate and Helena—both so outgoing and friendly—chose to live on this island. I deduced that Adam must have been paying them a bundle. But did the island really need a "manager" and someone to run such a low-volume café? Perhaps Adam wanted them here to ease his own loneliness? Or were Nate and Helena out here because they were hiding something? Maybe something related to the mystery? This last thought reminded me that I had yet to call my dad to ask him about the call records from the pay phone that had once stood at the Harbour Falls bank.

I grabbed my phone and, catching my dad at his office at City Hall, summarized for him what I'd found in the case files. "Do you think they're still floating around somewhere?" I asked when I'd finished.

"I can look into it, but it's been a long time. Those records—if they ever existed—were probably lost or destroyed."

Thinking out loud, I blurted, "Funny the police never followed up."

My dad was silent, and I suspected he was bristling. "Our police department never had the kind of manpower needed to head up that kind of an investigation, Maddy. You know that."

"I know," I conceded. It was true; the Hannigan disappearance had strained all of the resources in our small community.

"Anyway," I continued, "we know what time she made the call. If we could just get a list of numbers that were dialed out that night, we could find out who Chelsea was talking to."

"I'll see what I can do, honey," my dad promised, and then we quickly wrapped things up, since he was running late to a community meeting of some sort.

Fueled by the progress I was already making on this cold case, I fired up my laptop and began to scour my files for a good, clear photo of J.T. O'Brien, one I could take to Billy's.

Browsing through the old photos brought back waves of memories. I randomly clicked a thumbnail to expand a picture from back when I was fifteen. It was a close-up of Ami and me, smiling and sunburned at the local pool. The caption read: Red as Lobsters—But Happy as Clams. I recalled that day perfectly; we'd forgotten to bring sunscreen, and consequently had been burned to a crisp. But damn, we'd had fun.

Still smiling, I clicked another image—this one was of J.T. and Ami standing in a line at a local amusement park. I'd caught them off-guard as the three of us, so close back then, had waited to ride what had been deemed, at the time, to be the latest and greatest roller coaster in the area. I stared at the photo and shook my head. Where had the time gone? How had my friends changed so much?

With a sigh, I closed the image and opened a folder labeled "Summer after Graduation." And it was there I stumbled upon the mother lode of J.T. photos. Most had been taken down on Cove Beach, a few days following commencement. I remembered that day like it was yesterday. One of my graduation gifts from my father had been a digital camera, and J.T. and I had gone down to the beach to try it out.

There were several photos of J.T. goofing around near the water, but I ultimately chose a clear headshot, a sliver of blue sky the only background. I sent the photo to the printer and wondered what had happened to the friendly, shy boy I'd once called a friend. Was he the mystery man who'd been with Chelsea at Billy's? Doing drugs together? If so, what kind of relationship had they had? Had their commonality of substance abuse brought them together? Had it torn them apart? After my strange interaction with J.T. on the ferry, it wasn't hard to imagine something minor setting him off. There was something different about him now, something broken. Like a part of who he'd once been was lost. So maybe it wasn't so farfetched to imagine he had played a role in Chelsea's disappearance?

In any case, the suspect list was growing. Because if it turned out J.T. was once involved with Chelsea, then Jennifer was a suspect too. She loved J.T. and would have been insanely jealous had she known. Had she retaliated? Revenge was the oldest motive known to mankind.

I couldn't rule out Adam's sister, Trina, either. According to the case files, she hated Chelsea and hadn't wanted her brother to marry her. Why? Was it reason enough to have given her a motive? I'd have to find out.

And then there was Adam. If Chelsea had been blackmailing him, as rumored, then he may have had the strongest motive of them all. And that's what scared me.

The ride to Cove Beach on Monday morning was piloted not by Jennifer or J.T. but by Brody Weston, Jennifer's cousin. As he helped me on board, I tried to remember Brody's story. He'd been orphaned as a toddler and had come to live with Jennifer's family. In a way he was more like a brother to Jennifer. But, to my delight, Brody was nothing like his cousin. Nor was he like J.T.

Courteous from the moment I stepped on the ferry, he asked a few perfunctory questions and then left me alone. This was just as well since I was stressing out.

After all, I was heading to Billy's—not the nicest place around—to more or less conduct an interrogation. And I had no experience in questioning people. Sure, I'd written enough about it, but I had no idea how to effectively do it in real life, especially without arousing suspicions. I had no great plan. I was just going to wing it and hope I could pull it off.

Once we reached the mainland, Brody was sweet enough to help me back my car out of the garage by the dock. After thanking him, I headed over to Harbourtown.

Billy's was located in a warehouse district down by the river docks. Not the greatest part of town. The place itself was little more than a rundown, wooden shack that someone, probably drunk, had thought to paint a garish shade of purple. I shook my head as I drove by the entrance. The name "Billy's" was spelled out in big, red script letters that scrolled across the front edge of the roof. It looked like each letter was wired to light up at night, though, based on their condition, they were probably a fire hazard. The dot on the "i" was missing, and the "s" was listing forward, ready to topple over if a good, strong wind kicked up.

I parked around the side of the building behind the only other vehicle in sight, a motorcycle. When I reached the propped-open front door, the "s" creaked ominously above my head, making me hesitate. Maybe it was a sign to scrap this crazy plan? As I stood in the entrance, the smell of stale beer and sweat wafted out. But there was something more, something base and vile—Billy's reeked of desperation.

A part of me wanted to get back in my car and drive away, but I was here for a reason. So I went in. There was a guy—way too young to be Old Carl—wiping the top of the dark oak bar with a dingy-looking cloth that had seen better days. He was humming along to an old seventies song—something about lying eyes—as he lazily worked the rag down the length of the bar.

He looked up as I approached and, upon noticing he had a potential customer, reached below the bar and turned down the music. "Oh, hey. What can I getcha, Miss?" he asked, a stringy swath of dark hair falling across his gaunt face.

"Just water would be fine," I replied, as I pulled out one of several wooden bar stools and sat down.

The too-skinny bartender flipped the hair from his face and eyed me dubiously, so I hastily changed my order to a beer. He nodded approvingly and then made his way down to a silver cooler at the other end of the bar. "Glass?" he called back as he reached into the cooler.

"Just the bottle is fine," I replied, glancing around to get a lay of the land, so to speak.

There was a back room off to the left, housing several pool tables and a few of those dart machine games. A sign with an arrow was taped to the wall, and someone had written in black marker "Restrooms." I couldn't see much more back there, as the lights were off. So I focused back on the bar area. Besides the tall stools at the bar, there were a few tables and chairs scattered about. The wall behind the bar was one large mirror, making the place appear larger than it was. Several neon beer signs, some illuminated, some not, adorned the dark wooden valance above where I sat. As my eyes scanned the shelves before me, jam-packed with liquor bottles, I noticed the kid was on his way back to my end of the bar.

He stopped in front of me, twisted the cap off the bottle, and slammed the beer down in front of me. His dark eyes raked over me, and though I'd dressed down, I cursed myself for wearing designer boots.

"You sure you're in the right place, Miss?" he asked, snickering. "'Cause you're not really lookin' like you belong in here."

I took a deep breath, figuring I wasn't fooling the kid, so I might as well get down to business.

"Um...Yeah, right. I'm not really here to drink." He shot me a look that screamed, *No shit.* "I, uh, have a friend who I think used to come here. A guy. I'm kind of looking to find out if he really did hang out here. And if so, who he used to hang with. I think I may have known her, too, if it's the girl I'm thinking of." The kid eyed me cautiously, his dark eyes wary, but I stammered on. "I mean, she used to be kind of a friend too." *OK, so that part's a huge lie; Chelsea had never been my friend.*

The time stretched on, and the kid said nothing, so in an effort to put him at ease, I added, "I'm Maddy, by the way." I smiled my friendliest smile and held out my hand.

At first he continued the silent treatment, but then he quietly said, "I'm Jimmy." He reached hesitantly for my outstretched hand.

"There used to be another bartender here back then. He may know better who I'm talking about?" I offered, the pungent smell of disinfectant from his hands growing stronger as we shook.

I jerked my hand back, but he seemed not to notice. "Oh,

you mean Old Carl," he stated matter-of-factly. "Yeah, he doesn't work here no more. Quit a couple years ago."

"Oh," I said, "do you know where I could find him?"

"Nah, he doesn't live 'round here no more. Said he was goin' to California or some shit. No one's seen him since." Jimmy picked up the dirty dishrag and resumed his earlier task of wiping down the bar. "Maybe I could help? I've only been bartendin' here for a year, but I've been comin' here for a lot longer 'an that. Pretty much know every face that's been in and outta here the last few years."

"This would've been five, maybe six, years ago though," I said, doubtful that this kid was going to be much help. He looked too young to have been coming here back when Chelsea, and maybe J.T., had been frequenting this place.

But Jimmy insisted, "I'm tellin' ya, I've been comin' here since I was sixteen." He looked proud to share this admission. He leaned forward like we were in on it together and whispered, "Just don't be tellin' the boss."

"Wouldn't think of it," I mumbled into my tilted bottle, hoping he'd not catch my sarcasm, and then I downed a big gulp of cheap beer.

"This dude you askin' about, you gotta description?" Jimmy persisted.

Oh hell, it was worth a shot; maybe the kid *did* know something. So I said, "Better, I have a picture." I pulled the photo of J.T. out of my bag, and Jimmy tossed the dishrag aside before grabbing the picture and giving it what appeared to be a good, long look.

At last he lowered the photo, and his narrowed eyes met mine. "You're not some kind of a cop or somethin'?"

"I'm not a cop, I swear."

"Reporter then?"

"No," I said emphatically.

Jimmy glared at me, glanced back down at the picture of J.T., and then flicked the photo back at me. It landed faceup on the bar, and he turned away with a mumbled curse.

"So?" I asked Jimmy's back.

"Uh, never seen him before," he replied flatly, while showing a sudden interest in straightening the liquor bottles on the shelves behind the bar. The one with the turkey on it apparently didn't belong next to the one with someone's—I squinted—old granddad on it. Yeah, right.

I met Jimmy's eyes in the reflection from the mirror; the lie was written all over the kid's face. "Come on, Jimmy," I pleaded. "Tell me what you know."

He turned back around but kept his eyes down while muttering, "You know, I could tell 'ya, but business has been kinda slow here lately." He nodded to a tip jar nestled between two bottles. "Hard to remember things from the past when you're worried about makin' this month's rent."

OK, so the kid was shaking me down to pay for whatever information he had. I wasn't entirely surprised, and luckily I'd brought extra cash in anticipation of this exact sort of thing. I pulled out a wad of bills and peeled a fifty off the top. Jimmy's tongue darted over his chapped, peeling lips as I pushed the crisp bill across the bar. I thought I saw him salivate a little.

With his hand hovering above the money, he hesitated. "Ya know, you wouldn't believe how much it costs for a dump around here."

The kid was like a pro. I huffed and peeled off another fifty. I resignedly threw the bill atop the other one. Jimmy quickly grabbed the money and stuffed it into the tip jar which—a few seconds ago—had held only coins. He fished out a crumpled pack of cigarettes and a lighter from the pocket of the threadbare jeans that hung too loosely on his slender frame.

I tapped the heel of my boot impatiently against the leg of the bar stool, waiting while, with his lips, Jimmy pulled a cigarette out of the pack. He lit it, and drew in deeply. "OK, OK. Yeah, that guy used to come in here," Jimmy said, exhaling.

"And…" I prompted.

He shot a glance around the bar, which was still quite empty, but he lowered his voice anyway and said, "The guy in your picture used to come in here with that girl who disappeared. Chelsea, uh, something."

"Hannigan," I whispered.

"*She* was a friend of yours?" he asked, eyes widening.

"Kind of," I lied. "It's a shame what happened to her. Gone missing, and all."

"Hell, I'm surprised something didn't happen sooner, to tell you the truth," Jimmy chortled, cold and uncaring.

"Why do you say that?" I asked, a little sickened by his callousness.

"Well, for starters, that girl did some crazy-ass shit. Things that are bound to catch up to ya."

"Drugs?" I ventured.

"What do you think?" Jimmy snorted, blowing smoke in my direction. "But that was just the tip of the ol' iceberg with her. She'd pick up guys here and do 'em right in the backroom after we closed up." He nodded to the room with the pool tables. "Bet you didn't know *that* about your friend, huh?"

I shook my head. Holy hell, this was much more than I'd expected.

"She brought that guy in a bunch of times," he said, pointing to the picture of J.T., still on the bar, with his cigarette. "People used to talk. Said that guy got married on the rebound after she dumped his ass to get engaged to some rich prick that was away at college. Boy, that dude had no fuckin' clue what his girlfriend was up to back home."

Or did he? I wondered. That might explain Adam's supposed reluctance to marry Chelsea. Not to mention lend credence to the blackmail theory. *Oh, Adam, how much did you know?*

Jimmy stubbed his cigarette out on the floor, picked up the dishrag, looked at it like he didn't remember why it was even there, and then threw it back down on the bar. "You wanna know somethin' even funnier?"

I took another fortifying drink of beer. "What's that?" I asked, trying to keep my voice even.

"She still brought that guy in here even *after* he got married, and she was engaged to that college dude. Guess a girl like that doesn't give a shit 'bout things like marriage and engagements, huh?"

"Guess not," I whispered, glancing down at the picture of J.T. He looked so young, so innocent. Not like a guy who'd end up doing drugs and cheating on his wife. Had I ever really known him? What else was he capable of?

"Hey, you OK?" Jimmy asked.

"Yeah, fine," I replied heavily as I crumpled the photo and stuffed it into my bag.

I drank the last of the beer, which had grown warm, and readied to leave. But as I pushed the empty bottle away, Jimmy said, "Oh, hey, there was someone else she used to bring in here once in a while." I raised a questioning eyebrow.

"Not a guy though." Jimmy smirked.

"You remember a name?" I asked.

"Nah, but the chick sure was hot." He whistled. "Had a killer body and sexy long blonde hair."

"Was that it?" I asked, fighting the urge to roll my eyes.

Jimmy shook his head, a lecherous smile turning up his lips. "No, there's more. I remember this one time…"

I stood, waiting. Hell, I'd paid a hundred bucks for information; I wasn't going anywhere until he finished. Jimmy shuffled around behind the bar, acting strangely excited. "And?" I said impatiently.

"Yeah, so like I said, Chelsea was wild." He paused, all the while looking like maybe he was replaying in his head whatever tawdry tale he was about to tell. "So this time I'm talkin' about, she was here with that hot girl…the blonde…and they're both really drunk. Hangin' all over each other." Jimmy snickered. "Shit like that, you know what I mean?"

He looked at me, waiting, so I decided to humor him. "Sure."

"So it's late…like closing time late. Only people left are me, Old Carl, Chelsea, and her friend." Jimmy leaned on the bar, continuing in a low voice, "So Old Carl pulls out one of them Polaroid cameras from behind the bar. He tells Chelsea he'll let her bar tab slide for the rest of the week if she makes out with her friend. Oh, and lets him take some pictures, of course."

"Of course," I said dryly.

"Hell, she wasn't offended or nothin'," Jimmy said, snorting. "But it sure as hell wasn't like she needed a pass on her bar tab. Everyone knew she had money. No, her ass was all over that shit just for kicks. Full on tongue action too, man. And Old Carl got his pictures. A bunch of 'em too."

I perked up. Who was this mystery blonde? Nothing like this had been mentioned in the case files. Maybe it would turn out to be nothing, maybe she was just another wild girl who happened to meet up with Chelsea that night. But no, according to Jimmy, they'd been in here more than just that one time. She had to have been someone Chelsea knew. And that made me wonder why the police had never found her, never questioned her. What if she held some kind of key to the case? How much more had she known about Chelsea's secret life? Without a doubt, I needed to find out the identity of the girl.

"Do you know what he did with those pictures?" I asked Jimmy.

"Don't know what that old perv did with his, but he did give *me* one."

It was looking like my hundred bucks was about to pay off after all. "You still have it?"

"Yeah, somewhere, I think. I'll have to look for it, but I could call you if I find it."

"That'll work," I said, writing my cell number on the back of a coaster.

Jimmy picked up the coaster, but as I got up to leave, he stopped me. "Oh wait. I remember one more thing about that night. It was somethin' I overheard Chelsea sayin' to her buddy."

"What was that?"

"Right as Chelsea leans in to lay one on her friend, the girl starts pulling away…suddenly acting all uptight and shit." Jimmy took out another cigarette. "Then I hear Chelsea whisper something to her, like 'just go with it, nobody knows who you are here,' and 'it's not like we haven't done this before.'"

I blinked a couple of times, stunned, and stared blankly at Jimmy.

"That's it," he said, lighting his cigarette.

"Uh, OK, thanks," I said hastily.

I practically ran for the exit. I needed some air, and I needed it fast. Chelsea had obviously been *way* more out of control than I'd ever dreamed. *Poor Adam*. She'd been messing around with J.T. for a long time, their presence at Billy's confirming it. So that moved J.T., and probably Jennifer if she'd known, further up my suspect list.

But had Chelsea also been cheating on Adam with a *woman*? It was more important than ever to find out the identity of the blonde. I hoped Jimmy would truly search for the picture. Maybe he'd put some extra effort into it, thinking he'd make another quick hundred.

How could Adam not have known about Chelsea's many extracurricular activities? Surely he had to have heard the rumors. Why on earth had he still been planning on marrying such an unfaithful bitch? There was really only one explanation: Chelsea *must* have had something on him. And what she had on Adam must have been huge. Like, *life-ruining* huge. But what could it have been? The police had turned up nothing unsavory in Adam's past. But Chelsea obviously knew something more than they did.

But the question that haunted me the entire drive back to Cove Beach was this: Was this secret devastating enough for Adam to want to make Chelsea *disappear*?

Chapter 7

The following day, after my dad called to tell me he was making some progress in tracking down those pay phone records, I stopped by the café to visit Helena. Seated at a table near the front, staring out the picture window to her left, Helena was absently tapping her perfectly manicured fingernails on the side of a porcelain coffee cup.

"Helena?" I queried softly, reticent to intrude on what appeared to be an introspective moment.

She started at the sound of my voice, her hand fluttering to her chest. "Oh, Maddy, you startled me." She laughed a little. "I'm sorry, I was just daydreaming."

"I can always come back later," I offered.

"Don't be silly. Have a seat." Helena stood, smoothed out the long, white cardigan sweater over her black leggings, and began walking back to the coffee bar, black heels tapping out a staccato rhythm. "What can I get you? Cappuccino?" she called back over her shoulder.

I shimmied out of my trench coat and replied, "Just regular coffee's fine," before taking a seat.

Helena returned with the coffee. "I'm glad you stopped by," she began as she sat down across from me. "Nate left Sunday evening with Adam on a business trip, and it's been entirely too quiet around here."

I was more than a little surprised to hear Nate was traveling with Adam. As manager of the island, it seemed unlikely he'd be expected to accompany Adam on business trips. Maybe this particular trip had something to do with "managing" an island? After all, I felt pretty certain it had been Nate interrupting our time at the lighthouse. Perhaps it was all related.

Focusing back on Helena, I asked, "Well, I guess you're happy they'll be back tomorrow, huh?"

Helena flipped her blonde tresses back, shot me an all-too-knowing glance, and took a tentative sip from her cup. "Hmmm, bet I'm not the only one who's happy." Instead of answering, I too took a careful sip. Undeterred, Helena continued, "Nate tells me you're going on a date with Adam tomorrow night." I nodded. "Flying down to *Boston* even," she finished, one eyebrow arched.

"Yep, we are," I confirmed, trying to play it cool.

"Excited?" she pressed.

I shrugged, and Helena sighed exasperatedly. "Come on, Maddy, *Adam Ward* asked you out. On a date. He's taking you to Boston, for heaven's sake," she said, her voice raising an octave following each sentence. "So spill it, girl!"

I was secretly relieved and ecstatic to finally have someone to gush to about just how incredibly excited I actually was. So I squealed out an "I *know*," as I fully reverting back to a teenage girl level of enthusiasm.

Helena either had an Oscar in her future, or else she was genuinely thrilled for me, because she grabbed my wrist and squeezed. "Do you realize how momentous this is? Adam never asks anyone out. Like *never*."

Well, this was surprising news. "Really?" I asked, incredulous. "You mean Adam hasn't dated since…" I hesitated. "Well, since Chelsea? I mean that's a long time to go with no, er, physical contact." I was shocked—but kind of pleased—by the possibility that Adam was not out there actively pursuing female companionship. *Well, other than mine, that is.*

Helena gave me a measured look. "I didn't mean *that* exactly. I'd hardly characterize Adam as some kind of a monk. I'm just saying he never *dates* anyone."

A sick feeling began to form in the pit of my stomach, and jealousy reared its ugly head. The thought of Adam touching some other woman like that just bothered me to no end. Irrational as it was, I felt oddly possessive of Adam. Another sure sign

I was falling for the man. *Damn.*

Helena's expression softened once she noticed my dejected demeanor. "Don't let it bother you. You know Nate was just saying the other day that Adam hasn't even seen Lindsey for a couple of months. So I think that ship may have sailed."

"Lindsey? Who's Lindsey?" I cringed. "If you know her name, it must have been something ongoing, something long-term, right?"

"It's not as bad as it sounds," Helena insisted. "Just listen."

"Oh, don't worry. I'm waiting with baited breath."

Helena ignored my sarcastic tone. "Adam met Lindsey in Boston—"

"Oh great, Boston," I lamented, while dramatically resting my forehead on the table. "Maybe she can meet us while we're on our date. How cozy." I knew I was being ridiculous, but it just *bothered* me.

"Maybe we should talk about something else?" Helena muttered.

"No, no. Go on," I mumbled into the surface of the table. "I can handle it."

"Look," Helena continued, "Adam met Lindsay a while back, but it was never anything serious. It was just a physical thing. And it really sounds like it's over from what Nate says."

When I really thought about it, I knew I shouldn't be worried about this Lindsey-person, hookup, whatever. After all, she was in Boston, and I was here. And Adam hadn't *dated* her, according to Helena. But he had asked me out on a date.

I appreciated Helena's candor, and I couldn't help but wonder how much more she knew about Adam. I lifted my head from the table and sat back. "Can I ask you something, Helena?"

"Sure," she replied.

I nervously traced the rim of my coffee cup. "It's about Adam, and if you don't want to answer, or you don't know, I'll understand."

Helena reached over and stilled my hand. Our eyes met, and she said, "Maddy, just ask. I'll tell you what I know."

I took a deep breath. "Was Adam still in love with Chelsea when she disappeared?"

Helena's lips set in a hard line, and her face grew serious. She answered with a simple, "No."

Well, if that had been the case…

Curious about the other part of the allegation from the anonymous sources, I asked, "Do you know then if they were still, uh, sleeping together?"

Helena shook her head and barely whispered, "No, Maddy, they weren't."

"Then *why* was he going through with the wedding? In fact, why was he even still engaged to her?" I asked, desperately hoping she had the answers.

"I don't know, Maddy. I really don't," she said, looking away.

"But you must have some idea? Was there any indication of trouble? There had to have been something? Anything?" I pressed. "Please, Helena."

Helena leaned back in her chair and rubbed at her temples. Finally she cleared her throat. "Chelsea knew something about Adam. Something nobody else did…and I think she was leveraging whatever it was against him to get her way." She hesitated, biting her lower lip. "I don't know what it was, Maddy. Neither does Nate. But I'm sure it was bad, because I'm absolutely positive Adam did not want to marry that girl."

"You have no idea what it could have been?"

"None," Helena whispered, voice cracking and tears welling in the corners of her eyes. "I just wish I'd never introduced them. Some days I feel so guilty. Like all of this could have been avoided. But Chelsea wasn't that horrible early on. Sure, she could be bitchy, but she was nothing like the person she ended up becoming." Helena wiped a tear from her cheek.

I wasn't sure if Helena was crying over Chelsea's disappearance, guilt over introducing her to Adam, or something else entirely. I placed my hand over hers. "Helena, it's not your fault. You can't blame yourself. You had no control over what happened."

"Yeah, but Chelsea hurt Adam in *so* many ways." She blinked back more tears and then met my eyes. "Like did you know she had an affair with J.T. O'Brien?"

"Really?" I squeaked, pretending to be unaware. "Did Adam know?"

"He found out right around the time they got engaged." *This* I had not heard. Helena continued, "Adam was home for spring break, and the four of us went out one night in Harbourtown. We ended up getting wasted and calling a cab. But instead of taking us home, Chelsea directed the driver to take us to some rundown bar down by the river."

Billy's, I thought.

"J.T. was already there. Just sitting at the bar, all by himself. But he kept glancing over and giving us these weird looks. It was actually kind of creepy. Anyway, at some point, Chelsea said she had to go to the bathroom. About ten minutes passed, and Nate had to go too. Adam asked him to find out what was taking Chelsea so long to return." Helena stopped long enough to take a drink from her cup, and then she took a deep breath. "Well, Nate found out what was taking her so long when he walked into the men's room, because there was Chelsea. Down on her knees in front of J.T."

"Oh God, no," I gasped.

"It's true." Helena paused, as if even in retelling the story she still couldn't believe it had happened. "Nate threw J.T. up against the wall outside the bathroom, and, get this, Chelsea started screaming at Nate to leave *J.T.* alone. Adam and I witnessed the whole exchange when we ran over to see what all the commotion was about. Then, worse yet, Chelsea had the nerve to ask Adam to make Nate stop. She kept saying it was all a big misunderstanding."

"Oh, Helena," I said, shaking my head. Though it may have been foolish, my heart ached for Adam. Nobody deserved to be treated like that. "What did Adam do?"

She sighed. "He just turned and walked away, disgusted. He knew then, Maddy. Everything he'd ever suspected, rumors he may have heard, everything. In that instant, he knew it was *all* true."

"That's terrible," I mumbled.

Helena raised an eyebrow. "You think that's bad? It got crazier two days later."

"Why? What happened?"

"Chelsea calls to inform me she and Adam had just gotten *engaged*."

"What?" I said. "That doesn't make any sense."

"Tell me about it." Helena shrugged her shoulders. "I don't know. But think of it this way: If someone knew something about you, like, maybe it's something nobody else in the whole world knows. Maybe it's too dangerous to reveal." I was mesmerized as Helena continued, "If that person who knows your secret threatened to expose it, would *you* have a choice? Other than to go along with whatever that individual wanted?"

"I guess not," I said, shaking my head. What *was* this secret?

"There's one more thing." Helena leaned in close to the table. "Nate confronted Adam a few days after the official engagement announcement."

"What did he say?" I asked.

"Nate asked him outright if Chelsea was blackmailing him, because there was no other possible explanation. Not after what went down at that bar with her and J.T. O'Brien." Helena made a face of disgust.

"Did he have an explanation?" I leaned in close to the table as well.

"He didn't deny it, but Nate told me it was the one and only time he ever feared Adam." Helena met my eyes.

"Why?" I was on the edge of my seat. Literally.

"He said Adam was defensive, not like himself at all. He insisted Nate drop it. But it was the *way* Adam said it that bothered Nate. He told me he knew then that whatever it was Chelsea was holding over Adam, it was probably going to end badly."

I swallowed hard. "You don't think Adam—"

"Of course not," she cut in.

I didn't want to entertain the possibility of Adam playing a role in the disappearance either, so I changed direction. "Well, do you think Chelsea was still seeing J.T.? I mean, after that night?" I thought about how Jimmy had said she started bringing J.T. back to Billy's. Even after he was married to Jennifer, after Chelsea and Adam were engaged.

"Maybe not at first," Helena said thoughtfully. "But I always suspected it started back up again not long afterward. The crazy thing is that two weeks after that whole incident in Harbourtown, J.T. ran off with Jennifer Weston to Vegas to get married."

"That's odd," I said, trying to sound like I hadn't already been privy to this information too.

"Yeah, poor Jennifer. Guess J.T. married her on the rebound, probably to one-up Chelsea for getting engaged."

"Oh, Helena." I sighed in resignation. "It's so much more complicated than I even imagined." I rested my elbows on the table and put my head in my hands.

"I know, Maddy," she replied in a soothing tone. "But it's all in the past. Adam really is a good guy. Don't let those ghosts from the past haunt the present."

I ventured a tired glance up at Helena. "You're probably right."

"Trust me, I am," she said.

More than anything I wanted to believe Adam was a "good guy." My heart believed it, but my head was spinning, filled with uncertainty. How much had Adam known? Obviously his suspicions were confirmed by what he'd witnessed at Billy's. But had he also known when Chelsea and J.T. resumed their relationship? And though I'd not breathed a word to Helena about what I'd discovered at Billy's, I had to wonder if Adam had been aware of *everything* Chelsea was up to, including the random men...*and* the mystery blonde.

Lies, blackmail, affairs, deceit.

Not to mention were things really over between Adam and Lindsey? I certainly had no intention of becoming Adam's new side dish.

The earlier excitement I'd felt about my impending date

with Adam was waning. Sure, the man was incredibly appealing, but it seemed like I was being repeatedly reminded of why I should back off. Like fate was trying to warn me.

But instead of backing off, I chose to dive in deeper.

Chapter 8

Despite my misgivings, I couldn't help but feel a surge of anticipation when I heard Adam's Porsche pull into the driveway of my cottage. Seven o'clock sharp, the clock in the front hall confirmed with a series of lyrical chimes.

I smoothed the long, lacy sleeves of the black, crinkled-silk couture dress I'd fortunately thought to pack before leaving LA. Turning to check out the back view in the full-length mirror that hung on the wall near the front door, I was pleased to find the dress fit snugly in all the right places, the short hemline showing off a fair amount of bare leg. *Definitely quite a sexy little dress*, I thought, hopeful that Adam would agree.

Just then the doorbell chimed. I quickly stepped into my black leather stiletto heels with the trademark red soles. With a nervous touch to the tendrils of my upswept hair that were framing my lightly made-up face, I took a deep breath and opened the front door.

Nothing could have prepared me for the breathtaking sight of Adam dressed in an impeccably tailored black suit; crisp, white button-down shirt; black silk tie; and a pair of what I was sure were exorbitantly expensive black dress shoes. I looked up and caught Adam's deep blue eyes darkening as they *oh so slowly* descended down the curves of my body appraisingly.

After a moment of pretty much blatantly ogling me, Adam raised his unapologetic gaze to meet mine. A surge of warmth coursed through my veins, while a crooked, knowing smile played at his lips. "Maddy," he said in a velvety voice, "you look absolutely ravishing tonight."

"Thank you, Adam," I replied, thinking the same thing applied to him. But I kept it to myself; he was cocky enough.

Adam's eyes stayed on mine for a beat longer than necessary, making me wonder if he could guess all the sinful things I'd already dreamt of doing to him. *See, cocky enough,* I thought, looking away.

Adam extended his hand in a formal gesture. "Are you ready?" he asked. "Walker is back at the hangar, and Boston awaits."

"Walker?" I questioned, picking up my black velvet clutch in one hand, while placing the other in Adam's. The name was familiar; *Oh yeah, I read it in the case files.* Walker was the name of Trina's boyfriend back then. Could it be the same guy?

"Walker will be flying us to Boston tonight," Adam answered as we walked to his car.

He opened the passenger door for me, moving his free hand to the small of my back. "Would this be the same Walker who once dated your sister?" I asked, sliding into the car.

Adam looked down at me, scrutinizing my face briefly. *Oops, Adam had never mentioned* that *bit of information before.* As he closed the car door, I heard him mumble under his breath in annoyance, "Helena."

Nope, Adam, it wasn't Helena who told me, I thought to myself.

Adam slid into the driver's seat and turned the ignition. As the powerful engine roared to life, he responded, "Yes, it's the same Walker, but he's not just my sister's boyfriend anymore; he's her fiancé. In fact, they're getting married in the spring."

"And he's your pilot?" I asked. "I thought you flew your own plane?"

"I do, usually. Walker's a commercial pilot by trade, but he helps me out when I'd rather be focusing my attention…let's say, *elsewhere.*"

"Oh," I said, fidgeting slightly.

"Like tonight," Adam added, flashing me a dazzling smile before placing the car in reverse and peeling out of my driveway.

Driving to his private runway, which was located on the far east side of his property, took only minutes with Adam behind the wheel.

"Maddy," he chuckled when we pulled to a merciful stop at the end of the runway. "I sure hope you're more comfortable with flying." Adam nodded to my iron grip on the passenger door handle.

"*You're* not flying the plane tonight, right?" I inquired, only half-mocking.

"Ha-ha. Funny girl," Adam replied as he smoothly exited the car, just as graciously as he'd gotten in.

A Gulfstream III corporate jet sat idling on the runway, bright lights blazing against the backdrop of a teal and charcoal-streaked twilight sky. A smaller Cessna aircraft, most likely the plane Walker flew in on, was visible in the open hangar to the right of the runway.

Adam opened my car door and once again offered me his hand. "Nervous?" he asked.

"About?"

"Flying, of course." Adam caressed the back of my hand with his thumb. "What else would I mean, Madeleine?" he added with a wink.

"Ha-ha. Funny boy," I retorted, throwing his earlier words back at him as I swung my legs out of the Porsche in such a way as to afford him an eyeful of thigh. He sure was in fine form tonight, but so was I.

Adam's eyes raked up the full length of my body. A wicked grin spread across his face as I steadied myself on my heels. "Are you *coming*, Maddy?" Adam asked in a low, husky voice, leaning in close enough for me to see the mischievousness in his eyes.

Guess two could play at the innuendo game. I blinked up at him as he straightened to his full height. "Coming?" he asked again, this time with no hint of sexual innuendo. But my mind was still replaying the way he'd said it the first time.

"Uh-huh." I nodded weakly.

Adam laughed, and then we made our way across the runway. "So you really own this jet?" I asked as we reached the base of the aircraft's metal stairs.

"I really do," Adam replied.

"Impressive," I whispered to myself because, really, it just was.

Walker met us at the top of the stairs, and while Adam engaged him in weather condition and flight path-related conversation, I craned my neck so I could glimpse into the cabin interior.

Wow! The jet was equipped with all the expected—as well as some unexpected—passenger luxuries. Plush, oversized leather seats lined the sides of the cabin, some with small tables between them, bolted down to the floor of the plane, of course. Fresh-cut flowers in crystal vases topped most all of the tables, an obvious addition for tonight.

There was one longer table situated in front of two connecting seats that bore a closer resemblance to a loveseat than to any kind of standard aircraft seating. Atop that particular table, a bowl of fresh fruit, a bottle of iced champagne, and two flutes rested.

Adam cleared his throat, drawing my attention back to the tawny-haired, brown-eyed man in front of me. "Maddy, this is Captain Walker Adair." Our pilot extended his hand, and Adam continued, "Walker, Ms. Madeleine Fitch."

We shook hands, his grasp firm yet gentle. There was a kindness in his demeanor, and I found myself instantly liking Captain Adair. "Nice to meet you, Ms. Fitch," he said.

"Nice to meet you too," I replied. "And please, just call me Maddy."

Walker nodded and excused himself to the cockpit. Within moments the sounds of soft jazz filled the cabin. Adam led me to the two connected seats—the ones that looked like a loveseat—and I sat down on the side closest to the window, sinking into the soft, buttery leather.

Adam sat down in the seat next to me and proceeded to swiftly uncork the bottle on the table. "Champagne?" he offered, a crystal flute poised in one hand.

I nodded, and he poured us each a glass as the plane began to taxi down the runway. Our knees accidentally touched when

Adam handed me my flute, and a rush of electricity pulsed through my body. "Shall we toast?" he asked, raising his glass.

"Sure." I raised my glass to his.

Adam hesitated and then said, "To a wonderful start to what I hope will be a memorable evening. Cheers."

"Cheers," I said, tapping my glass to his as the plane lifted into the air.

Adam and I tipped our glasses back simultaneously, but while I took a dainty sip, Adam emptied his flute. He then settled back into his seat, loosened his tie, and closed his eyes with a sigh.

Angling to get a better view of him, I shifted in my seat, all the while sipping my champagne. But far more delightful than the sweet, bubbly liquid in the glass, I drank in the glory of Adam Ward at rest. Even dressed in his fine attire, his raven-black hair was still a sexy mess. I longed to run my fingers through it, much like I'd seen him do the night I'd been caught on his property. I bit down on my lip and sighed when my eyes fell upon his full lips, glistening with a touch of wetness from the champagne. Replaying the teasing, feather-soft kisses from our time at the lighthouse sent more tingles through my body than any amount of alcohol ever could. Even so I tipped my head back and drank the last bit of bubbly from my glass.

Leaning forward, I placed my glass on the table. When I sat back and glanced next to me, I was surprised to find a seemingly amused Adam, eyes open and a knowing smirk on his face. A blush rose to my cheeks because, eyes closed or not, he was clearly aware that I'd been checking him out.

"How was it, Maddy?" Adam's voice was even and betrayed nothing, but his eyes danced wickedly.

"How was what?" I asked innocently.

"The champagne, of course." Adam leaned his head back against the rest and waited, watching, for my response.

Two could play at this game, so I licked my lips and said, "Mmm, it was *amazing*. The aroma...the full bouquet...I'd have to say it may have been the most *suc*-culent thing I've ever tasted."

Adam cocked an eyebrow, and a smile tugged at the corners of his mouth. *It would seem our dear Mr. Ward was quite enjoying this little exchange.*

Reaching into the bowl of fresh fruit on the table, he purred, "Personally I prefer a sweeter juiciness against *my* tongue."

I was rendered momentarily speechless by Adam's suggestive words, and surely that had been his intention. Holding up a plump, ripe strawberry, he added smugly, "I'm talking about the strawberry, Maddy. Would you care to try one?"

I swallowed hard, nodding. Good God, he was killing me. I reached for the strawberry, but Adam pulled it away, short of my grasp, at the very last second.

With a dark smile, he crooned, "Uh-uh-uh. It will be much better for you like this."

Adam poured champagne into his empty flute. He then lightly dipped the strawberry into the fizzing liquid, tapping the side of the fruit to the rim of the glass before lifting it to my lips. "Open your mouth," he demanded, in such a way that I readily parted my lips.

Adam brushed the strawberry across my bottom lip, held it still for a beat, and then used the champagne-moistened fruit to lightly trace the outline of my lips, his darkened eyes meeting mine. "Lick the tip," he said, his voice low and silky.

Eager to comply, I tentatively touched the end of the strawberry with the tip of my tongue. Champagne sweetness hit my taste buds. What we were doing felt sinful and thrilling. Emboldened by the decadence of it all, I artfully swirling my tongue around the tip of the strawberry and met Adam's gaze.

He pulled the strawberry away. "Close your eyes," he whispered. I readily acquiesced and felt him shifting in his seat—the heat of his body closing in on mine. A swirl of liquid, a light tapping against the crystal rim of the glass. "Do you want it, Madeleine?" Adam asked, every word laced with the suggestion of so much more.

I nodded demurely, and Adam purred, "*Tell* me you want it."

"I want it, Adam. Please." And, holy hell, I'd never wanted

it so badly in my life. I didn't care about the damn strawberry itself, but every fiber of my body was on fire, and I wanted Adam to be the one to give it to me. "*Please,*" I whispered again.

Suddenly the champagne-moistened fruit was at my lips—tracing, teasing, taunting. I let out a stifled moan, and Adam stilled the movement of the strawberry. "You're not peeking, are you?" he asked.

I shook my head, my lips brushing against the pebbly texture of the fruit. "OK, be a good girl now"—Adam prodded my lips open with the fruit— "and suck."

I squirmed in my seat and obediently wrapped my mouth around the whole strawberry. When I dragged my lips along the length of the fruit, I heard Adam whisper a barely audible "fuck" that stirred me even further. I repeated the same action, and Adam growled, "Just bite the fucking strawberry, Madeleine."

I bit the tip off the strawberry, and Adam pulled the fruit away. I could hear him biting into what remained.

Just as I was about to open my eyes, heated, strawberry – and champagne-moistened lips crashed into mine. We both moaned as our mouths moved hungrily together. He tasted divine, and I wanted more. I trailed my hands lazily over the lapels of his suit jacket, before curving them up and around to the nape of his neck. Adam's fingers teasingly brushed the sides of my breasts as he snaked his hands down to rest on my waist, and, in response, I raked my fingers into his hair, pulling him closer.

Amid noisy gasps and hot breaths, Adam deepened our kiss, tenderly parting my lips until our tongues met—all strawberries, champagne, and the thrill of uncharted exploration that only those first kisses can deliver.

My body ached for more, much more, but unfortunately the plane was beginning to descend. We'd soon be in Boston. Adam, who must have felt the change in altitude as well, began to slow our kisses.

"You're so beautiful," he breathed out against my lips.

I longed to hear more; I longed to say something in return.

But Walker's voice rasping out over the intercom brought me back to reality. "Mr. Ward, we'll be on the ground in about five minutes. Please prepare for landing."

We broke apart, leaned back in our seats, fumbled for our seat belts. As the plane touched down, Adam took my hand and brought it to his mouth. "So did you enjoy the flight, Ms. Fitch?" he asked, his lips brushing over my knuckles.

"Immensely," I responded, smiling. *And, boy, had I ever.*

Still in a daze from the champagne, the strawberries, but mostly the kisses, I barely noticed as we made our way from the plane to a sleek, black limousine that was waiting for us on the runway. As we pulled away from the jet, I heard Adam instruct the driver to take us to some exclusive, members-only dinner club that was located in a skyscraper in downtown Boston. I'd heard of it before but had never been there.

The club—which took up the entire upper floor of the tall building in which it was housed—was all dark wood paneling, maroon carpeting, brass adornments. Oil paintings in the style of the Old Masters lined the walls. Everything about the place screamed old money, power, prestige. It was obviously a place for only the absolute wealthiest of the wealthy.

The maitre d' led us through the main dining room and back to a private dining area. As we stepped into a room, decorated in the same dark wood and maroon palette, Adam informed me he had reserved the whole area just for us.

I glanced around. Floor-to-ceiling windows allowed for the lights of downtown Boston to sparkle before us. Classical music played softly in the background, and the soft glow of candlelight flickered all around. "Adam, this is very, *very* nice," I remarked as we took our seats.

"I'm glad you approve," he replied, a smile playing on his lips.

Just then a wine steward entered the room, and Adam engaged him in a quiet discussion. I nervously fumbled with my napkin while they spoke. When the wine steward left, Adam directed his attention back to me. "Maddy, I have a bit of a request."

"And what would that be?" I asked quietly, somewhat distracted by how painfully gorgeous Adam looked in the warm glow of the candlelight—shadows playing across perfection.

"I've ordered a special vintage for us, which I think you'll enjoy." Adam paused. "But, if you don't mind, I'd also like to take the liberty of ordering dinner for the both of us."

I'd never had a man order dinner for me before, but Adam had impeccable taste, so, trusting him, I said, "Of course. That would be fine."

A waiter came in with a set of menus, but Adam ordered without even opening one. Observing the interaction between the two—the waiter listening attentively and respectfully as Adam commanded his full attention—I felt the obvious power Adam held over so many people. It was truly impressive, and it allowed me to see why he was so successful.

After the waiter left, the steward returned with the wine and poured a small amount into a glass. Adam took a contemplative sip and nodded to the steward, who then poured us each a glass before leaving the room.

I took a small taste and found it to be, as promised, quite delightful. Curious as to what exactly I was drinking, I leaned across the table, albeit awkwardly, to try to read the label on the bottle which was resting in an ice bucket.

Adam cleared his throat, and I glanced up to meet his amused stare. "Oh, sorry," I said, quickly leaning back in my chair.

He chuckled amusedly. "It's a Bollinger Vieille Vienes Françaises, 1999, Maddy."

"Mmm." I finished the last of the fine vintage and put down my glass. "Well, I have to say, it's quite tasty."

"I'm glad you like it," Adam replied, smiling as he poured me another glass.

I was already feeling a little heady, but whether it was from the alcohol—or my date—I couldn't be sure.

The waiter arrived with our first course, foie-gras-stuffed morels. Not surprisingly they were a perfect complement to the wine Adam had chosen. As we finished up, and before the entrees arrived, the waiter placed tiny, dainty liqueur glasses filled with sorbet in front of each of us.

Adam placed his small spoon in my glass and scooped a small amount of sorbet onto it. "May I?" he asked, holding the spoon to my lips.

I said "uh-huh" and allowed him to place the icy, lemony treat on my tongue. I closed my eyes and was instantly reminded of the strawberry on the plane and how that had led to kissing Adam. A tiny sigh escaped my lips at the memory. I opened my eyes and glanced at Adam, who was smiling surreptitiously while spooning more sorbet onto the tiny spoon.

"Adam, why are we having dessert *before* the main course?" I inquired quietly, while glancing at the doorway to make sure the waiter was not within earshot.

Adam laughed. "Maddy, it's not dessert. The sorbet is to cleanse your palate *before* the main course."

"Oh," I giggled, licking the icy goodness from the spoon Adam again raised to my mouth. I actually knew that, had seen it in a movie, but the wine was making me silly and giddy. Besides, it was just too much fun to play with Adam.

And it seemed Adam was all set for *his* next move, for he dipped my spoon into his own glass of sorbet and licked it, just as I had done. Only he did it very, very slowly. Our eyes met, and I melted a little at the playful, but utterly seductive, sparkle in his blue, blue eyes. He held my gaze as he dug the little spoon into the last bit of my sorbet, preparing to feed it to me, once again.

"You know, a girl could get used to being pampered like this," I remarked.

"Could you?" Adam asked, setting down the spoon.

I searched his face, not sure if this was all part of Adam's seduction strategy—which was *really, really* effective, to be honest—or if he was genuinely interested in me, Maddy Fitch. My heart tightened in my chest, because, of course, I wanted to be pampered like this by Adam Ward. I wanted desperately for him to have more than a passing fancy for me. But I was worried that my heart could end up broken. I didn't want to be his new Lindsey, so I answered, "Maybe," as I cast my eyes downward.

"Maddy," Adam sighed, his tone serious. I waited for more, but the main course arrived, effectively silencing whatever he'd been about to say.

Adam had chosen a turbot with lobster sauce. Turbot, he informed me as we ate dinner and engaged in less serious banter, was a type of fish. And I found it to be surprisingly good. After dinner and a dessert of red velvet petit fours, Adam slid open one of the glass panels, and we walked out onto a large balcony overlooking the city.

For late September it was unusually warm, and I savored the mild, ocean-kissed breezes as they swept over me. Walking to the iron railing encircling the balcony, I was astounded by the amazing view of downtown Boston. "Wow," I mouthed to myself.

Adam came up behind me, and wrapped his arms around me. I leaned back into the warmth of his body, relaxing into him as his lips began to ghost along the side of my neck. But then he stilled. Turning me around to face him, fingers splayed out over my hips. I placed a hand on his chest and looked up into his inquiring eyes. "Do you trust me?" he asked.

"Um…" I glanced away, and then down. "I think."

Adam chuckled a little. "Guess that's a start." He lifted a hand from my hip and nudged my chin up so that I was looking at him. "I'm going to be honest with you, Madeleine." Was this what he'd been about to tell me at the lighthouse? "I was attracted to you back in high school, and I should have dumped Chelsea and asked you out." My heart skipped a beat. "But I was young and naïve."

I moved my hand to trace the smooth contours of his face. "I would have loved to have gone out with you back then, Adam," I admitted.

"What about now?" he whispered, his lips lowering to mine. "Better late than never."

Adam kissed me, softly at first and then with more passionate. His hands moved slowly over my curves. I moaned into his mouth and pushed my breasts into his chest.

Adam's mouth moved to my neck—sucking, kissing, nibbling. I groaned, and he pulled me closer to his body. I could feel the clear outline of his substantial hardness close to my own heat, and, throwing caution to the wind, I gasped, "God, let's get out of here."

Adam pulled back, eyes ablaze. "Are you sure?"

A quick image of Adam seated on one of those oversized leather chairs on the plane, hiking up my dress while I stood before him played through my mind, and I hastily answered, "Yeah, I'm absolutely positive."

We left the dinner club hurriedly, and Adam and I pretty much made out like we were kids back in high school during the limo ride to the plane. There was a lot of groping and grinding, but apparently, he wanted to wait as much as I did until we got into the air for the real fun to begin.

As we boarded the plane, Walker gave us a knowing smile as we tried, unsuccessfully, to keep our hands to ourselves. "Guess I'll be keeping the cockpit door *closed*?" I heard him say quietly to Adam as I continued to my seat. I didn't hear Adam's reply, but he spent a few extra minutes talking with Walker, so I could only imagine.

"Do I have time to go to the restroom before we take off?" I asked once Adam settled in next to me.

"Yeah, sure, it'll be a few more minutes before we take off."

I grabbed my clutch and went into the airplane lavatory, closing the door behind me. Fumbling through the contents, I finally found some gloss to apply to my lips, deliciously swollen from all the kissing. When I threw the tube back in, my cell blinked. I had several missed calls, all from my dad.

The voicemails he'd left said variations of things like "Maddy, call me back; it's important," or "Madeleine, this is your dad. Where are you? Call me *now*." I really didn't want to call my father back, not now, but it sounded urgent. So, sighing, I dialed his number.

"Maddy!" my father exclaimed upon answering on the first ring. "Where in the hell have you been? I was—"

"Dad," I interrupted, keeping my voice low. "I can't really talk for long, but what's going on? Are you OK?"

"Yeah, I'm fine. I didn't mean to worry you. I was just calling to tell you I tracked down those records from the pay phone at the bank here in town."

"Oh? *Ohhhh*," I said. "So what did you find out?"

I could hear paper rustling on the other end of the line, just as the engines of the Gulfstream whirred to life. "Dad, hurry," I pressed.

"OK, OK, here it is…" More rustling papers, and then, "One forty-three second call to a cell phone number. Ah, let's see, a local number, it seems."

"Dad! *Who* was Chelsea calling that night?" I pressed.

"It says here that the cell phone she was calling was registered to Adam Ward."

No!

I was silent, and my dad repeated, "Looks like Adam was the last person Chelsea talked to right before she disappeared."

This was not good, not good at all. Had those records truly been missed by the police? Or had they been buried? I knew of one person with enough money to make that happen. And it made me sick to consider it.

One thing for certain, I'd made a huge miscalculation by going on this date. To be honest, I'd misjudged everything. I had been deluding myself. You couldn't go back in time, people change. This night was a lie. Who was Adam, really? He'd been calling Chelsea less than an hour before she disappeared. And what did that mean? Nothing good, I was sure.

Despair washed over me as I sunk to the lavatory floor. And in that moment I think my heart broke just a little.

Chapter 9

Things were a mess. Better put, I was a mess. Over a week had passed since my date had been cut short by my dad's discovery that *Adam* was the person Chelsea had called from a pay phone in Harbour Falls shortly before she was never seen—nor heard from—ever again. Yes, you could say that little tidbit of information put quite a damper on the evening.

The flight from Boston back to Fade Island that night had gone from awkward, once I returned to my seat for takeoff, to tense by the time we landed on the island. I'd tried to play off my sudden icy demeanor toward Adam as an unfortunate side effect of some kind of stomach upset. True, I'd been feeling rather ill but not from eating something that hadn't agreed with me. Despite my act, by the time the plane landed, Adam had correctly suspected there was something more behind my sudden cool and distant attitude.

On the short ride back to the cottage, he repeatedly tried to get me to tell him what had caused my change of heart. After all, we'd gone from almost becoming lovers to barely speaking. The whole episode served to remind me that I'd been moving entirely too fast with Adam.

Silent at first, I eventually stated I had nothing to discuss. Trust me, I wanted an explanation for the last known phone call Chelsea had ever made, but the problem was I'd have to offer up a reason of my own for even *knowing* about that forty-three second call to Adam. I had no desire to witness his reaction if he found out I was on the island to investigate his one-time fiancée's disappearance. And, worse yet, write a book using the information I uncovered.

Just why had Chelsea been calling Adam after midnight that night? The files made mention that they'd argued earlier in the evening. Had she called to make things right? Why hadn't she returned to the hotel? After all, the wedding was just hours away. More importantly, why had Adam never said anything about that call to the police? Unless, of course, he had something to hide.

Adam had grown increasingly frustrated, and definitely irate, by the time he screeched his Porsche to a halt in front of my house. As I'd swung open the passenger-side door to get out, I turned back to him and said, "I'm sorry, Adam. This just isn't going to work."

Then I slipped off my heels and hurried to the front door before he could stop me, not that I noticed him trying. Later that night I cried myself to sleep, soaking my pillowcase with tears.

Since then I'd avoided Adam rather handily by holing up in my cottage and barely talking to anyone. It helped that he'd gone on another business trip the day after our abbreviated date. I learned of his travels from the many texts and voicemails he left, telling me he was out of town but asking me to please tell him "what the hell had gone wrong" and how could he fix it.

A part of me wanted to talk to him. After all, I still had so many questions. Apart from the whole phone-call mess, I had never gotten around to asking Adam if he was still seeing Lindsey, the woman Helena had told me about. Another reminder that I'd behaved recklessly on my date with Adam.

Helena had somehow found out about our interrupted date, probably from Nate, who I was sure had heard about it from Adam. Helena had already left almost as many voicemails as Adam himself. When I didn't respond to any, she threatened to drive out and break down my door if I didn't, at the very least, let her know I was OK. So I texted back that I was hanging in there, and I'd talk to her eventually, but I just needed some time to myself. That seemed to have calmed her.

Running low on food, I reluctantly placed a small grocery order online but then couldn't bring myself to open the door when Nate knocked. Standing on one side, peering through the peephole, I waited until he finally gave up and placed the groceries on the step. "Maddy, I know you're in there," Nate had said. "I'm going to leave these here, but locking yourself away from the world isn't healthy, you know."

"I know," I'd whispered, leaning my head against the smooth wood door and listening as Nate drove away.

My father was another issue entirely. He wanted to rush out to Fade Island and move me back to Harbour Falls as soon as possible. He only relented when I solemnly promised to stay away from "that Ward guy," as he had put it.

So far keeping that promise was proving to be a snap.

As September faded into October, I discovered holing up in my cottage gave me a lot of time to think. And I waffled back and forth, wondering what I should do. Give up on the case? Scrap the book idea? Forget about Adam? I wasn't sure what to do with any of those things.

The day after the date-that-had-gone-all-to-hell, I became so despondent that I called my agent, Katie, since she was also my best friend. Barely holding back tears, I'd told her that I was ready to break my lease and return to Los Angeles. I was done with Fade Island and everything associated with it. She reminded me that Maddy Fitch didn't give up so easily. I made a commitment, and I should stick with it. Besides, the case really did have the makings of a great book. Her words gave me pause; I promised to reconsider. However, that didn't mean I was ready to jump right back into the investigation.

Instead I found a better hiding spot for the case file—under a loose floorboard in the living room—and forgot about the Harbour Falls Mystery. Or maybe I just pretended to forget as I kept myself preoccupied with mundane tasks.

Busy, busy, busy, I was like a whirlwind, cleaning the already-spotless cottage daily. In eight days I'd done the laundry—four times, reorganized my closet twice, alphabetized my shoes, and when I'd run out of domestic projects, I had plopped down on the sofa and eaten all four tubs of Häagen-Dazs chocolate-chocolate chip ice cream Helena had so thoughtfully snuck in with my grocery order.

With nothing left to do, it was no surprise I now found myself bored. Bored to tears. I paced around the living room, back and forth, back and forth. Enough. Tentatively I went to the front door and opened it a crack. I'd not been out of the house in days.

Indian summer was now upon us, and it was beautiful outside. The two white-flowering chrysanthemum plants from Max still rested on the doorstep. *It's as good of a day as any to finally get them planted in the window box*, I said to myself as I eyed the pots.

Yes it was.

So I slammed the door and jogged up the stairs to change my clothes. I threw on an old, faded pair of jeans and a black tee. The jeans sat kind of low on my hips, and the tee was cut off at the midriff. It was a little risqué for gardening with that much exposed skin, but it wasn't like I was expecting company. Nope, not on this island. There was little chance I'd even be seen. So I slipped on some old, beat-up Chucks, found an old, but still usable, garden trowel under the sink, and went outside to get to work on the flowers.

I knelt below the window box and worked the plants free from their plastic pots. I then carefully placed one mum—and then the other—in the rectangular structure. There was dirt already in the box, and as I worked, I found the sun-warmed soil a soothing balm for my frazzled nerves. A light ocean breeze rustled through the leaves, and I leaned my head back, allowing the sun to warm my face. Despite my indecision in the days leading up to this one, it was at that exact moment I knew, without a doubt, I would stay on the island until I found *all* the answers I was seeking. I'd finish my investigation, no matter what.

Resolved, I stood, swiped my hands clean, and brushed away some dirt from my jeans. I stepped back from the window box to admire my handiwork, and just then I heard a familiar—and currently unwelcome—sound of a car engine. I glanced over my shoulder just in time to see Adam's Porsche pulling into the driveway.

"No way," I hissed through gritted teeth, while quickly calculating the distance to the front door, wondering if I could get there faster than Adam if I made a run for it.

"Maddy, wait," Adam's voice rang out as I bolted for the door. *What the hell is he doing here? Had I not made it clear I didn't want to see him? Persistent, much?*

Obviously he was back from the business trip. He'd never mentioned where he'd gone. Maybe back to Boston? Where Lindsey lived. As I lunged for the doorknob, I had myself convinced his trip had probably included a visit to his former hookup. Especially since I'd left him hanging on date night. *Bastard*, I thought as I worked myself into quite the angry frenzy.

Just as I was shouldering the door open, almost in the clear, Adam's hand glanced down my arm. "Fuck. Just stop for a minute, OK? This is getting to be ridiculous."

I shrugged his hand away and spun to face him. "No, you are getting to be ridiculous," I spat. "Don't you fucking get it? I want to be left alone."

Adam's eyes flashed in anger, his jaw clenched. "Maddy," he said sharply, "you can't stay away from me forever. After all, you do live on *my* island."

I crossed my arms across my chest, and Adam's eyes glanced down to my exposed skin, making me feel oddly excited instead of angry. "What do you want anyway?" I huffed.

His eyes met mine. "At the very least, you owe me an explanation."

"I don't owe you anything," I said, marching into the cottage with Adam right on my ass.

"*Get out!*" I yelled, turning and pushing at his shoulders. But I couldn't budge him. The man was more solid than a damn rock.

I gave up on trying to get rid of him. Instead I grabbed the front of his white button-down shirt and said icily, "Why don't you leave me be? Forget about me, and just go fuck your little skank."

"What are you talking about?" Adam snapped, genuine

confusion in his tone.

I laughed derisively, tugging at his shirt as I said, "Oh, I don't know. Does the name Lindsey ring a bell?"

Adam looked positively pissed. "Who told you about her?" he demanded as he attempted to pry my clenched hand from his shirt. But I held on tightly and glared.

"Fucking Helena," he mumbled under his breath when he saw I wasn't going to answer.

Releasing my grasp, at last, I took a step back. "So it's true then?"

"Maddy, I don't have to answer to you." Adam chuckled darkly, looking down as he casually tucked his now-rumpled shirt back into his black dress slacks.

"You do when you practically asked me to be your girlfriend last week. Or were you just lining me up to be your newest piece of ass?" I accused.

"Is that what you think?" Adam asked in a disturbingly calm voice, his blue eyes meeting mine and flashing something far from calm.

I had to look away. "Uhh."

"Answer me," he said, quickly closing the narrow gap between us.

"I-I don't know," I stammered, taking a step toward the open door.

With lightning speed Adam slammed it shut, quickly spinning us around so that my back was up against the wood. His hands slid from his hold on my shoulders down to the bare skin at my waist. I inhaled sharply, surprised at how good his strong hands felt, despite how heated our argument had become. Or maybe that was why it felt so good? The fact that I could make him this angry sort of thrilled me.

"Did I somehow leave you with the impression that I was looking for just a piece of ass?" I tried to look away, but Adam nudged my chin. "A piece of ass that you were about to give up, I might add," he said smugly.

"Shut up," I said, but it sounded unconvincing, even to me.

Easing me back against the door, Adam pressed his firm

body to mine. "Do you think I just want to *fuck* you, Madeleine?"

I stifled a moan, and he laughed softly. "Or is that what you're looking for? A good, *hard*"—Adam rocked against my hips—"fuck."

Despite my protestations, Adam's intensity was enticing. The danger, a thrill. My breathing quickened, and I rasped, "No."

"No, what?"

"No, that's not all I want."

"And," Adam pressed, "do you really believe that's all I want from you?"

"No, I don't think that's all you want either," I finished, raising my hands from my sides to find purchase at his trim waist. This exchange was leaving me weak-kneed.

"Good," he said softly, relaxing into me. "See how much nicer things are when we agree."

Adam was so warm, so solid. He was right. Agreeing with him was much nicer. I sighed and shifted so that our lips were almost touching. But Adam pulled back and grinned wickedly. "What are you doing, Maddy?"

The laughter in his eyes told me he was no longer angry, so I admitted, "I'm trying to kiss you, dammit."

"Madeleine," Adam scolded teasingly. "I think we still have some things to discuss before we start back down that road."

Good God, the voice of reason.

I leaned my head back against the door and rolled my eyes. "Fine, I'm still mad at you anyway," I reminded him, although *I* was the one who obviously needed reminding.

Adam stepped back but, to my twisted delight, kept his hands on my bare waist.

"Yes, exactly *why* are you so angry with me? Surely not because of some woman Helena told you about. Did she also remember to tell you I haven't seen that particular woman in quite some time?"

Oh shit. While I was elated to hear Adam hadn't been in touch with his Boston babe lately, confirming what Helena had said, I still had to think of a plausible explanation for my behavior over the past week. I couldn't exactly tell him I'd had my dad snoop into old phone records relating to his missing fiancée. Or that we'd found out that *he* was the person she'd been calling.

"Um, I don't know if I can explain..." My voice faltered.

Adam sighed. "Does this have something to do with the real reason you're here on my island? Did you come across something in your little investigation for your book that scared you off and made you run?"

I swallowed, *hard*. "What? You know why I'm here?" I gasped, stunned.

"Yes, I know exactly what you've been up to. Writer's block, my ass," he scoffed.

"How did you find out?" I asked meekly, and then thinking of the others on the island, I added, "Oh God, does anyone else know?"

"Maddy," Adam began, "it's my fucking island. When someone—especially an author who writes *mysteries*—shows up wanting to spend three months here in the off-season, I make it my business to know why." He paused, eyeing me intently. "And to answer your other question, you can relax. Nobody else knows about your little project."

"Are you mad?" I whispered, closing my eyes to escape the intensity of those stormy eyes.

Adam slid his hands down to my hips and pulled me roughly to him, muscles flexing enticingly. "Open your eyes," he practically growled.

Frightened, I did but was surprised to see a softening in his gaze. He squeezed my hips gently. "No, not anymore, But I was plenty pissed at first, especially when you wouldn't tell me yourself. I certainly gave you plenty of opportunities. The first night I drove you back, the lighthouse." Adam paused and kissed my forehead, his lips lingering. "But no, I'm not mad at you. Not now."

"Besides," Adam continued. His lips traveled down to mine, where he paused and whispered, "Why would I be angry when I have nothing to hide?"

"Um, yeah, about that…" I trailed off, turning my head.

I had to think straight. Adam had a way of using my attraction to him to manipulate me. If I was ever going to get an answer out of him, it had to stop now.

Adam stilled, his fingers clenched on my hips. With hot breaths caressing my cheek, he asked softly, "Is there something else you want to tell me?"

"Uh, ask you, actually," I said, my voice shaky but resolute.

Adam pulled back, his interest seemingly piqued. "Is it the reason for your behavior on the flight back? And why you've been avoiding me this past week?"

"Yes," I said in a near whisper.

"Do go on then."

I was afraid to ask him the question, but I was more afraid of the answer. Adam cocked an inquiring eyebrow and waited. I tried to slide away from his grasp before phrasing my question, but he tightened his grip on my hips, effectively pinning me to the door. It was clear there would be no escaping Adam Ward.

"I, uh, I found something out the other night. Um, while we were still in Boston. Right before takeoff actually."

"What was it?" Adam sounded like he was running out of patience.

"It was about a phone call. A phone call, uh, Chelsea made…" I swallowed. "*That* night."

Adam closed his eyes and breathed in deeply. "*What* night would that be, Madeleine?"

He wasn't making this easy. "You know, the night before she, uh, disappeared."

My voice had grown so faint by this point that I didn't know if he had heard, but then, eyes still closed, he asked, "OK, so what phone call are you talking about?"

"A call she made from a pay phone at a bank in Harbour Falls."

Adam said nothing for at least a solid minute. And then he opened his eyes, his penetrating, indecipherable stare falling on me once more. My pulse raced, my heart pounded. I had nowhere to go; Adam had me trapped. Moments earlier I would have been aroused by his proximity, but finally I sensed the peril I could be in. And I was kind of terrified.

"You certainly are thorough, aren't you?" he said at last.

"She called *your* cell phone, Adam," I blurted. "Did you talk to her?"

"Yes, I did," he answered, his tone impassive.

No. No. No!

I started to squirm, attempting to break free. "Let me go," I demanded, but Adam was unyielding.

"Quit trying to get away, Maddy." He grabbed my flailing hands, sighed, and then pressed his body to mine in an attempt to stop me from fighting him. "You're not running away *this* time."

Exhausted and defeated, I slumped in his arms. "What did you do, Adam?" I cried, causing him to loosen his hold. "God, please tell me it wasn't you. Please tell me you had nothing to do with whatever happened to her," I sobbed and slid down to the floor.

He knelt down beside me, placing his hand on my cheek. I put my hand over his and let out a choked sob. Everything had finally caught up to me.

"I didn't have anything to do with what happened to Chelsea. I swear," Adam said, his voice tired and defeated.

I glanced up at him, and I just wanted *so* much to believe him. "I'm sorry, I just don't know what to think," I choked out.

Adam, helping me up and leading me to the sofa, said, "Shhhh, calm down." He took my face in his hands and, with his thumbs, wiped away the stray tears. "What do you want to know?"

The tears subsided, and slowly I got ahold of myself enough to ask, "What happened when she called?"

Adam leaned back into the cushions and sighed. "There's not much to tell. I was asleep at the hotel. Nate, Helena, and I had been drinking, and I passed out when I got to my room. Chelsea's call woke me up." He took a deep breath. "She started yelling, and I yelled back. I ended up hanging up on her." He paused. "We'd had a fight earlier that night."

"What was she yelling about?" I looked over at him, watching his features, beautiful still, even as he recalled *that* night.

"Most of it I couldn't make out." Adam ran his fingers through his hair. "It was a short call, but there were a couple of things I caught. She wanted me to tell her to stop whatever it was she was about to do." He shrugged. "And something else, like, she'd turn around and come back if I'd tell her I still loved her."

"And did you tell her you still loved her?"

"No," Adam said, pained. "I told you, I hung up on her. I didn't love her anymore, and I couldn't lie."

I wanted so badly to question him further about why he was marrying someone he just admitted he no longer loved, but frankly I was afraid. There had to be another way to investigate the validity of the blackmail claims. Asking Adam point blank about that particular rumor was just too intimidating.

So, instead, I focused on the phone call. "What did she mean when she asked you to tell her to stop whatever it was she was going to do? What was she up to?"

"Good question. I don't know, probably nothing. Chelsea had a flair for drama."

I looked down and asked softly, "Why didn't you tell the police about the call, Adam?"

"What good would it have done? That call didn't shed any light on what may have happened to her. It didn't even make sense. And the police were already focused on me as the primary suspect. Why would I give them yet another reason to not even consider other possibilities?" His hand was at my chin again, urging me to look into his eyes. "Maddy, I need for you to believe me. I had nothing to do with her disappearance."

I held his gaze, searching for any indication of guilt. He seemed so sincere.

"Do you believe me?" Adam quietly asked.

My heart and mind were at war, but my heart won this round. "I believe you, Adam," I said softly.

His pained eyes filled with gratitude. He leaned down and curved his lips to mine in a simple gesture that spoke more intimately than any of the lust-filled kisses we'd previously shared. "Thank you," he murmured, looking exhausted as he pulled away and leaned his head back against the sofa.

Thankfully our conversation drifted into less emotionally charged territory. We talked about the trip he'd been on. Making my earlier concerns that he'd used his trip as an excuse to see Lindsey seem even more foolish, he told me he'd not been anywhere near Boston. His business had been in Washington, DC. He didn't elaborate on the nature of his business there but instead talked of restaurants and museums, and how we should fly down there some time so he could take me to those very places. Eventually we both grew weary and found ourselves stretching out on the sofa, my back to his chest, his arm draped over my shoulder.

In the waning hours of the afternoon, silence descended, and I fell into the best sleep I'd had in over a week, wrapped in the comforting warmth of—what I hoped was—an innocent Adam.

When I woke up, it was dark. Everything was quiet, except for Adam's steady breathing coming from behind me. My stomach rumbled, reminding me I'd not eaten for hours. Delicately I extricated myself from Adam's arms, being extra careful not to wake him, and then I tiptoed into the kitchen, where I began to rummage around for something to eat.

I was pretty certain Adam would be hungry as well, so I decided to make some pasta and a salad. I put water on to boil and took some vegetables out of the refrigerator, all the while trying to be as quiet as possible. Unfortunately I dropped a wooden bowl as I was setting the table, and minutes later a disheveled Adam appeared in the doorway. Sleepy and tousled but still one fine-looking man.

"Hungry?" I asked, holding up a head of lettuce and a tomato.

Adam stretched, and my eyes were drawn to the way the

fabric of his shirt pulled taut over his well-muscled torso. "Starving," he replied, yawning.

He chuckled when he caught me staring at his body, so I quickly looked away and said, "It won't be long if you want to have a seat."

Adam pulled out a chair and sat down, stretching his long legs out in front of him. "Is there anything I can do to help?" he asked.

I could not think of a single thing for him to do—other than just sit there and continue to look incredible—so I went with, "No, I think I have it. But thanks for offering."

Soon the pasta was ready, so I drained the softened noodles, scooped some onto each of our plates, and ladled tomato sauce overtop. Adam thanked me as I placed our dinner on the table, and I smiled in return as I sank down into the chair across from him.

It took me a few minutes into our meal, but I finally worked up enough nerve to bring up the case once again. I still had a few questions. And I had an offer of my own.

Since Adam already knew why I was on the island, I told him I was willing to share all I'd uncovered so far in my investigation. He'd been honest; now it was my turn to reciprocate. On a roll I even confessed that I had a copy of the case files and, going one step further, offered to let him read through them. But surprisingly Adam waved it off. "I've already seen all those files—"

I gasped, interrupting him. He rolled his eyes. "Do you honestly think you're the only one with the right connections, Maddy? I read those files a long time ago."

"Oh, OK," I mumbled dejectedly, crunching into a bite of salad.

"Anyway," Adam continued, "I have no desire to rehash the details of the case. It's part of my past, and I'd like to keep it that way. Do what you need to do, but keep me out of it, got it?"

"Sure, I can do that. But you really don't mind if I continue to look into it?" I asked, somewhat baffled that he wasn't asking me to shut down my investigation. Maybe this was proof enough that he was innocent.

Adam twirled his pasta unconcernedly. "It's just research for a novel, right?"

It suddenly dawned on me that, of course, Adam would naturally assume I was writing another work of fiction. He probably thought I was utilizing the case files as some kind of general outline. I was suddenly grateful I'd not gone off about my trip to Billy's nor revealed that there was a mystery blonde Chelsea had been photographed kissing.

I had to rethink things. Maybe it was best to keep my real plans—to write a nonfiction account of the Harbour Falls Mystery—a secret after all, so I responded with, "Yeah, just the usual background research I do before sitting down to write."

Adam held my eyes for a moment, searching. I kept my expression neutral, and he finally said, "In that case I don't foresee any problems."

After we were finished eating, and Adam helped me clear the table and load the dishwasher, we sat back down at the kitchen table. "I hate to eat and run, but I really do have to get going," he said.

I glanced at the florescent-blue digital readout on the stove; it was only a little after eight. Nights were boring and lonely at the cottage, and had been especially so during my week of seclusion.

"Already? Why?" I blurted, and then added in a softer voice, "I'm sorry. I was just hoping you'd stay longer. I thought maybe we could watch a movie together."

"I wish I could, I really do. But there are some things I have to take care of before tomorrow morning." Adam reached over and caressed my cheek. "Trust me, I'd much prefer spending the evening watching a movie with you than catching up on work. But duty calls."

"That's fine, I understand," I said.

Adam must have detected the disappointment in my tone, because he offered, "Maybe another night?"

"What about tomorrow night?" I paused, and then added, "It is a Friday after all, the start of the weekend."

"Sounds like a plan," he said, smiling. "How 'bout I get here at seven?"

"Perfect," I replied.

When Adam left he did so with only a chaste kiss to my cheek. *Tease*, I thought, when I noticed him suppressing a smile. Was he still withholding kisses? We'd see just how long that would last. I smiled as I envisioned movie night with Adam Ward...curled up on the sofa.

But I wanted to look more appealing than this. I glanced at my apparel—yeah, the wrinkled tee and dirt-smudged jeans look was not going to cut it if I wanted to *really* capture Adam's attention. Although the exposed skin at my midriff had not gone unnoticed by him, I wanted to wow him with a sexier look. Silk couture, a la date night, might be a bit much, but I'd have to find something more enticing for tomorrow night.

While I sat mentally sifting through potential outfits, guilt began to nag at me. Reminding me that honesty—not some contrived outfit—was the real foundation of a burgeoning relationship. Adam had been honest with me about the phone call. It seemed wrong to let him go on believing I was planning on writing some fictional novel. But what choice did I have? I feared he'd ask me to stop if I told him the truth. And honestly, I didn't want to give up on the investigation. I didn't want to give up on the idea of a nonfiction book about the disappearance, and more than anything, I really didn't want to give up on Adam.

So what would happen if—or when—he found out I'd lied to him? I'd cross that bridge when I came to it, and if it did come to pass, I surely hoped he'd understand.

Chapter 10

Friday afternoon was spent fully emerging from my week of self-imposed isolation. First I called Helena to let her know everything was fine and promised to stop into the café sometime the following day. The trill of conversation punctuated the background, and when I asked who was there, Helena said Jennifer had brought somebody over on the ferry, and she was in the middle of filling their order for two lattes to go. Before I had a chance to question her further to find out who had arrived on Fade Island, Helena yelled out a hasty, "I gotta go, talk to you later," and disconnected.

My next call was to my father. He kept stressing that Fade Island was a lot closer to Harbour Falls than Los Angeles, but sometimes it didn't seem that way. So after catching the hint that my father was missing his daughter, I made plans to head over to the mainland and visit him on Sunday afternoon. That seemed to brighten his day considerably.

After I hung up, I glanced over to where I'd hidden the case files, in their new spot under a loose floorboard by the bookcase. I knew I should go back over the material, review it some more, but I wasn't really up to delving back into the mystery. Not just yet.

For one thing, I was too preoccupied thinking about the night ahead—movie night with Adam. And after the week I'd just had, I wanted one night where I could pretend there was no mystery, no missing person, no unsolved case. I wanted to be Maddy Fitch—a girl who was looking forward to spending a fun, flirty evening with a guy she was falling for. Tonight I didn't want to be Maddy Fitch—the writer investigating a complicated cold case and getting in way over her head.

With those thoughts in mind, I went upstairs to find something more appropriate than my current ensemble of baggy sweats and crummy T-shirt. After rummaging through half my wardrobe, searching for something casual, yet sexy, to change into, I finally settled on charcoal twill pencil-leg jeans; funky, black, open-toed ankle boots with lots of sassy straps; and a cute, black-lace, corset-style top with satin ribbons up the back. Yeah, this outfit was definitely hot, and I was pretty certain it would get Adam's attention.

It was approaching seven, so I quickly showered and got dressed for the evening. I left my hair down and applied more eye shadow, liner, and mascara than usual to give my eyes a smoldering, smoky appearance. Satisfied, I went back downstairs to double-check the provisions for the evening.

There was beer in the fridge—a respectable import—and a frozen pizza in the freezer. That was going to have to do if we got hungry. After all, it wasn't as if there was pizza delivery around the corner here on the island.

Since this was, in a way, our second date, and the first one had ended so badly, I felt a little apprehensive and nervous. Pacing around the kitchen wasn't settling the butterflies in my stomach, so I went back into the living room, put on a mellow CD from some indie band, and popped open the cold beer I'd grabbed from the fridge. Sitting down on the floor in front of the TV cabinet, I began to organize my somewhat-limited DVD collection into categories. I sorted eight into "comedy," four into "horror," twelve into "drama," and two into a special category I deemed "Hell-no-Adam-mustn't-know-I-own-this."

Falling into that last category was, first, a classic Disney movie. It was really cute, but Adam did *not* strike me as the Disney type. So Simba, Timon, and the gang got tossed under the sofa. The second DVD was a romantic drama, a real tearjerker. One of my favorites, in fact, but I feared Adam would suspect I was trying to send him some kind of message about how I expected *our* relationship to go. *Yeah, definitely too soon for that one,* I thought. I hesitated, though, because I really loved that movie.

Sitting there, DVD poised in hand, the glare of car headlights suddenly flashing across the living room wall drew my attention. Was it Adam arriving early? If so I had to get rid of the tearjerker flick. So I quickly jammed it under the sofa to join the Disney show.

I rose and went over to the window to look out. Adam's car was, indeed, closing in on the cottage, but the Porsche was coming from the direction of town, not from Adam's house. *Odd, maybe he'd gone into town first for some reason.* As the vehicle slowed around the bend near the cottage, I saw Adam driving. But what was strange was that there was someone in the passenger seat. A woman, for sure. One with short, dark hair. What the…?

The car sped off toward his house, and I went back to sit on the sofa, dumfounded. Why would Adam be driving by my cottage with a *woman* in his car? Fifteen minutes before he was supposed to be here to watch a movie with me. Something was definitely off. And I didn't like it one bit.

I went into the kitchen, slammed the empty bottle down on the table, and defiantly grabbed another one out of the refrigerator. And then I began to pace, the heels of my boots clicking across the linoleum floor. My mind went into overdrive. The woman wasn't Helena or Ami, not with the dark hair. It couldn't have been Jennifer either. This woman had short hair. Besides, I suspected Adam and Jennifer were not particularly friendly. How could they be with the J.T. factor thrown in? So who was in the car with Adam?

Lifting the bottle to my lips, I drank down the last of my second beer. I attempted to toss the bottle into the trash but missed. Damn, I was a lightweight when it came to drinking. I went over to pick the bottle up off the floor and froze. *Oh no!* What if the unidentified woman was Lindsey? From what Helena had said, I'd gotten the impression Lindsey didn't come *here* to see Adam; it sounded more like a convenient tryst for when he was in Boston. But maybe she'd come up to the island to find out why Adam had stopped seeing her. Hell, I would have. And hadn't Helena said Jennifer had brought somebody over from the mainland earlier today? I kicked myself for not calling Helena back earlier to find out who'd been ordering that latte with Jennifer. *Shit.*

Things rapidly went from bad to worse when I noticed it was three minutes after seven. My heart dropped. Not only was Adam with another woman, but he was apparently standing me up. Now determined to drown my sorrows in alcohol, I grabbed another beer. And that was when my cell phone began to buzz.

Adam, the screen indicated.

Oh, this ought to be good, I thought to myself as I took a long drink and then said "Hello" in a none-too-happy voice.

"Maddy, it's Adam." *No kidding.* "I got delayed, but I'll be there in—"

"You're late," I interrupted, promptly sipping more beer in the ensuing interlude.

"I know, and I apologize. Something out of my control came up—"

"Oh, I bet *something* came up," I said bitingly. Being a smartass was better than crying, and the beer made it all too easy.

Adam paused. "Maddy, are you alright? You sound kind of, I don't know, not yourself."

"Never been better," I answered, before downing the last of my cold beverage.

"Uh, if tonight's not a good night…" he trailed off, uncertainty in his voice.

I wanted an explanation—in person— so I hastily replied, "No. In fact, how soon can you get here?"

"Ten minutes?"

"See you then," I said flippantly, before hitting *end*.

I waited until I heard his Porsche pulling into my driveway to get up from the kitchen chair I'd settled into. *Whoa, steady there,* I thought as I held tightly to the edge of the table for a few extra seconds. The alcohol I'd consumed had caught up to me, and I was definitely feeling it.

Tottering in my heels, I negotiated my way to the front door. Once I made it there without incident, I fluffed out my hair, bit down on my lips to give them some color, and pushed up my corset to further enhance my already-prominent cleavage. *Let him see just what he'll be missing once I kick him to the curb.*

But when I opened the door, I was met with a breathtakingly gorgeous—albeit slightly blurry—Adam. Dressed in a deep blue pullover that complemented the color of his eyes and faded jeans that hugged him in all the right ways, he was quite a vision of handsomeness. "Wow! You look hot," I blurted and then mentally slapped myself for complimenting him when I was supposed to be mad.

Adam chuckled, and I caught him steal a glance at my ample cleavage. *Score one for me.*

"*Com*ing in, Adam?" I giggled, throwing his words from the night on the runway back at him, while leaning against the doorframe for support.

Adam eyed me curiously, brow furrowed, "Have you been drinking, Madeleine?"

"Aw, just a little," I pshawed. I grabbed his hand and tugged. "Come on in to my humble abode. Or should I say *your* humble abode."

Adam allowed me the illusion that I was dragging him across the floor and into the living room, but in reality he was helping me keep my balance. "Maybe you should lose the heels," he said when I almost tripped.

"Trying to get me out of my clothes already, Adam?" I teased, swaying.

"Come here, Maddy," he said gently as he led me to the sofa, where I promptly fell back into the cushions. He knelt down on the floor in front of me, while wrapping a hand around one of my heels. "Lift," he prodded.

Sighing, I complied, and Adam unzipped my boot. "So I had a little too much to drink," I protested. "It's your fault anyway."

Dropping the boot to the floor, he wrapped his hand around my other ankle as his oh-so-blue eyes met mine. "My fault?" he asked, nonplussed as he unzipped the other boot. "Why's that?"

I held up my index finger. "One, you're late."

"Only fifteen minutes, and I apologized." The second boot dropped to the floor.

"That was only the first reason," I said, waving my finger and raising a second. "Number two, and this is a big one." Adam cocked an eyebrow. "I saw you driving by with another woman."

Adam laughed—and damn if he didn't look more gorgeous than ever. This man was maddening. But I forged on. "Who was she, Adam?"

He curled his hand around my calf, smiling. "You're cute when you're jealous."

"It's not funny," I huffed. "And I'm not jealous."

"You are," he said as he rubbed my calf gently. "But you have no reason to be. That was my *sister* in the car. She was supposed to come in tomorrow, but she came up from Boston early."

"That was Trina?" I squeaked out, realization dawning on me that she was the person Jennifer had brought over today. *Oops.*

"Who did you think it was?" Adam asked, unmistakable amusement lacing his tone.

"Oh, I don't know. Nobody, really…" I trailed off.

Not only did I have no intention of sharing my misinterpretations with him, but his hands were wrapped around both my calves now, and whatever he was doing with his fingers felt amazing.

"Yeah, sure." A smile played at the corners of his mouth.

"It's not important anyway," I said as I relaxed back into the sofa. "We should just pick out a movie and forget about it."

"We should but first"—Adam swiftly pulled me into his lap—"we should do this." His lips crashed down on mine, and I maneuvered my legs to either side of his.

Soft and warm those tender kisses were until they turned ravaging. Desperate, hungry, I couldn't get enough of Adam. And caught off guard, he responded.

With his fingers tracing the laces on the back of my corset,

Adam broke away long enough to breathe out, "This is *very* hot." His hands trailed down to curve around my bottom. "God, Maddy, do you know how much I want you?"

In response I let out a stifled moan and grinded myself down against him. *Please, don't stop.* And though I could *feel* his body didn't want to, Adam hesitated.

I sighed in frustration, and he moved his hands to the sides of my face. "What is it? What are you thinking?"

I shrugged. "Why'd we stop?"

He kissed me softly, and against my lips, he said, "If we keep going, I might not be able to stop." He pulled back and our eyes met. "It's just... Maddy, I know you want more than—"

"Adam," I broke in, "I don't have any expectations. I mean, I do, but..."

I didn't know what I wanted, not really. And that was the problem. Yes, I wanted Adam. But not like this. Not under the influence of alcohol, although my buzz was wearing off. But Adam was correct; I'd regret a hasty action.

Ducking my head, I muttered, embarrassed, "You're right. At least one of us is thinking tonight."

"Hey, hey." Adam wrapped his arms around me. "We can talk about this stuff later. Why don't we watch that movie?"

I nodded my head against his shoulder and held on, enjoying his warmth, a minute more. When we broke away, I scooted off of Adam and rose to my feet, straightening my clothes in the process.

Adam tried to be coy, but I caught him sneaking another peek as I adjusted my corset top. "What?" he asked, playing innocent oh so well.

"Nothing," I replied, shaking my head. "I'm going to grab something to drink. Do you want anything? Beer? Coke?"

Adam cocked an eyebrow. "What are you having?"

I was done with drinking for the night, so I answered, "I think I'm switching over to Coke."

"Coke sounds good," he said. "I'll have the same."

I started toward the kitchen, and halfway there I called back, "Oh, I have food too. If you're hungry, I can heat up a pizza."

"Sure." I heard Adam say. "Do you need any help?"

"No, no, I've got it," I yelled back. "Go ahead and pick a movie. There are some in the TV cabinet on the bottom shelf."

Having reached the kitchen, I grabbed two cold Cokes out of the fridge. And then I pulled the pizza out of the freezer, unwrapped it, and slid it into the oven. The back of the box indicated it would take twelve to fifteen minutes for the pizza to be ready, so I set the timer and went back into the living room.

"How long is your sister staying on the island?" I asked Adam as I handed him one of the cold sodas. He was crouched down in front of the TV cabinet, thumbing through my limited DVD collection.

"Just 'til Monday," he replied.

He opened the soda and took a drink, while I walked back to the doorway and leaned against the jamb. I had promised myself that I'd forget about the case for this one night, but if there was ever going to be an opportunity to spend some time with Trina, this weekend could be it. So I casually inquired, "Will Trina be at the café this weekend?"

"She's hanging out with Helena most of the day tomorrow, so, yeah, probably," Adam said as he rose from his kneeling position, two DVDs in hand.

Perfect! I thought, but to Adam I said, "Find anything good?" I nodded to the cases he held.

Holding up both a comedy selection and a classic Hitchcock film, he asked, "Funny or suspenseful?"

The oven chimed before I could answer, and Adam walked back to the sofa. The toe of his shoe hit something on the floor, and he stopped. To my dismay I saw it was one of the DVDs I didn't want him to see. Crap, I thought I'd pushed them both under the sofa. Adam bent to pick it up, and I froze, catching the image on the cover. *Oh no*, it was the romantic tearjerker. "Um, we don't have to watch that one," I said in a rush of words.

"Is there some reason this one is halfway hidden under the sofa?" Adam smirked as he skimmed over the back cover.

"Um, no," I muttered.

"Hiding your chick flicks, eh?" Adam teased in return. He

was enjoying this way too much.

"I must have dropped it," I mumbled, embarrassed for the second time in one night, because we both knew that wasn't true.

The timer buzzed, so I made a quick escape to the kitchen. I'd literally been "saved by the bell." Or maybe not. As I was getting the pizza out of the oven, Adam came into the kitchen. He grabbed the paper plates I'd set out on the counter, and I slid the pizza onto a large cutting board. "I bet you'd never guess," Adam said softly, "but I've always wanted to see that movie."

"The chick flick?" I looked up, shooting him a look of disbelief.

Adam tapped the paper plates against the counter and smiled. "I'll admit, maybe it won't make my life complete. But judging from your reaction, it seems like it would be something you'd enjoy watching."

"It's only one of my favorite movies, like ever," I said under my breath as I pulled a cabinet drawer open and rummaged for the pizza slicer.

Adam's hand stilled mine. "Then let's watch it."

I couldn't believe it. I couldn't believe I was going to watch such a romantic movie with such a gorgeous guy. Maybe he was starting to fall for me too. A girl could only hope, right?

In the end we watched the "chick flick." And not surprisingly I cried at all the touching and sad parts, of which there were many. And Adam was sweet, wiping my tears away and showering me with tender kisses. By the end of the movie, I was curled up with Adam on the sofa, wrapped up in his strong arms, feeling happier than I'd felt in a very long time. If only things could have remained so blissful.

Chapter 11

The next afternoon, as I hurried into the toasty warmth of the café, a cold shiver coursed down my spine. Unfortunately it wasn't just a reaction to the icy drizzle and frigid temperatures that had blown in off the sea. Though the weather did indeed add to my uneasiness, I had this feeling I just couldn't shake that something bad was about to happen. But I had to put my worries aside for now.

Helena was behind the coffee bar, leaning on the counter and laughing along with a tall, smartly dressed woman with short, dark hair. Though she looked different than I remembered—more chic, more polished—I recognized that she was Adam's sister, Trina.

Glancing up as I approached, Helena called out a cheerful, "Maddy!"

Trina smiled as I reached the counter, and Helena turned to her and asked, "You remember Maddy Fitch, right?"

"Of course I remember," Trina said warmly. "It's good to see you again."

The next few minutes were spent engaged in reintroductions and small talk. Trina confirmed she was staying until Monday and then confessed she had come up to the island a day early because she'd gotten into an argument with Walker. Helena asked her if it had been about anything serious, but Trina said no. They'd just been getting on each other's nerves with all the planning for the upcoming wedding.

"Men," Helena said exasperatedly, shooting Trina a look of solidarity.

"Speaking of which," Trina said slowly as she turned to face me, her stunning blue eyes so similar to Adam's that I had to keep myself from staring. "I want to know your secret for getting my boring brother out on a Friday night. If he's not out of town on business, he's usually holed up in his study working."

Helena broke in with, "Aha, I heard you two had made up. But Nate didn't tell me you had another date."

"It wasn't really a date," I explained. "We just watched a movie together at my place."

"That sounds cozy." Helena nudged Trina's arm. "Come on, tell us all the gory details."

"Uh, maybe not everything, Maddy." Trina grimaced. "We are talking about my *brother* here."

"It's not like that anyway," I insisted. "We watched the movie, and then Adam left."

Sure there'd been a little bit more than that, like some amazing kissing, but I had no desire to share those details.

"Oh sure," Helena said with a roll of her eyes. "Editing for Trina's sake is fine for now. But you know I'll be expecting the unrated version later."

"Um…" I trailed off.

Thankfully Trina saved the day when she said, "Really, Helena, leave Maddy alone. You really need to get off this island more often."

Helena laughed and agreed, and I jumped at the chance to ask how she and Nate had come to live on Fade Island.

She explained that after college, Nate, who'd been trying to get picked up as a quarterback, was drafted by an NFL team across the country. But during training camp, he suffered a career-ending injury, thus halting their plans to move west. Adam, who had moved out to the island following Chelsea's disappearance, then asked Nate if he'd be interested in "managing" Fade Island. Nate had a degree in a computer-related discipline as well, so Adam went even further, offering Nate a chance to do some work for him on the side. Made sense, and I'd already suspected as much. Nate and Adam had been computer whizzes back in school. But it made me wonder once again just how involved Nate was in Adam's business. That would better explain why they so often traveled together.

As for the "managing" the island offer, Nate was immediately interested, but Helena wasn't so sure. When she expressed concern that there'd be nothing for her to do on the island, Adam came up with the idea of running the café. Though it would be dead in the winter, the summer clientele promised to keep her plenty busy. Still waffling, Nate and Helena made up their minds without further ado once they saw Adam's more-than-generous final offer. They quickly accepted, moved onto the island, and never looked back.

"I do love this island, don't get me wrong, But it does get boring from time to time," Helena confessed.

"You could always come down to Boston for a break," Trina offered, her expression hopeful. "Help me with wedding stuff. There's so much to do before spring."

"Hmm, maybe," Helena began. "This time of year, Adam wouldn't care if I closed up the café for a week or two." She paused and then, smacking her hand on the table, said, "Yeah, let's do it!"

Trina looked delighted. "Oh, Helena, I promise we'll have lots of fun. I'll keep you plenty busy." She then turned to me. "Maddy, you should come down for a few days too. You must be getting kind of bored yourself here on the island."

"Oh, thank you," —I had to think fast to get out of this one— "but I really need to stay here. I'm supposed to be trying to write—"

"Yeah, Maddy came here to cure her writer's block," Helena interrupted.

Uh-oh. Despite Adam's claim that nobody but he knew why I was really here, I couldn't help searching Helena's face for any sign that she was onto me and my phony cover story. But thankfully she appeared to be none the wiser to my ruse.

"That's right! You're a writer," Trina said. "I'm definitely going to check out your books as soon as I get back to Boston."

"I started the first one," Helena chimed in, surprising me completely with her admission. "It's really good." I met her eyes, and she smiled warmly. "I highly recommend them."

How sweet! I thought. Helena was rapidly becoming my *second* favorite person on the island. Eventually the conversation veered away from my novels. Helena and Trina started to complain about their significant others, and I felt more and more out of place, having nothing to contribute.

"Just think," Helena said, "give it a few more months with Adam, and you'll be sitting here bitching about him right along with us."

Certain I was blushing profusely, since Adam and I were nowhere near that point, I lowered my eyes. Helena must have forgotten that I had signed a lease for only three months. It was way too early to be making assumptions about where my relationship with Adam was heading. Not to mention she didn't know the other half of why I was even here.

"Uh, I don't know about that…" I trailed off.

"Well, I beg to differ," Trina said, jumping into the conversation. "I know my brother, and he is definitely into you."

"Did he say anything?" Helena asked, taking the words right out of my mouth.

"He doesn't have to say anything. I can tell." Trina paused. "Let's just say he looks happier than he has in a long, *long* time."

My heart soared to new heights thinking I could possibly be the reason for Adam's newfound joy.

Trina patted my hand. "And, Maddy, you are the kind of woman Adam needs. Not someone like that wretched Chelsea," she huffed, making a face.

Here was my chance to possibly uncover some more info. "You didn't like her?" I ventured.

"Didn't like her? Hell, I *hated* her." Trina's eyes darkened. "She was the worst thing that ever happened to my brother."

Helena glanced away, biting down on her lower lip. After what she'd told me the other day, how she somehow felt she was to blame since she'd introduced Chelsea and Adam, I knew how hard it had to be for her to hear this.

Unaware, Trina said vehemently, "Thank God, the bitch is gone."

Her tone was so cold and dispassionate as she uttered those

words that a heavy silence fell over our table. It didn't appear Trina was going to be as forthcoming with her reasons for hating Chelsea as Helena had been. The air was tense as none of us seemed to know what to say next.

Breaking the tension at last, Trina said, "Listen, I'm going to the ladies room." She pushed back her chair. "And then I'm going to make us some cappuccinos, and when I get back we are *so* changing this subject."

Helena and I both nodded in hearty agreement. Once Trina closed the restroom door, Helena began to quietly fill me in on *why* Trina despised Chelsea so very much. I thanked the heavens above that the beautiful Helena Jackson had a penchant for gossip when she began to tell this story:

Trina had never been fond of the flashy Chelsea Hannigan, but she grew to despise her when she started to believe Chelsea viewed Adam as just another prize possession to hold onto. In high school and throughout his early college years, Adam had genuinely cared for Chelsea. His intentions had been nothing but honorable back in those early days. As time wore on, though, he too grew to distrust Chelsea. He heard the rumors, but every time he'd confront her, Chelsea denied any wrongdoing. But, of course, his suspicions were confirmed with the incident at Billy's.

Trina, like Nate and Helena, was absolutely stunned when Adam didn't immediately break things off with Chelsea. Hell, she'd been caught red-handed. And adding insult to injury, she'd defended J.T. O'Brien. It was then that Trina came to believe Chelsea had something she was holding over Adam. There was no other plausible explanation for his behavior. Adam had never been one to allow himself to be told what to do, or be controlled in any way by anyone, particularly not Chelsea. It had always been Adam in control, calling all the shots. So it came as an even bigger shock when Adam asked Chelsea to marry him…just two days following the whole J.T.-Chelsea spring break fiasco. And as he'd done with Nate, Adam told Trina to mind her own business when she questioned his bizarre decision to get engaged to an unfaithful girlfriend.

But beyond that Trina had another reason to hate her brother's fiancée. Apparently Chelsea had once tried to seduce Walker. Shortly following the engagement announcement, Adam had gone back to MIT. But while Adam's spring break had ended, Trina and Walker's had just begun, and they soon found themselves back in Harbour Falls.

Two days following their return, Chelsea called Trina—drunk and asking for a ride home from a bar in Cove Beach. It was after three in the morning, so Trina sent Walker to pick her "drunken ass up"—as Helena put it—and bring her back to the Ward house. That would allow Chelsea time to sleep it off, and Trina and Walker could drive her back to her car in the morning.

Trina heard Walker returning with Chelsea, but when it seemed to be taking entirely too long for him to come back to their room, Trina got up to see what was going on. Making her way down the hall, she heard giggling coming from one of the guestrooms. When she flung open the door, she found a half-dressed Chelsea pressing herself up against Walker in front of the bed, trying to kiss him. And even though she knew nothing had happened *yet*, Trina—not one for subtlety—had marched right up to Chelsea, spun her around, and smacked her hard across the face.

The next day she told Adam everything. Trina became even more convinced that something was horribly awry when Adam *still* refused to dump Chelsea. In fact, he wouldn't even consider calling off the engagement.

Helena stopped talking when Trina came out of the restroom and went behind the bar to start on our cappuccinos. After having heard this new information, I made a firm resolution to get the nerve up to talk to Adam. It had to be done. I needed to know what Chelsea had been holding over him. I couldn't continue to pursue this relationship with him, knowing he'd been blackmailed and not knowing why.

When Trina returned to the table with the cappuccinos, the three of us sipped our steaming, hot drinks, and sat and talked until darkness began to fall. As our conversation began to wind down, Helena's cell phone buzzed. It was Nate, calling to inform her that he was still with Adam, and they were running late. Unsure as to how much longer they would be, he asked if she could drive Trina back to Adam's house.

I was readying to go myself, but Helena asked if I'd stay at the café until she got back. "I hate to ask," she said, "but Brody Weston is supposed to be stopping here to pick up some hard-to-find part for the ferry that Nate tracked down for him." She checked the time on her cell. "Actually he was supposed to by now, but I guess he got held up."

I told her I had no problem with staying awhile longer and that I'd give the part to Brody when he arrived. Helena thanked me and placed a small cardboard box—I assumed it held the part for the ferry—on the counter.

After they left I paced around the café looking for something to do. I was wired from all the caffeine and consequently restless as hell. There was a pile of unfolded cloth napkins on the other end of the counter, so I reached over, pulled them to me, and began to fold them. Soon I had a row of neatly folded napkins before me. Just as I was working on the last one, I heard the café door swing open.

I turned, expecting to see Brody or possibly even Adam and Nate. But instead my eyes fell on J.T. O'Brien. Judging from his unsteady stance and the fact that he was wearing only a thin T-shirt and long shorts despite the cold, wet weather, I suspected he was drunk…or on something.

I placed the napkin I'd been folding down and keeping my voice even, said, "Hey, J.T. Are you here to pick up the part for the ferry?"

He walked toward me, his expression dark and troubled. "What the fuck are you talking about, Maddy?" he slurred, his tone gruff.

Obviously he wasn't here for the part, so why was he here? When he was only a few feet away, I noticed he was holding an almost empty bottle of amber-colored liquid against his leg. "Why don't you give me the bottle?" I said, sighing and reaching for it. "I think you've had enough."

"*You* think I've had enough?" J.T. snorted, pulling the bottle out of my reach. "Sorry, but I don't take orders from someone who hangs out with a killer."

I knew what he was insinuating. "Shut up, J.T., you don't really believe that," I said, turning back to the counter, hoping maybe he'd just leave.

"You don't know anything!" J.T. bellowed from behind me. Ignoring his outburst, I muttered, "You're an ugly drunk."

Suddenly the whiskey bottle he'd been holding whizzed past my head, missing me by mere inches. It crashed into the wall behind the coffee bar, raining down shards of glass and dark, sticky liquid. I spun around, my hands reaching back to grip the edge of the counter as I cowered away from an approaching drunk and furious J.T.

"God, J.T.," I gasped, horrified. "What the hell is wrong with you? Stop it!"

He closed in on me, halting only inches away, close enough for me to smell the whiskey on his breath. "Stop it," J.T. mimicked in a high-pitched voice. His dark eyes were wild and flashed menacingly. I knew I was in danger. "Maddy, as I see it, *you* are in no position to tell *me* what to do."

His lip curled up into a nasty sneer, and he leaned over me. Trying, and succeeding, to intimidate me. I turned my head to the side, my sweaty hands slipping as I struggled to keep hold of the counter behind me. "J.T., please," I whimpered.

In my face J.T. yelled, "Please *what?*" He slammed his hands down on either side of me.

"P-p-please stop," I stammered, tears welling up, despite my effort to suppress them.

J.T. laughed what could only be described as a sinister laugh, throwing his head back and chortling. Seeing an out I tried to duck under his arm. But he was too quick. He stopped me by grabbing the front of my shirt and bunching the material up in his fist. "And where do you think you're going?" he growled. "Trying to run so you can go find your rich, murdering new friend?"

I didn't answer, and J.T. continued. "You do know you're

just another piece of ass for Ward to pursue?" He cocked his head to the side, sizing me up. "Shame too. I always pegged you for having better taste."

He touched my cheek, and I raised my hand and slapped him across the face. "Fucking bitch," he roared while slamming me back forcefully against the counter.

A sharp pain cut across my lower back, and J.T. was back in my face. "Tell me, Maddy, what is it about Ward? Is he that great of a fuck?"

I closed my eyes, and tears streamed down my cheeks. I hadn't even gotten to that point with Adam, but I knew it wouldn't matter to an enraged J.T. O'Brien. "Answer me," he demanded, his hot whiskey breath nauseating me.

A choked sob escaped my lips, and just when I feared the worst might happen, J.T. was violently yanked away from me. As I slid down to the floor, eyes still tightly closed, I heard a loud crash and the sound of punches being thrown.

"Get the fuck off me, you murderer," J.T. protested, sounding frightened and pained.

"Fuck you." —More punches, J.T. coughing— "Don't you *ever* fucking touch her, you hear me?" I knew that voice, so I wiped at my teary eyes and glanced up to see a glowering Adam looming over a curled-up J.T. on the floor.

"Don't worry. I won't ever touch her again. I don't want any more of your sloppy seconds anyway," J.T. laughed.

Adam's hands clenched at his sides, and J.T. flinched. "Go ahead, Ward," he challenged, his voice thick with blood. "Hit me again."

Adam spat in J.T.'s direction. "You're not worth it, asshole."

"Whatever. You still can't change the fact that I was fucking your fiancée almost the entire time you were away at college," J.T. yelled defiantly.

Adam's expression turned murderous. "Get up, you pathetic drunk. Get up and fight like a man." His voice, now, disturbingly calm.

But instead of getting up, J.T. rolled to his side and suddenly choked out, "You took away the only girl I ever loved, you fuck."

Well, this was news. J.T. had *loved* Chelsea? As J.T. lay sobbing on the floor, drunk and defeated, Nate emerged from the shadows to stand next to Adam. Had he been there the entire time? If so, Nate had had Adam's back throughout the duration of the fight. Not that I was surprised.

"What do you want me to do?" Nate asked Adam.

"Get him out of here before I end up really hurting him," Adam said shakily, cracks showing in his controlled veneer. "Take him to Max's."

"Why'd you do it?" J.T. bellowed, spitting blood. Nate pulled him up and began to drag him to the door. "*Why?*" J.T. croaked.

"Wait," Adam said.

Nate halted, J.T. in tow. "I didn't kill her, you fucking idiot. Did you ever consider that maybe she just left?" Adam paused, eyeing J.T. carefully. "Chelsea didn't love you any more than she loved me. Chelsea only loved Chelsea, so quit wasting your time—and your life—pining away for her."

"She didn't leave," J.T. said quietly as Adam was turning away.

He spun back around. "Is that a confession, O'Brien?"

"Fuck you!" J.T. shouted, and Nate tightened his grip on him. "You know I didn't kill her."

"Do I?" Adam asked.

His stance, expression—just everything—was eerily calm. J.T. must have noticed the same thing because he said nothing more. Nate pulled him up and out the door.

With both men gone, Adam rushed over to where I sat on the floor, legs pulled up to my chest with my arms wrapped tightly around them.

He knelt down in front of me. "Are you OK, Maddy? Do you want me to fly you to the hospital? I can—"

"Adam," I interrupted. "I don't need to go to a hospital. I'll be fine, I'm just a little shaken up."

He took my face in his hands, scanning for any signs of harm. "Are you sure you're not hurt? When I was coming in,

I saw him slam you back into the counter." I winced, suddenly cognizant of a dull aching across my lower back.

"Maddy?" Adam asked. "Where does it hurt?"

"My back. But it doesn't hurt *that* much."

Adam touched the hem at the back of my shirt. "Do you mind if I take a look?"

"Go ahead," I whispered.

Adam scooted behind me and lifted up the back of my shirt, just enough to see what kind of damage had been inflicted.

"Fucking J.T.," he muttered under his breath.

"How bad does it look?" I asked, worried since Adam's hand seemed to be frozen in place.

He sighed. "There's some bruising, but that's the worst of it." He lowered my shirt back into place. "It still makes me wish I'd fucked him up more than I did. He had no right touching you, let alone hurting you."

I turned to face him, my eyes meeting his. "You saved me, Adam," I said softly. "If you hadn't come in…"

I shuddered at the thought of all that could have happened, and Adam put his arms around me, carefully avoiding the bruised part of my back. I snaked my arms around his neck, whispering, "Thank you."

He really had saved me.

"I'll do whatever it takes to protect you, Maddy," Adam said softly. "That is, if you'll let me."

I held onto this man I was falling for, his embrace comforting me. I believed his words, but I hadn't forgotten my earlier resolution. I needed to steel myself and ask him for the truth. I needed to know *what* Chelsea had been holding over him. I wanted Adam to protect me—and he had tonight—but I couldn't trust him completely. Not until *he* trusted *me* enough to share this big secret. I mean, now that Chelsea was gone, was it even still relevant?

"Adam, I need to, uh, ask you…something," I said in a tiny voice.

He pulled back, his expression curious, "Yeah?"

"Uhh…" I hesitated.

Asking Adam a question of that magnitude—while staring into his striking blue eyes—was not a simple thing to do. I closed my eyes, took a deep breath. *OK, here goes.* "Was there, uh, somethin—"

Just as I was getting to the question everybody seemed to want an answer to, I heard the café door open. I opened my eyes and looked up.

And then I groaned in exasperation, because I realized I wouldn't be asking my question. At least not anytime soon.

Chapter 12

Helena scanned the mess that was her café. Broken chairs, overturned tables, shattered glass littering the floor, blood and whiskey spilled. "My God," she uttered. "What happened in here?"

Her eyes flickered our way as Adam straightened and helped me to my feet. "J.T. O'Brien is what happened here, Helena. He showed up drunk."

Understanding seemed to dawn on Helena; she shook her head and sighed. "Are you two OK?" she asked quietly.

Before we could answer, the café door swung wide. Nate had returned from dropping J.T. off at Max's house. So after we were seated, the three of us took turns giving Helena a detailed account of the events that had transpired in her absence. I filled in the blanks in the timeline, explaining what had happened from the time Trina and Helena had left up until Adam and Nate's well-timed arrival to the café.

I didn't miss the number of times Adam shifted irritably, blue eyes flashing in ire, as he listened to the vivid details of J.T.'s unprovoked attack. When the story was finished, Helena pulled me into a tight hug. And then she strongly encouraged me to press charges against J.T.

But I was torn on what to do. On one hand, nothing too terrible had occurred, thanks to Adam's intervention. But on the other hand, it frightened me to envision all that could have happened. And I knew J.T. should have to face the full repercussions of his criminal behavior.

"What happened to the sweet guy I once knew? We were actually *friends* at one time," I lamented, still in disbelief over the actions of a J.T. I no longer recognized.

Helena voiced what I already knew in my heart. "Drugs and alcohol have a way of changing people, Maddy. And it's never for the better."

Nate proceeded to tell me that if I pressed charges, J.T. would then be forced to enter a Harbour Falls mandatory drug and alcohol dependency rehabilitation—in lieu of doing any time—since he was already on probation for drug charges in the past. "It'll actually be the best thing for him." Nate said.

When I asked about the specifics, he explained that it would be a six-week program, with two weeks of inpatient therapy and four weeks of outpatient support. It sounded like it would, at least, be a starting point for J.T. to get some help.

"Do I have to go over to Harbour Falls to press charges?" I asked. Fade Island and Cove Beach both fell under the jurisdiction of Harbour Falls.

Adam cleared his throat. "No, actually Max can take your statement. He's actually an officer with the Harbour Falls PD."

This was news, though I couldn't say I was completely surprised by the admission. After thinking it over for a few more minutes, I decided to press charges. J.T.'s problems were serious, and I had to face the fact that he could have very easily been the one behind Chelsea's disappearance. His fury had been truly terrifying. It wasn't difficult to imagine *that* level of rage leading to something like—I hated to admit it—murder.

I shuddered as we all rose, and in response Adam put his arm around me. Before we left the café, he told Nate to make the necessary arrangements for me to meet with Max in the morning. I broke in, saying I didn't want to go alone to Max's bungalow to enter my statement. Max and I had made amends, but I didn't really care to show up at his home all by myself. Needless to say, I was relieved when Adam said he'd go with me.

Stepping out into the cold night air, Adam pulled me close as he led us to his Porsche. "Maddy?" he questioned when I hesitated on the sidewalk.

"What about my car?" I nodded to the Lexus parked in front of his car.

"Don't worry, I can take you down to the dock after you meet with Max, and then Trina and I can pick up your car sometime tomorrow. We'll drop it off at your cottage while you're with your dad."

Oh shit! *My dad!* I'd forgotten all about my plans to visit with him Sunday. I'd mentioned it in passing to Adam the night before, and thank goodness I had. Or I'd have ended up inadvertently blowing off my poor father. Of course Adam had no clue I had no plans to mention *his* name to the mayor. My dad was still under the impression I was staying away from "that Ward guy," as he had requested. However, I suspected that once my father found out the details of what had happened at the café—and he surely would—there was little doubt in my mind that he'd be more concerned with me staying away from J.T. O'Brien.

Ugh! Statement in the morning, my dad in the afternoon. All this when all I really wanted to do was just spend some time alone with Adam. After all, I needed to ask him about the blackmail allegations. With that in mind, and not really caring to spend the night alone at my isolated cottage after the café incident, I blurted out, "Will you stay with me tonight?"

Adam was opening the passenger door for me and shot me a curious sideways glance. I quickly amended, "Oh stop. I just don't want to be alone tonight."

I got into the car, and once Adam was seated, he said, "Why don't we stay at my place. You can sleep in my bedroom." I raised my eyebrows, and he threw my words back at me mockingly, "Oh stop, Maddy."

Happy to be laughing so soon after what had happened, I smacked his leg playfully. "Smart-ass," I muttered.

Adam started the car and said, "Seriously, you can have my room. I'll sleep in one of the guestrooms."

I would've been content with a guestroom but didn't protest. Besides, I was too preoccupied wondering how one casually brought up the subject of blackmail.

We neared my cottage, and Adam asked if I wanted to stop. I didn't have anything to sleep in, no toothbrush, nothing really, so I said yes. Adam waited in the car, and I ran inside and threw some essentials into an overnight bag. I rushed back out to the car, and we started up to Adam's place.

I thought about asking my big question but decided to wait until we were settled in at his house to broach the tricky blackmail subject. I could wait a while longer, but tonight was definitely going to be the night. I had to find out exactly *what* Chelsea had been holding over him.

When we entered the spacious foyer at Adam's place, the first thing I heard was Trina's voice lilting from down a long hallway to the right. She sounded like she was on the phone with someone. Adam explained that she was in his study and probably talking to Walker. I hastily whispered that I'd rather not have to recount the café incident for the second time in less than an hour. He nodded understandingly, and we hurried up the long, curving staircase, where he led me down another hallway to his bedroom suite.

The large, high-ceilinged bedroom resonated with the same masculine style as the living room. But while the living room had boasted gleaming hardwood floors and Persian rugs, this room was blanketed in plush carpeting that was as white as freshly fallen snow.

Stepping over the threshold, my feet sunk into the heavenly pile. To my right there was a massive, black marble fireplace, complete with a cozy sitting area. The entire far wall was made up of ceiling-to-floor windows with long, slate-gray curtains that were drawn for the night. A bed, much larger than a king-sized, spanned half the distance down the wall across from the fireplace. It was covered in luxurious-looking black and gray bedding and far too many pillows to count. The only bright colors in the room were contained in the abstract art on the walls.

"Um, is there a bathroom?" I asked, suddenly anxious to get out of clothes that reeked of whiskey.

"Over there." Adam pointed to a door just beyond the fireplace.

I hoisted my overnight bag up higher on my shoulder and went into the bathroom. Flipping the light switch on, I closed the door and dropped my bag to the floor.

Wow, now this is a bathroom, I thought as I strolled around the spacious room. A huge walk-in shower, hexagon-shaped and sporting multiples nozzles, took up one side of the room. And in a recessed area, under a set of small, frosted windows; a glossy, black porcelain tub—equipped with whirlpool jets, no less—sat sunken into the floor. Wow, Adam sure liked his amenities.

There was an array of shampoos and body washes along the ledge at the back of the tub. I had to smile to myself because, surely, Trina had put those items there. I just could not picture Adam mulling over scented body washes nor shampoos that promised "thick, luxurious" hair.

Turning away from the tub, I faced a wall of mirrors. I unbuttoned my ruined shirt and let it fall to the floor. Turning my back to the mirror, I craned my neck to see the damage J.T. had wrought. A row of yellowing, bluish-black bruises marred my lower back. *Ouch!* Although, as bad as it looked, there didn't appear to be any major swelling, and the aching had mostly subsided. Sighing, I finished undressing. After washing up some and brushing my teeth, I put on the hot pink cami and black silk shorts I'd brought from home.

Tentatively I stepped back into the bedroom. Adam was standing by the bed, and he looked like he had freshened up as well. In fact, he looked amazing. He wore a pair of navy pajama bottoms that hung low on his hips and absolutely nothing else. *Oh my.*

No doubt sensing my ogling, Adam looked up, blue eyes alight. "Maddy." An ebony lock of hair fell across his forehead, and he raked it back into place. "I brought up some ice" —he held up a bag that was loosely wrapped in a dark hand towel— "for your back."

My feet seemed to be stuck in place, and my thoughts were muddled. *Yeah, Adam—half-naked and unwittingly oozing sex appeal—had that effect.*

"Maddy?" he questioned, concern streaking across his features. "Is something wrong?"

"Sorry," I mumbled, getting a grip and making my way across the room. "I was just lost in thought."

I took a seat on the edge of the bed, next to where Adam stood. It was then that I noticed abrasions on the knuckles of his right hand. Marks he'd received from defending me.

Adam adjusted the hand towel around the ice pack and sat down next to me. "May I?" he asked, gesturing to my back. I nodded, and Adam lifted the back hem of my cami, just high enough to apply the ice.

Wincing, more from the cold than the pain, I said, "I saw your hand, Adam. You should get some ice for that too."

"I'm fine," he replied. "O'Brien deserved worse than I gave him for what he did to you."

Still coming to terms with the fact that someone who used to be one of my closest friends had done something so terrible, I asked softly, "Do you think I'm doing the right thing?" I paused and looked down. "Pressing charges, that is."

Adam nudged my chin. "Yes, I do," he said as our eyes met.

"J.T. will get the help he needs this way," I murmured, unconvinced even as I said it.

Adam breathed in deeply and then exhaled a long sigh. "He needs more help than what some half-assed, overcrowded Harbour Falls facility can offer. But let's just hope it sticks this time."

Well, it was pretty clear Adam didn't expect J.T. to get any better. With all the bad blood between them, it didn't surprise me. "You knew, didn't you?" I asked quietly. "About J.T. and Chelsea, I mean. You knew when they started seeing each other? Again, after the engagement."

I glanced over to find Adam staring at me intently, his body tense. "Yes," he said, "I knew."

"When did you find out?"

He raked his free hand through his hair and over his face, while the hand holding the ice bag shifted. "I found out shortly after it started back up. I knew every time they saw each other. *Every* time, Maddy, right up until the end."

I reached back and pulled the ice out of his hand. After placing it on the bedside table, I turned so we were facing one another. "How did you know so much?" I asked, my voice hardly more than a whisper.

Adam hesitated, his expression dark, and then said, "Suffice it to say, I have my ways."

"Did you know about the other…men?" My voice weakened on the last word, and then I whispered, "And the drugs?"

Our eyes locked, his full of a fury that spoke of betrayal. "Yes, I knew," he said curtly, his jaw tensing. "It took awhile, but eventually I was made aware of all those things."

This was it. This was the opportunity I'd been waiting for. There'd never be a more perfect time to ask. Spurred on by all he'd shared so far, I steeled myself, sat up straighter. "Why were you still going to *marry* her? You knew all those things, yet you got engaged. You were still going to go through with the wedding. Why, Adam, why?"

Adam shifted away, rubbing his hands over his face once more. Although this time they remained over his face. "It's complicated," he mumbled, his words muffled.

I took a deep breath. "She had something on you, didn't she? I hate to ask, Adam, but I have to know." I paused, the silence deafening. "Was Chelsea blackmailing you?"

He dropped his hands listlessly to his sides and lay back on the bed, staring at the ceiling. "I was wondering when this was going to come up," he said, bitterness creeping into his tone.

Time ticked away slowly, Adam silent as he continued to stare up at the blank ceiling.

"Adam?" I said at last, my voice shaky. "Are you going to say something?"

He sat up abruptly and fisted one of the many pillows on the bed. With his blue eyes stormier than I'd ever seen, he leaned forward and held my gaze. "Why, Madeleine, would I tell *you* something that I definitely do *not* want to see exploited in some book?"

His harsh words cut to the quick. "I'd never publish anything like that!" I protested loudly.

Adam laughed derisively. "Really, Maddy?" He cocked an

eyebrow. "Isn't that the sole reason for you even being here?"

It was, but it was no longer the *only* reason. Yes, I was here to research the mystery so I could write my next novel. But now that I was involved with Adam, I knew adjustments would have to be made. I wouldn't be able to just recklessly recount everything I'd discovered. After all, I was starting to care for some of these Harbour Falls Mystery players. Especially one in particular...and it hurt to realize he trusted me so little. Because, really, all he'd told me up to this point were things I already either knew or suspected.

"I'd never write anything that would end up hurting you," I said quietly, biting down on my lip and looking away.

My words were true. I had no intention of divulging secrets that could destroy him. Maybe I'd have to reconsider, go back to writing a work of fiction. I could use the information I'd obtained but change the details, fictionalize it. After all, I was a fiction writer.

Adam suddenly cupped my chin, urging me to meet his eyes. Deep, deep blue, the darkest blue, tormented. Did he want to tell me? What was holding him back?

With his hand in place, I couldn't turn away. Adam said very slowly, "Ask me the question. *Again.*"

My heart raced. "Was Chelsea blackmailing you?"

"Yes." Adam paused, releasing my chin but keeping his eyes trained on me. "There's your answer. Are you happy now?"

I shook my head. "No, of course not."

I felt queasy. It was difficult to hear him confirm what so many had suspected.

"Aren't you going to ask me what it was?" Adam chuckled, though it was an empty action, devoid of humor. "That's always the next question."

"Um, was it something illegal?" I croaked.

Adam looked at me like I was an idiot. "Hmm, you could say that."

His eyes were so intense that I dropped my gaze to focus, instead, on a light smattering of freckles that peppered his right shoulder. I cleared my throat. "Did you hurt somebody?"

I was terrified to hear his answer, so I counted freckles in time with my beating heart. *One, two, please say no. Three, four, please say no.*

"No, Madeleine, I did not hurt anyone." Adam paused, and I released a *whoosh* of air I hadn't even realized I was holding. "In fact, I can assure you it's probably none of the things you're thinking."

Relief and gratitude washed over me in the knowledge that whatever it was, at least he hadn't injured—or done worse to—God forbid, some innocent person. Throwing caution to the wind, I wrapped my arms around him, the heat of his bare skin permeating through the thin material of my camisole. "Thank you," I whispered.

I wasn't exactly sure why I was thanking Adam. I guessed it was because he had actually answered my questions, and so far it didn't really sound like he'd done anything too horrific. Maybe what he'd done wasn't even anything illegal? Or maybe it was something that had been illegal at the time? Then again...

Relieved and lost in thought, I brushed my lips over that peppering of freckles on his shoulder. Adam lay back once again, absently curving my body to his while resting a hand on my hip.

Between butterfly kisses down his shoulder, over his bicep, I decided to press my luck and push for more information. "So Chelsea knew this secret...and she threatened to expose it...if you refused to marry her?"

On my hip his hand flexed. "Uh-huh," he mumbled wearily.

I really was incredibly intrigued. How had Chelsea uncovered this terrible secret? Had he confided in her? Or had she somehow stumbled upon the damning information?

When no more information was forthcoming, I sat up suddenly. Adam's hand fell away from my hip. I searched for clues in his perfect features. I willed him with my eyes to share. My mind screamed: *What was it?*

Adam, perceptive as always, sighed, "Maddy, I've already told you more than I've ever told anyone. You do understand why I can't give you any more details, right?"

I shrugged. "It's not like I'd run and tell the world, Adam. I just told you I wouldn't write—"

Adam cut me off and sat up. "Why would I even put you—or myself—in a position like that?"

"So it's a matter of trust?" I accused, stung. "You want *me* to trust *you*, but you don't trust me. At all."

"Oh, you trust me?" he shot back dubiously. "Because as I recall in Boston, you said you *thought* you trusted me, but then you refused to even tell me what the fuck was going on when you found out about a phone call from four fucking years ago!"

"I *did* tell you!" I yelled, outraged.

"Only after I chased you down and pried it out of you," he yelled back.

Leaning his head back, he closed his eyes and pinched the bridge of his nose. In a lowered voice, he asked, "So which is it, Maddy? Do you trust me? Or not?"

How had this turned into a conversation about me?

"I trust you, Adam," I said quietly, casting my eyes down. And I did trust him. To a point.

I continued, "I know you're just trying to protect us both, but"—our eyes met—"if we are ever going to have a chance, *eventually*, Adam, you are going to have to trust me enough to tell me the truth. All of it."

He took my hand and pulled me to him, and then he eased us down into the pillows as he reached up and turned off the bedside lamps.

"Maddy, Maddy. *Eventually*, huh?" he asked, the playfulness back in his voice. "You're willing to wait?"

I nestled into him and nodded. "Yes, I can wait, for now. But eventually, yeah."

His fingers ghosted over the thin strap of my cami, sending a warm shiver through me. Despite being extremely tired, a part of me desperately wanted to stay awake. All the heightened emotions were fueling my desire to feel physically close to Adam. I hooked a leg over him and pressed myself to his firm body, eliciting a surprised, shaky exhale of air from him. Encouraged, I ran my hand down his chest until I reached his abdomen.

Adam placed his hand over mine. "Maddy, don't start something you aren't willing to finish," he said in a husky, low voice.

I really was too exhausted to enjoy much of anything if I continued down this path, literally and figuratively. It had ended up being a trying day, and we were both in dire need of some sleep.

Adam must have sensed my reticence, because he said softly, "We should sleep, for now."

"Yeah, I guess," I agreed as I moved my hand back up to rest on the smooth planes of his chest. "Will you stay though?"

I didn't want to sleep alone, not tonight.

"If it will help you sleep better, of course," he said.

Propping himself up on an elbow, he leaned over to press his lips to mine. We kissed—oh so slowly and gently—until I was positively dizzy. Pulling back, Adam said in a low voice, "Oh, Maddy, the things I'm going to do to you."

He caressed my cheek, his hand drifting down to my neck, over the swell of my breasts, a brush of fingers across my stomach, and then lower, lower, until his hand rested dangerously close to… A moan escaped my lips, and I asked breathily, "When?"

Adam plopped back against the pillows, chuckling. "Oh, I don't know," he said slyly. "Let's say…*eventually*."

I huffed, feigning indignation, and tried half-heartedly to roll to the other side of the enormous bed. But he easily caught me in his arms and eased me back to lie against him.

We'd reached an impasse, of sorts, but, for this night, I was fine with where we were.

"Good night, Adam," I said, closing my eyes.

"'Night, Maddy."

Chapter 13

I woke up only once in the middle of the night, entangled in Adam—stretched across his bare chest, his arm draped over my shoulder, I tilted my head back just enough to watch him sleep. He seemed so peaceful, so at rest. Wishing for Adam to find that kind of contentment in his waking life, I laid my head back on his chest and allowed his steady heartbeats to lull me back to sleep.

The second time I woke up, though my eyes remained closed, I could tell it was morning. Something velvety trailed across my cheek, tickling my skin. I lifted my hand to brush it away, smiling, and heard Adam chuckle. Opening my eyes, the first thing I saw was Adam and, in his hand, a vibrant red rose.

Tentatively I touched the petals, the texture as velvety as when he'd brushed them across my cheek. Adam stretched out across the bed, already dressed for the day in jeans and a long-sleeved T-shirt. "For you," he said, handing me the flower and wowing me with one of his drop-dead smiles.

I took the rose and inhaled the sweet fragrance of the bloom. "How'd you locate a red rose here on this island on such short notice, Adam?"

He leaned close, trailing kisses along my cheek, following the path he'd made with the rose. "For you, Maddy, I can make anything happen," he murmured.

No doubt he could. "Thank you. It's beautiful." I smiled, truly appreciative of his sweet gesture.

"Oh, there's one more thing." He rose from the bed and made his way over to the doorway. As he disappeared into the hallway, he called back, "I hope you're hungry."

I was kind of hungry, now that he'd mentioned it, so I sat up and craned my neck to see what Adam was doing in the hallway. He soon appeared in the doorway, holding a breakfast tray laden with a delectable presentation of food. "Wow," I mouthed, impressed by the presentation, not to mention the image of this gorgeous man bringing it to me.

Once Adam reached me, he placed the tray across my lap and sat down next to me. "A vegetable omelet, toast, fruit, and orange juice," he said, pointing to each of the items on the tray as he listed them off. "Hope this meets with your approval, Ms. Fitch," he added as he slipped the red rose from my fingers and slid it into a slender, water-filled vase on the corner of the tray.

"Thank you. It looks delicious," I said, touched that the powerful Adam Ward was serving me breakfast in his bed.

I took a tentative bite of the omelet and found myself pleasantly surprised at just how mouthwatering it was. "Mmm, Adam," I said between enthusiastic bites. "This is *so* good. Did you make this yourself?"

"I did," he replied, chuckling. "Is it that shocking that I can cook?"

I thought it over for a minute. "I guess not. You certainly seem to excel in everything you do."

Adam cocked an eyebrow, and I rolled my eyes, despite the fact that I was actually rather anxious to find out just what kinds of *other* things Adam excelled in. But instead of sharing those thoughts with him, I said, "You know what I mean."

"I do," he purred. "But believe me, Maddy, I make it my mission to excel in everything I do." He trailed his hand down my bare arm, leaving goose bumps in his wake. "And I do mean *everything*."

I wanted Adam in every way imaginable. I was sure he knew his words made my body ache for his touch. But it was more than that. Despite everything I was clearly falling for Adam a little more with each passing day. I just didn't know if he felt the same way. True, he'd made it clear he didn't view me as just some new sexual plaything, like Lindsey. But could he ever truly fall for me?

Lost in those thoughts, I failed to respond, and Adam coughed a little. Sensing my hesitation he smoothly changed the subject. "We'd actually better get going soon. Max is expecting us."

"Right," I mumbled into my orange juice. I'd almost forgotten about pressing charges against J.T. Almost.

Before Adam drove me back to my cottage to change, I reluctantly threw on the clothes I'd worn the day before, grimacing when the smell of stale whiskey hit my nose. And after showering back at my own place, I was only too happy to throw the offending shirt in the trash. Actually a part of me wanted to burn it. Damn J.T., what an ass.

Wanting now to get this over with and forget about it, I hurried back downstairs. I practically ran to the front door, passing by Adam as he stood waiting for me in the living room. "OK," I yelled over my shoulder. "I'm ready."

Adam caught up to me. "You don't have to do this, Maddy. You know that, right?"

"No, I do. I really do," I whispered, leaning my forehead against his chest. My voice was soft but full of conviction.

So we drove down to Max's modest bungalow, where it took only ten minutes for him to take my formal statement. I basically recounted exactly what had transpired at the café, while Adam held my hand. After I concluded, Max pressed the stop button on the recorder he'd set out on the coffee table and then informed us that J.T.—who was back in Cove Beach—would be taken into custody later in the day. Max explained how J.T. would be processed and then admitted to a rehab facility. As opposed to the alternative, jail, it seemed more than fair.

After we left Adam drove me down to the dock. My father was still expecting me today, though I dreaded the visit. Adam must have noticed my solemn mood, because he offered to ride over with me on the ferry to Cove Beach. Without hesitation I took him up on the offer. Apart from it being an opportunity to spend more time with him, I was kind of secretly hoping Jennifer would be piloting us over. I couldn't wait for her to see *who* was with me. I highly doubted she'd be her usual bitchy self in front of the owner of the island.

Unfortunately, though, the wrong Weston was at the helm today. As usual Brody said very little, and the ride over was uneventful. After we docked Adam instructed Brody to wait for him before heading back over to the island. We then walked over to where my car was stored.

Adam lifted the door to the garage and looking in, said, "Oh, Maddy, I see you've been holding out on me." He nodded to my car. "A BMW, eh? And a pretty sweet one at that."

Knowing that Adam could easily afford an entire fleet of the model I owned, the M6, I laughed. "This from a man who drives a Porsche. And not just any Porsche, mind you. Let's see..." I furrowed my brow in mock concentration and began to list off the stats, the facts rolling off my tongue smoothly. "The 911 GT2 RS...620 horsepower...only about five hundred in the world."

"I'm impressed." Adam arched an eyebrow. "Someone must be reading their *Car & Driver*."

"Not exactly," I admitted. "I looked it up on the Internet."

Adam chuckled. "Resourceful girl," he said with a wink.

Oh, if only he knew...

I was reluctant to part, so I wrapped my arms around him. He held me tightly and said, "Just text me when you're on your way back, and I'll pick you up at the dock."

"I'll be back before dark," I promised, pulling back.

Adam kissed me until I was breathless, and then he opened the driver's side door for me. "Have a nice time with your father."

"I will," I replied, getting in.

In my rearview mirror, I watched as Adam walked away. And then I was off. Half an hour later, I was parked in front of my dad's stately, white frame house in Harbour Falls. The home I'd grown up in.

My dad and I spent only a short time at the house—mostly I tidied things up for him—and then we headed over to one of the local steakhouses. I suggested it because I knew my dad's beloved Patriots were playing, and that particular place had a big screen TV.

My dad appreciated the gesture, but he had no idea I had another, more selfish reason for suggesting the steakhouse. I was hoping that if the mayor was occupied with the football game, he'd be less likely to inquire about whether or not I was staying away from Adam.

And it went pretty well for a while, with no mention of Adam. Then at halftime he brought up the investigation. "So, sweetie, you finding all you need in those case files to work on that book of yours?"

"Mmm, yeah," I muttered as I focused intently on cutting a piece of steak. "They've been really helpful," I added, probably with more enthusiasm than was warranted.

I wasn't lying though. The case files had been helpful. But not enough to prevent me from snooping around, and I knew that was what my father had hoped to prevent by giving me those files. No doubt my dad would kill me if he knew I'd already paid off a shady bartender for information the police didn't even have.

"That's good." My dad took a drink of his soft drink and then setting the glass back down with a *clink*, continued, "I want you to stay under the radar, Madeleine, if you're going to continue to live on that island."

Huh? "What do you mean, Dad?"

"Well, I've been thinking about those pay phone records."

"And?"

"Ms. Hannigan didn't once use her cell phone after leaving the hotel, but we know it was in her possession." The mayor paused meaningfully. "However, as we know, she did make a call from the pay phone at the bank…to Mr. Ward."

Uh-oh.

My dad eyed me curiously when I suddenly coughed. "Is something wrong, Maddy?"

"No, no." I cleared my throat. "So you were saying."

"Ms. Hannigan made that call and then attempted to make another in Cove Beach."

"At the convenience store," I added helpfully.

My dad nodded. "And we have no way of knowing how

many other calls she made that night that weren't caught by any surveillance cameras."

"Exactly!" I agreed. "I thought the same thing when I read the files."

My dad leaned forward, while looking around to make sure nobody was listening to our conversation. "I think it's safe to assume Ms. Hannigan was calling people from these other phones because she didn't want them traced back to her." I nodded, and my dad continued, "I have two theories: One, the most obvious is that she was covering her own ass in case the authorities ever got ahold of her cell records. This way they'd show nothing damning."

"Yeah, I'm sure her drug dealer wouldn't have appreciated her calling from an easily traceable phone, like her cell." I added. "Nor would Chelsea want that drug dealer traced back to her."

"Yes, but maybe she was calling someone *other* than some drug dealer from these other phones."

"Like who?"

"Maybe she was calling a lover," my dad said, his face reddening.

I was just as embarrassed as my dad. We never talked about those sorts of things.

I quickly said, "So she was calling, er, someone else." I paused. "And you think she was protecting herself—and that person—from the authorities?"

"Not from the authorities." My father held my uncomprehending gaze. "This is where my second theory comes into play."

My ears perked up because, when it came right down to it, the mayor really was incredibly wise. "The flaw in the first theory is that we're assuming Ms. Hannigan was being proactive in case the authorities ever caught up to her. But based on all her prior behavior, I think we can safely say she viewed herself as being above the law."

That much was true. Chelsea had done plenty of illegal and immoral things with *no* regard for the consequences.

"What are you getting at, Dad?" I asked, kind of at a loss.

"By not using her cell phone, Ms. Hannigan was behaving as if she had every expectation that those records *would* be seen, seen by someone *other* than the police." My father looked at me pointedly.

I swallowed hard. "Who would have been checking her cell records, Dad?" I asked meekly, afraid that I already knew the answer.

"My guess? Her husband-to-be, Adam Ward."

"But she called him from the pay phone at the bank," I protested. "Why didn't she just use her cell to call Adam? What was the point of using the pay phone?"

"I wondered that as well," he said. "But maybe she was originally planning to call someone *other* than Mr. Ward from that pay phone and then had a change of heart once she started to dial." I bit down on my lip, while my dad added, "After all, we still don't know why she detoured to Harbour Falls. It seems she was planning on doing something there and changed her mind at the last minute."

This was good stuff. Very plausible. I wanted so badly to share with my dad what Adam had told me about the strange things Chelsea had said to him during their short exchange. Asking him to tell her to *not* do something, telling him she'd turn around and go back to the hotel if he'd just tell her he loved her. But I couldn't betray Adam's trust. Not this soon after he'd been so forthcoming with me.

And what was Chelsea doing in Harbour Falls anyway? Maybe my dad was right. Maybe she'd originally planned on calling someone else from that pay phone and then changed her mind at the last second. It certainly fit with her bizarre, cryptic comments to Adam that night.

The rest of my dad's theory made sense too. If Chelsea truly suspected Adam was checking her cell records, then by using pay phones that night she could be certain he'd see only what the police had ended up seeing: No calls were made from her cell phone.

But Chelsea had been trying to call *someone*. It had to have been someone she spoke to often. Why else would she have attempted to make those surreptitious calls that night? And Adam, if he'd been working on tracking that person down through her cell records, must have suspected she was in contact with someone she was hiding from him. But who could it have been? Not J.T., Adam knew all about him. So who?

By blackmailing him, Chelsea had taken away something Adam was used to having—control. Maybe he'd been leveraging to catch her in her many lies, so he could turn the tables and get out from under her hold. It was starting to look like Adam and Chelsea had been playing a game of cat and mouse, with Adam closing in on her. If only she'd used her cell that final night…

"Honey," my dad said, breaking me out of my reverie. "Are you OK? You look a little peaked."

I pushed my hair behind my ears. "Yeah, I'm fine. I was just thinking about what you said. I think you may be onto something."

"Well, the most important thing is" — I met my dad's concerned, fatherly gaze— "for you to continue to steer clear of Adam Ward. Any man with that much power is capable of anything."

Too late for that, and time for a subject change. I nodded distractedly and glanced up at the television, mounted on the wall, where the football game was in progress. "Look, Dad, I think we just scored!"

That was all it took, and the mayor, thankfully, dropped the subject. The game soon ended, and my dad paid the bill, and then we headed back to the house.

I knew it was only a matter of time before my dad found out about my relationship with Adam. I couldn't keep it from him indefinitely. I was certain he'd also soon hear about what had happened at the café with J.T. And then he'd probably push for me to give up on the investigation and move off of Fade Island. But I was in way too deep. I wasn't about to give up. Not now.

I dropped my dad off at the house. But before I started back to Cove Beach, I detoured over to the bank on the edge of town, the one where Chelsea had made that last call. There really wasn't much out here. Besides the bank, there was a sub shop, a small neighborhood where Sean and Ami lived, and Hensley Discounters, Sean's family-owned business.

First I pulled into the bank parking lot. A patch of unkempt grass and weeds occupied the space where the pay phone had once stood. It was quiet out here, especially today, since the bank was closed. I glanced around, but I knew there were no answers out here.

With a sigh I pulled out of the bank parking lot. Hensley Discounters, located a block away, made me think of Ami. At the last second, I turned into the gravel lot and parked. I hadn't heard anything from her since the day I'd signed the lease. And that had been almost three weeks ago. By my calculations, the baby would be here any day now. Maybe Sean was working today. If so, I could get an update on Ami. Not to mention I hadn't seen Sean in ages. Spending the afternoon with my dad had made me feel a little nostalgic, and I longed to stay connected with the few people from my past that, unlike J.T., hadn't changed.

It was Sunday and close to closing time, so when I walked into the store, the first thing I noticed was how empty it was. A young girl of about sixteen was ringing up a sale, while the only other customer—an elderly woman with gray-blue hair—was rummaging through a sale table overflowing with discounted backpacks.

Once the teenage boy who'd been checking out left, I approached the young girl. She was plain but cute, with long dark hair and a name tag that read, "Cami."

"Hi," I said, smiling. "Is Sean Hensley in today?" The girl eyed me up and down suspiciously, probably wondering who the hell I was. So to avoid any misunderstandings, I added, "I'm an old friend of both his wife and him."

"Oh, that's cool," she said, interest apparently waning. "But he's not here today. Neither is his wife. Sorry."

Damn. "Can you tell them Maddy Fitch stopped by?"

"Yeah, sure," Cami answered distractedly. "But it'll have to be after they get back from their trip."

Trip? They? I thought. As in Sean *and* Ami were away? Instantly I had the sense that something was amiss.

But just as I was about to question Cami further, the elderly lady with the blue-tinged hair called her over to the sale table. "Honey, I need some help over here picking out a backpack for my grandson." Cami brushed past, effectively halting my opportunity to dig for more information.

Back behind the wheel of my car, I sat, ignition off, lost in thought. How could Ami be traveling with Sean? She'd been huge; she'd told me her due date was only a month away. That would've put the expected delivery at no more than a week from now, give or take. I couldn't shake the feeling that I was missing something vital. Turning the key in the ignition, I made a mental note to ask Adam about Ami once I was back on the island. Surely he'd know something, since she was, after all, one of his employees.

Brody took me back over to Fade Island, and Adam met me, as promised, at the dock.

Never one to miss much, he immediately noticed something was off. "What's wrong?" he asked as we got into the Porsche. "You look distracted. Did everything go well with your dad?"

"Everything was fine with my dad," I replied, fastening my seat belt.

I'd eventually get the nerve up to ask Adam if he'd been checking Chelsea's cell phone records, but at this moment, the strange Ami development took precedence.

So I said, "There is something kind of bothering me."

Adam turned to me, the car idling, and raised a questioning eyebrow.

"I stopped by Hensley Discounters on my way back. Uh, to ask about the baby—"

"Baby?" Adam interrupted, his tone clearly troubled.

"Yeah, Ami's baby."

Adam sighed and raked his fingers through his hair. "Did Ami tell you that she was pregnant?"

"Adam, yes," I looked at him in disbelief. "I mean, haven't

you seen her lately? It's kind of obvious."

"Maddy," Adam said softly. "There is no baby. Ami is *not* pregnant."

My first thought, which I voiced loudly, was "Oh my God, did something happen to the baby?"

Adam placed his hand over mine, and said, "No, nothing happened. There never was a baby."

"Yes, there was," I insisted. "I saw her! She was definitely pregnant, Adam."

"No, Maddy," Adam said slowly, as if I wasn't comprehending what he was saying. "Sean and Ami can't have children."

That sick feeling was back. "Adam, what's going on?" I asked, my voice shaking.

Squeezing my hand gently, he said, "I think I'd better tell you about what happened to Ami Dubois-Hensley a few years back."

Chapter 14

Before delving into the tale of Ami Dubois-Hensley, Adam drove me back to my cottage, where he pulled in behind the Lexus he and Trina had, as promised, picked up earlier from the café. With a turn of the key, the purr of the Porsche's engine silenced. In the shadows I watched as Adam breathed in deeply and then shifted his tall form so that he was angled toward me. "I should have told you sooner," he said, sighing. "But I had no idea it had started up again."

"Adam, you're scaring me. What's wrong with Ami?"

In the darkness of the car, lit only by the ambient glow of a half moon, Adam told me Ami's story. And what a story it was.

Unbeknownst to me, my former best friend had suffered some kind of a mental breakdown four years earlier. Ami had ended up in a mental health facility that autumn. After locking herself in the master bathroom of the house she shared with her husband, she'd attempted to commit suicide by downing a crazy cocktail of prescription pills and booze. Luckily Sean had come home from work early that day and found her lying unconscious on the cold tiles of the bathroom floor.

At the hospital, after her stomach had been pumped, Ami was moved to the psychiatric ward for observation. Following a series of tests, exams, and sessions with a psychiatrist, she was deemed to be a danger to herself but not to others. So she'd been moved to a Harbour Falls mental health facility for further, more intensive treatment.

Searching for a possible catalyst for her breakdown, which appeared to have come out of nowhere, the new psychiatrist treating her began to suspect it stemmed from her inability to have children—a condition which she and Sean had discovered that summer after a year of failed attempts to conceive.

Following two more months of treatment, Ami was finally released and initially appeared to be "cured." She'd gone back to her house and her loving husband, and even returned to her job at Harbour Falls Realtors.

"I didn't have the heart to fire her," Adam explained, "She'd been a model employee, and I saw no reason to let her go. In fact, I hoped if she returned to a normal routine, it might actually help."

"Did it?" I asked, though by Adam's pained expression I sensed it hadn't.

He explained that, at first, she really had seemed like her old self. But then one day, after showing a property located in Harbour Falls to a nice young couple who were expecting their first child, Ami was seen later sporting a rather impressive baby bump. In this "condition" she went to a local grocery store and a gas station. She later confessed she'd purposely sought out opportunities to talk with people about her "pregnancy."

For example, a man at the grocery store had allowed her to go ahead of him in the checkout line. She thanked him and then proceeded to tell him how much she appreciated his kindness and how she'd just been *so tired* lately with her due date coming up. At the gas station, she'd waddled in to pay with cash and then spent ten minutes talking about babies with the young lady working at the station.

When she returned home, Sean was out in the yard raking leaves. "You can imagine how he felt when Ami got out of the car and Sean saw she was 'pregnant.'" Adam slouched in the leather seat and leaned his head back on the headrest.

"That's terrible," I lamented.

Adam shook his head in what I guessed was dismay. "She confessed everything to Sean that night and even asked him to take her back to the hospital. He called me to let me know why Ami was going to be missing more work. That's how I found out what had happened." Adam paused. "He was so upset he even told me that Ami had admitted to sneaking into the high school and stealing one of those prosthetic pregnancy suits that had been used in a school play."

"Oh, Adam." Tears welled up in my eyes as my heart went out to this broken woman who, as a girl, had once shared so much with me. "She didn't end up at Willow Point, did she?" I asked, shuddering.

Willow Point was a mental health facility that housed patients deemed to be a danger to themselves and/or others. It was located over in Bangor, perched high atop a hill overlooking the small downtown area. Even without the knowledge that it housed the insane, the old gothic structure itself was just plain creepy. In fact, Willow Point had inspired many a lurid tale. Almost everyone who'd grown up within a hundred-mile radius of the place had heard the terrifying stories of what went on at Willow Point. Many of the stories were true. Back in the sixties and seventies the place had been so overcrowded that beds were placed in the hallways. The atrocities that had occurred with patients essentially running amok were truly hair-raising. Reforms were passed, though, and conditions improved. But it still was a place that inspired terror.

"Maddy," Adam said, throwing me an exasperated look. "Willow Point is for the *criminally* insane. Ami didn't commit a felony; she just needed more help."

According to Adam, despite more treatment Ami still periodically regressed back to these false pregnancies. Over time, though, the episodes appeared to occur with less and less frequency. So the doctors felt it'd be best to just allow things to play out. Especially since her farce never lasted for more than a day or two. Consequently, people who knew better just played along, and people who didn't know—like me—remained none the wiser.

"Should we call someone?" I asked. "Let them know she's at it again?"

Adam shook his head. "No. I'm sure Sean knows anyway. That's probably why he took her out of town. To get away for a few days."

So he *did* know they were gone. "Do you know where they

went?" I tried to keep my voice even.

"No idea," he replied. "She just asked for a few days off." I bit down on my lip and stared out the passenger-side window. Noticing, Adam added, "Maddy, if you're that curious, I can find out where they are."

There really was no reason, so I shook my head. "This is just a lot to take in," I murmured, leaning my head against the cool glass of the passenger window.

I kept thinking of the time I'd recently spent with Ami. She'd seemed so excited about the nonexistent baby. The whole thing was just heartbreakingly sad. So much had changed since I'd left Harbour Falls. Everyone was so different, their lives so full of complications. Me, I just wanted to go inside and forget this whole day.

Adam put a comforting hand on my knee. "It is a lot to digest," he agreed. "And I'm sorry I didn't tell you sooner. I didn't think it'd be an issue."

"It doesn't matter. I know now, that's what counts." I put my hand over his. "We can talk more about everything tomorrow."

"Uh, actually we can't," Adam said. "I'm leaving tomorrow morning."

I resisted the urge to groan. I was beginning to hate all these business trips of his. But after suppressing my irritation, I asked, "Where are you going? Boston?"

"No, I have some more business down in DC."

"When will you be back?"

Adam hesitated. "Not until Thursday evening."

"Oh," I sighed.

Four long days with no Adam. And then I caught myself. I was definitely starting to rely on Adam's presence far too much. But when Adam reached over and pulled me to him, I didn't resist. A few heated kisses later, we reluctantly pulled apart and said our farewells until Thursday.

Later that night I woke up, and when I couldn't get back

to sleep, I padded down to the living room. After lifting the loose floorboard, I pulled out the case files and paged furiously through the reams of material with renewed interest. The past twenty-four hours had been eye-opening, and surely that was contributing to my current case of insomnia.

There had been Helena's tale of why Trina hated Chelsea; J.T.'s attack that had, if nothing else, highlighted his substance abuse problems and anger issues; Adam's confession that Chelsea had indeed been blackmailing him; and then my dad's theory that Chelsea may have been hiding her calls from Adam. On top of all that, now I had to come to grips with the fact that my former best friend was a mental mess. Little wonder my mind was in overdrive.

I sat down, right there on the hardwood floor, and began to reread the files. When I reached the particulars of Chelsea's last visit to Billy's, I was reminded that I'd not heard anything from Jimmy. Obviously a return visit to Billy's was in order. Maybe Jimmy had misplaced my cell number, or maybe he'd forgotten all about the alleged photo of Chelsea kissing some blonde girl. In any case a little reminder—and possibly another cash infusion—might be enough incentive to get him moving.

There was something about the blonde mystery woman that was bothering me. There had been no reported rumors—like with Chelsea and J.T.—about Chelsea and this individual. Adam had known about J.T. and Chelsea for quite some time. And he had been made aware of the other random men, and the drugs. Had he known about the mystery blonde as well? Or had Chelsea kept that part of her life successfully hidden?

I knew I should have just asked Adam, but I was reluctant. What if that night at Billy's had been a one-time event? Or what if Jimmy had lied about what he'd overheard Chelsea and the mystery blonde saying? Hell, he could have made the whole thing up. Besides, hadn't Adam made it clear he didn't really care to discuss the things I was uncovering in this investigation?

That seemed strange too. *Unless* he didn't really anticipate I'd discover anything that hadn't already been reported in those files. If that were the case, then it only served to make me want to dig deeper and solve this damn thing, once and for all.

Somewhere along the line this investigation had become much more than "research." Now it was personal.

Early Monday morning my father called. Yes, as expected, he'd found out about what had happened with J.T. O'Brien. It took nearly twenty minutes to calm him down. The only good thing that came out of it was that he reluctantly agreed Adam had saved me from further harm. I guessed it made him feel better about me staying on the island, because he didn't threaten to come over and drag me back home. Although, I half-expected that to still happen.

On Thursday I drove down to the dock. Dressed in some raggedy jeans and an old flannel shirt that I knew would make me fit right in at Billy's, I was all set to pay Jimmy another visit. As I made my way to the waiting ferry, I inwardly groaned when I noticed Jennifer Weston was at the helm. I was in no mood to deal with her today.

"Oh yay," I muttered to myself as I stepped aboard.

Jennifer appeared to be as excited to see me as I was to see her. "If it isn't Madeleine Fitch." Sarcasm dripped with every word as she purposely blocked my way. "Must be my lucky day," she snapped.

Pushing past her, I took a seat. "Back to the mainland so soon?" she continued, starting up the ferry. "Running low on people to press charges against? Or is island life just too boring when your rich boyfriend isn't around to beat the piss out of someone?"

OK, so it was clear Jennifer had taken issue with the J.T. incident. *No surprise there.* She obviously still had feelings for him. Ignoring her comments, I rummaged through my bag, searching for the book I'd brought along to pass the time.

Without warning the ferry lurched forward uncharacteristically, and Jennifer shot me a look of satisfaction, surely pleased at startling me. "J.T. was right about you, you know," she said.

"Oh, this ought to be good," I muttered, pulling out my

book.

    Jennifer snickered. "We had a bet on how long it was going to take for you to end up in Ward's bed."

    I rolled my eyes. What was it with her and J.T.? I hadn't even slept with Adam…yet. Well, I'd slept with him in the literal sense, but I was sure they meant more. Just the thought of it, when it did happen though, brought a secret smile to my lips.

    "That's what I thought," Jennifer snarked, misinterpreting my smile. "Looks like I won. I said less than a month."

    "Whatever," I huffed dismissively.

    "It won't last, you know," Jennifer continued, undettered.

    Oh, it was going to be a long ride to the mainland.

    "You don't know anything about my relationship with Adam." I should have just ignored her, but I felt compelled to say something.

    "Relationship?" she spat. "If it makes you feel better to call it that, then fine."

    I opened my book and began to read in an attempt to end the unpleasant conversation. But Jennifer would not shut up. "Do you want to know what I can't figure out, Fitch?"

    No, not really, I thought, pretending to be deeply engrossed in the book when, really, I'd not read a single word.

    "You don't seem at all like what Ward usually goes for. Odd," she mused out loud, clearly baiting me as she feigned a lost-in-thought expression.

    I put my book down. She sure had my attention now. "What's *that* supposed to mean?" I asked, returning her glare.

    "Let's just say, I know plenty more about Adam Ward than you do."

    "Sure you do." I laughed and taunted, "You're so well-informed."

    "I know this," Jennifer hissed. "Ward is a powerful man who prefers beautiful women." She eyed me up and down, like I didn't make the cut.

    When I rolled my eyes, she continued, "Not to mention" —Jennifer tapped her finger to her chin mockingly, pretending to be in deep thought— "he's a man with a voracious appetite that I doubt *you* could keep up with. You seem a little too, I don't know, bland maybe." She winked knowingly, and my eyes widened.

How in the hell would Jennifer know something like that, unless… I narrowed my eyes at her, and she said pointedly, "Oh please, Fitch, drop the look of dismay. I never touched your precious Ward. I'm just saying I've heard things."

Heard things? Like what, I wanted to ask? And from whom? Jennifer had certainly not been friends with Chelsea. Did she know Lindsey? No, I doubted it. But I didn't know who all Adam had been with over the years and whose paths had crossed with Jennifer's. I didn't care to dwell on it either. But it just bothered me to no end. *Who* would have confided in *Jennifer*?

"I'm not particularly interested in whatever crap you've heard," I said, trying desperately to sound unfazed and uninterested.

"Suit yourself," she countered. "But did you ever consider you might be being played?"

I bit my lip, turning my head away. "Shut up, Jennifer."

But apparently she was just warming up. "You're a novelty to him, Fitch. You're nothing but a between-inning stretch. What do you think is going to happen?" She snorted unattractively. "Do you dream of the great Adam Ward falling for you? Why would he want *you*, when he could have anyone he wants? Face the facts, bitch, he's out of your league."

As much as I was trying to fight them, tears threatened. Jennifer was awakening all the insecurities I'd ever had. "You don't know anything about me," I said quietly, blinking back tears.

"I know you once had a schoolgirl crush on Ward. Just remember, you're not in high school anymore."

What? How could Jennifer know that tidbit? Her words left me stunned. The only person who'd ever known about my crush on Adam was Ami. But Jennifer and Ami weren't friends. Were they? I mean, it seemed unlikely since they'd barely spoken to one another on that first ferry ride over to Fade Island. Of course, Helena now probably suspected I'd always had a crush on Adam. And maybe she'd told Trina? But were Trina and Jennifer friends? What about Helena and Jennifer? I hadn't gotten the impression they were pals.

But God, how'd Jennifer know about Adam's supposed sexual prowess? Who else could she have been friends with? Maybe she had been buddies with Chelsea, despite everything? That would explain at least part of how she knew these things. So I asked, "Who told you those things about Adam? The part about his…" I winced. "…voracious appetite? Chelsea?"

As soon as the words were out of my mouth, I regretted them. Jennifer cut the engine, leaving us to drift quietly on the water out in the middle of the ocean. She approached, and I hastily stood up.

"Let's get one thing straight." Jennifer was in my face. Close. Too close. "That fucking piece of shit slut was no fucking friend of mine. So don't ever even *think* it."

I took a shaky step backwards, the sound of the waves sloshing against the sides of the ferry seemingly amplified in the silence. "OK," I responded meekly.

Jennifer cocked her head to the side, as if examining me. "What *are* you doing here, Fitch?" I shuddered, and before I could answer, she added, "You're not poking around in things that don't concern you, are you?"

I shook my head emphatically. "No, I'm not."

"Are you sure? 'Cause if you are…" She trailed off.

"I'm not," I insisted.

Jennifer suddenly backed off, laughing smugly. "Wouldn't it be poetic if you found out you were sleeping with the enemy, so to speak, in this little scenario?"

"Adam didn't do anything to Chelsea," I stated with conviction.

"Maybe, maybe not." Jennifer's eyes were black and unblinking, her voice cold. Even colder when she added, "Personally, I hope he fucking offed the bitch."

This was getting to be too much. Something bad was going to happen if I didn't snap her out of this tirade. "Um, I need to get to the mainland, Jennifer," I squeaked out in a meager attempt to diffuse her fury.

She snickered. "Of course you do. What do you think I'm going to do? Throw you overboard?" Her eyes flashed to the water as if she were considering it.

But to my relief, she returned to the pilot's house and set the ferry back into motion. I sat back down, trembling. *Maybe I should tell Adam about this incident.*

The rest of the way to Cove Beach, I thought about ways I could broach the subject without having to divulge the more sordid things Jennifer had said about him—that he was playing me, that he was the enemy. *Jesus.* By the time we reached the dock, though, I decided it'd be best to keep quiet. I'd already sent J.T. to rehab; and I didn't want Adam to retaliate against Jennifer, too, and make things somehow go from bad to worse.

With all that had transpired on the ferry replaying in my head, I got my car out of the garage and drove to Billy's. Except this time, as I traveled along the two-lane state route, I kept getting the distinct impression that I was being tailed. I checked my rearview mirror. There were a few cars behind me, but when I slowed, they passed without incident. Hitting the gas I concluded I was just feeling extra paranoid due to Jennifer's behavior on the ferry. Still, when I reached Billy's, I parked the car directly in front of the door and practically ran into the establishment.

Jimmy was standing on a step stool behind the bar, stringing up Halloween lights. Rock music played in the background, and his head bobbed up and down with the beat as he secured the string of lights.

When Jimmy flipped a switch on the cord, a wash of orange and purple bathed the bar area. "Looks good," I said, startling him.

"Hey." Jimmy jumped down from his perch and folded up the step stool. "Didn't see ya there." He picked up an almost-spent cigarette in the ashtray behind the bar, took a drag, and stubbed it out. "What can I getcha?"

Before I could answer, movement from the back room caught my eye. Damn, I wasn't the only customer today at Billy's. This would make it harder to get information out of Jimmy, especially since his eyes kept darting to the back room.

"Um, a beer would be fine," I said, and Jimmy's attention returned to me.

As Jimmy made his way down to the cooler to retrieve my drink, I craned my neck to catch sight of the other customer. And then I wished I hadn't.

There was no other way to describe the guy in the back as anything other than a bad-looking dude. He was huge, bigger than Nate even, maybe about the same size as Max. He had on jeans and a navy muscle shirt that showed off his bulging arms. Tattoos ran up and down his arms, but he was too far away for me to make out what they were.

I watched as he ran his hand over his closely shorn, white-blond hair and took a swig from a mug of beer. He picked up a pool cue—I guessed he was playing alone as there were balls all over the table. Suddenly he pointed the cue stick at me. "Bang," he mouthed.

I quickly averted my eyes, ignoring him. *Crap!* Had he known I'd been watching him the whole time?

Jimmy returned and placed the bottle on the bar. He'd left the cap on, so I twisted it off with a huff. But he didn't even seem to notice. It seemed my bartender-pal was distracted, as he kept glancing over at Mr. Cue Stick in the back room.

I cleared my throat. "Did I catch you at a bad time?" I asked, curious as to what was going on here.

"Nah." Jimmy shot another furtive look to the back and then lowered his voice. "Hey, listen. I haven't found that picture yet. And I figure that's why you're here. But today's probably not a good day for you to be here—"

Before Jimmy finished, a rude voice interrupted, "Who's the fresh meat?"

It was the guy from the back. He slammed his empty mug down on the bar, and though I kept *my* eyes on the bar, I felt his bore into me.

I heard Jimmy say, "Let her alone, man. She's not lookin' for what 'ya think she is."

What the hell was Jimmy referring to? Drugs? No doubt.

The man laughed. "Hell, Jimmy, everyone can use a little pick-me-up from time to time." He paused, and I reluctantly glanced over. He tapped his nose. "Isn't that right, sweet thing?" He cocked his head to one side, examining me like a specimen. "Or maybe you're just looking for a little tweak?"

His eyes were so dark, almost black. I couldn't hold his stare, so I dropped my gaze. The tattoos on his right arm—screaming skulls with dark snakes writhing out of their eyes—seemed to be looking right at me. If the artwork hadn't been so disturbing, I would have thought it beautiful in its intricacy. But as it was, I shuddered. There was something very wrong with this guy. I sensed he was still staring, so I glanced up. A shiver ran down my spine as those black eyes met mine.

I looked away, and he laughed. "I got all kinds of goodies to loosen up a tight little piece like you. You let me know if you change your pretty little mind."

Still keeping my eyes averted, I found myself nodding out of sheer terror. The man laughed louder. "Don't worry about the price either. I got all kinds of payment options for customers who look as good as you do." I cringed at the thought, and he added, "Aw, don't look so scared. You come spend a few minutes with me in the back, and I'll get you so high you'll think you're in heaven."

More like hell, I thought.

"Zeb," Jimmy interjected, though his rattled voice betrayed his fear. "Leave her alone."

I looked up to see Zeb turning to Jimmy, fury emanated from him. "*You* don't tell *me* what to do, you got that, man?" Jimmy nodded meekly as he refilled Zeb's mug, his hand trembling. "You just worry about getting me what you owe me, or we're gonna have some real problems on our hands."

Thankfully Zeb was more focused on Jimmy now. He stared intently at him as Jimmy slid Zeb's now-full mug toward him. As Zeb picked up his beer, his eyes never left Jimmy. Not even as he headed back to the back room. Finally he looked away.

A few minutes later, when Zeb disappeared into the men's

room, Jimmy leaned toward me and whispered, "Listen, Maddy. You better get outta here."

I had every intention of hitting the road before Zeb had another chance to harass me, but first I wanted to take care of something. It was clear Zeb was a dealer, and Jimmy owed him money. I couldn't help but feel bad for the kid. He probably needed as much help as J.T. A part of me wanted to talk to him about getting his life together, but I knew Zeb would be back soon. Right now, the only thing I could offer was some help to get him out of financial trouble with the scary dealer.

I stood up, readying to go. "How much do you owe him?" I asked Jimmy in a hushed voice.

He cast his eyes down. "Five hundred, but he'd leave me alone if I could get him sumthin'."

I didn't have five hundred dollars on me, but I pulled out the extra money I had brought. Sliding two one-hundred dollar bills across the bar, I said, "Here, take it. But God, Jimmy, try not to buy from him again."

"Hey, I'm not some charity case, 'ya know," Jimmy protested.

"Then think of it as an advance," I offered. "For the picture."

He hesitated but ultimately snatched the money up. He sounded deflated when he said, "I'll get 'ya whatcha need, I promise."

"Can I ask you one thing before I leave?"

Jimmy nodded, and I whispered, "Was that Zeb-guy Chelsea's dealer?"

He looked like he wasn't going to answer, but then he glanced at the money in his hand. "Yeah," Jimmy said quietly. "Anyone here who needs sumthin' they go to Zeb. Always have, probably always will."

Considering Chelsea's drug habits, I wondered if she'd ever taken Zeb up on any of his special "payment options." I was going to ask, but Jimmy glanced uneasily to the back. "You better go."

So I nodded and rushed out of Billy's. When I slipped back into my car and adjusted the rearview mirror, I caught a glimpse of a man ducking behind one of the warehouses. Unfortunately he was too quick for me to get a clear view. But there was no more doubt in my mind that I was being tailed. But *who* would be following me? And *why*? I debated whether I should get out and confront the person. But then I thought of Zeb. I took action, all right—I got the hell out of there.

Even though I thought of a bunch of good retorts to throw back at Jennifer the Bitch on my drive to Cove Beach, I was, nevertheless, relieved to see that Brody, not his sister, would be taking me back to the island.

Once back on Fade Island, I hopped into the Lexus and drove back to the cottage. Pulling into the driveway, my eyes were drawn to a small square of paper taped to the front door. Fluttering in the breeze as I approached, I could see it was a handwritten note of some sort. I peeled it loose. It was a simple message from Adam; he wanted me to stop by his place as soon as I had a chance.

Curious as to what was up, but wanting to freshen up after my time at Billy's, I took a quick shower. Then I changed into a nicer pair of jeans; a long-sleeved, mocha-colored tee; and a pair of ballet flats. After brushing out my hair, I left for Adam's house.

Trina was back in Boston, so I knew we'd have the place to ourselves. Something I was definitely looking forward to. I knocked on the front door and waited.

When Adam opened the door, my breath caught in my throat. *Wow*. He looked exceptionally hot, even though his expression betrayed a brooding kind of anger. Still I lowered my eyes to the ground and began a slow, appreciative ascent up his physique— starting at the expensive-looking black shoes he wore, up to the alluring way his dark gray slacks fit him in ways most men wished for, and to the black button-down shirt he was wearing, top buttons undone. Finally my eyes came to rest on his face.

It was the first time I'd seen Adam with a shadow of stubble, which was definitely working for him. I met his eyes, and they flickered in annoyance. Something was definitely not right, because this look was far different from his usual expression of amusement when he'd catch me blatantly ogling his magnificence.

"Maddy, are you going to just stand there, or are you coming in?" Adam snapped, impatience coloring his every word.

Huffing, I brushed past him into the foyer. "Geez, somebody sure is cranky," I muttered under my breath.

He sighed and ran his fingers through his hair. "We need to discuss something." He turned and began walking down the hallway. "Follow me," he said. "We can talk in my study."

Aah, the study, I thought. *Must be serious.*

Trailing behind him, feeling more like I was off to the principal's office, I sighed. "What's going on, Adam?"

"We'll discuss it in here," he said brusquely. We'd reached the door, and he pushed it open.

Adam's study was smaller than most of the rooms in his place, but it was by no means tiny. Tastefully decorated, the study was a cross between a traditional Old World study and an executive's office.

He led me to a plush, burgundy leather chair that faced the front of his ornately trimmed dark wood desk. "Sit," he commanded.

Maybe due to Adam's no-nonsense demeanor, maybe due to the air of authority with which the atmosphere pulsed, I couldn't be sure. But, in any case, I quickly obeyed, gently placing my bag on the floor next to me. Adam took a seat in an elegant, black leather chair behind his desk. What an image—the powerful Adam Ward in his element.

Evening was rapidly approaching. The light from the large, single window in the room—overlooking the ocean through a break in the thick pines surrounding Adam's compound—was waning.

Adam clicked on a desk lamp, and I cleared my throat. "There's obviously something wrong," I began. "Are you mad about something?"

Instead of answering Adam shot me a pointed look, and then he withdrew a key from his pant pocket. Reaching down, he inserted it into the bottom right-hand desk drawer.

"I'm not mad at you, Madeleine," Adam said distractedly, head down as he turned the key and entered a code into what I assumed was a keypad built right into the drawer. "However, something has come to my attention with which I'm not particularly pleased."

The drawer sprung open, and I waited, still having no idea what Adam could be referring to. When he looked up, his serious gaze met mine. In his hands he held a stack of photos. Of what I didn't know, but I had a feeling I was about to find out.

"Can you do something for me?" His voice was even and smooth, businesslike.

"Sure, anything," I replied.

Adam slid the photos across the vast expanse of the desk. "I know you're set on this little quest of yours to research my ex's disappearance. But I'd prefer if you stayed away from *this* place." Adam nodded to the pictures, so I picked them up.

There were about a dozen four-by-six-inch color photos, all of me going into (and coming out of) Billy's. They'd been taken earlier today. *Unbelievable!*

Instantly I was furious. "You had someone follow me?" I accused, my voice raised. I tossed the photos back at Adam, scattering the glossy images across his otherwise tidy desk.

"Maddy, calm down," he said reproachfully.

"No! I'm not going to *calm down*. I knew I was being followed today, but I never expected you were the one behind it."

Adam's expression betrayed his displeasure with my outburst. "There's no reason to get this upset. I asked Max to follow you for your own safety."

"Max again?" I scoffed. "And I'm supposed to believe you're that concerned with my safety?"

"Madeleine," Adam said warningly. "Need I remind you of the other night with J.T. O'Brien?"

That gave me pause, because maybe it wasn't *that* crazy to believe Adam had had Max follow me for my own protection. After all, it wasn't like Billy's was exactly safe. An image of Zeb pretending to "shoot" me with the pool stick flashed through my mind.

I shuddered and said, "But pictures, Adam? Really? Don't you think that's a bit much?"

His eyes held no apology. "I wanted to see what you were up to anyway," he stated matter-of-factly. *Ah, there's the real reason.* "And I'm going to reiterate, I do *not* want you going back there. End of story."

"God, who do you think you are?" I said, incredulous and infuriated at his demand. "Maybe your, your *minions* obey your every command, but I, Adam, am not one of them. I make my own decisions," I stated with conviction. "You got that?"

Maybe I should have held back. Adam's eyes flashed in anger, boring into me. "Yeah, I *got that*, Madeleine. Far be it from me to try and save you from your own damn self."

Fleetingly his mask wavered, and I saw concern cross his features. God, maybe I was overreacting. Was it guilt for keeping my visits to Billy's secret that had me so worked up? Maybe Adam had been thinking of my safety?

Confused and humbled, I backed down. "I'm sorry for snapping at you," I said, my voice soft. "I know you're only looking out for me." I put my head in my hands and mumbled, "I guess it's just been a long day." It was a weak excuse, but it was all I had.

"Come here, Maddy." Adam's voice had eased, his anger dissipated.

I glanced up, and he beckoned for me to come around to his side of the desk. I got up and went to him, and once I reached him, he spun his chair to face me and leaned his head back. "Kiss me, Madeleine," he purred.

His charm was irresistible. And the tension from our fight lingered—we both needed a release. So I bent down and curved my lips to his. Such a perfect fit. Our mouths moved together—tongues touching, dancing, darting—until Adam made a growling noise and pulled away.

Before I knew what was happening, Adam had shifted my body so that my backside was pressed against the edge of his desk. He stood, hovering over me as he kicked his chair back.

"Want to make a friendly wager?"

Standing on the tips of my toes, I brushed my lips across his. "Yeah, sure," I breathed. Hell, anything sounded good at this point. "What are we betting on?"

With no warning and to my delight, Adam slid his hands up under my shirt, his strong hands encircling my ribcage, his thumbs tracing over the lacy edge of my bra. My breathing hitched, and I leaned my head against his chest as his long fingers trailed up and under the straps, poised ever so teasingly on bare skin. I arched my back, wishing he would slide his hands down to my breasts that ached to feel his touch.

But as if knowing what I craved, he did the opposite—slid his hands back out from under my shirt. "First, if I win, you have to promise you will *never* go back to that bar under *any* circumstances." The businessman was back, making a deal. He eased me back onto the surface of the desk and stood towering above me.

I looked up at him in his position of power. "And if I win?" I asked breathlessly, slick, glossy photos sliding beneath my jean-clad bottom.

Adam parted my legs and eased between them. *Oh. My. God.*

Chuckling, he said, "Then you're free to do whatever you want. I'll promise not to interfere." He leaned down, cupping my face. "But Maddy, I will win."

And then he kissed me like he'd never done before. His mouth was hungry, demanding, angry. His hands roamed, touching, taking—under the shirt, over the shirt, over the jeans, under the waistband. The top button popped. "Oh God," I gasped, arching into him, aching to *feel* how much he wanted me.

But Adam shifted, and I felt his hot, urgent breaths at my ear. "Want to know how I'm going to win?" he asked, his lips skimming my neck.

I nodded furiously, plunging my fingers into the silkiness of his hair.

He chuckled, pulling back slightly. He turned his wrist, and we both glanced at his very expensive watch, noting the time. *OK, whatever.* At that exact moment, I couldn't have cared less.

Dizzy, I leaned my head back on the desk, and Adam slid down my body, lifting the hem of my tee and placing a warm, wet kiss on my exposed hip. He knelt down between my legs, yanking me to the edge of the desk. His mouth returned to my hip, his tongue lazily trailing a wet path across my abdomen. And then his hand cupped my core. "Oh God," I gasped.

"I win, Madeleine, if in sixty seconds or less, I can get you to beg me to take off these jeans," Adam purred, and then he began to kiss lower and lower.

The bet was on…

Chapter 15

Not surprisingly Adam won the bet by a rather significant margin. Yeah, don't bet against Adam Ward. But right as I was begging him to take my jeans off *now* so he could do all the amazing things he was doing with his mouth without the damn denim in the way, someone knocked on the door of his study. Adam yelled, "Go the fuck away."

But the knocking continued and was soon accompanied by the apologetic-sounding, yet urgent, voice of Max.

I yelped and hurried to make sure everything was zipped and buttoned, while Adam straightened his own disheveled attire. On his way to the door, he let a litany of creative curses fly. Once decent I plopped down in Adam's chair and pretended to be examining those damn pictures, most of which were now scattered *all* over the desk. Adam shot me an apologetic look as he opened the door just enough for him to speak to Max. Good god, how embarrassing. Not to mention frustrating.

After a few moments of mumbled conversation—I had no clue what they were discussing, nor did I care—Adam closed the door and turned to me. "Maddy, I have to take care of something with Max. Will you be OK in here for about fifteen minutes?" I hesitated, and Adam added, "Unless you want to go home, of course."

I didn't want to leave for two reasons. First, I didn't relish walking past Max. Not only had he been spying on me earlier in the day—though at Adam's request—but I also felt sure he knew he'd interrupted something just now. *Yeah, way too embarrassing.* But the more pressing reason I had for staying was a fervent hope we'd pick up where we'd left off once Adam returned. Things had just been getting interesting. Suppressing a smile I was certain Adam deciphered, I said, "No, I don't mind waiting."

So Adam went out into the hallway with Max, closing the door behind him, but not before shooting me a look full of promise that we would indeed be continuing what we'd started. I glanced down at the scattered photos before me, many of which were now bent and crinkled from my writhing around on top of them. Smiling at the naughtiness of what had occurred, I began to gather the photos into a pile on Adam's otherwise uncluttered desk.

Even though I'd lost the bet—meaning I was to never step foot in Billy's ever again—I knew I'd have to break that promise at least once if Jimmy located the picture. But I'd worry about that when—and if—the time ever came.

Adam sure had been adamant about me staying away from that bar. Perhaps he didn't relish the thought of his new girlfriend frequenting the establishment where his old girlfriend had committed so many acts of betrayal. Based on that assumption, it seemed prudent to keep looking into the mystery blonde on my own.

Once I'd organized the photos back into a pile, I spun around once, twice. Dizzy, I tried to imagine what it must be like to be Adam Ward. Being that rich and powerful tended to make people do exactly what you wanted. Even I hadn't been immune to Adam's charisma. It had to be intoxicating to be him. Hell, I felt it just by being in his presence.

I swiveled the chair left and right, and took a moment to inventory the study. Packed bookcases lined the room, an eclectic mix of literature and technical manuals. A few museum-worthy oil paintings graced a couple of the walls, and on a credenza under the window, there were framed photos of Adam's parents as well as his sister.

There was a work area on the opposite side of the room, and by the looks of it, it was a tech-lover's dream. Elaborately set up computers and peripherals, routers, and other hardware that held little interest for me. So I directed my gaze to the large window on the far wall, the one with the view of the ocean through the trees.

Night had fallen, but the blinds remained open. It was a little unnerving to think that someone—like Max—could have been out there watching us. Even though it was unlikely, and I was being a little paranoid, I still wanted them closed. But as I rose from Adam's chair to do just that, something on the floor by the desk drew my attention. One of the photos had apparently fallen to the floor.

I reached down to pick it up, and that was when I noticed the bottom drawer—the one Adam had pulled the photos from—stood ajar, the tiny key resting innocuously in the keyhole, the digital keypad dark and disengaged. Adam had forgotten to lock it back up, probably since we'd been otherwise engaged.

At that moment I had a choice to make. I could just ignore the unlocked drawer, or I could open it and see what other things Adam was keeping in there—the only drawer with a lock on it. *God, would he be pissed if he knew I was even contemplating going through his private things.*

I held my breath and listened. Everything was quiet, Adam apparently still busy with Max. Only a few moments had passed, so I knew I probably had a good ten minutes more to snoop. I breathed out and sat back down in the chair, tapping the edge of the photo on the desk. *What to do, what to do.* Oh hell, the temptation was just too much. Tossing the picture aside, I wrenched the bottom drawer open and peered in.

Stacks of thick file folders and large A4 envelopes were piled high. With my hand shaking, I reached down tentatively and flipped the top folder open. It contained what appeared to be some sort of a business contract. Nothing too interesting, just boring legalize.

In fact, as I made my way through the pile, it seemed several of the folders and envelopes contained the same things: contracts, lots of contracts, and reams of transcribed notes from business meetings. There was one folder labeled Hensley Files, but I paged past it. I assumed it detailed the stuff Adam had already told me about Ami, plus I didn't really have time to peruse everything. All of this stuff was obviously private papers. But nothing seemed damning, until I reached the very bottom of the pile. There, three things caught my eye.

One was a file folder stamped "confidential."

The second was a large, ivory-colored A4 envelope with the name "Trina" scrawled on the front in Adam's neat script.

And the third was a gun—a .38 revolver. Loaded, based on the weight in my hands as I picked it up and turned it over and over.

OK, so Adam owned a gun. It didn't seem unreasonable for a man of his professional stature to possess a weapon for home defense. I tried not to over-think the firearm as I carefully placed it back in the bottom of the drawer. With the gun safely secured, I focused instead on the first item of interest: the file folder marked "confidential."

It contained pages and pages detailing a stock trade Adam had made during the winter months, almost seven years earlier. I nearly dropped the entire contents when I saw the amount of profit he'd made on that single transaction on a stock he'd held for less than two months. *Wow!*

Attached to one of the earnings summaries was a worn, yellowing page from a newspaper I'd never heard of—The News Record of Cambridge. Skimming through the articles from six years earlier, it appeared to be some sort of tiny publication, maybe just for the students of MIT. Why had Adam kept something so insignificant under lock and key? When I reached the bottom left-hand corner of the newspaper page, I had my answer.

SEC Investigation Comes to an End for Promising MIT Student

Due to a lack of evidence, current undergrad Adam Ward has been cleared of any wrongdoing in a fortuitous stock transaction that netted the young MIT computer whiz 18.7 million dollars.

Following an intense two-month investigation by the Securities and Exchange Commission, it was determined that the young Mr. Ward's incredible windfall had more to do with diligent research, and possibly a bit of beginner's luck, than with trading on an illegal insider stock tip, as was originally suspected.

The SEC became suspicious after Mr. Ward withdrew a significant chunk of his trust fund monies to purchase an exorbitant number of troubled TechnoDyne Inc. shares only six weeks before the small, New York-based software development company was purchased by an industry leader, thus sending the stock price soaring.

When Mr. Ward unloaded all of his holdings and collected his tidy profit, the SEC swooped in and opened a case to investigate the transaction.

However, no illegal activity was uncovered; so pending the discovery of any new information to the contrary, the case is now officially closed. And the young, very rich Adam Ward is now free to spend his previously frozen assets however he wishes.

Oh my Lord! Hastily I slipped the clipping back under the shiny, new paper clip that had held it and placed the file on the desk. I'd never come across any information detailing stock trades Adam had made. Since this article was nothing more than a blurb from the back pages of some little-known paper, it made sense I'd not found anything like this in my research. But I could see how the Securities Exchange Commission would become suspicious, as 18.7 million dollars was a huge amount of money to attribute to "beginner's luck."

And that made me wonder... Had Adam been tipped off by someone about the buyout prior to the information becoming public? That would certainly have been illegal, falling squarely into the definition of insider trading. Could this be the "illegal" thing Adam had done? Was this his big secret? It had to be! I knew it in my heart.

And had Chelsea known? It dovetailed into the timeline perfectly. Is that what she'd been blackmailing him with? The threat of going to the SEC with what she knew?

If she had gone to the SEC with solid information, the case would have been re-opened, and Adam may have had to face a jury trial. Depending on how damaging her testimony was, Adam could have been found guilty and possibly faced prison time. Without a doubt, that would have ruined his life. The article was dated right around the same time he'd gotten engaged. Coincidence? I doubted it. In fact, I *knew* this had to be the secret. That was why it was under lock and key.

Feeling both elated and terrified at discovering this, I shakily picked up the second item of interest, the ivory A4 envelope—the one with "Trina" written on the front in Adam's own handwriting. I tipped the envelope, and two letters—addressed to Chelsea's Harbourtown apartment—fell onto the desk. Both had June postmarks from only one month prior to her disappearance. Things were going from bad to worse.

Each envelope contained a short, handwritten note, both written in a feminine cursive.

The first one read:

Chelsea, I don't know what you have on my brother, but I do know you're going to end up ruining his life. Adam doesn't love you. He hasn't for a long time. You've become an evil person, and someday you're going to get exactly what you deserve. -Trina

The second one, written one week later, read:

You are a bitch. I can't believe you're actu-

ally going to go through with this farce of a wedding. You can't love Adam. If you did, you'd never do this to him. Call the wedding off, Chelsea, or I'll personally make sure you're sorry you didn't. -Trina

With my heart in my throat, my hands would not stop shaking as I grasped the letters tightly. So Trina had been threatening Chelsea. While I was aware there'd been no love lost between those two after the incident with Chelsea and Walker, it was still disturbing to read Trina's vitriolic words.

And how had Adam ended up with these letters in *his* possession? The police reports hadn't mentioned anything about threatening letters. And surely they would have, had they known. Was Adam protecting his sister by keeping them hidden? Had she actually followed through on her threats and done something to Chelsea to prevent her from marrying Adam?

Frazzled, and with time running short, I shoved the file folder with the stock information back into the bottom of the drawer, on top of the gun, and left everything as it had been. I held onto the letters, however, placing them back into the ivory A4 envelope. I wanted those letters in my possession until more information came to light. If Trina had really done something to Chelsea, I couldn't just sit by and allow Adam to continue to cover for her.

My head was spinning, and my pulse was racing from anxiety. I wanted to go back to my own place. I needed some time alone to think over the implications of both matters I'd discovered tonight. Clutching the envelope containing the letters, I stepped into the hall, and closed the study door behind me until I heard a soft *snick*.

I looked left, I looked right; the coast appeared to be clear. I hurried down the hall, through the foyer, and suddenly realized I'd left my bag in the study. And my car keys were in the bag. *Damn.*

So I turned around and rushed back, shouldering my way into the study's half-open door. *Odd, I thought I had closed that door.* With no time to contemplate, I hurried over to where I'd dropped my bag to the floor.

But it wasn't there.

I knelt down on the floor and checked under the desk. Nothing.

Suddenly a low, irate voice broke through the silence. "Looking for something, Madeleine?"

I rocked back onto my heels quickly, the ivory envelope containing Trina's letters clearly visible in my left hand. I attempted to slip it under my knees and, in the process, glanced up to see Adam in the doorway. And, holy hell, did he look pissed.

He stood perfectly still, my bag dangling from his right hand. Which way had he come in? Not through the front, as I would have run right into him. And how long had he been back? Long enough to have seen me snooping around?

I bit down on my lip, hard enough to draw blood. Adam's hard-muscled body was all the more pronounced with the way the desk lamp light fell on him. Coupled with the expression of fury on his face, I felt tiny and vulnerable from my vantage point on the floor. He dropped my bag and took three long strides, and then he stood before me.

I lowered my gaze, fearful to meet his dark, angry eyes. "Give me the envelope *now!*" he said, his voice steady but firm.

I held it out to him with absolutely no hesitation.

Snatching it from my hand, he scolded, "I'm extremely disappointed in you, Madeleine." He circled around me, not unlike a stalking predator. "Going through my private papers, *stealing* from me." Adam placed the edge of the envelope under my chin. "Look at me," he demanded.

I reluctantly met his glare, and though his eyes were full of fury, there was also something else. Hurt? Betrayal? Whatever it was, I felt incredibly guilty for what I'd done. Adam had asked me—more than once—if I trusted him. And I had vehemently questioned his trust in me. Yet here I was, the one betraying him. How ironic.

Yes, Adam had secrets—and I'd wanted answers—but

sneaking around in his private files was just wrong. Who was the bad person in this scenario? I knew the answer. It was I.

"I'm sorry, Adam." I whispered, my voice cracking but not solely from fear. I was also ashamed. I truly was sorry, and in that moment, all I desired was his forgiveness.

Holding my gaze, he growled, "You've really gone too far this time. I have half a mind to terminate your lease and kick you off the island."

"No," I cried. "Please, Adam. I don't care about the past. Even if your sister did something to Chelsea—"

"Trina did *not* do anything to that bitch! Fuck, Maddy, there are how many suspects out there?" Adam yelled, running his hand through his hair in apparent frustration. "Why are you so fucking set on blaming a Ward?"

"I'm not," I tried to explain. "I believed you when you told me you were innocent. I still don't think you hurt Chelsea. But those letters, Adam."

"These letters" —Adam held the envelope up menacingly— "mean nothing. Trina was trying to scare Chelsea. My sister could never hurt anyone. She was only trying to protect me."

"And you were protecting her in return," I whispered.

"Yes, I was protecting my sister from having the police think exactly what you're thinking right now. I intercepted these letters before Chelsea ever saw them, thank God." Adam tossed the envelope onto the desk. "After she disappeared I started keeping them under lock and key."

"I'm sorry," I muttered, "for everything. If you want me to leave the island, I will…" My voice faltered, tears in my eyes.

I didn't want to leave the island. And I definitely didn't want to leave Adam. I longed to tell him I was falling in love with him, but I was fearful of being rejected, especially after tonight. And one thing for sure, I certainly wasn't about to bring up the stock trade information I'd also discovered. *No way.* Not tonight.

"Stand up," Adam ordered, his voice firm but less angry than before.

I stood up, shaky, and Adam took my hand. I looked up into

his tormented blue eyes. "I don't want you to leave the island, OK?"

"It was wrong of me to go through your stuff," I said, knowing, and believing, it now more than ever before.

"It was," he agreed, letting go of my hand.

"I should go."

Adam didn't protest. He led me out of the study but not before putting the envelope containing Trina's letters back into the desk drawer and, of course, making sure it was locked this time.

We walked down the hall, through the foyer, out to the driveway, all in silence. At my car Adam stopped me. "Madeleine, I have business over on the mainland tomorrow, but I'll stop by the cottage in the morning." I looked at him quizzically. "We have one more matter to discuss," he clarified.

There was no need to ask what he meant. He knew I'd seen more than Trina's letters in that drawer. He knew I'd read the SEC stuff.

I drew a deep breath. "Adam—"

"Not now, Maddy." Fingers on my lips, silencing me. "It's late. We'll talk tomorrow."

I didn't argue. I got in the car and drove back to the cottage. Let myself in, dragged myself upstairs, peeled off my clothes, fell into bed.

Had Adam traded on insider information? If so, had Chelsea blackmailed him with her knowledge of it? How much would Adam tell me? And where did we stand after tonight? Would he forgive my snooping?

I didn't know, but I'd surely find out tomorrow morning.

Chapter 16

Unfortunately sleep didn't lessen the guilt I felt for going through Adam's private things. He'd been more irate than I'd ever seen him. Well, maybe he'd been angrier at J.T. that night at the café. But Adam had never been that angry with me. The only bright spot I could find was that whatever feelings he had for me, Adam's actions demonstrated that they were, without a doubt, full of passion.

That brought up the question of just what did Adam feel for me? Could he be falling in love with me? Like I was with him. Or was this something entirely different for him? This last possibility was the one that worried me.

But after what had happened last night, maybe it didn't even matter. Sure, Adam had said I could stay on the island, but that didn't mean he still wanted to see me.

I thought about the folder containing the stock trade information and the old, yellowed newspaper clipping outlining the SEC investigation of Adam. Had he truly forgotten to lock that drawer? Or had he wanted to share his secrets with me, and that was the only way he knew how? We'd gone back and forth on the trust issue. Had he been testing me? Had I failed miserably, or had I actually, in some crazy way, passed? After all, he hadn't kicked me off his island. No, it appeared Adam wanted me to know, wanted to keep me close. The phrase "Keep your friends close, but your enemies closer" came to mind. The only thing was that I was not the enemy. And I hope Adam knew that.

The doorbell sounded, and I raced to answer it. It was a little after seven, but I'd been up for two hours, waiting for Adam to arrive.

And now he was here, all dressed for business in black tailored pants, a crisp white dress shirt, dark tie, and black shoes. "You look nice," I said lamely as I stepped aside so he could come in.

Adam's eyes traveled over the charcoal-gray leggings, black tunic-style sweater, and Chucks I'd thrown on after showering. "And you look...comfortable," he replied. A smile played at the corners of his mouth, and I started to believe we might just be able to work this out. Maybe he'd forgive me after all.

We walked into the living room, but neither of us sat. Adam spoke first, "There's no point in pretending, Maddy. We both know what you found in that drawer."

I dared to meet his gaze, expecting fury, but instead he just looked tired. He sighed. "No more games, OK? There's one thing you have yet to ask. So just get it over with, ask me."

"Are you serious?" My voice was incredulous. I hadn't expected this.

Adam's eyes, dark as cobalt today, met mine. "Deadly," he replied coolly.

"OK." I drew in a deep, calming breath. "Did you trade on insider information?"

"Yes, I did."

My heart skipped a beat. Good Lord, what other illegal things had Adam done? *He does have that gun.*

I shook away those thoughts and spoke quickly, "And Chelsea somehow found out about it? That was what she was using to blackmail you, right?"

He nodded. "Yes, that was it."

"But I don't understand," I said. "Why would you ever trust someone like her with something so important?"

"I didn't *tell* her, Madeleine," Adam replied, irritation creeping into his voice. "Chelsea was the one who gave me the insider information."

"You're kidding," I murmured, astounded. "How did someone like her come across information like that?"

Adam loosened his tie and sat down on the arm of the sofa.

"Chelsea overheard her father talking on the phone to a business associate about the impending buyout. I have no idea how he'd obtained that kind of information, but I can only imagine. Anyway Mr. Hannigan, wisely, never acted on the tip."

"But you did."

"Yes, Maddy, I did. I made a fuckload of money in a very short time. But I also brought a lot of unwanted attention to myself. I regretted it, but it was too late to undo it."

"Did *she* encourage you to make that trade, Adam?" I asked, taking a hesitant step closer to him. I longed to comfort him in some way. But would my overture be welcome?

Adam closed his eyes, his beautiful features pained. "It doesn't matter. I ultimately made my own decision."

"Why would she use it to blackmail you though?"

"My relationship with her had degraded into one of habit, I guess. We certainly didn't love one another anymore, but every time I tried to break up with her, she threatened me. It seemed the more I didn't want her, the more she held on." Adam was quiet for a moment—reflective, maybe—and then he continued, "When I caught her with J.T. O'Brien, I told her that was the final straw. But she said she'd never let me go. She said she'd rather see me in prison than with someone else. She wanted to get engaged, and she threatened to go to the SEC and offer her testimony against me if I refused."

"God, Adam, I'm sorry." I reached for his hand.

Adam caught my hand and lifted it to his lips. "Don't feel sorry for me." He ghosted a single kiss across my knuckles. "My mistake was in listening to her in the first place."

I squeezed his hand to reassure him, but his face grew somber. "The irony is that Chelsea may not have sent me to jail, but after she was gone, I ended up in a different kind of prison—one with walls of suspicion and doubt."

"Oh, Adam," I whispered, my voice pained.

"It doesn't bother you?" His eyes searched mine. "Knowing these things about me?"

I wasn't about to hold something he'd done years earlier against him. Chelsea had tempted him with the prospect of easy money, and he'd been young and rash. I secretly wondered if she'd done it on purpose in an effort to trap him. After all, he had ended up paying a high price for his actions.

Adam cleared his throat. "Maddy?" he asked, awaiting my response.

"No," I answered honestly. "It doesn't bother me."

It didn't seem possible, but his expression grew even more somber. With a grave tone, he stated, "This is a one-time discussion. It's not something I ever speak of, and I expect it to stay that way."

I looked into his eyes and hoped he could read the truth in mine. "I'll never betray you, Adam. I swear on my life, no matter what you tell me, it will stay between you and me."

He pulled me roughly to him and kissed me hungrily. His hands found purchase on my hips, his long fingers pressed gingerly into my flesh. There was urgency in these deep kisses, and I sensed it had nothing to do with lust. It was about acceptance. Soon, too soon, he loosened his grip, composed himself, and slowed the kisses. I leaned my head on his shoulder, and we held onto each other, both of us silent.

After several moments, he chuckled, murmuring into my hair, "There is one good thing that came out of it all. I was able to buy this island."

I pulled back. "Weren't you worried it would draw attention to you? Making such a large purchase?"

"Not at that time. The island didn't go up for sale until months after the whole SEC investigation had concluded. My assets were no longer frozen, and I'd always planned on investing in real estate. So…"

"So you bought an island." I smiled, brushing a dark lock that had fallen across his forehead back into place.

"I always loved this place, the beauty, the ruggedness, the privacy. My family used to vacation over here when I was a child." He paused, and his expression darkened. "Of course, Chelsea hated this place. She told me she'd never live out here. I didn't move here until after she was gone."

"And here we are," I said quietly.

"Yeah, here we are." His fingers caressed my cheek tenderly. "I've never told a soul that whole story."

"Would you have told me had I not..." I leaned into his warm touch. "Uh, you know."

"Yes, *eventually*. Remember?" Adam said playfully.

I had to smile at his lighthearted reference to our words from the other night. This new openness between us made me feel brave enough to ask, "Adam, what's going on between us?"

He hesitated, pulling back. "This is a conversation we should save for later. I have to go if I'm going to make my meeting over on the mainland."

"I know," I said, "I just thought..."

Adam cupped my face, kissed my lips, and then said, "I should be back at the dock by about six. Let's meet at the café, and we can talk there, sound good?"

That sounded good to me, so I told him so. Adam stood, and after one more long and lingering kiss at the door, he straightened his tie and left for his meeting over on the mainland.

Once he was gone, I checked my cell for messages I may have missed, since I'd turned it off yesterday evening before going up to Adam's. Oddly enough Katie, my agent, had left two voicemails and three texts asking me to call her as soon as possible. So I sat down at the dining room table and dialed her number.

She picked up immediately. "Maddy, where have you been? Why didn't you call me back last night?"

"Um, my phone was charging," I lied, cringing at my pathetic excuse. And before she had a chance to question me further, I added, "Why? What's going on?"

"Well," she stated slowly, "some woman from Maine stopped by the office late yesterday afternoon. She said she was your friend, and—"

"Wait, what? She said she was my friend?" I interrupted, baffled. "From where? Here?"

"Yeah," Katie continued, "from Harbour Falls. Her name is Ami. She was with a clean-cut-looking guy with kind of sandy-colored hair. I'm guessing he was her husband?"

Whoa, wait a minute. "Ami and Sean are in *Los Angeles*?"

Things were getting stranger and stranger. California was where they'd gone for their little trip? *Bizarre.*

"You do know them then?" Katie asked.

"Yeah, but what are they doing there?"

"Oh, you're going to love this," my agent continued, clearing her throat. "First her husband just kind of hung out in the background, looking uncomfortable and kind of apologetic."

"Apologetic?"

"Yeah, I guess because this Ami was going on and on about how I needed to step in and put a stop to, oh wait, how did she put it?" Katie paused for a beat. "Uh, this was it, word for word: I should 'put a stop to whatever the hell Maddy is doing on Fade Island before she ends up hurt. She's in serious danger.'"

"Oh Lord," I gulped. "Katie, not to sound insensitive, but the truth is that Ami has some serious mental issues."

"No kidding," she said, "I kind of guessed as much."

But I had to wonder what Ami had been referring to? And why would she involve my agent? *She must think Katie is my boss and can tell me what to do.* Did Ami really believe I was in "serious danger"? And was it serious enough to warrant a trip out to LA in some convoluted attempt to protect me? It just felt like something was off.

"You didn't tell her anything, right?" I asked.

"Of course not. But, Maddy, she was really worked up. God only knows who else she's been in contact with out here."

There was only one other person Ami knew of from my life in California—my ex-boyfriend, Julian—and I could only hope she'd dare not look him up. I put my head down on the table. "Ugh, what a mess," I mumbled.

"Oh, honey, don't worry. I'm the only one out here who knows what you're doing in Harbour Falls. I'll keep you posted if I hear anything, especially if she comes back to the office."

"Thanks," I said resignedly. What more could I do from here, other than wait to see what Ami's next move would be?

"Maddy?"

The sudden seriousness in Katie's voice grabbed my attention. "Yeah?" I responded.

"Be careful up there, you hear me?"

I assured Katie I would try my best to stay safe, even if it wasn't exactly true. The last thing I needed was a worried agent thinking Ami's crazy ramblings held validity. After we disconnected, I sat, cell phone in hand, wondering how Ami Dubois-Hensley fit into this whole Harbour Falls Mystery mess. Sure she was unstable, but did she really think I was in some kind of danger? Why else would she want me off the island? Did she have some kind of tie to the case? I couldn't recall her ever having had any sort of association with Chelsea. But who knew? One thing I was learning, sometimes painfully, was that around here *nothing* was ever as it seemed.

At around four o'clock in the afternoon, I drove down to the café to visit Helena before Adam got back. "Maddy!" Helena exclaimed when I walked through the door. "I've been bored to tears all day. You sure are a sight for sore eyes."

She came out from behind the coffee bar in the back to greet me, and I met her halfway, where she pulled me into a warm hug. "Adam's meeting me at six," I said, stepping back. "But I was hoping we'd have a chance to talk before he gets here."

Helena gestured to one of the tables. "Here, let's sit." She paused. "Oh, did you want anything to drink?"

"No." I shook my head, while sitting down. "I'm fine."

"So is something going on with you and Adam," she asked, slipping into the seat across from me. "That is what you want to talk about, right?"

I had absolutely no intention of divulging even a hint of the many things Adam had shared with me, but I was curious to get her opinion on the things Jennifer had said. And, since she and Nate knew him so well, see if she had any insight into Adam's feelings for me. After all, Nate was Adam's closest friend, and he'd confided in him in the past. And sure, I'd be talking with Adam soon enough, but one could never have too much information. Especially when it came to matters of the heart.

So I began with, "I don't know what to think, Helena. I mean, I know how I feel about him, but I'm not sure he feels the same."

Helena patted my hand reassuringly. "Adam's interested in you, Maddy. We've known him a long time, and he's different now that you're in his life. Even when he speaks of you…" She trailed off, considered, and then said, "You just make him happy, even Trina thinks so."

"I know, but…" My voice faltered.

"What?"

"It's stupid," I said, casting my eyes down. "Just some stuff Jennifer Weston said yesterday. I shouldn't let it bother me, but it does."

"What did that miserable bitch say to you?"

I needed to talk to someone, at least about the things I could, so I told her some of the things Jennifer had said, mostly the comments about how I was "just a novelty" and how "it would never last." But I was careful to leave out Jennifer's angry reaction when I'd mentioned Chelsea's name.

When I finished, Helena said, "Jennifer is a bitter, unhappy person. She's been that way for years, and the whole J.T. mess made her even meaner. She enjoys needling people and saying things to purposely hurt them. Don't let her get to you. Adam is not using you."

"Yeah, but Lindsey obviously meant very little to him," I countered. "He dropped her without a second thought. Who's to say he doesn't do the same to me?"

"I told you, that relationship was different from the one you and Adam have."

I knew she was right, but I was looking for reassurance. After everything Adam had shared with me, I should have been confident that he cared very deeply for me. But the one thing nagging me was that he'd told me only after I'd snooped around and discovered those things.

"Why don't you talk to him? Just ask him how he feels."

"I did," I replied. "We're supposed to discuss it tonight. That's why he's meeting me here."

Helena smiled triumphantly. "See, just the fact Adam even

agreed to have a 'relationship discussion' speaks volumes."
"I suppose."
"It does, trust me." Helena lowered her voice to an almost whisper. "And between us, I think you're helping Adam learn how to love again."

God, I wanted to believe she was right, especially about the love part. Adam had forgiven me rather easily when he'd discovered my duplicity. Now the ball was in my court to prove to him I could be worthy of his trust and, hopefully, his love.

Helena and I talked for a while longer. She told me she was going to close down the café on Monday for a couple of weeks, so she could go down to Boston and help Trina with wedding preparations. She invited me to join her for the trip, but I declined. With a little prodding though she did get me to commit to spending a day with her and Trina. She said it'd be easy enough since Adam flew to Boston on business all the time. I could just fly down with him, spend the day with the girls, and fly back that night. I told her I'd discuss it with Adam, and if we could coordinate it, then I'd love to come down and spend a day with her and Trina.

When Adam arrived—still dressed for success in his business attire and looking particularly debonair—Helena readied herself to leave. She claimed she needed to run over to the house because Nate was cooking dinner and might burn down the bungalow if she didn't check on him. I knew she was just giving us time alone, and I appreciated her all the more because of it.

Once Helena was out the door, Adam leaned down and kissed me with far more passion than I was prepared for. *Wow!* By the time he pulled away and sat down across from me, I finally caught my breath. Adam seemed to be in rare form this evening.

"So," he began, something naughty sparkling in his blue eyes as he loosened his tie. "Did you have a pleasant afternoon?"

I decided to play along. Smiling, I responded, "Pleasant, Adam?" He chuckled. "Yes, my afternoon was quite pleasant.

And how was your meeting on the mainland?"

Adam traced the inside of my forearm with his long fingers. "It sucked," he said silkily.

"Why was that? The potential client didn't sign?"

"Oh no, Maddy, he signed. But let's just say I had *other* things on my mind." Adam leaned forward, his voice low and sultry. "Would you like for me to show you some of the things that were occupying my thoughts?"

Would I ever, I thought. Meeting his lust-filled gaze, I offered, "Maybe we should get out of here?"

"Fuck that. Maybe we should lock the door and—" But, before he could finish, the café door swung open. Adam, his back to the door, groaned in aggravation.

Jennifer Weston darkened the threshold, holding the door ajar with her hip. "Oh, what perfect timing," she exclaimed. Was that smugness in her tone? "I just brought a visitor over, and he cannot wait to see you, Fitch."

Adam shifted in his chair to face the café entrance, his expression none-too-pleased. *Uh oh*. Jennifer continued, undeterred by my lack of response, "In fact, it's someone who is quite worried about your well-being up here on this lovely island."

Adam shot me a look, raising an inquisitive eyebrow. I shrugged, having no clue what Ms. Miserable was going on about. Just then, Jennifer made a grand gesture of pushing the door open as wide as it could go, thus allowing the mystery passenger she'd ferried over from the mainland to step into the café.

A tall man with a strong physique stopped just inside the entrance—hair the color of caramel and, as usual, in need of a cut, deep brown eyes that I hadn't seen in months.

Oh...my...God. My words caught in my throat, but I somehow squeaked out, "Julian?"

Chapter 17

Julian's eyes moved from me, nervously, to Adam and then back to me. "Maddy, what the hell is going on here?"

Just as I was about to ask my ex the same question, Adam turned back to me, the legs of his chair scraping harshly against the wooden floor of the café as he pushed it away. Standing, his eyes burned into me, a mixture of fury and disbelief. Without speaking a single word or waiting for any kind of an explanation, Adam turned his back on me.

Heading over to where Julian and Jennifer were standing, he paused momentarily but then walked past them without a word. Both Julian and Jennifer moved aside to give Adam a wide berth. Yes, an angry Adam was not to be toyed with. That much was certain.

After Adam left, Julian's expression changed to one of confusion, while Jennifer just looked victorious. "You're a fucking bitch," I yelled, directing my comment at Jennifer as I rose from my chair.

I could no longer control my own anger. She had set this up somehow. I was sure of it.

But how? I had no clue, yet. But I was going to get to the bottom of it once I had a chance to talk with Julian—alone. But first I'd deal with Jennifer.

"No, Fitch," she hissed. "From the priceless look on Ward's pretty face, I'd say you are the *fucking bitch*, Bitch."

"You did this," I accused, stepping closer to where she stood near the door.

Julian, who I'd almost forgotten was there, interrupted, "Is anybody planning on telling me what the hell is going on?"

Jennifer spun on her heels. "You should ask Fitch since I have to go." She giggled maniacally, reaching for the door handle. *Crazy bitch.* "It looks like you two have a lot of catching up to do."

With that she was gone, leaving Julian staring at me with a look of befuddlement. *What a mess.* I stepped back and sank into my chair, defeated. This was just too much. Instead of having a discussion with Adam to define what was going on between us, I was stuck here with my ex-boyfriend. And based on Adam's reaction, it was starting to look as if we might never be having that relationship discussion.

Julian came over to where I sat. "Maddy, what's going on? Are you all right?"

His voice held nothing but genuine concern, making it even more likely he was being used as a pawn by someone. Jennifer? Ami? *She is in Los Angeles,* I thought.

I sighed. "Julian, what are you doing here?"

He slid into the chair across from me, the one Adam had been sitting in. "Your friend from up here tracked me down." *Ami,* I thought. "She told me you were here. She said you're in danger." His voice dropped. "Maddy, we may not be together anymore, but I'll always be here for you. If you need help getting out of here, I'll do whatever I can to help. If that guy is—"

"Julian," I interrupted, "I'm not in any danger." *Small lie.*

I explained how Ami was unstable and had obviously overreacted for whatever reason. With the nagging fear that—maybe—she *did* know something, and I really was in some kind of peril, I tried to convince Julian I was fine. I explained I was just here working on a book.

Naturally he didn't buy it.

"Really, Maddy?" He looked at me skeptically. "Are you here working on a novel...or working on that guy who just left?"

Both, I thought but answered, "I'm working on my next novel. That's all."

Julian still didn't look as if he believed me, but he nodded nonetheless. Quietly he said, "I can go back over to the mainland tonight if that'd be better for you."

Although I knew it would be better, based on Adam's behavior, I couldn't just dismiss Julian after he'd traveled all this way just to make sure I was OK. Besides, I was certain Jennifer had left for the night, so he'd have no way back anyway.

"No. You can sleep at my place tonight. The ferry will be here tomorrow morning. You can go back then." His eyes questioned mine, and to avoid any confusion, I hastily added, "I have a really comfy sofa. You can sleep there."

We left the café, and by the time we'd reached my cottage, I felt so bad about the whole situation that I insisted I stay on the sofa and Julian take the bed. It took awhile for him to agree, but he finally acquiesced. I quickly showed him around upstairs, grabbed a pair of pajamas from the dresser, and left Julian to his own devices in my bedroom. Hurriedly I made my way back downstairs.

After enough time had elapsed for Julian to fall asleep, I dialed Adam's cell phone. It went straight to voicemail, so I left a message, asking him to "please call me as soon as possible" so we could talk.

Once I shrugged out of my clothes, I slipped on the comfortable, oversized flannel pajamas I'd brought down from upstairs. With little cartoon dogs and cats all over them, they were the unsexiest ones I owned, making them a perfect choice in case Julian wandered downstairs for something. Encouraging him was the last thing I wanted to do. Drowsy, I turned out the lamp and lay back on the sofa. With a throw pillow beneath my head and a quilt thrown over my body, sleep came quickly.

At some point in the middle of the night, I woke up abruptly, certain I'd heard footsteps close by. "Julian?" I whispered, allowing my eyes to adjust to the shapes and shadows in the room, illuminated only by slivers of moonlight pouring in through half-closed blinds.

"Not your ex-boyfriend," a voice purred from close by, startling me.

I shot upright and pulled my legs up to my chest, but then the shape at the foot of the sofa came into focus. "Adam," I ventured. "W-w-what are you doing in here?"

Stepping around the arm of the sofa, he sat down beside me. My heart began to race in both fear—and anticipation—of what was coming next. I noticed Adam had changed clothes; he now wore all black—black leather jacket, black low-hanging jeans, black T-shirt that clung enticingly to the lean muscles of his chest. He looked dark and dangerous. And, I hated to admit, sexy as hell.

"Shhhh." Adam's tone was low and mocking. "You don't want to wake up your houseguest, now do you? After all, your ex-lover probably wouldn't approve of my being here."

"He was more than a lover, Adam," I snapped, glancing to the staircase. It was clear Adam knew *exactly* who Julian was, so I added, "How did you know who he was anyway?"

My uninvited guest chuckled as he shucked off his jacket, the scent of leather...and Adam...wafting my way. "I certainly hope you don't allow just any guy who happens upon the island to sleep in your bed," he chided.

"Seriously, Adam," I said. "How did you know?"

"Maddy, Maddy, so naïve," he tsked, draping an arm casually on the back of the sofa. "Do you really think I wouldn't have thoroughly checked out your previous, uh, suitors?"

A flare of anger blazed through me. Was there anything Adam didn't know about my life? Irritated, I hissed, "What are you doing here? I know I locked the doors, so how'd you even get in?"

He held out a keychain with several keys attached. "Madeleine, do you really need to ask?" He jangled the keys softly. "*Nothing* on this island is off-limits to me."

I swallowed hard, the implication of his statement not lost on me. As if to punctuate his meaning, Adam stood, kicked off his shoes and pulled his shirt over his head. His sculpted bare chest, bathed in silvery moonlight, held my eye. At least until he casually threw his shirt to the floor, flipped open the top button on his jeans, and then dropped back down to the sofa in a crouch.

I gasped as he crawled up the sofa toward me, trapping

me in a cage created by his arms. I curled my knees tighter to my chest, but he reached out and adjusted each one—none too gently—to either side of his body. With one arm, muscles taut, holding him up, and his other hand on my knee, he whispered, "So Madeleine, who invited your *friend* to my island?"

"Not me," I answered, biting my lip, my eyes drawn to his flexing chest muscles as he lowered himself until our bodies were pressed together. "It was Ami," I continued. "Uh, she's in Los Angeles. She told him I was in danger," I breathed out, excitement mounting as Adam trailed soft, warm kisses along my jaw and down my neck while I was speaking.

"Ami, huh?" he mumbled distractedly against my skin. "In California, eh? Crazy girl."

This was a side of Adam I'd not yet seen, and though it frightened me, it also thrilled me. I knew I should make him stop, make him go—after all, what right did he have to break into this place?—but I couldn't do it. The danger, the wrongness of it all with Julian just up the stairs. I had to admit, those things excited me.

I ran my hands along Adam's bare skin, up his back, to his broad shoulders. God, I felt so small beneath him. He lifted up just enough to begin unbuttoning my pajama top—from the bottom up. Warm fingers grazed the skin of my abdomen, lighting tiny fires in their wake. Adam seemed more fixated on getting my clothes off than in discussing why Ami might be in LA. And at this point, so was I.

"How chivalrous of... Julian, is it?" Adam didn't wait for an answer, though his fingers stilled at the second button from the top. "How chivalrous of Julian to rush all the way out here to my island to rescue you."

"Adam," I said, my breath quickening as he undid those last two buttons, "we both know I don't need rescuing."

"Oh, I beg to differ," he murmured darkly.

My top gaped open and Adam pressed his chest to mine, skin to skin. He felt so good that I forgot about Julian sleeping upstairs, forgot about Ami and whatever she was up to. I just wanted Adam, all of Adam.

Arching up, our hips met, and I felt how very ready he was. "I want you, Adam, so much."

For a moment I didn't recognize my own lust-filled voice. But then a second of clarity made me say, "I don't know if this is a good idea, though. What with Julian—"

"I happen to think it's a great idea," Adam rasped.

He reached down and grasped the waistband of my pajama bottoms. "Not to mention we have some unfinished business we never got to last night." And with that he adeptly slid the bottoms—along with my panties—down my legs in one fluid movement.

Mmm, maybe for a moment, I thought.

Adam settled his full weight on me, and I wrapped my legs around him. Our lips met, the kisses sloppy and desperate. My hands explored the hard planes of his toned body, and though I was almost naked, his damn jeans were still on, and getting in the way. Groaning in lust and need, I clumsily sought the zipper, pulling at it until I was able to reach in and feel—Adam moaned—his thick and heavy shaft. "Oh God, Adam." My words were jumbled and incoherent as he pumped into my hand, jeans sliding lower and lower with each thrust.

Adam's fingers sought my own heat, and soon they were sliding along folds wet with desire. When his fingers entered me, my body moved and rocked with the frantic rhythm. Skin to skin, dampened with sweat, we twisted and grinded against one another. Raw and primal, this was no act of love. Adam was here to stake his claim, mark his territory. And I was all too willing to submit. Angling my body, I got close enough to rub my wetness against his hard shaft. With a sharp intake of breath, he stilled my hand. "Maddy," he said, his voice low, his breaths ragged. "Slow down."

Clarity came to me. Suddenly everything we were doing felt not wrong, but not right either. Feeling a sudden need to cover my nakedness—out of embarrassment or out of guilt, I wasn't sure—I pushed Adam away from me. He complied, and I buttoned my pajama top, my fingers clumsy as I scanned the floor for the rest of my clothes. Adam, seemingly knowing what I was looking for, handed me my pajama bottoms from the other end of the sofa, the panties still tangled up in the mess of material.

"What were we thinking, Adam?" A lump rose in my throat. Blinking back tears, voice unsteady, I hissed, "God, my ex is just up the stairs. Do you realize how wrong this is?" I sat up and awkwardly tugged my panties and pajama bottoms on.

Adam moved away from me and adjusted himself back into his jeans. Quietly he said, "This was a mistake. I shouldn't have come here tonight."

"No, you shouldn't have," I agreed. "Why did you? Why, Adam?" I'd gotten the tears under control, and now I was angry. "Did you come here to check up on me? Or are you here to make some kind of male territory-bullshit statement?"

Adam didn't answer at first. But as he finished dressing, he said, "I'm sorry, Maddy. I guess I thought… Whatever I thought, I was wrong. It shouldn't be like this." He raked a hand through his already-mussed hair but said nothing more.

"Just go," I said, disgusted. It was so obvious his reasons for coming here were rooted in nothing more than jealousy.

Adam left, but before he did, he slid the key he'd used to come in off the key ring and tossed it onto my coffee table—all without saying a single word. Whether that meant he was sorry for having broken in or that he wasn't coming back, I had no idea.

I awoke early the next morning, and though Adam had left hours earlier, his scent—leather and just pure male—was all around me. I hurriedly dressed, throwing on the same leggings, sweater, and Chucks from the night before. Not wanting to revisit the events of last night, I rushed into the kitchen and toasted a couple of bagels, made some coffee, and waited for the inevitability of Julian making his way downstairs.

Just as I was pouring coffee into a cup, I heard a sleepy voice from the doorway, "'Morning, Maddy."

"Good morning, Julian," I answered, trying to sound chipper as I kept my back to him and grabbed another cup from the cabinet. Julian yawned, and unable to face him, I softly added, "Did you sleep well?"

"Great, actually," he answered, thankfully oblivious to what had occurred in the living room.

I took a deep, steadying breath and turned to him. "Coffee?" I tried to smile as I held the steaming cup out to him.

He stepped forward, taking the cup and saying, "Thanks."

I hesitated and then said, "Julian, you shouldn't have come all the way across the country to see if I was OK. You could have just called, and I'd have told you everything was fine."

He leaned against the counter. "Maybe I just needed a reason to see you, Maddy."

I took a step away to further the distance between us. My emotions were already all over the place. This was the last thing I needed to deal.

I guessed Julian could see it in my face because he said, "You're seeing somebody, aren't you?"

"Yes," I nodded, glancing away. "I'm sorry, Julian."

"Hey, it's OK," he said softly, and actually he did sound OK with it. "Is it the guy who was with you at the café?"

I raked my fingers through my hair, much like I'd seen Adam do so many times. "Yeah, that's him."

Julian's eyes, a touch of sadness in them, met mine. "All I've ever wanted was for you to be happy." He took a deep breath. "He's a lucky man," he said wistfully on his exhale.

"Thank you," I whispered.

Now, I *really* felt guilty for messing around with Adam while Julian had slept, blissfully unaware, upstairs. I wondered if he'd be so gracious and understanding if he knew what I had done. Worse yet, Julian probably thought Adam and I were in love. And while there was no doubt in my mind that I loved Adam, I still had no clue if he loved me in return. Just because he'd come here, jealous, to "claim" me with Julian under the same roof did not mean that what he felt for me was love. He was just letting me know that he had access to everything on this island, including me. Hell, he'd even let himself in, using a key I hadn't even been aware he possessed.

In almost complete silence, things more awkward than before, we finished our coffee, and I drove Julian to the dock. After he was gone, I returned to the cottage.

It was an unseasonably warm day for mid-October, and I felt like I should stay outside, allow the fresh air to clear my jumbled thoughts. Maybe even go for a run. But I was too exhausted, so I lay on the sofa, pulled the quilt over my spent form, and drifted off to a dreamless sleep.

When I finally woke up, it was late afternoon. Some clouds had rolled in, but after a quick peek outside, I found the temperature was still quite mild. I went upstairs, changed into sweats and a T-shirt, then laced up my running shoes, and pulled my hair back into a ponytail. Before leaving the cottage, I checked my cell. No messages from Adam. Not a single one, nothing. Not even after last night. *Jerk.* He was really starting to piss me off.

Suddenly I snatched the key Adam had tossed onto the coffee table and stomped out the front door. Hurt, angry tears pricked at the corners of my eyes. *Fucking bastard.* Maybe I wasn't cut out for this kind of a relationship. Maybe Jennifer was right, maybe the powerful Adam Ward was just playing me.

Knowing exactly where I was heading, I started north along the path that led to Adam's property. Picking up speed with every step, I soon broke into a full run along the trail, branches scraping unmercifully at my bare arms. Tears, previously held back, streaked down my cheeks. Adam's actions last night played over and over in my head, along with Jennifer's harsh words. *Novelty, my ass.* I'd show him.

The ground was wet, and mud splashed up onto my legs as I pushed myself harder and harder. My own sweat intermingled with the dried sweat from last night that I'd not yet washed away. Sweat that Adam and I had created together.

Finally I reached the end of the path and began to sob. Stumbling forward, I fell to my knees, my hands pressing into the cool earth at the edge of Adam's driveway. My lungs burned, my mind was muddled, and my heart ached. Everything was finally catching up with me. And I, Maddy Fitch, had reached my breaking point.

The Porsche was parked in the driveway, its presence a cruel taunt. He was home. Why hadn't he contacted me? Did he care so little?

The rain that had been threatening for the past hour began to fall, and I rocked back on my heels. Running a muddy hand over my tear-streaked face, I pushed away the stray hair that had escaped from my ponytail.

What was I doing here? What was Adam Ward doing to me? I wanted to go to his door and scream at him to give me answers. *Fuck the mystery.* I wanted—no, I *needed* to know how he felt about me. And I needed to hear it from him, not through the opinions and conjectures of others.

With the rain falling harder, I got to my feet and marched to the front door. I had no regard for the mess I surely was. If anything, my physical appearance would be an excellent indicator to Adam of the mess I was inside as well.

Hell with the doorbell! I pounded on the door, leaving muddy rivulets in my wake. I watched as they trailed down, though they were quickly blurred by a fresh surge of tears.

Adam opened the door, eyes widening. "Jesus, Maddy! What the fuck happened to you?"

With a sob I collapsed into his arms, muddying his immaculate white T-shirt and faded jeans. He held me upright, blue eyes darkening with concern as he scanned over my body. "What happened? Are you OK?"

I closed my eyes, tired and broken, and pressed the key to the cottage—his key—into his hand. When he looked at me with confusion, I uttered the only words that came to mind, "I don't think I can do this anymore, Adam."

Chapter 18

With no hesitation Adam swept me into his capable arms. But when he tried to carry me upstairs, I balked. "No, I want to go home."

I really meant back home to California, but the cottage would have to suffice for now. So I amended in barely a whisper, "Just take me back to the cottage."

I thought he'd argue, but surprisingly, Adam just nodded and carried me out to his car. Once buckled in I slumped in the passenger seat, leaning my head against the cool glass of the window. A muddy clump of hair flopped onto my cheek, and I lazily brushed it back. Glancing down at my mud-smeared sweats and rain-soaked T-shirt, I mumbled off-handedly, "I'm sorry I'm getting your car all dirty and wet."

"That's a ridiculous thing to say, Madeleine," Adam retorted dryly as he glared over at me. "Do you really believe I care so little about you that I'd be more concerned with a little mud and rain water?"

I shrugged, and in response Adam peeled out, barreling down his long driveway to the main road. "Unbelievable," he muttered.

When I failed to respond, he said no more. The rest of the way was all darkening skies, empty road, and silence.

Once we arrived at the cottage, I jumped out and scampered to the door, but then I realized I hadn't brought my own keys. And I'd given the one Adam had used back to him. So I had no choice but to move aside as Adam approached the door.

He used the key I pressed into his hand back at his house to unlock the door, and I snapped, "You might as well keep that key, although I'm sure you have plenty more, seeing as you have access to *everything* on this island."

Pushing past him—and, boy, did he ever look annoyed—I went into the living room and plopped down on the sofa. "The scene of the crime," I mumbled, loudly enough for him to hear as he followed me into the room.

"Are you done?" Adam asked.

I ignored him and pulled at the sides of the clinging, muddy T-shirt that was sticking annoyingly to my skin. "I can get you a change of clothes from upstairs," Adam offered, his demeanor softening as he headed over to the sofa." You really should get out of those wet clothes."

He knelt down beside me and gently lifted the hem of my shirt, but as he began to tug it up my torso, I stopped him. "No," I croaked, clumsily smacking his hand away.

"Maddy," Adam scolded. "Quit behaving like a petulant child. You're filthy—"

I pulled my shirt back into place and crossed my arms.

"—*You* make me feel filthy, Adam!" I cried out, choking back a sob. "What are you planning to do? Clean me up so you can keep on playing me? I'm done with being used. I need more."

I was upset and angry, and I wanted my words to cut to the quick. I glanced up, and Adam's eyes, for a moment, were pained. But only briefly.

His expression of hurt rapidly morphed to anger. "Stupid girl," he growled, yanking my shirt unceremoniously over my head, while snapping my bra off in one swift move. I yelped in surprise, covering my bare chest with my arms as I attempted to scoot away from him.

Pulling the quilt from the sofa and wrapping it around me, he pulled me back to him. "I'm *not* using you," Adam soothed, stroking my head and sliding my loosened ponytail holder down until my hair cascaded to my shoulders. "I'd never do that to you."

The tone of his voice hinted more at exasperation than anger, so I relaxed against him. "But you used Lindsey," I protested.

"Shhh," he calmed, fingers gently combing through my tangled locks. "Things are different with you. Everything is different with you. Haven't you realized that by now?" He traced along my cheek with his fingertip, urging me to meet his gaze. It was at points such as these that I usually caved. But not tonight. I wasn't going to let him off so easily. Adam was going to have to give me more than this.

"How is it different?" I pressed, breaking away from his captivating eyes and tightening the quilt around my body.

Adam shook his head resignedly. "You know I've shared things with you," he said quietly, "that nobody knows."

Shamefully I cast my eyes down to my muddy sweats, and Adam continued, "If you could only comprehend the magnitude of my telling you my secrets, you'd already know the answer to your question."

In my heart I felt the impact of his words. I thought about it. True, a man as shrewd as Adam Ward would not have done such a thing without thoroughly examining the consequences. And if you loved somebody, surely you'd want to share yourself—good and bad—with that person. Right? Did that mean Adam was just as in love with me as I was with him?

Vastly different from the secret crushes we'd had on one another in high school—and even more intense than the undeniable lust we shared—there was a deeper connection developing. Despite everything, or maybe *because* of everything, it felt as if we were destined to be together. Did he feel it too?

"Why? Why did you tell me your secrets, Adam?" I whispered, staring at an especially prominent streak of mud that had dried on the right knee of the sweats. "Did you let me find those things in your desk?"

Adam's lips brushed the top of my head, and I looked up. "In business," he said, "sometimes you have to take a calculated chance. Sometimes the potential reward outweighs the risk."

"This isn't business, Adam," I reminded him.

Adam chuckled humorlessly. "You're right, it's not. It's life, it's love. And it's not going to be perfect, Maddy. If we're really going to make this work, you have to accept that I'm not going to do all the right things, nor say all the right things." He paused. "But I do know I want to make you happy."

"Why?" I whispered.

"Because you make me feel something I thought I'd never feel again. So I'm willing to take this chance with you." His voice faltered somewhat, and then he added in a quiet voice, "Even if it means my ruin."

Adam stilled, and I held his fiery gaze, filled with raw emotion. What I saw touched my heart. Though I was the one physically half-unclothed beneath the quilt, it was Adam who was emotionally naked and, surprisingly, vulnerable. Not even in confessing his secrets had he let me in like he was doing at this moment. I knew with every fiber of my being that Adam was allowing me to see a part of his soul. It was a part of him to which no one else was privy, that much I was certain. He was sharing something bigger than his secrets; he was sharing his true self with me. And, in that moment, whatever doubt I'd been harboring, regarding his true intensions, dissipated.

Reaching out and tracing the perfection of his features with my fingertips, I found myself in awe. He had never appeared more beautiful than right now. "I'm falling in love with you, Adam," I admitted, my voice soft.

My words were simple and honest. I was no longer asking for anything in return. But Adam still delivered. He flattened my palm against the light stubble on his cheek and simply said, "You may be falling, but I already fell. I love you, Madeleine Fitch."

My own eyes filled with tears upon hearing those words from his mouth. I felt foolish for ever having questioned his intentions toward me. "I'm sorry," I said softly, a single tear trailing down my cheek.

Kissing the stray tear away, Adam said, "I haven't made this easy, I know. I'm the one who should be apologizing."

"It's just been, I don't know, confusing," I admitted.

"I know, and I'm sorry. I really am."

Adam pulled me to him, his lips finding mine. He kissed me, sweetly and tenderly, until I felt him smiling against my

mouth. "What?" I asked, pulling back slightly and smiling too.
Adam chuckled. "I was just thinking, since I'm new to this relationship thing, I'm probably going to fuck up...a lot."

"New to this relationship thing?" I echoed, confused. "But you were with Chelsea for a long time."

Adam shook his head. "That was a lifetime ago. And, sure, I thought I loved her at one time, but it was never like this."

My heart soared, making me giddy with joy. "Well"–I nodded to my mud-splattered T-shirt on the floor, the dirty sweats sticking to my legs, both reminders of the meltdown that had led me to his house—"you can't do much worse than I've already done."

Adam laughed, brushing my hair back behind my shoulders. "Speaking of which, you probably should get cleaned up, and you have to be starving." He hesitated, and then gestured in the direction of the kitchen. "I can make something while you shower. Sound good?"

"Sounds great," I responded as Adam helped me to my feet.

Fifteen minutes later, after a hot shower, I padded back down the stairs, clothed in a fresh pair of gray sweats, a white long-sleeved tee, and a black hoodie. A pair of thick, wooly socks completed my comfortable outfit. The one thing I'd decided while in the shower was to ask Adam about the blonde mystery woman. We'd been so honest with one another that I was certain if he knew anything he'd tell me.

"Smells good," I said, entering the kitchen just as Adam was ladling steaming tomato soup into bowls he'd set out on the table, next to where he'd already plated grilled cheese sandwiches.

"Your gourmet experience awaits, milady," he teased, gesturing dramatically to the table.

Laughing, I sat down. I took a bite of the sandwich, a sip of the soup. "Delicious," I gushed as Adam sat down across from me. "But I expect nothing less."

My tone was light, but Adam must have sensed there was something more on my mind because he said, "What's up, Maddy?"

I set my spoon down. "I wanted to ask you something."

"Anything."

Tensing, I cautioned, "It's about the case."

Adam sighed deeply but said quietly, "I'll answer whatever question you have. If I can, that is."

This wasn't an easy question to ask, but I forged ahead. "Um, did you ever hear anything about Chelsea possibly, uh, messing around with a *woman*? A blonde?"

Far from the reaction I expected, he laughed out loud, clearly finding my question amusing. "A woman?" he said, disbelief in his tone. "Chelsea may have been promiscuous, but she was definitely not into women, Maddy."

Adam sounded so sure. Was it due to a male ego that couldn't comprehend such a thing? Or had Chelsea kept that particular indiscretion well hidden? The one drunken incident at Billy's supposedly captured on film the only lapse.

But there was also another possibility, one I had to consider. Jimmy could be jerking me around. Especially since there had been cash involved when he came up with his tale. Making that possibility more likely, I had yet to come across one scrap of evidence corroborating his claim that Chelsea had been messing around with some blonde female.

I was about to drop it completely when Adam took a sip of soup and then casually asked, "What did you uncover that made you think something like that?"

I almost lied. *Almost*. But things were different now. It was like we had turned a corner in our relationship, and I didn't want to be the one to set it back. So I was truthful. "I heard a rumor about a picture."

"A picture? Of what exactly?" Adam had been eating up to this point, but now he set his spoon down next to his bowl of soup.

"A picture of Chelsea supposedly kissing some blonde girl."

Adam eyed me intently, interest piqued. "Have you seen this picture?"

"No," I said. "I told you it's just a rumor. It probably doesn't even exist."

He held my gaze. I knew Adam was contemplating something, probably how much deeper to dig. Sure enough, he asked, "And just where did you hear about this alleged photograph, Madeleine?"

Well, now what? I didn't want to start weaving another web of lies, so I admitted, "The bartender at Billy's told me about the picture. He said Chelsea was there one night with this blonde friend of hers and agreed to make out with said friend so the bartender—a different one at that time—could take pictures."

Adam rolled his eyes and picked up his sandwich, though he didn't take a bite. "Did this bartender offer Chelsea something? Like make a bet with her?"

"Sort of. Jimmy said that the bartender told Chelsea he'd let her bar tab slide for the rest of that week if she'd do it."

"Well, that's why she did it then," Adam said, biting into his sandwich nonchalantly.

I had given up on my own meal. Pushing the plate aside, I said, "But it's not like she was on a budget or something. She certainly didn't need the money."

Adam swallowed and wiped his mouth with a napkin. "It was never about money with Chelsea. It was about winning. At any cost."

His words made sense, and he had known Chelsea probably better than anyone. The possibility that Jimmy's claims were an exaggeration—especially the one where he'd supposedly overheard Chelsea saying to her blonde friend that they'd "already done a lot more" than kiss—was more than probable. And knowing what I'd learned so far about my young bartender friend, it was probably nothing more than some perverted, wishful fantasy. I made a quick decision to not even bother telling Adam those sordid details.

"So," I clarified, "you think there really could be a picture out there, but that it doesn't depict anything more than Chelsea following through with some kind of a wager?"

"Exactly," Adam confirmed, reaching over the table to smooth back a damp piece of hair that had fallen to my cheek. "So Madeleine, there is absolutely no reason for you to go back to that bar. Don't forget you made a promise when you lost a bet of your very own." He cocked an eyebrow. "Remember?"

"Yes, yes." My cheeks flamed. "I remember." How could I forget the bet I lost—the one where I'd ended up begging him to take off my jeans?

"Maddy," Adam warned, "I hope you intend to keep your promise."

Maybe one little white lie isn't too bad? "Of course," I muttered.

He seemed to consider my response, watching me closely. At last those stormy eyes calmed. I was off the hook, for now.

We finished our dinner and then moved into the living room to watch some television. After awhile I curled up in Adam's arms and drifted off. He must have fallen asleep as well, because we both started when my cell phone buzzed across the coffee table. I grabbed it, quickly silencing the text-alert tone.

"Who is it?" Adam asked, his voice thick with sleep.

There were three consecutive texts from Helena. She'd set up our day in Boston for Wednesday, and apparently she and Trina already had the shopping itinerary planned out. I shared the information with Adam, showing him the texts, and asked what his upcoming work week looked like.

"I actually have meetings all day on Wednesday in Boston. You could fly down there with me in the morning," Adam offered.

Adam went on to detail how I wouldn't even have to bother planning transportation to Trina and Walker's downtown loft apartment, since his driver could easily drop me off on the way to his morning meetings.

"Oh, that sounds like a plan," I cooed in response, and then texted Helena with the good news that I'd definitely be joining her and Trina on Wednesday.

Shortly thereafter Adam left, and I went up to bed. Unlike before, now I was really looking forward to the Boston excursion. Helena would be closing down the café for the next two weeks until the first of November. And Adam had several business trips coming up; he'd informed me he was working on closing a deal with a big client located in Boston. That was why he'd had so many meetings there lately.

With no Helena and very little Adam, I feared the next few weeks were going to be extremely dull here on the island. But as I drifted off to sleep, little did I know how incredibly wrong that assumption would end up being.

Chapter 19

As planned I flew out Wednesday morning with Adam. Oh, how that man looked smoking hot sitting there in the pilot's seat in the cockpit of his jet, aviator sunglasses on, the early morning sunlight reflecting off the mirrored lenses.

Adam flipped a few switches, and the engines sprang to life. I placed the copilot's headset on my head and pretended to press a few buttons on the control board.

"Madeleine," Adam scolded playfully, while moving my hand back to my lap. "Behave!"

I lowered my chin, peering over the top of my own cool sunglasses. "Or what, Captain?" I teased.

Adam shot me a sidelong glance, smirking. "Or else the copilot is going to have to be punished."

"Oooh, promise?" I squealed in delight. "Sounds like that could be fun."

Adam laughed and shook his head. "Naughty girl," he muttered.

"Only for you, babe," I replied, leaning back into the copilot's seat and adjusting my sunglasses. "Only for you."

The plane taxied down the runway and then lifted into the clear, blue sky. There was nary a cloud marring the azure horizon. We really could not have planned for a more ideal day to fly to Boston.

The flight was short, and upon landing, I noticed there was a limo waiting for us out on the tarmac. Adam directed the driver to Trina's downtown loft apartment that she shared with Walker. When we pulled up to the sidewalk, Adam and I said our farewells in the idling limo, punctuated by a fairly steamy make-out session. We broke apart only when we heard the driver clearing his throat, loudly. Yeah, being in love was awesome. I waved a good-bye and practically skipped into the tony apartment building. When I reached the elevator, I pressed the button for Trina's floor—the fourteenth—and finally came down from my Adam-induced high.

Trina's apartment was at the end of the hallway—a corner unit. The door swung open almost as soon as I rang the bell. "Maddy, hi," Trina exclaimed. "Come on in."

Stepping over the threshold, I noticed Trina was dressed to the nines in a pale blue blouse and navy pencil skirt ensemble that accentuated her trim figure perfectly. She was tall, like her brother, but the dark blue suede pumps she wore added even more height.

"Helena, Maddy's here," Trina called out over her shoulder, and then she gave me a quick hug. Stepping back, she added, "You look great, by the way."

"Thanks." Glancing down at the maroon crepe dress and black Louboutin pumps I was wearing, I was happy I'd chosen appropriate attire for this shopping excursion.

Trina led me into the living room, asking, "How was the flight down?"

"Smooth," I replied. "It's such a beautiful day."

Trina nodded. "Yeah, perfect for flying but even better for shopping."

The living room was all high ceilings and lots of open space. Funky, Scandinavian-style furniture was scattered about the room. The overall look was eclectic but in a very put-together way. It suited Trina, just as Adam's décor suited his personality.

Helena, standing in front of a curved-back chair with chocolate brown cushions, looked as glamorous as a runway model in a chic black dress, black tights, and black, thigh-high boots. She came over to give me a hug. "Maddy, I'm so happy you're here. We are going to have so much fun today."

"Aw, thanks for inviting me," I said, stepping back.

I felt genuinely welcomed as we spent some time chatting in the living room. Before we knew it, it was time to go, so we headed over to a local bistro Trina and Helena had chosen for lunch. "You're going to love it," Trina said as the hostess seated us. "The salads here are the best in the city."

After we perused our menus and placed our orders, Helena feigned a gravely serious expression and stated, "Maddy, I hope you're ready for some seriously hardcore shopping this afternoon."

Trina giggled and added, "Yeah, you haven't shopped until you've shopped with us, honey."

The waiter returned to our table, filling our glasses with fresh ice water. "Well, I guess it's a good thing I brought my platinum card," I said, laughing.

"Oh," Trina said, "you should have borrowed Adam's black Amex. No limit, you know."

The salads arrived, and spearing a piece of endive with my fork, I muttered, "Um, I think my own card should be enough."

Helena raised her eyebrows in mid-bite. Hurriedly she swallowed, forked poised in the air, and said, "Speaking of Adam, how are things going with you two? I'm guessing you worked everything out after the unexpected visit from your ex?"

I hadn't mentioned Julian's visit to Helena, so I assumed Adam had told Nate.

Trina glanced up, confused, so I quickly filled her in on the unexpected visit from my ex-boyfriend. I didn't mention Adam's late-night break-in at the cottage nor my subsequent breakdown. I only confirmed that Adam and I had worked it out.

"I still don't get how this Julian-guy knew where to find you." Trina said.

Helena took a sip of water. "Yeah, Maddy," she said as she lowered her glass. "I could see him looking for you in Harbour Falls, but Fade Island is so remote. How'd he know you were there?"

I saw no harm in sharing how Julian had discovered my whereabouts. In fact, I hoped maybe the two of them could offer some insight into crazy Ami and her antics. But I had no intention of going into detail about the reason for his visit: thinking I was in some kind of danger on the island. Revealing that might clue them in to my true intentions.

"Uh, Ami Dubois, er, I mean, Hensley, told Julian where I was living. She and Sean are vacationing out in Los Angeles, and I guess she looked him up." I paused, rolling my eyes, and adding for effect, "God only knows why."

"How strange," Helena said, her voice oddly flat. "That poor girl sure has problems. I guess she didn't hear that you and Adam are dating."

Trina nodded. "Yeah, I've only met her a few times, but Adam told me all about her, uh, *problems*. It's just so sad."

Remembering how Jennifer had mentioned my schoolgirl crush on Adam—something only Ami had known—I asked Helena, "Do you know if Ami is friends with Jennifer Weston?"

"I don't think so," Helena replied, eyeing me with curiosity. "Why do you ask?"

The waiter returned to clear away our plates, so I took a sip of water and then continued after he was out of earshot. "Jennifer mentioned something about a crush I had on Adam back in high school. Ami was the only one who ever knew about that crush."

"Hmmm..." Helena seemed contemplative, but something about her demeanor still felt off. "That is bizarre. Who knows? Maybe they are friends, but I've never seen them hanging out together."

With a shudder Trina asked, "Speaking of Jennifer, what's the latest with that creepy J.T. O'Brien?" She shot me an apologetic look. "Is he still in rehab?"

Helena glanced uneasily to me and said quietly, "Actually, Nate said he got out yesterday."

I nearly knocked my glass over. "What? I thought he was in for at least two weeks?"

Helena placed her hand over mine in a gesture of support. "He was supposed to be, Maddy. But that facility is overcrowded, so J.T. was released into the outpatient program early."

"Great," I mumbled sarcastically.

"That's ridiculous," Trina chimed in. "He's another one

with some serious issues. They really should just lock him up and throw away the key. In fact, all the things he's done in the past, I'm surprised he's not at Willow Point."

OK, so it was clear Trina disliked J.T. O'Brien as much as her brother did. I had little doubt it was due to J.T.'s past involvement with Chelsea. But Willow Point? Even I wouldn't wish for J.T. to end up there.

Trina, now on a roll, continued, "Maddy, it was terrible what he did to you at the café. Adam asked me not to bring it up, but really, just thank heavens he and Nate got there in time."

"Yeah," Helena added. "If Adam hadn't arrived, you could have ended up like Chelsea." She snapped her fingers. "Poof! Just disappeared into thin air."

Trina gave Helena a pointed look, and Helena glanced to me apologetically. "Sorry, I got carried away."

It was crystal clear who Helena believed was responsible for Chelsea's disappearance. Not that I disagreed with her. J.T. O'Brien could've very easily been behind Chelsea's unexplained departure. Crime of passion and all that.

And now he was out.

A silence fell over the table as we all absorbed the impact of Helena's words. I glanced over to Trina, who was nervously playing with a dangly earring, eyes downcast. Flashes of the letters I'd discovered in Adam's desk flipped through my mind. I couldn't rule Trina out as a suspect either, despite her brother's insistence of her innocence.

And I couldn't figure out why Adam continued to hold onto those incriminating letters. Unless he believed his own sister had followed through on her threats. Did he plan to confront her someday with that evidence? Or would he be so cold as to use it to exonerate himself if he ever were arrested? God, I hoped not. It seemed unlikely, though, since he could have used those letters ages ago when the police were really bearing down on him.

Then there was Helena, another suspect. The case files revealed her alibi to not be nearly as ironclad as Nate's. Just because she *claimed* to have gone to the bathroom down the hall from the rental office of their former apartment complex did not make it a fact.

But did I really think Helena or Trina were more likely suspects than someone like J.T. O'Brien? *No.* But I also couldn't blindly ignore the evidence I'd uncovered thus far.

In any case I didn't want our day to be ruined by the damn Harbour Falls Mystery, so I said, "Maybe we should change the subject. Agreed?"

Helena and Trina nodded emphatically. Both seemed relieved, and we began to discuss less serious topics. Like which stores we'd be hitting up on our shopping extravaganza. Trina excitedly listed off a dizzying array of shops and boutiques in the area. I hadn't been shopping since before I'd left LA, so I was kind of excited to get started.

After leaving the bistro, we walked down the block to the first boutique on Trina's list, and then the next and the next. Trina's list was inexhaustible, it seemed. Our shopping spree continued down the corridor of fashionable shops. There was no end in sight until we finally, as late afternoon approached, entered a trendy boutique specializing in women's business wear. Exhausted, we all agreed to make it our final stop for the day.

The shop was very small, and there was only one other customer—an exceptionally attractive blonde woman. The sales clerk placed a handwritten receipt in a tiny envelope and then handed that, and a bag, to the woman.

When the blonde woman turned to us, Helena shot Trina a look I couldn't decipher, and then she grabbed my hand. "We should just skip this store," she said, pulling me toward the door. "In fact, I think I've maxed out my credit card."

Trina came up from behind me—blocking my view of the store—and nervously added, "Yeah, me too."

Something more was happening. I wasn't buying the suddenly maxed-out credit card stories. My suspicion was quickly confirmed when a soft, very feminine voice rang out from behind us. "Trina? Is that you?"

Trina groaned and stepped aside, and I came face-to-face

with the petite, flaxen-haired beauty that'd been at the register. I stepped back, catching Trina and Helena glancing uneasily at one another before simultaneously looking to me. Apparently they were anticipating some sort of a reaction, though I had no idea why.

At least I didn't until Trina said to the diminutive woman standing there, "Hi, Lindsey. How have you been?"

Lindsey? As in Adam's *Lindsey*? Oh God, I instantly felt self-conscious. This woman was extremely attractive, although in a more subtle way than Chelsea. One thing for sure, Jennifer had not been lying—Adam had obviously dated nothing but incredibly beautiful women in the past. Chelsea. Lindsey. Who else? I couldn't help but wonder, *what in the hell does he see in me?*

After Lindsey introduced herself to Helena, she flipped her long, very straight blonde hair over her shoulder and turned to me. "I'm sorry. I don't believe we've met, though you do look familiar." She scrunched her beautiful face in thought for a second and added, "I'm Lindsey, by the way."

"I'm Maddy—"

"Maddy, as in *Maddy Fitch*," Helena interrupted. "You know, the best-selling novelist."

I knew what Helena was doing, trying to keep the conversation diverted away from Adam. But even with Helena proudly touting my vocation, I couldn't shake the feeling of inadequacy in comparing myself to this stunning woman who, up until very recently, had been sleeping with Adam. Satisfying his— what had Jennifer said?—voracious appetite.

Ugh. I felt ill as Jennifer's words haunted me. Perhaps this woman had been Jennifer's source of information regarding Adam. Did she know Lindsey? Maybe Lindsey had visited Adam on the island. After all, Helena recognized her. But Trina had introduced them as if they didn't know one another. Had Helena seen a picture of Lindsey then? It was all too confusing.

"Oh," Lindsey said, some kind of recognition registering on her face. "So *you* are Maddy Fitch. Hmm…" She eyed me up and down. "…very interesting."

From her tone of voice, I knew she'd just realized I was

Maddy Fitch—not so much the mystery writer—but rather Maddy Fitch, Adam's new love interest. *Guess word had gotten around to her.*

I glared at Lindsey, daring her to say more. Trina and Helena exchanged a worried look, and Trina said, "Well, we really should get going, it's getting late."

"But you just got here," Lindsey protested, in a sweet but phony voice. She turned to Trina, keeping her doe-like eyes trained on me. "How is Adam doing? You really must tell him to get back in touch with me." She shot me a haughty look. "I miss all the *fun* we used to have together."

Trina rolled her eyes, and Helena flipped her own beautiful, blonde tresses back. "I wouldn't hold my breath, Lindsey," she interjected. "I do believe Adam has finally been tamed."

Trina glanced away, stifling a giggle. My own eyes widened. *Leave it to Helena.*

Lindsey wrinkled her pert, little nose in disgust and stared directly at me. "Hmmm, perhaps he's been tamed…for now. But Adam gets bored rather quickly, especially if one can't keep up with him."

"Being in love is hardly boring," Helena shot back at Lindsey.

Lindsey bristled, clearly stung by Helena's words. For a moment I almost felt bad for her. She'd probably been strung along by Adam, hoping he would fall for her. And all along he was just using her for his own pleasure.

Yes, for a moment I felt bad for her, but then it quickly passed. Instead I began to feel empowered. Adam loved me. My own subtle beauty had somehow captured his heart. I stood up a little straighter and declared, "Sorry, Lindsey, but Adam isn't going to be calling you, getting back in touch, whatever." I waved my hand dismissively. "After all, he's going to be too busy keeping up with *me*," I added with a wink.

That seemed to be the final straw for Lindsey. She dispensed with the snarky comments, said good-bye to Trina and Helena, nodded curtly to me, and scurried for the door.

"Way to go, Maddy," Helena said proudly as the door

swung shut.

Trina laughed. "You definitely got the best of her, that's for sure."

Though I felt victorious, part of me was less than thrilled to have run into one of Adam's past hookups. It seemed like every part of his past was always catching up to us.

What next?

An hour later, after we'd returned to Trina's place, Adam arrived to pick me up. Trina pulled her brother inside and started whispering to him. Adam leaned against the closed door, listening intently, and I knew, without a doubt, Trina was filling him in on the details of our run-in with Lindsey.

Helena caught me watching them and, in an effort surely designed to prevent me from eavesdropping, began to help me gather my many shopping parcels. She paused as she pressed the bag handle of one of my purchases into my hand. "Maddy, Adam loves you. He never had feelings like that for Lindsey. You remember that."

I nodded, appreciating Helena's vote of confidence.

Helena made so much noise with the bags (surely purposely) that I couldn't hear, but my eyes were still drawn to Adam as he listened attentively to his sister. He was as striking as ever in his dark gray suit, leaning casually against the door, loosening his tie. He must have sensed my eyes on him, because he looked over and met my gaze, smiling one of those amazing smiles that I loved so very much.

In that moment it was like we were the only two people in the world. Only Helena's nudge to my arm brought me back to reality. "See," she said softly, leaning close. "Now there is a man clearly in love."

Yeah, and I love him. Hell with Lindsey, I thought.

After Trina and Adam wrapped up their conversation, they rejoined us in the living room. Before we left, Helena, Trina, and I gushed about how much fun we'd had throughout the day—the run-in with Lindsey excluded—and how we'd have to do it again soon. Once Adam finally extracted me from the love fest, we made our way down to the waiting limo parked at the curb.

As soon as the driver saw all the bags, he rushed out to load them into the trunk.

Slipping into the backseat, Adam draped his arm around my shoulders and asked cautiously, "Everything go OK today?"

"Everything was fine," I replied, meeting his deep blue eyes, filled with concern as he searched my face. "Why do you ask?"

"Trina told me you ran into Lindsey." He sighed, raking his fingers through his hair. "Maddy, I don't want my past upsetting you." He pulled me close, kissing the top of my head, and whispered, "You're the only one for me. You know that, right?"

I tilted my head and leaned my cheek to his. "I know, Adam. And I'm fine." And in that moment, I was fine. In fact, everything was fine.

If only it could have lasted.

Chapter 20

When we reached the small regional airport we'd flown into that morning, Adam went out to the tarmac to where the Gulfstream was waiting. While he checked on things for our flight back, I was left to my own devices in the hangar. Remembering that my cell was still on vibrate, since I'd not wanted my day with the girls to be interrupted, I fished the phone out of my bag and began scrolling through the texts.

There was a new one from Helena—sent just minutes ago—reiterating how glad she was that I had joined her and Trina for the shopping trip. Smiling, I shot a quick text back, assuring her that I'd had a great time as well.

With a smile still lingering in recollection of what a fun day we'd all had, I checked voicemail. There was a short message from my dad, just asking me to call him when I had some free time. Nothing urgent. So far, so good.

But then I began to listen to a voicemail from Jimmy.

With a shaky voice, he began with, "Maddy, hey it's me, Jimmy. From the bar." Nervous laughter. "I ain't found that picture yet, but I'm still lookin'. But I got some other info I think 'ya might wanna know. Call me, 'kay?"

He'd left the message at 11:20 this morning, probably during the start of his shift at Billy's.

I touched the screen to replay the message, but then I heard Adam approaching. I hastily threw the cell back into my bag and spun to face him. He eyed my bag and hesitated, a flicker of suspicion crossing his face. "Everything all right?"

Feigning innocence I replied, "Mm-hmm, I was checking messages. You just kind of startled me."

"Sorry," he said, but he didn't sound sorry in the least. His blue eyes were intense, trained on me. "Have any?" he asked curtly.

"Any what?"

"Messages, Maddy." Impatience colored his tone.

"Oh," I answered, hoping to appear nonchalant. "Yeah, actually, um, Helena texted, and my dad left a voicemail." Adam looked as if he didn't entirely believe me, but just as he was opening his mouth to say something more, his own cell phone buzzed. *Thank God.* He raised the phone to his ear and began to talk.

I shifted and blew out a breath of air. Adam glanced at me, so I pointed to the restrooms in the far corner of the hangar to let him know that was where I'd be. He nodded and then redirected his attention back to whomever he was speaking to on the phone. Hurriedly I raced to the ladies' room. Not because I had to go. I just needed a private place from which to call Jimmy back.

The ladies' room was sparse and industrial, one stall, a metal wash basin with a plastic soap dispenser attached to the wall, and a hand dryer that looked as if it had seen better days. Standing just inside the door, I dug my cell phone back out of my bag. But then I paused. The bathroom door, made of some kind of metal, seemed kind of thin and flimsy. Someone standing on the other side would surely hear anything I said. To prevent that very thing from happening I stepped over to the basin and turned the water on full blast. In such a small space, the water echoed noisily off all the metal surfaces.

With a hand over one ear so I could hear Jimmy and not the water torrent, I raised my phone to my other ear, calling Jimmy in the process. "Hey, Maddy," he said, answering on the first ring.

"Jimmy," I said softly, hoping he could hear me over all the noise. "I only have a minute. What's this info you have for me?"

Jimmy laughed. "I can barely hear 'ya. Where 'ya callin' from? A damn rain forest?"

"Ha-ha," I replied. I didn't have time for jokes, so I hurried him along. "Just tell me why you called. I'm really in a hurry."

"Sure thing." Jimmy's voice grew serious. "Thought 'ya might be interested to hear your friend was here at Billy's last night."

"Huh? What friend?" For a minute my heart stopped, thinking it'd been Chelsea.

But then he said, "That dude you was askin' about." He sounded exasperated. "He was at the bar. First time I've seen 'im here since before that girl disappeared."

Well, this was certainly a curious development. His first day out of rehab and J.T. O'Brien shows up at a *bar*. And not just any bar but Billy's.

"Was he drinking?" I asked.

"Maddy, the dude was at a bar. What do 'ya think he was doin'?" Jimmy scoffed. "Thought you might also wanna know he spent some time with Zeb too." He didn't come right out and say it, but I knew he was trying to tell me J.T. had bought drugs.

Looks like Adam was right; rehab doesn't stick for J.T.

"By the way that guy is a real dick," Jimmy added, almost as an afterthought, but with a suddenly venomous edge to his voice.

"Why?" I asked. "What happened?"

"I had to shut the dude off. Wasn't holdin' his liquor. At all. He was fallin' off the stool, real pathetic-like. So I tell him, 'That's it, bud. You're done for the night.'" Jimmy lowered his voice. "Dude didn't like that one bit. Told me I'd better watch my back. He sounded pretty serious, if 'ya ask me."

Interesting. Since J.T. had been messed up, I probably would have told Jimmy it was just an empty threat and not to worry. But after experiencing an enraged J.T. firsthand at the café, I wasn't so sure. J.T. O'Brien had a dark side and was capable of violence. But I didn't know where J.T. drew the line. Or if he ever even did.

"Did he say anything else?" I asked.

"Nah, but that was enough. He had a look in his eyes"—I knew that look all too well—"Dude just gave me the creeps, that's all."

The bathroom doorknob began to jiggle. *Damn, it had to be Adam.*

Desperate to wrap things up, I whispered, "Jimmy, I gotta go."

"Cool,' he said, unperturbed. "I'll call you if I ever find that picture."

The doorknob jostled more urgently. "Thanks," I said quickly and then added, "And Jimmy, please be careful."

Jimmy was laughing and saying, "Sure thing, see 'ya around," when I hit the *end* button.

Adam's voice rang out from the other side of the closed door. "Maddy? Are you OK in there?"

I tossed the cell into my bag, crossed the small space, and flipped the lever to unlock the bathroom door. Instantly it flew open, and Adam, standing on the other side and not looking happy, eyed me up and down. "What's going on? You've been in here for an awfully long time."

"Uh," I began. The water was still blasting away, making things look even more suspicious. Adam walked over to turn it off, and I followed him, saying, "Nothing is going on. I was just...washing my hands."

Adam was no fool, and the look he gave me confirmed it. "Madeleine, the water's been running for a good ten minutes. I could hear it outside the door."

Our eyes met. "Can we just get out of here?" I asked, sighing. "We can talk about it on the flight back."

He held my gaze and then relented. "Let's go. But, Madeleine, you *are* going to tell me exactly what you're up to. Is that clear?"

I reluctantly nodded, and Adam turned away. I walked behind him, keeping my eyes on his broad shoulders, tension evident in every stride. *Damn!* He was not going to be pleased to find out I'd been corresponding with the bartender at Billy's, especially now that J.T. O'Brien was back in the mix.

We boarded the plane in silence, no witty bantering in the cockpit this time.

Once we were airborne, Adam switched the controls over

to autopilot and swiveled in his seat to face me. "So, what were you doing in the restroom back at the hangar?"

Here we go.

"Talking on the phone," I replied, staring beyond Adam to watch the sun sink on the horizon, a fiery orb of red that appeared to sizzle into the skyline.

"And to whom were you speaking that you felt the need to leave the water running at full power? You obviously wanted to keep someone from hearing what you were saying, and I'm sure that someone was me," Adam said coolly, but the accusation burned as hot as the sinking sun.

I swallowed hard. "Um…"

"Madeleine."

"OK, OK." I met his gaze. "Remember when I told you about the bartender at Billy's?"

Adam rolled his eyes. "That place again," he muttered to himself and then asked, "The guy who *supposedly* has the alleged photo of my ex kissing some blonde, correct?"

"Yes."

"And this was why you were on the phone with him?" Adam's tone turned mocking. "Because, let me guess, he still can't find this alleged photo. But nevertheless he had the burning need to check in with you. Surely to keep you engaged in whatever game he's playing."

Either Adam didn't believe a picture of Chelsea kissing a blonde woman existed, or he was trying to downplay its significance by focusing on Jimmy and his supposed ulterior motives. Good thing I hadn't told Adam about the cash I'd given to the kid, or he'd really have something to run with.

"He didn't find the photo," I softly confirmed. "But he called to tell me about something else that happened at the bar."

Adam was starting to look quite aggravated. "Really, Maddy, I'm running out of patience here. Just tell me why you were talking to that guy?"

I took a deep breath. "You're not going to like this."

"No doubt," he chuckled.

I took a deep breath. "He told me J.T. O'Brien was at Billy's last night. He was really drunk, maybe even doing drugs." I paused. "Wait, you do know he got out of rehab early, right?"

Adam shot me a look that said, "*Are you serious?*"

I still wanted an answer, so I waited and he confirmed, "Yes, I'm well aware of O'Brien's early release."

Of course.

"Well, anyway," I continued, "he threatened Jimmy. That's the bartender's name, by the way."

Adam shook his head. "Nice to know you're on a first name basis with the lowlifes at Billy's," he chided, his voice laced with disapproval.

I bit down on my lip to keep from uttering some kind of a smart-ass retort. Adam was irritated enough with me. I ignored his comment and instead asked, "Do you think J.T. meant it? Do you think Jimmy is in any danger?"

"No, I'm sure your new pal will be perfectly fine."

"Adam," I huffed, "he's not my new *pal*. He's just trying to help me—"

"With the case," Adam finished, sounding angry. Suddenly his hand was at my chin, urging me to meet his stormy, irate eyes. "Madeleine, you better not be planning on returning to that bar."

I shifted in my seat, uneasy. "If a picture turns up, I want to see it," I protested.

The storm in Adam's eyes lingered but then abated. "You really want to know who's in that picture with Chelsea, don't you?" he laughed.

"I do." I searched his face. "Aren't you the least bit curious?"

"I'm really not." He sighed, dropping his hand from my chin. "Even if a picture like that exists—and I have my doubts—I certainly don't believe it has anything to do with whatever happened to Chelsea." He ran his hand over his face. "It was probably some random Harbourtown girl that Chelsea kissed in order to... What did you say before? Get free drinks all week?"

I nodded. "Maybe you're right, but..."

"Just let it go," Adam warned. "Stay away from that place."

If you keep going there, you *will* end up in hot water, especially if O'Brien is back to frequenting the place."

That much was true. If Jimmy did locate the photo, I'd have to make sure J.T. wasn't around when I picked it up.

"I'll let it go," I lied, even though it made me feel terrible to do so.

Adam reached for my hand, and I slipped it into his grasp. He squeezed lightly, and we stayed like that—quietly lost in our own thoughts—the rest of the flight back. I didn't know what I was doing anymore. I'd come here to investigate a cold case mystery and write a book using the facts I uncovered. But things had changed. I hadn't planned on falling in love with the primary suspect. I also hadn't planned on becoming friends with Helena and Trina—two other possible suspects.

I no longer cared about writing a book based on the Harbour Falls Mystery. And I couldn't help but wonder if Adam sensed that I'd had a change of heart. It was probably the reason why he so seldom asked for details. And part of the reason why, besides having fallen in love with me, he'd divulged so many of his own secrets.

Maybe that had been his crafty plan from the start? Get close to me so that I'd never end up writing about the mystery. *His* mystery. My imaginative writer's mind couldn't help but wonder. But even if that were the case, it didn't matter. He had a right to keep his past private. And even without Adam's possible machinations, I was losing the desire to write about the people I'd come to care about.

On the other hand, though, I did still desperately want to *solve* the mystery. For the exact same reasons that I didn't want to write about it—I cared for these people. I wanted closure for them. And, more than anything, I wanted closure for Adam. He'd lived with this mystery hanging over his head far too long. It affected everything around him, including us. I wanted Adam to be able to move forward, without the question of what had happened to his ex-fiancée haunting his life. I wanted answers for him, for me…for all of us.

Somewhere along the line, this had become intensely personal. It almost felt as if I was part of the case. And at that time, I didn't know it, but I was about to become an integral player in my own right.

Chapter 21

Several days following the Boston trip, I found myself sitting alone at the kitchen table, absently stirring cereal that had become soggy fifteen minutes earlier. My mood that day? Dreary as the late October morning had proven to be, the circumstances as depressing as the heaviness in the atmosphere that the wet weather had wrought.

Adam was away on business—again. In fact, after dropping me off at the cottage after we'd flown back the day of the shopping excursion, Adam had had to turn right around and fly back down to Boston. He was making tremendous progress in securing that lucrative deal with the client there, and that was good and all. But it was taking up a lot of his time, putting a crimp in the time we spent together and effectively stalling our relationship. Though it had been moving too fast initially, our physical relationship was at a standstill now. Apart from a few heated make-out sessions, we'd gone no further than the night he'd broken in, the night Julian had been sleeping upstairs. In fact, if I were to be honest, Adam seemed distracted. And I was having trouble discerning whether it was due to the stresses of his work or something else entirely. I planned to ask tonight though. Adam was returning to the island and had promised to be back in time for a late dinner.

Which reminded me, I had yet to thaw out the eggplant Parmesan I'd made over the weekend. One of many, many culinary creations I'd whipped up over the past few days. Yep, I'd been cooking up a storm ever since Adam had not so subtly suggested I take a break from the case for a while. *Just to clear your head*, he'd said. I, however, sensed it had more to do with him wanting me to stay away from Billy's than with his desire for me to be operating with a "clear" head.

I let the spoon in my hand drop back into the cereal, a splash of milk the sole protest. Who was I fooling with these distractions? Had all the cooking helped? *Nope.* It sure hadn't helped the other day. With the aroma of simmering tomatoes and garlic and herbs wafting through my cottage, I'd pored over the case files that day. Wishing for something to pop out at me, something I may have missed. I was trying harder than ever to figure out what could have happened to Chelsea Hannigan.

The way she'd disappeared without a trace had me considering the possibility that maybe she'd just left town and started a new life somewhere far, far away from Harbour Falls. Had she wanted to do something like that, she certainly would have had the resources. Hell, she could have been setting things up and planning for months. I recalled how Adam had said to J.T. on the night of the attack that maybe she'd "just left."

But people like Chelsea didn't just leave. Not when they were getting everything they wanted right where they were. And since she'd never been spotted anywhere, not even once, it seemed unlikely. All the national networks and publications had covered the story and still replayed the details on the anniversary of her disappearance. Chelsea Hannigan's phenomenally gorgeous face had been made famous…or infamous, as it were. It would be next to impossible for someone so stunning to escape notice unless she'd dramatically altered her appearance. But I couldn't imagine her doing that either. Chelsea's looks had been her crowning glory, and it was doubtful she'd trade them away in order to start a new life somewhere else. Again, what purpose would it have served?

That left only one other possibility: someone had murdered her. But who? And why?

The list of potential suspects was long, as were the multitudes of motives.

I tried not to dwell on it, but the fact remained that Adam had the most compelling reasons to want Chelsea out of the picture. I could just imagine her holding that illegal stock trade, and the threat of going to the SEC with what she knew, over him like a dagger ready to plunge at any second. I couldn't fathom what that must have felt like for Adam to have only two options: One, obey Chelsea's every whim, including staying with—and marrying—her. Or, two, leave her, thus giving her the opening to make good on her threat to go to the authorities with incriminating testimony against him. Then he could have lost everything and, if convicted, gone to prison. *Yeah, great options,* I thought bitterly.

Despite such a strong motive for murder, I just didn't feel in my heart that Adam had done anything to Chelsea. Maybe I was blinded by love, but that was what I believed.

Besides, the list of suspects didn't begin and end with Adam. Not by a long shot.

Chelsea had led a wild and dangerous life, making numerous enemies along the way. Even Adam's own sister despised the woman. I still wondered what had motivated Trina to send those threatening letters. Had she really been trying to frighten Chelsea into backing out of marrying Adam? And why had Adam intercepted them? Despite what he'd said, maybe he actually believed Trina had taken matters into her own hands and followed through with those threats. In that case he surely wouldn't have wanted those letters floating around, implicating his own sister.

Then there was J.T. Had Chelsea met up with *him* that fateful night? Was that what she wanted Adam to tell her not to do? And since he'd not dissuaded her, what if she had met J.T. and something had gone wrong? J.T. O'Brien was volatile and unpredictable. I'd been on the receiving end of his temper, and it made me shudder to recall the rage alight in his eyes that night at the café. And just days ago, he'd threatened Jimmy. It seemed J.T. was a walking time bomb, ready to explode at the slightest provocation. Yeah, when it came to Chelsea's disappearance, a crime of passion could not be ruled out.

And, of course, there was also Jennifer Weston—another suspect. She certainly had her own demons and anger issues. That fact had been made clear throughout almost all of my limited interactions with her, particularly on the most recent ferry ride I'd shared with her. Apart from her veiled threats, it made me wary to know she was aware of private things pertaining to Adam.

Someone had told her, and based on her angry reaction that day on the ferry, I was fairly sure it had not been Chelsea. But someone had hinted at Adam's sexual prowess in the bedroom. Who would know something like that? Someone who'd been with him sexually...or someone who'd *known* someone who had been intimate with Adam?

Jennifer had known about my high school crush on Adam, and there was only one person I'd ever divulged that information to: Ami Dubois-Hensley. Maybe she was the source of Jennifer's information. But did that mean...*God, no!* My stomach churned at the thought of Ami ever having been with Adam. Though she certainly fit the bill of what his "type" had been prior to meeting me. Ami was beautiful, and she had long, blonde hair.

Hmmm, maybe he had slept with her. But Ami had all those mental issues, and I just couldn't see Adam exploiting them by seducing her. Not to mention she was married. And she was his employee, which brought up a whole host of other potential problems. After evading an insider trading charge, surely a sexual harassment suit was the last thing Adam would have wanted.

No, if Ami had been the one to tell Jennifer those things, then she had heard them from someone else. I felt certain of this, but I wondered who would have shared that kind of information with Ami Hensley.

And how bizarre was it that she'd gone out to LA to contact my agent...and Julian? Telling them I was in danger here on the island. From what? From whom? Was Ami really trying to protect me? How much did she know? Did she have knowledge of what had happened to Chelsea Hannigan?

Good Lord! This whole thing was so confusing that a part of me wished something would surface to prove Chelsea had been the victim of some random stranger passing through town. But no, that wasn't going to happen. There were too many suspects right here. And they all had motives.

And then there was the mystery blonde, the woman kissing Chelsea in the picture. She never came forward, so the likelihood she held some kind of pertinent—and probably damning—information was very high. I needed to find her so I could question her. She had to know something, especially if she'd known Chelsea, well, intimately. But Jimmy hadn't recognized her as someone who frequented the bar. He said she'd been there only a few times, and always with Ms. Hannigan. Who was she?

A blonde mystery woman...

For a fleeting moment, I considered Helena. But how crazy and unlikely would that be? She was my friend now, and why would someone wishing to remain anonymous be so forthcoming with so much information? *Almost a little too forthcoming,* a little voice whispered in my head. And Helena's alibi was less than ironclad. But Helena and Chelsea? Did I really want to start down that path? It was just too outlandish. She'd never do something like that to Adam. And she'd definitely not hurt Nate; she clearly loved him too much.

Adam was probably correct—the mystery blonde would turn out to be just some random Harbourtown resident Chelsea had hooked up with. Maybe.

I still felt the picture held the key to solving this whole thing. Adam had dismissed its significance, but I wasn't so convinced it was useless. Whoever was in that photograph had miraculously managed to avoid suspicion for far too long. And as far as I was concerned, it was up to me to make sure that no longer remained the case. Yeah, I couldn't wait to get my hands on that damn picture.

And here I was again, rehashing the facts as I knew them in my head. Clearly it was time for a diversion. I dumped my cereal down the disposal, gave it a whirl, and put my bowl in the sink. Next I took the eggplant Parmesan out of the freezer and plopped it onto the counter with a resounding thud. There.

Even though it was dreary out, the rain had stopped, and

the temperature was mild. *I should get out and enjoy the day*, I thought. Sitting around here was just making me crazy, and for the love of God, I was sick and tired of cooking. Cooking hadn't helped, but maybe a little exploration here on the island would "clear" my head.

I had yet to check out the heavily forested, mostly impassable, east side of the island. The car would be useless, but hiking on a mild October afternoon like this one sounded like a welcome respite. So I laced up my hiking boots, smoothed out my jeans, and tied a light jacket around my waist in case the thin sweater I had on proved inadequate.

After grabbing a bottle of cold water out of the fridge, I left the cottage and started north. This time I stayed off the trails and stuck to the paved main road. It was the most direct route anyway, and I soon reached the western boundary of Adam's property.

In Adam's absence Max was spending time patrolling up here, just generally keeping an eye on things. I'd seen him drive by my cottage in his dark green Hummer a number of times over the past several days. I figured Adam was behind all the surveillance. It seemed silly and overdone to me, because the few residents who were on the island were Adam's trusted friends. But I supposed it was the individuals who traveled back and forth on the ferry, and their possible passengers, he was distrustful of.

I continued along the edge of the road as it curved past Adam's driveway. I now knew the long, winding lane—wider now that the undergrowth had died out in the changing season—split off in two directions a few hundred yards ahead. One lane led to Adam's house and the other to a set of garages where his other vehicles—more sports cars and a black Range Rover that was mainly used in the winter—were kept.

I stopped, considering if I should head up the driveway and see if Max was around. Adam would surely want him to know that I was heading into the wilderness on the east side of the island. But then he may discourage me from going or, worse yet, go with me. I certainly did not require a babysitter. Besides,

I had my cell in my pocket, and Max's number was still in my contacts. I'd call him if I needed him. So I resumed walking, believing everything would be fine.

A mile from the driveway, there was a gravel turnoff. I recalled it to be the one leading back to the runway and hangar on the far eastern edge of Adam's compound. I smiled as I recalled my first date with Adam, the experience with the strawberries and champagne. How I longed to re-create that experience, this time with no interruptions.

Lost in my lust-muddled thoughts, I tripped at the point where the pavement, and consequently the main road, ended abruptly. I glanced around. At last I'd reached the east side of the island. And it sure was desolate.

Before me, a nearly impassable access road—really just a widened trail—snaked deeper into the forest of ancient oak and thick pine. From my research I knew the access road meandered through the woods in a southerly direction, eventually coming out near the lighthouse area.

I took a few cautious steps, navigating the uneven terrain and the many muddy puddles. The access road was in worse shape than I'd anticipated, rutted and overgrown with wiry, coiled tangles of skeletal-looking branches. Towering pine trees grew in densely packed clusters on either side of the path, creating an overhead canopy that made the overcast day appear even darker. But I forged ahead, keeping safely to the middle. Dried leaves, clinging lifelessly to the trees, rustled all around me. I heard the scurrying of animals and the occasional bird chirp, but the forest was much too thick to actually catch sight of any of the island fauna.

After traveling what I estimated to be about two miles, the woods quieted. No more rustling leaves, no scurrying animals, no more chirping birds. It was actually kind of creepy, and I started to wish I'd stopped, after all, to let Max know where I was heading. Breathing in deeply, the smell of rotting leaves particularly pungent now, I fished out my cell phone to reassure myself Max was only a phone call away. But a sick feeling of dread passed through me when I saw I had no signal over here on this side of the island. *Stupid for not checking first*, I thought. I knew if I continued, I'd eventually reach the cliffs above the lighthouse. Recalling how Adam had told me there were hidden caves in the wall of cliffs, I shuddered. *Uh, definitely not going down there all alone.*

Although there was plenty of daylight left, I'd had enough. It was too quiet and devoid of life here. And I had no cell service. Worse yet I was starting to get a bad feeling. I stopped, took a swig of water to calm my nerves, and turned around.

I began to walk quickly but halted when I heard a weird *clang* noise, like metal hitting metal. *What is that?* Somewhere off to my right, coming from behind a cluster of particularly dense pine, it sounded again. *Clang!* And then a few seconds later, *Thunk! Thunk!* This time it sounded like something metal pounding at the ground. What the...?

Besides Max, Nate was the only other person who was supposed to be on the island today. Helena was still in Boston. But why would Max or Nate be over here in the deep woods on this side of the island?

Against my better judgment, I crept to the edge of the rutted road and crouched down at the treeline, the cool smell of pine filling my nose, in the hope of catching a glimpse of the source behind the steady, rhythmic noises that had yet to abate.

What I saw made my hand fly to my mouth to stifle a gasp. *Oh God!* Several yards away, there was a man—in muddied jeans and a dark hoodie— and he appeared to be burying something. He was just about finished with his task, patting down the dirt neatly to obscure the digging he had done. Clutching my water bottle tightly, my hands grew sweaty, because I recognized this person. Though his face was mostly obscured, I knew, without a doubt, that the man patting down the dirt was J.T. O'Brien. And, hell, if I didn't need to get out of here—fast.

I looked furtively left and right. Of course, nobody else was around. *Oh God, this isn't good.* Here I was, stuck deep in the woods with my former friend, but more recently my assailant. Thankfully, J.T. appeared to be deeply engrossed in what he was doing, which, at this point, was kicking fallen leaves over the now barely noticeable mound of dirt.

"Get out of here!" my mind screamed.

Quickly I stood—my limbs trembling—and backed away cautiously. My heart was taking up residence in my throat as memories of J.T.'s assault at the café flashed through my mind. Only this time there would be no Adam to save me. I turned and crept away silently, rapidly putting as much distance as possible between J.T. and me.

When I was certain I was out of his hearing range, I broke into a run. I needed to get the hell out of there as quickly as possible, but I still ventured a glance over my shoulder, my pace barely slowing. Relief washed over me once I confirmed I was not being followed. No J.T. in pursuit as I'd feared.

After what felt like forever, the forest a blur, I reached the entry to the access road, breathless and with my heart pounding. Gasping for air I slowed to a walk as my feet hit the paved surface of the main road. Safe, at last.

With fear taking a backseat, my thoughts turned to what I'd seen. What was J.T. O'Brien *doing* back there? *Bizarre.* Why would he be burying something out here on Fade Island? Whatever it was, I'd been fortunate he'd not caught sight of me. One thing for sure, J.T. O'Brien had certainly been engaged in some crazy behavior since his short stint in rehab. Showing up at Billy's for the first time in ages, buying drugs, and getting so messed up he threatened Jimmy for shutting him off, and now, digging around out here on the island. Yes, J.T. was up to something. I hoped to God he hadn't caught wind of my investigation. Suspecting I was poking around would be bad enough, but if J.T. actually knew specifics—like my visits to Billy's—then that could spell big trouble for me. Especially if he was trying to hide something, and I was getting too close.

When I finally reached the cottage, I was a sweaty mess. I went in, showered, and changed clothes. Adam would be arriving soon, and I had to decide if I was going to share this new development with him. But there really was no choice; he had to be told that J.T. had been on the island burying something. But Adam would surely be upset with me. Not only had I not cooled it with the case, I'd put myself in danger, once again.

Later that evening, as I plated the eggplant Parmesan I'd reheated, the doorbell sounded. Wiping my hands on the apron I'd thrown on over my jeans and sweater, I hurried to the door and let Adam in.

He greeted me with a kiss that started out soft but soon deepened. Leaving me somewhat breathless, he pulled away way too soon for my liking. "Miss me?" Adam asked, his tone soft.

"More than you could imagine," I replied.

His brow furrowed. "Is everything OK?"

I waved a hand dismissively. "We can talk while we eat," I said. "Dinner's on the table, and it will get cold."

I was biding my time, waiting for an opportune time to bring up the day's events. Now didn't feel right.

We sat down to eat, and Adam talked of his business in Boston. He wasn't pressing me to elaborate on my earlier comment, but he seemed to notice I was preoccupied.

Cutting into a piece of eggplant, he asked, "Maddy, are you with me here? You look like you haven't heard a single word I've said."

I looked up from my own plate, meeting his questioning gaze. "Um, not really." I admitted. "It's just that…"

Adam put down his fork, wiped his mouth with a napkin. "Did something happen while I was away?"

I lifted a glass of water to my lips and took a long drink. Putting the glass down, I nodded. "Yeah, something did happen. When I was hiking down the access road over on the other side of the island, I saw some—"

"Jesus Christ," Adam interrupted, running a hand through his hair in frustration. "What were you doing over there? You know it's not safe to be traipsing around on that side of the island. Hell, it's almost impossible to even get cell service over there."

"Adam," I said, huffing in indignation, even though everything he said was true. "Please."

I rolled my eyes at him, and he replied sharply, "You couldn't find anything else to occupy your time?"

"What like cooking?" I pushed my plate away, my appetite lost.

"What about *writing*, Madeleine?" Adam's voice was harsh, cold. "That is what you're here to do. Remember?"

Yeah, I remember, I thought, but I didn't share with Adam all the second thoughts I'd had recently. Instead I said, "Look, I know you want me to take some kind of a break from the case, but I'm not going to sit around here locked up in this cottage all day like some kind of prisoner."

"You're hardly a prisoner," Adam's voice softened. "It's just that anything could happen to you in those woods. If you fell or got hurt, we'd have a hell of a time even locating you." Pausing, he added, "Did you at least tell Max where you were going?"

Uh-oh. He'd just settled down, and now he was going to be pissed all over again. And I hadn't even gotten to the J.T. part yet.

I shook my head, staring at my plate of unfinished food. "Um, no, I didn't tell anyone where I was going."

Adam was silent, so I glanced up. His eyes held, not anger as I expected, but disappointment and sadness. I suddenly felt genuinely bad for being so foolhardy. "I'm sorry," I said softly.

Adam reached over and covered my hand with his. "Don't apologize, OK? I just worry when I'm not around to protect you. Next time,"—I was sure those words were killing him, because he knew there'd always be a next time with me—"just please tell Max."

I took a deep, steadying breath. "I will, Adam, but, uh, there's more." He looked weary, so I added, "Promise me you won't get angry when I tell you what else happened."

"Just spit it out, Maddy."

"Ok, uh," I sputtered, "J.T. O'Brien was there today, in the woods on the other side of the island." I cringed, dreading Adam's reaction.

But instead of an angry outburst, he took a small drink of water and leaned back in his chair. "Do you really have so little regard for your own welfare?" He shook his head. In disappointment, I imagined.

"I never expected to see *him* out there," I said in my defense. "Besides, he didn't notice me. He was...preoccupied."

"With what?"

"Digging, maybe burying something. He was covering the area with leaves, covering something up." I raised an eyebrow of my own for emphasis. "That's what I've wanted to tell you this whole time. I'm sure whatever J.T. was doing, he was up to no good." I paused. "And I think we should find out what—"

"We, Madeleine?"

"Well, maybe not we," I acquiesced. "But someone should check it out."

"You're right. O'Brien has no right trespassing over there. He's well aware that side of the island is completely off-limits," Adam said, clearly aggravated. "I'll have Max take a look around. Do you think you could pinpoint the location for him?"

"I don't know, maybe. If we head down there before it rains I could probably find the mound."

The look Adam gave me told me I'd misunderstood. "I meant pointing out where you were on a map," he said quietly.

With that, I nodded. But I knew I'd never be able to pinpoint the exact location on a map. I'd been so scared, I'd be lucky if I could find the right spot even if I did go with Max—though it sure would be more likely.

But I'd try it Adam's way...for now.

The next morning I gave Max the best directions I could, trying to remember the exact lay of the land in the area where I'd seen J.T. The map was really no help at all. I could estimate, but I wasn't sure how far down I'd traveled. I ventured a guess that I'd been about halfway to the lighthouse. When I mentioned that tidbit, Adam and Max exchanged an odd glance. Then Max folded up the map and took off in his Hummer.

When Max returned later that day and told us he'd been unable to locate any signs of the ground having been disturbed where he'd searched—no mound of dirt, no disturbed leaves—it came as no surprise to me. I insisted I'd have to go with Max if there was any hope at all of pinpointing the exact spot J.T. had been. But Adam quickly vetoed that plan. Instead he came up with an alternate plan to be employed the following day. The three of us—Adam, Max, and I—would go back and investigate the area as a group.

Unfortunately the weather had other ideas. Heavy rains moved into the area that night, making the likelihood of our getting back down the rugged access road—even in Max's all-wheel drive vehicle—slim to none. So we delayed the plan for the following week. It was necessary anyway, because Adam was leaving for Boston the next morning for *another* three-day business trip. He was so close to closing the deal that I couldn't help but be excited for him. Even though I'd be lonely until he returned on Sunday, which just happened to be Halloween. At least I'd have one treat to look forward to, Adam's return.

So things were on hold.

I knew in my heart J.T. had been up to nothing good in those woods, and I suspected Adam felt the same way. Why was J.T. digging around in the most remote part of an already remote island? He was obviously burying something he intended to keep secret. Or maybe—and this one made my blood run cold—he'd been digging up and *re*burying something.

Yes, maybe J.T. O'Brien was reburying a long-hidden secret, because he feared somebody was close to discovering the truth. And that somebody was me. So if J.T. knew what I was doing, and I was getting close to uncovering secrets meant to stay hidden (or buried), then what exactly did that mean for me?

The question was: Did I really want to find out?

Chapter 22

Sunday, the last day of October, started out ordinarily enough. The mild temperatures we'd enjoyed the previous week were long gone, and we now found ourselves dealing with a bout of horrendous weather—ice-cold blowing winds and a relentless driving rain. It was the type of weather that had earned Fade Island its reputation as a most inhospitable place this time of year. Standing at the window in my sweats, a warm mug of cocoa in my hand, I watched the downpour from the comfort of my living room. Yeah, it appeared fairly certain I'd be spending the day in the toasty warmth of the cottage.

Sometime in the early afternoon, Nate arrived with a small grocery order I'd placed online the day before.

"Happy Halloween, Maddy," he exclaimed cheerfully, despite his semi-soaked attire, when I answered the door.

"Oh geez, Nate, hurry and get in here," I said, stepping aside so he could get in out of the weather.

"I completely forgot it was Halloween," I continued, catching up to Nate as he headed to the kitchen with the two bags of groceries in tow, a trail of big, wet footprints in his wake.

"Easy to do around here," he began, but just then a booming crash of thunder shook the foundation, making us both jump. "Then again, maybe not," he amended.

I laughed in agreement and stopped next to the table as he set the bags down. "Do you want a cup of coffee before you go back out in this mess?" I asked.

"No, thanks. There's plenty back at the café."

"Oh, that reminds me," I began. "Helena will be back tomorrow morning, right?"

The café had been closed for two weeks now with Helena still in Boston visiting with Trina.

"Nope," Nate said, his tone indicating this was not a subject he cared to spend too much time discussing. "Actually there was a change in plans. Helena's back in the area, but she's been staying over in Harbour Falls with her mom."

"Oh, is everything OK?" I ventured, recalling all the trouble those two had once endured at the hands of her abusive stepdad.

Nate, usually so easygoing, tensed. "Uh, yeah, no worries. She'll be back by Tuesday."

Silence descended, the sound of the heavy rain pelting the slate roof of the cottage punctuating the lull. Uncomfortable, I grabbed a package of cookies from the top of one of the bags and set it on the table. "Adam is supposed to be coming back today. But who knows with this weather," I flung my hand toward the window, and then continued to ramble as I began to take groceries out of the bag closest to me. "He may be stuck in Boston until tomorrow. He's trying to close some kind of deal." A can of green beans I'd been grasping slipped from my hand, clattered to the floor, and rolled toward Nate.

"I know," Nate said as he picked the can up and placed it on the table.

I shot Nate an apologetic look, hoping he realized I hadn't meant to pry or bring up an uncomfortable subject when I'd asked about Helena.

Thankfully he smiled and, back to his usual form, said, "Last I heard, this rain is supposed to clear out sometime later today, so I'm sure Adam will make it back by tonight."

The rest of our conversation remained upbeat. No further mentions were made about why Helena had returned from Boston early to spend time with her mom. But after Nate left, the unexpected tension that had crept up between us nagged at me. It reminded me I was alone and made me miss Adam more than ever.

The last few days, Adam and I had been talking and texting often, but it wasn't enough. I didn't feel safe on the island without his being here. Despite Max and Nate being around to keep an eye on things, just the fact that J.T. O'Brien knew his way around so well—well enough to have been burying something over on the godforsaken east side—gave me pause.

I also hadn't forgotten about the plan to go back down the access road to see if I could pinpoint where J.T. had been digging. But nothing could be done until Adam returned. And then, only if the weather cooperated.

I booted up my laptop to peruse the latest weather reports. First I checked the forecast for later today, and just like Nate had said, it was supposed to clear up. *Good, that means Adam will be able to fly back as planned.* I breathed a sigh of relief.

I scrolled through the extended forecast. A huge storm was due to hit on Wednesday. That gave Adam, Max, and me either tomorrow or Tuesday to return to the east side. After a rain as heavy as what was being predicted, the chance of finding the spot J.T. had been digging at would be next to nil.

I hated the thought of a big storm hitting the island. Everything would be disrupted. Adam wouldn't be able to fly in or out, the ferry service would be suspended, and things were usually just an all-around headache. I reminded myself that tomorrow was the first day of November, and this was just a taste of things to come.

Resigned, I closed my laptop. I leaned back on the sofa just as my cell sounded. I hoped it was Adam, as I had yet to hear from him today. But as I checked the display, I saw it was someone I'd not heard from for over a week: Jimmy.

When I answered Jimmy began to speak in an enthusiastic voice, "Hey, I'm glad you picked up. I got some news."

"Uh-oh, what is it?" I asked worriedly. "Not another visit from J.T.?"

"No, no, nothing like that," he responded. "Dude hasn't been back since I talked to 'ya last. But I got somethin' way better."

He grew quiet, probably going for dramatic effect, so I prodded, "OK, so what is it?"

Jimmy's excitement emanated through the connection as he

said, "I found the picture."

Oh. My. God.

Four little words I wasn't expecting to hear. Jimmy found the picture! A picture I'd considered, at times, didn't even exist or would *never* be found. But the young bartender had come through—Jimmy had found the picture.

I felt like screaming *hallelujah*, but instead I said, "You're kidding."

Then, for a few seconds, I feared Jimmy might be playing a practical joke—some kind of Halloween trick. Thankfully, that was not the case.

"Nope, I really found it," Jimmy assured me.

He sounded so pleased to be giving me the good news, and in that moment Jimmy seemed so much like the kid he actually was. "I have it, so whenever you want to swing by—"

"Tomorrow!" I interrupted. "I can come to Harbourtown tomorrow."

What I really wanted to do was hang up and go pick up the picture right now, but there were too many obstacles in my way. A) The ferry wouldn't be running until the weather cleared, and by then Adam would most likely be back. And B) It was Sunday, so Billy's was closed. Which meant if I were to somehow get to the mainland today, I'd have to go to Jimmy's place—wherever that was—and pick up the picture in person. Apart from having no clue where he lived, I cringed at the thought of Adam's reaction if he ever found out I did something *that* stupid. No, it was bad enough I'd be breaking my promise to stay away from Billy's. Better to not tempt fate.

So many things could go wrong between today and tomorrow. So just in case my plans were somehow derailed, I asked Jimmy, "Hey, can you do me a favor?"

"Depends on what it is."

"Can you make a copy of the photograph and send it to me here on the island?" I asked.

"You think I'm gonna change my mind and not give it to 'ya?" he chortled.

"Of course not," I retorted, though it had crossed my mind.

"It's just an insurance policy. I have to see that picture, Jimmy. It's important. And I'd just feel better knowing we have a backup plan."

To my surprise Jimmy agreed to make the copy. His apartment was located next to an office supply store, he informed me. How fortuitous. I thanked whatever gods had intervened to finally make something go smoothly. Jimmy even promised to make the copy as soon as we got off the phone. He said there was a mailbox outside the store. So if all went as planned, it would take Jimmy only about fifteen minutes to make the copy and drop it in the mail. Before we ended the call, I gave Jimmy my Fade Island address, making him read it back to me three times to make certain he got it right.

Things were really starting to happen, but I wouldn't rest easy until the picture was in my hands. If there was any hope of pulling this off without Adam finding out what I was up to, I had to tread carefully and pay special attention to every detail. Otherwise he'd put a stop to it. Now I wished Adam wasn't returning later in the day, as it was going to make things trickier to get off the island tomorrow. His first full day back, I was sure he planned on spending it with me. But I had to get to Harbourtown, even if it was just for a short period of time early in the day. Therefore, I needed a plan to prevent Adam from catching on to what I was up to. I ran my fingers over the keys on my cell. Nate said Helena was in Harbour Falls...

Inspiration struck.

I hastily typed a text to Helena, explaining that I was going to be in Harbourtown tomorrow. I asked if she wanted to drive over from Harbour Falls and meet me for lunch. Of course I planned on telling Adam we'd be having lunch closer to Helena's mom's house to hopefully allay any suspicion.

After I hit send, I crossed to the living room window. As predicted the rain was starting to lighten up. But brisk winds were blowing the freshly fallen leaves, spinning them into tiny tornadoes that hinted at a bigger storm to come. A feeling came over me with a sudden ferocity, a feeling of dread. Closing my eyes I breathed in deeply, chalking up my skittishness to the

Halloween heebie-jeebies. Strangely enough, though, it was at that exact point things started to get, well, strange.

First Helena didn't respond for a solid hour. Usually I never had to wait more than five minutes for her to text back. *Odd.* And then the only thing she wrote in her return text was: *Why are you going to be in Harbourtown?*

The tenor of the text was off. Helena never asked questions like that, nor did she write such short, clipped replies. Something was wrong. Did Helena suspect something? How could she? Knowing how easy it was to misread the intent of the written word, I brushed it off.

With my fingers on the keys, I contemplated my reply. Helena wouldn't be running into Adam over the next twenty-four hours. *Hmm.* My thumbs flew over the keys, I texted that I needed to go to Harbourtown to pick something up for Adam. Hoping she'd not ask what, I hit send.

Another lengthy twenty minutes passed, and then Helena texted: *Let's meet at the little Italian bistro on the corner of Leaf and Ninth. I think the name is Peppio's. Is 2 o'clock good?*

I knew the restaurant—it wasn't far from Billy's—so I confirmed with a return text, and then I placed the cell next to me on the sofa.

Well, that was unusual. Maybe Helena had been distracted, seeing that she was at her mom's house and all. Apparently something was going on there, especially with the usual calm and cool Nate acting so tense earlier.

From the cushion next to me, my cell buzzed once again. This time it was Adam.

"Hey," I answered, smiling, even though he couldn't see me.

"Hey," he replied curtly.

I ignored his seemingly annoyed tone and asked, "How're things going? What time do you think you'll be back?"

Adam cleared his throat. "Yeah, about that..." He hesitated. "Uh, I won't be back until tomorrow."

I glanced out the window, and though it was already almost dark, the rain had stopped completely. "Why aren't you coming back tonight?" I pressed. "The storm passed."

"It's not the weather, Madeleine," he snapped. "Something has come up that I have to take care of."

"OK," I said softly, cowed by his sharp tone.

Adam sighed, and I could imagine him running his fingers through his hair. "I'm sorry, Maddy. I'm just stressed out with wrapping up this deal."

"It's fine," I replied, even though I did feel slighted. "I understand."

We talked awhile longer, but there was something off throughout the rest of the call. When I hung up, I felt even more alone. Everyone was acting strangely—Helena and now Adam.

I tried to see the bright side of the situation. I mean, I hadn't had to mention my lunch plans with Helena to Adam. He didn't even need to know that I planned to go to Harbourtown. He'd obviously been in a bad mood, and there'd been no point in exacerbating the situation. Hopefully I could take care of my business tomorrow at Billy's, meet Helena for lunch to preserve my cover story in case it ever came up, and be back on the island before Adam even returned.

But I couldn't help but wonder if Adam's bad mood was truly a result of his stressing over the Boston deal. He was usually in high spirits when discussing anything related to the deal—assuring me it was as good as done. Until today.

So what could have happened to have made him so agitated?

I slept fitfully that Halloween night, my sleep plagued with nightmares...

I'm down by the lighthouse, and bloody waves of water crash over the black rocks. Red over black, red over black. And then I'm back at the café, and J.T. is attacking me, only Jimmy's voice is in the background, whispering the threatening words J.T. had said to him. And then suddenly J.T. is gone. But Jennifer is there, seated at a table and drinking cappuccino. When I turn away from her sneering face, I notice there are more women, all seated at the tables. Helena, Trina, even Lindsey.

Only instead of cappuccino, they're drinking champagne from fluted glasses. Strawberries are scattered all over the tables, the chairs, the floor, everywhere. And the women are laughing...at me.

Adam steps into the café, and I run to him, pleading with him to get me out of there. He leans down to kiss me, telling me everything will be fine. But as our lips move together, I suddenly feel the air being sucked out of my lungs. Gasping, I open my eyes. And I'm not kissing Adam. I'm kissing Chelsea. And she's pale, cold, and dead.

Monday morning was cold and dreary, a light drizzle ushering in November. Jeans, layers of long-sleeved tees, a beige wool sweater, and my trusty hiking boots, and I was ready to face the day. Ready to go to Billy's—hopefully for the last time—and get the picture from Jimmy. My heart raced with the anticipation of finally discovering who was in the Polaroid with Chelsea.

Nervous, but resolute, I locked up the cottage and headed down to the dock, scanning the area to see who was around. The café nightmare had made me especially uneasy at the prospect of having to deal with Jennifer or, God forbid, J.T. this early in the morning. But to my relief, J.T. and Jennifer were not around.

Instead it was Brody who waited for me to board the ferry. Always a gentleman, he smiled and helped my aboard, and then we were off. I was uncharacteristically chatty, surely due to nervousness, but Brody seemed preoccupied and tired, yawning almost incessantly. I got the hint, so I buried my head in a magazine I'd brought along to pass the time.

Once we reached the mainland, I quickly surveyed things. No sign of J.T., no Jennifer. Excellent. I hurriedly got the BMW out of the garage and raced toward Harbourtown. This excursion needed to be quick and anonymous, and so far, so good.

Paranoid that Adam had somehow discovered what I was up to, I kept a check on the traffic behind me, periodically glancing up to the rearview mirror. But there was no Max trailing me. In fact, I had the road mostly to myself, unlike the last time I'd traveled this route. Or the first time. With such light traffic, I reached Billy's in no time at all. I parked along the side of the building, got out, and locked my car doors. It was always lonely down here, but today seemed exceptionally desolate, with no other cars or people in sight in the area around the bar. I guessed Halloween had been quite the party night down here by the docks, and now the revelers were all home recovering.

I hustled to the entrance. As I shouldered the door open and stepped inside, an unexpected chill ran down my spine. Breathing in the smell of stale beer and sweat I'd come to associate with Billy's, I detected an unusual, underlying scent. Something so pungent I skidded to a stop just as the door slammed shut behind me. What I smelled was the scent of fear and... something else, something metallic.

I glanced around, my eyes adjusting to the dim interior. The string of Halloween lights Jimmy had strung up behind the bar was on, giving everything an eerie orange and purple cast. But otherwise everything looked normal. Well, as normal as Billy's could look. A half-empty mug of beer rested on the bar, but not a soul was in sight. It was quiet, too quiet. Jimmy always played music, but today the only sound was a steady drip of water coming from somewhere in the back room.

"Jimmy," I called out, taking a tentative step forward. "Is anybody here?"

My hollow voice echoed, and I sensed there was something terribly wrong. My heart raced, but I continued to take small, shuffling steps, forcing myself to keep walking toward the bar. Closer, closer, but then I slipped, quickly grabbing hold of a bar stool to steady myself.

I glanced down to the dusty, wooden floor. A piece of white paper or something was stuck to the heel of my hiking boot. Reaching down, I peeled it away. It wasn't a piece of paper after all. It was an envelope. A shaky, childlike "M," printed on the front in black marker, the only marking on it. A lump rose in my throat, because I knew in my heart that the "M" was for Maddy, and Jimmy had been the one who'd written it.

This was it—the picture! I turned the envelope over and lifted the flap, all the while my hands trembling. But the envelope was empty. There was no photo, nothing.

Had Jimmy dropped the envelope before having a chance to put the photo in it? No, that wasn't right. Panic set in. Why was the envelope even on the floor? Had someone removed the photo and dropped the envelope? That was looking like the most likely scenario. But if so, who?

"Jimmy?" I called out once more.

Nothing.

Dizziness overtook me, so I closed my eyes. *Count to ten... breathe slowly.* I slid my hands from one bar stool to the next, letting them be my guide to the end of the bar. When I reached the final stool, I opened my eyes. Coming here was a mistake, a terrible mistake. I felt it with every fiber of my being. And when I leaned around the edge to look behind the bar, my fears were confirmed.

Lying on the floor, in a widening pool of blood, was Jimmy—a single bullet hole marring the pale skin of his forehead.

Chapter 23

The shock of it all knocked the wind out of me, I truly couldn't breathe. I dropped to my knees, my heart hammering in my chest. My gaze swept over Jimmy's still form. Nobody could lose this much blood and be alive. My mind refused to accept it though. I placed a shaky hand along the cool skin of his neck, feeling for a pulse. *Please, even a weak one*, I prayed.

But nothing, nothing. Jimmy was dead.

I yanked my hand back and watched helplessly as the pool of blood beneath his head slowly widened. Sickened, I scooted away and fumbled in my bag for my cell. Once in my shaky grasp—with Jimmy's blood on my hands, literally and figuratively—I dialed 911. And then I dropped the phone back into my bag and waited.

So much blood, there was *so* much blood. In my left hand, I was still clenching the envelope I'd stepped on. Loosening my grip, I glanced down. The "M" on the front, now smudged with Jimmy's spilled blood, taunted me. Though the envelope was empty, I was sure it had once contained the photograph I'd come to pick up. But now that picture was gone. And Jimmy was dead.

Was he dead because he'd been trying to help me with the case? God, I prayed not, but my instincts told me that was the case. I felt numb. Someone had taken a drastic step to ensure the picture remained hidden. Who would murder someone over a picture? *The person responsible for Chelsea's disappearance,* my mind whispered.

Yeah, that—or someone close to the individual responsible. The fact that a person would go to these lengths strengthened my conviction that the picture somehow held the key to Chelsea's disappearance. That blonde mystery woman knew something.

I knew it was wrong, but I couldn't help but hope Jimmy had remembered to make a copy of the photo and mailed it to me. Because now it was my only chance of ever finding out who was in that picture with Chelsea Hannigan.

The wailing of the sirens grew closer and closer, until the cacophony was joined by the flashing of red and blue lights as they pulsed through the single glass block window cut into the front of Billy's. Several officers of the Harbourtown police department burst through the front door, but I was unable to move. So I stayed where I was—kneeling on the dusty, wooden floor, next to a kid lying dead in his own blood. My left hand twitched, and I realized I was still holding onto the potentially incriminating envelope. Only it wasn't just an envelope, it was Jimmy's death warrant. And it had been signed, so to speak, with my initial. It had to go. I scanned the area for a place to dispose of it.

The police were approaching, and I panicked. Fearing that I'd be implicated in Jimmy's murder, I crumpled the envelope—inadvertently smearing more blood along the front and back—and quickly tossed it into a trash container tucked beneath the bar.

When I glanced back up, a young officer was before me, offering his hand. I searched his face to see if he had seen what I'd done, but there was nothing to indicate he'd caught me throwing the envelope into the trash can. In fact, he graciously helped me to my feet and then told me his name, asked if I was OK.

Did I look like I was OK? The name went in one ear and out the other, but I did have the wherewithal to nod that I was—at least physically—unharmed. He led me away from Jimmy's lifeless body to a table in the back room. He wanted me out of the way, but in a place so small, I still had a pretty good view of the Harbourtown PD as they moved around the body like bees around a hive, processing the crime scene.

I sank into a wood chair at the table, and the young officer told me to remain where I was. He said a detective would be over to speak with me shortly. I nodded absently, but I don't think he even took notice. He was too busy staring at my bloody hands. He pulled several napkins from a metal dispenser atop the table, handed them to me with a shake of his head, and then left me alone.

The blood on my hands—so sticky, still wet—made my stomach roil. Disgusted, I scrubbed at the gloppy, red mess as best as I could. I wanted it off, off, off. But even as my hands grew sore from the intense rubbing I employed, they still retained a faint pink tint. I choked down the lump rising in my throat and tossed the soiled napkins into a pile on the edge of the table. I surveyed the rest of my body. Besides a long, diagonal streak of blood smeared across the front of my beige sweater—I must have wiped my hand without realizing it—there was no more evidence of Jimmy's demise marking me.

Now that I was as cleaned up as I was going to be until I could take a shower, I resumed watching the flurry of activity surrounding Jimmy's body. More importantly I listened carefully to what was being said...

Jimmy Kingston—,whose last name I'd never taken the time to learn—was pronounced dead at 12:48 p.m., though the coroner who had arrived on the scene a few minutes before, and was now barking this information out, estimated the actual time of death to have occurred roughly an hour prior.

That meant I had just missed the killer. A chill ran down my spine at the thought.

Cause of death: a single bullet wound to the head. Ballistics: Jimmy was shot with a .38 caliber weapon, at close range.

The gun I'd come across in Adam's desk drawer flashed through my mind, but I quickly dismissed it. After all, lots of people owned that particular type of firearm.

No sign of a struggle.

Jimmy had either known the individual who'd shot him, or he hadn't seen the individual as a threat. Someone pretending to be a customer, most likely. Or had it been someone he recognized?

An officer with a portable fingerprinting kit was lifting prints from the half-full glass of beer still perched on the bar. He was telling another officer that the only prints found, so far, belonged to the victim—Jimmy.

Maybe the killer had worn gloves? Or maybe Jimmy had poured the beer for himself?

Another officer chimed in that the surveillance video that would have captured the perp's entrance and exit from the bar was missing. It was becoming apparent that the person responsible for Jimmy's death had been smart and thorough.

No money was missing. So a robbery-gone-wrong was ruled out. It was clear from the snippets of conversation I picked up that the police were coming to the conclusion that Jimmy had been the intended target. Something I already knew.

And I was damned sure I knew the reason why, but I couldn't exactly tell the police. Hell, I'd been snooping around in an unsolved mystery, illegally obtaining case files from my dad, and paying cash for potential evidence in the cold case. Yeah, probably best to keep quiet.

I looked away, and when I turned back, a handsome, rugged-looking man with tousled brown hair was making his way toward me. A second later he was at the table. "I'm Detective Mitchell, homicide division," he said, introducing himself with a somber nod. "I'd like to ask you a few questions, if you feel up to it."

Saying I didn't feel up to it wasn't really an option, I knew this. Detective Mitchell was just being nice. He was going to make sure he got his answers, and he was going to do it before I had a chance to think too much about my responses. So I nodded and exhaled slowly. "Sure, that'll be fine."

The detective sat down and took out a small, tattered, spiral-bound notepad and a pen. The questioning then began.

"What's your full name? Miss…?" he asked.

"Fitch," I replied. "Madeleine Fitch."

He paused, looking up from where he jotted down my name in the tattered notebook, and met my eyes. "You related to Mayor Fitch over in Harbour Falls?"

"Yes." I choked on the word, wincing. "I'm his daughter." My dad was going to be hurt and disappointed that I'd hardly stayed "out of trouble."

"Mayor Fitch is a good man," Detective Mitchell declared, his light brown eyes softening. "So where do you live? Harbour Falls?"

I shook my head. "No, I live on Fade Island."

The detective's face grew troubled. "That your permanent residence?" He sounded doubtful.

"No," I answered, "my permanent home is in Los Angeles."

He scribbled something down in his notebook. "Occupation?" he continued without looking up.

"I'm a writer."

Detective Mitchell lifted his gaze, eyeing me with a sudden sense of recognition. He then asked quietly, "*Mystery* novels, right?"

I just nodded, noticing he didn't write anything down about that. He just continued to watch me, tapping his pen a couple of times on the table. *Tap, tap, tap.* I shifted in my seat nervously.

"Fade Island is a rather, uh, mysterious place in its own right." He paused, one sharper tap. "Isn't it, Miss Fitch?"

"I guess," I replied, hoping my voice didn't sound as shaky to him as it did to me.

Detective Mitchell's eyes didn't waver. "And what brought you to an establishment like Billy's today?"

"Ummm..." I faltered and then offered timidly, "A drink."

Detective Mitchell leaned back in his chair. "Were you acquainted with the victim, Jimmy Kingston?"

I glanced down at my blood-tinged hands, a fresh wave of guilt washing over me. "Only from being in here twice before," I said, my voice soft, unconvincing.

Two more taps of the pen from the good detective. "And why were you here those other times, Miss Fitch?" He hesitated and then added dryly, "For a drink, no doubt?"

"Yes," I lied.

A stretch of uncomfortable silence filled the air between us. "Tell me, Madeleine... May I call you Madeleine?" I nodded, and he continued, "Billy's is a little off the beaten path and really quite a hike from Fade Island. Do you always travel so far from home for a drink?"

I bristled, knowing Detective Mitchell was trying to trap me up. He surely suspected there was more to my visit, and he was right. But it wasn't like I could tell him the truth.

Mustering all the indignation I could—because really I needed to in order to sound convincing—I retorted, "Yes, Detective, I do when I'm meeting a friend for lunch here in Harbourtown."

I hated to drag Helena into my mess, but I couldn't see any way around it with this turn in the questioning.

Detective Mitchell snapped, "Does this friend have a name?"

"Helena Jackson."

A flicker of something—recognition, a memory?—crossed his face. Detective Mitchell was no rookie, and I suspected he'd seen all the evidence related to the Harbour Falls Mystery. Hell, he'd probably worked it.

"And you were meeting this Helena Jackson for lunch today?"

"Yes."

"When and where?" he asked curtly, his pen poised over his notebook.

I pulled nervously at the sleeves of my sweater. I hated the thought of Helena finding out I was not here in Harbourtown to pick something up for Adam. I hated that I'd lied to her, and I felt even worse for breaking my promise to Adam. In fact, I didn't care to even imagine his reaction when he found out what had happened. He'd repeatedly warned me to stay away from Billy's. If only I had listened.

Detective Mitchell was still waiting, so I said, "We were supposed to meet at two o'clock at Peppio's."

He raised his arm, glanced at his watch. When he lowered his wrist, I caught the time—1:40. Mitchell called over the young officer who'd helped me to the table earlier and gave him instructions to go to the restaurant to see if there really was a Helena Jackson waiting there for me.

The detective asked a few more questions and then, with a flip of his tattered notebook, informed me he'd like for me to accompany him to the station to enter a more *official* statement. Official statement, the police station, I knew those things didn't bode well for me. I needed an attorney and probably a very competent one at that. I asked Detective Mitchell if he was arresting me. He said no.

After he tucked his notebook and pen back into his pocket, he stood up and told me to meet him outside in five minutes. I was to leave my car here; he'd drive me to the station. OK, I wasn't being arrested, but there was no question the detective was making damn sure I'd be entering that formal statement today.

When he left, I pulled out my cell phone. I was much too humiliated to call my dad, so I pulled up Adam's number instead. My finger hovered over the keys. Was I really going to ask for Adam's help? Did I have a choice?

Taking a deep breath, I pressed *send*.

Several hours later I found myself, once more, seated across from Detective Mitchell. Only this time we sat in metal chairs, a rectangular table made of wood between us. We were at the Harbourtown police station in one of the bland interrogation rooms. Scuffed, eggshell-colored walls surrounded us, and a darkened mirror—two-way glass, no doubt—reflected my troubled visage back to me.

I looked down, scanning the items on the table. A recording device, a small microphone canted in a stand, a bunch of loose papers, and Detective Mitchell's tattered notebook, his pen clipped to the front cover.

The detective had softened somewhat on the way to the station. Apparently he and his partner, Detective Crowley, had known my dad for several years. Though they were not friends per se, he told me he liked and respected my father. No surprise, since most people did, but it didn't make me feel any better. In fact, I only felt worse. I'd disappointed my dad, and he didn't even know it yet. But once we arrived at the station, I knew that would soon change.

As Detective Mitchell had led me to the interrogation room, the inquisitive stares of the men and women in blue had fixed on me, recognition in the eyes of more than a few. Yeah, it was only a matter of time before someone picked up the phone and told Mayor Fitch his daughter was about to be officially questioned in the murder—yes, the murder—of Jimmy Kingston.

Sitting here now in interrogation room number two and imagining those conversations, my face heated. I glanced up at the big institutional clock on the wall—almost five o'clock. We'd been waiting roughly three hours since I'd been in touch with Adam, but he still wasn't here. I guessed finding a defense attorney on such short notice took time.

When I'd talked with Adam, he'd been surprisingly calm. Having just arrived back on the island, he took it in stride when he learned of my predicament. My broken promise, my lies, my new status as a suspect in Jimmy's murder, yeah, all that. I suspected Adam was probably just saving his wrath for when he saw me.

In any case he'd calmly informed me he'd contact a defense attorney he knew in Harbour Falls—a man named Elliott Hoffman. I'd heard of him from the newspapers and he was definitely the kind of attorney I was going to need. One who could get a person out of a jam. Adam's plan was to come over to the mainland, have Hoffman pick him up at Cove Beach, and then head over to the Harbourtown police station. I glanced back up at the clock, but only two minutes had passed.

"More coffee?" Detective Mitchell asked, nodding to the almost-empty paper cup clutched in my hands.

"No, thanks," I replied.

Mitchell grunted and resumed shuffling papers atop the table, and I choked down the last of my cold coffee.

Just then the door to the interrogation room opened. I breathed a sigh of relief when Adam stepped in, a short, balding man with unassuming features—the defense attorney, I presumed—trailing behind. I felt confident this Elliott Hoffman was more than capable, but when his sharp, unwavering lawyer eyes scanned the room like a hawk, I knew he was the perfect attorney for this situation.

Introductions were made, and I shook his hand. "Don't worry, Ms. Fitch," he said to me. "We'll get you out of here in no time."

He shot Detective Mitchell a look that said he meant business. I felt instantly relieved. I needed the best, and Adam had obviously brought me—and bought me—the very best. I felt confident this attorney would sooner have the Harbourtown police for dinner than allow them to detain me past the time it took to take my statement. Let alone if they tried to arrest me.

Confirming my impressions, his eyes on Mitchell, Hoffman said tightly, "Let's get this over with, Detective. I believe you've wasted enough of my client's time today."

"We'll see about that, Mr. Hoffman," Mitchell replied, handing him back the business card Elliott Hoffman had thrust into his hand during the introductions.

Adam cleared his throat. "Excuse me, gentlemen, but before you begin, I'd like a moment alone with Ms. Fitch."

I knew Detective Mitchell could deny his request, but he didn't. I couldn't say I was all that surprised, as Adam always seemed to get his way. The detective and the attorney left, closing the door behind them, and Adam came over to stand next to where I was seated.

I'd been careful to avoid meeting Adam's gaze up to this point. I had to admit I was ashamed that I'd brought this on myself, by not heeding his warnings to stay away from Billy's.

Adam coughed to get my attention, and I tentatively looked up. His pained blue eyes were locked on my bloodstained sweater. He reached out and traced the streak that had dried to a brick color, and then he swept me out of the chair and into his arms. "God, Maddy, are you all right?" His words were muffled as he held on tight with his head lowered, speaking into my shoulder.

I nodded meekly, tears filling my eyes at last. I hadn't cried once, until now.

"I'm so sorry, Adam. I should have listened," I choked, my tears moistening the smooth, light blue fabric of his button-down.

"Shhh," he soothed, lifting his head. "I'm just thankful you're fine. Let's just get this unpleasantness over with and get you back home. Sound good?"

I nodded, words eluding me. Adam's kindness was making me feel guiltier than ever for breaking my promise. I sobbed, fisting the back of his shirt in my hand as he tightened his hold. There was so much more I needed to say, and I wanted to stay wrapped up in his warmth forever, but a sharp knock on the door ended our embrace as well as any further time to talk.

Adam took a step back, hands on my shoulders. "Remember, don't answer *anything* Elliott advises you not to." His tone was gravely serious. "Understood?"

I bit my lower lip and nodded. "Yes."

Elliott Hoffman and Detective Mitchell stepped back into the room, and Adam trailed a finger down my cheek, wiping away the last of my tears.

As I sat back down, I overheard Mitchell telling Adam there was a waiting room down the hall where he could wait until we were finished with the interrogation. After Adam left, Hoffman sat down next to me, and the detective returned to his seat on the other side of the table.

The formal questioning was much like it had been at the bar—just variations of the same questions—but with the same gist. Hoffman took copious notes, nodding after each of Mitchell's questions, thus indicating it was permissible for me to answer each one. I sensed Detective Mitchell suspected there was more to my visit to Billy's, but he didn't press. Not with my new attorney present. But I was sure he'd do some digging, and when armed with more information, he'd confront me, attorney or not.

Just as Mitchell was wrapping up, the interrogation room door burst open. Another detective I recognized from earlier at the bar entered the room, and Mitchell rose to greet him. As they stood speaking in voices too low for me to hear, I tried to assess this new development.

Hoffman appeared to be unaffected, glancing up with a bored expression and then returning to his notes. But the detective having a heated discussion with Mitchell was definitely unhappy about something. This new detective was a tall man with gray-streaked dark hair. I estimated his age to be about mid-forties. And as his cold, dark eyes flashed to me, I started to get the feeling this man's displeasure had something to do with me.

Hoffman suddenly cleared his throat, startling me and interrupting the detectives. "Pardon me, but if we are finished here, I'm sure my client would like to get home after her very trying day."

Mitchell held up his hand. "Not quite yet, Counsel, we're going to need a few more minutes. My partner here, Detective Crowley, has a few more questions for Miss Fitch."

"Five minutes," Hoffman snapped, his tone firm. "My client has already proven to be more than cooperative."

Detective Mitchell appeared apologetic but not Detective Crowley. No, not at all.

Instead he approached the table, glowering at me. "Ms. Fitch," he began, pacing the floor with his fingers steepled in front of him. "Is it true your official statement is that you and the victim, James Kingston, had no more of an involved relationship than that of customer and bartender?"

Hoffman nodded to me, so I answered, "Yes, that's correct."

Crowley stopped and turned to face me. "If that is indeed the case, then tell us please, Ms. Fitch, why did the victim call *your* cell phone yesterday afternoon?"

Oh no! I looked to Hoffman, unsure of how to respond. He shook his head and answered for me, "My client has no comment."

Detective Mitchell—who had been relegated to a corner of the room—caught my eye. Disappointment was written all over his face. *Yeah, Mayor Fitch's daughter had lied to the police. Sorry.*

Detective Crowley addressed my attorney, smugness in his

tone. "Clearly, the record speaks for itself, Mr. Hoffman."

"There's no proof the cell phone you are referring to was even in my client's possession yesterday," Hoffman countered smoothly.

Oooh, he is good, I thought.

Crowley smirked at my attorney and said slowly, "There's also no proof that it wasn't in her possession." The detective paused momentarily and then redirected all of his anger back on me. "Ms. Fitch, are you familiar with terms like 'obstruction of justice' and 'tampering with evidence'?"

Hoffman stiffened but nodded for me to proceed. "Yes." My voice was no more than a whisper.

And then, to my absolute horror, Detective Crowley produced the crumpled, white envelope—tainted with Jimmy's blood—and threw it on the table. It was now sealed in a plastic "evidence" bag, but the printed "M" on the front was facing up, mocking my sad attempt at deception. I kept my eyes glued to the envelope, afraid to meet any of the questioning eyes I felt upon me.

"Would you care to explain why this"—Crowley tapped the incriminating evidence—"was found in a trash bin under the bar at Billy's?" When I didn't answer, he put his hands on the table and leaned toward me. "Your prints, Ms. Fitch, are all over it!" he hissed.

"I didn't kill Jimmy," I suddenly cried out, standing.

I felt Hoffman's hand on my shaking arm, silencing me, urging me to sit back down. "My client is invoking her fifth amendment rights," he said sharply, with a light squeeze to my arm to remind me to keep quiet.

Crowley laughed darkly. "Fine, but let me tell you this…" I glanced up, and his eyes locked with mine. "If Bill Fitch wasn't your father and a man I respect, I'd arrest you right now."

Detective Mitchell moved in to calm his colleague, while Hoffman interjected, voice raised, "You're out of line, Detective. I will not allow you to speak to my client in that manner. You have nothing here but circumstantial evidence at best."

"Bullshit!" Detective Crowley fumed, shucking Mitchell's

hand off his arm. "We have a body and a suspect who is lying. I can name you hundreds of cases where the defendant was convicted on far less!"

Mitchell grabbed Crowley again and this time pulled him back, all the while apologizing for his colleague's outburst. Hoffman's only response was to remind both detectives that the five minutes had elapsed, and that we were done here.

Detective Mitchell refused to meet my gaze as my attorney steered me to the door. But Detective Crowley threw me a parting glance that promised he'd not let this slide.

Hoffman led me gently out into the hallway, and I thanked him for everything. He offered to walk me down the hall to the room where Adam was waiting. On the way he assured me there was no need to worry. The evidence was weak. "Circumstantial evidence doesn't hold much weight with a jury, Ms. Fitch, despite Detective Crowley's claims to the contrary," he said.

I didn't really know what to say in return. God, I sure as hell didn't want things to get to the point of being arrested, let alone be faced with a trial.

As we walked Elliot Hoffman asked for clarification on a couple of the answers I'd given, but he never once asked me if I was innocent. I didn't think he really cared. He'd been hired to be my advocate, and he was going to do his job. And, no doubt, he'd do it well.

When we reached the waiting room, I stopped abruptly. I was done thinking about the events of the day. All I wanted to do was fall into Adam's arms. It was there that I felt safe and protected.

Unfortunately, when we stepped into the room, I realized my plans would have to be put on hold. Adam was not alone. There was somebody else in the room with him, waiting for me and looking less than pleased. It appeared my earlier fears had been confirmed. Someone had contacted my father, and now he was here.

Well this is going to be…awkward, I thought, sighing.

Chapter 24

My dad stood across from Adam, the full distance of the tiny waiting room, a gulf neither appeared willing to cross. Instead both acted as if the other wasn't there. Adam stood leaning casually against the wall closest to the door, raven locks falling across his forehead as he scanned a Wall Street Journal. The mayor was standing as far away from Adam as was humanly possible on the opposite side of the room. His arms were crossed, his posture stiff, and his eyes everywhere but on the man he'd asked me to stay away from.

My dad caught sight of me and hurried over, ignoring both Elliott Hoffman to my right, and Adam, who lowered the paper and met my apologetic gaze. Wrapping me in a hug, he said, "My God, Madeleine, what the hell is going on?"

"Mayor Fitch," Adam interjected, straightening.

I suspected this was the first either had spoken to the other in this small, enclosed space.

My dad spun to face him. "You!" he said through clenched teeth. "There's nothing you have to say that I care to hear."

Adam took a restrained step back, and my father moved toward him. "I knew my daughter would end up in some kind of trouble hanging around with the likes of you. I warned her to stay away."

"Dad, stop!" I pleaded, taking note of Adam's terse expression. "Dad, Adam is helping me, OK?"

"Yeah, I bet he is," the mayor said with a derisive scoff, sweat beading on his brow.

After the day I'd had, this was just too much to take. I didn't want the two most important men in my life at each other's throats like this. The only way to diffuse the situation was to speak with my dad alone. Hoffman had already made himself scarce, having retreated back out to the hallway. When I glanced over my shoulder, I saw he was busy with his Blackberry, paying absolutely no heed to the unfolding drama. *Geez, that man is cool as a cucumber.*

When I turned back, both Adam and my dad were watching me. I supposed they were waiting to see what my next move would be. And it was this: I asked Adam for a few moments alone with my dad. He nodded, shot a parting look of aggravation to my father, and then joined Hoffman in the hall. When the door clicked shut, I turned to face my irate dad. His eyes held all the disappointment I'd expected to see. Maybe more. He'd obviously been briefed, and I was sure no detail had been spared.

"Dad," I whispered, dropping my eyes to the floor in shame.

My father cleared his throat and said softly, "Madeleine, what kind of mess have you gotten yourself into? This whole thing is just some kind of a misunderstanding, right?"

"Of course," I reassured him. "But I can't explain everything just yet."

My dad's brow creased. "I hope you're not withholding information from the detectives." He sounded bewildered, an emotion he rarely expressed. "I've known those guys for years. They'll do right by you, sweetheart, but you have to level with them. Tell them everything. They don't believe you really hurt that boy."

I wasn't so sure about that, especially when it came to Detective Crowley. I must have looked skeptical, because my dad reiterated, "You can't keep secrets, Madeleine. These men can help you only if you're honest with them."

"I will tell them, uh, everything," I said without conviction, and then added in a whisper, "Later."

My dad obviously didn't hear my last word, because he launched into his next order of business. "How does Adam Ward fit into all of this?"

I started off by explaining that I was actually in a relationship with Adam—a relationship that was getting serious. But, as expected, this hardly comforted my father.

"Maddy, you promised me you'd stay away from that guy. And now you're telling me you're involved with the man? Unbelievable." He shook his head disapprovingly.

"Dad, yes," I hesitated and then just laid it on the line. "I'm in love with Adam. And he loves me. I'm sorry if that hurts you, but it's the truth."

"But, honey, he may be a murder—"

I held my hand up, stopping him in mid-sentence. "Don't say it. Please. I can't hear it from you." I begged with my eyes. "He's not who you think he is."

My father looked doubtful but held his tongue, so I continued, "Look at what's happening to me right now. You see how easy it is for someone to become a suspect for something they had nothing to do with..." I trailed off, and then the tears began to fall.

My father pulled me into a hug. "I love you, Maddy." He patted my back. "I'm just worried."

"I know," I mumbled. "I love you, too, but you're going to have to trust me on this one."

The mayor and I ended up reaching a truce. As long as I didn't ask for his outright blessing, he'd refrain from voicing his objections to my burgeoning relationship, particularly in the presence of Adam.

Speaking of Adam, I was anxious to reunite. But when we opened the door and stepped into the hallway, neither he nor my attorney were there. I told my dad I'd check for them in the front lobby, but the mayor said he had something he needed to do elsewhere in the station—speak with Detectives Mitchell and Crowley. Presumably to find out exactly where they stood on the question of my guilt, and I was sure he wanted to see what he could do to assuage their suspicions.

After we said our farewells, my dad walked down the corridor to the detectives' offices. And I went to the front lobby, where I found Adam—a weary-looking but still insanely gorgeous Adam.

"How'd it go with your father?" he asked, as I went to him and leaned my forehead against his chest. He wrapped his arms around me, making me feel infinitely better.

"It went as well as could be expected," I answered. "Just don't expect the mayor to be giving you the key to the city or anything,"—Adam chuckled—"but I think he's willing to give you a chance."

I hope he gives you a chance, I thought, but left unsaid.

Stepping back I noticed Hoffman was nowhere to be seen. I cast a curious glance to Adam, and he explained that my attorney had gone back over to Harbour Falls. I was certain we'd be discussing more tomorrow, but it felt good to be done for now. It had been a long, trying day, and I was sick of talking about the events that had transpired. I just wanted to go home.

Adam and I stepped out into the cold, biting air. The promise of winter resonated as we made our way to the parking lot.

Adam was kind of quiet, so I asked, "Aren't you wondering what went down in the interrogation room? I kind of figured you'd be expecting a blow-by-blow account."

Adam gave me a tight smile. "Elliot already filled me in."

"Oh," I replied. "Um, does that mean he told you, uh, everything?"

I felt a little conflicted. I mean, yeah, I realized Adam was paying the man, but Elliot Hoffman was still *my* attorney. What about attorney-client confidentiality and all that?

Adam must have guessed my thoughts, because he exhaled loudly and said, "Maddy, if you want to stay out of jail, it's imperative I stay abreast of all the developments." I sensed a flash of annoyance as he finished speaking, but he put his arm around me nonetheless and kissed the top of my head. Maybe I was just imagining things.

When we reached the first row of cars in the parking lot, I halted, suddenly realizing we had no transportation. "Wait," I said. "How are we supposed to get home?"

Adam had said Hoffman picked him up at Cove Beach and drove them both to the police station here in Harbourtown. Or so I assumed. In any case Hoffman was gone, leaving us with no options. Then again I knew Adam had cars at his disposal here on this side of the water too. So who knew?

"You drove here with Hoffman, right?" I asked, looking for clarification as we resumed walking.

Adam shot me a sheepish grin. "Uh, not exactly."

I frowned, and he amended, "Well, I was with Hoffman most of the way. He did pick me up at Cove Beach."

I was so busy looking at Adam—trying to figure out what he was intimating—that I hadn't noticed we'd stopped at a burgundy car—a burgundy BMW. *My* burgundy BMW. What the hell? Detective Mitchell had driven me to the station; I'd left my car at Billy's. How could it be parked here?

I turned to face Adam and asked that exact question, my tone wary. "How'd my car get here, Adam?"

"I had Elliot stop at Billy's so I could pick it up for you. I didn't think you'd want to go anywhere near that place after what happened there." I cringed at the fresh memory and nodded in agreement. "So we stopped there, got your car, and then I followed Elliott the rest of the way here."

"But…the keys," I asked, feeling for and finding the clear outline of the key fob in my bag. "How'd you get it started?"

I was stumped. Surely hot-wiring foreign imports was not among Adam's many talents. Although I doubted much would shock me at this point.

"Yeah." Adam raked his fingers through his hair. "About that…"

"Adam," I warned.

"I had a spare key made for your car," he confessed with no hint of apology.

God, this man continued to drive me mad, but I was too exhausted to get into it with him. I let it slide, even though it had been a very intrusive thing to do. Whatever, though. I had bigger things to worry about.

Adam produced the said spare key—complete with key fob—and unlocked the doors. Rolling my eyes, I got in on the passenger side and sank down into the seat. I leaned my head back and closed my eyes, listening as Adam slid into the driver's seat, a rustle of fabric against leather. And then the key turned in the ignition, the engine coming to life.

Adam's warm hand descended to my own chilled ones that I held clasped together in my lap. "Everything is going to be fine," he reassured me in a soft voice. "The police have nothing. It's all circumstantial bullshit."

With my eyes still closed, my breathing hitched as I said, "Adam, nothing is fine. Someone ended up dead today, because of me."

Adam was quiet, so I opened my eyes and shifted in my seat so I could meet his gaze, unreadable in the limited illumination of the instrument panel.

Honesty, I had to be honest. Hoffman may have filled him in on the details of the interrogation, but there were still things Adam didn't know. I needed to remedy that.

I cleared my throat. "Jimmy called me yesterday while you were out of town. I spoke with him for a few minutes."

Adam's expression twisted into something I couldn't discern. "Is that why you went back to Billy's?" he asked sharply. "Is that why you broke your promise, Madeleine?"

I winced because I knew this was the elephant in the room. Or in the car, as it were. I'd broken my promise. But look at what had happened. I'd certainly paid a high price.

Even so, Adam was obviously irritated, so I tried to explain, "When he called, he said he'd found it—Jimmy had finally found the picture. I only wanted to see who was in it." My voice turned bitter. "But it doesn't matter, not now. You were right. I should have left it alone and stayed away. Jimmy would still be alive today."

Suddenly consumed with guilt, I looked away. Adam nudged my cheek, and I turned back to him. His anger seemed to have dissipated. "Maddy, that bar is a dangerous place. That's why I wanted you to stay away. I may not be happy you broke your promise, but you sure as hell aren't responsible for that guy's death."—Adam's tone was now so full of understanding, I actually felt worse—"He was probably shot by a disgruntled customer, or some—"

"Stop," I pleaded, choking up. "There's more, Adam. More you don't know."

I squeezed his hand and quietly told him the other details he'd yet to hear. I explained how I'd found the empty envelope with the "M" on the front. With my face burning with shame, I admitted how I'd thrown it away in a panic, fearful I'd be linked to Jimmy's murder. How ironic that action had turned out to be. I continued, expressing my concern that once the police delved further into the phone records, they'd find my other correspondences with Jimmy. Like the conversation I'd had with him regarding J.T.'s recent visit to the bar.

I suddenly froze. "Oh my God," I exclaimed. "Do you think J.T. shot Jimmy? I mean, he did tell him to 'watch his back.'"

Adam seemed to consider it but shook his head. "No, I don't think so."

I, however, was not so convinced. "Well, did anyone see him around today?" I was thinking back to earlier in the day when I'd not seen him on the ferry or at Cove Beach.

"I don't know, Maddy. I was in Boston all morning, remember?"

Oh right. Adam continued as he put the car in gear. "Speaking of which, we'd better get started back. It's been a long, crazy day."

That was an understatement.

When we arrived at Cove Beach, we stowed my car in its assigned garage. But once we reached the dock, we bypassed the ferry. Instead Adam led me to a waiting speedboat.

"Oh," I said, surprised. I knew Adam had his own private boats, but I'd so rarely seen him utilize them.

"With everything going on earlier, I didn't have time to wait for a ferry," he explained. "This is a lot faster anyway. You'll see."

And it was. We reached Fade Island in no time at all, docking at the northern end of the island, where Adam's other boats were apparently kept.

Adam drove me down to the cottage, but I could barely keep my eyes open. I leaned my head on his shoulder, feeling a newfound kinship with this man I loved. Now I truly knew what it must have been like—these past four years or so—for Adam. With the purr of the Porsche engine lulling me to sleep, my last conscious thought was that *this* is what it felt like to be suspected of a crime you didn't commit.

Late the next morning, I woke up—alone—in my own bed. But I was all tucked in, even had on the pajamas with the little cartoon dogs and cats. Someone had obviously gotten me out of my bloodstained clothes and into my pajamas. I plucked at my flannel sleeve, smiling. Adam evidently had accomplished the task, all without stirring me from my slumber. Amazing. I really had been exhausted. Not that I felt much better now. But it was a new day, and I couldn't give up. I took a long shower, dressed, and made my way downstairs. With a strong cup of coffee in hand, I headed into the living room. Just as I sat down, my cell buzzed.

To my surprise the screen display indicated it was Ami. I'd not heard from her in weeks, and I still needed an explanation for her sending Julian to Fade Island, so I answered. "Maddy," she began. "I'm glad you picked up. I really need to talk to you. It's important."

"Yeah," I replied, "I'd like to talk to you too." I paused and then let her have it. "Why in the hell did you tell Julian I was in some kind of danger? What were you thinking? Do you know he flew all the way up here to Maine just to see if I was OK? All because of what you said. Hell, Ami, why were you even in California?"

Despite my tirade Ami remained unruffled. "It's a long story," she said impassively.

"Well, I'd like to hear it," I retorted. "I mean, Ami, why would you tell my agent—tell *Julian*, for God's sake—that I was in danger?"

"You *are* in danger!" she exclaimed. "Look at what happened yesterday to that kid in Harbourtown."

OK, so Ami had heard about Jimmy. In such a small community, the news was probably all over the place by now.

Ami was still rambling, "I mean, what if it had been you, Maddy? What if you were the intended target?"

Now she had my attention. "Do you know something?"—silence—"If you know anything at all, Ami, you have to go to the police. Do you realize they think I killed Jimmy?"

Ami remained quiet but then said in a soft voice, "Actually I may be able to help you. But it's too dangerous to talk over the phone. We should meet in person."

"Fine, when?"

"I can make it over to the island in an hour. Meet me at the dock at one o'clock."

After I agreed, we ended the call. I didn't have much time. I wanted to tell Adam what was going on, so I tried his cell. But it went straight to voicemail. I thought about leaving a message, but there was too much to tell, so I just disconnected.

How could Ami possibly help? What did she know? These were the thoughts that occupied my mind as I finished my coffee, rinsed out the cup, grabbed my jacket. *Shit!* I suddenly remembered my Lexus was down at the dock. Since we'd taken Adam's speedboat and docked on the northern end of the island, I hadn't even considered my car. But when I opened the front door, resigned that I'd have to walk all the way down to the dock, I got quite the surprise. The Lexus was in the driveway. Adam must have had Nate or Max return it to the cottage sometime within the past twenty-four hours. In any case I was just thankful it was there, so I hurried out, hopped into the car, and turned the key that was still in the ignition.

The drive down to the dock took no time at all. I passed the café, but it was still closed. It was Tuesday, the day Helena was supposed to return to the island. *She should be back by now*, I thought, *opening the café for business*. Maybe she'd gotten tied up in Harbour Falls. I hated that I'd lied to her about my real reason for having been in Harbourtown, but I wondered if my remorse would really matter to her.

Detective Mitchell had informed me that the young officer had indeed found Helena waiting for me at the restaurant. But he hadn't divulged what her reaction had been when she'd been told why I wouldn't be meeting her for lunch. Had she been angry with me for lying? Or mad that I'd involved her in my mess? Surely she had to be wondering why I'd been at Billy's. All the players in the Harbour Falls Mystery knew the significance of that place, so it was a certainty she'd put two and two together. Writing a book about the mystery had fallen off my priority list, but solving it was still at the top. Yeah, Helena was no fool, and she'd soon realize why I'd come to Fade Island. I just hoped she could forgive me when she did.

It was after one when I pulled into the parking lot down by the dock. The ferry was just coming in—fifteen minutes late—when I got out of the Lexus. Odd, since the ferries were quite punctual despite the motley crew that operated them.

I squinted into the glare from the sun to see if Ami was on board. But I frowned when I caught sight of the pilot instead. J.T. O'Brien. Ugh, why did it have to be him? I'd been hoping for Brody to be the one piloting the one o'clock ferry.

The possibility of a connection between Jimmy's demise and J.T. made my blood run cold. He was about the last person I cared to see today. Hell, I still had no idea what he'd been up to over on the east side of the island. Digging around, burying something, reburying something, who knew?

I shuddered as I approached the dock. J.T. glanced up as he secured the ferry to the dock. "Maddy Fitch," he said, expression grim. "What brings you down to the dock?" He lifted a dark satchel. "Are you really that anxious to get the mail?"

For a brief moment, I froze, panicked that J.T. somehow knew I was waiting for something from Jimmy. But he'd have no way of knowing such a thing. Besides, there was no way Jimmy's mail—if he'd remembered to send it—would be here so quickly. Mail service was notoriously slow around these parts.

Looking past J.T. and ignoring his comment, I said, "Where's Ami?"

He looked perplexed, but I couldn't discern whether if it was an act or not. "Who? Ami Hensley?"

I eyed him suspiciously. "Yeah, she told me she was coming over on this ferry."

"I don't know what to tell you, Maddy. The only thing I brought over is the mail," J.T. said flatly as he hoisted the satchel over his shoulder and pushed past me.

A shiver ran down my spine at the brief contact, and I took a step back. Before I could think better of it, I muttered under my breath, "Likely story."

J.T. dropped the satchel to the ground and spun around to face me. "You accusing me of something?"

"No," I replied, looking everywhere but at his face.

And that was when I noticed a deep scratch running down the length of his forearm. It looked like it had been inflicted by something sharp, like maybe a long fingernail, and worse still, it appeared to be a recent wound. Like really recent.

My stomach lurched as J.T. stepped to close the gap between us. Fear gripped every part of my being, and I held my breath, expecting the worst. But suddenly a black Porsche screeched into the parking lot, skidding to a stop. *Thank God!*

With his hot breath in my face, J.T. muttered, "Lucky bitch." I stepped back, and he hissed, "One of these days, your luck is gonna run out."

Calmly picking up the mailbag, J.T. snorted in derision and began walking toward the steep grade that led up to Main Street.

Adam got out of the car and shot J.T. a look of undisguised fury. But he kept on walking, ignoring Adam completely. Adam appeared torn on whether he should follow J.T. or come to me. In the end he headed in my direction.

"Maddy, what are you doing down here?" he asked in exasperation as he reached me, his eyes flickering to J.T.'s departing form.

"I thought Ami was coming over, I came down here to meet her," I explained and then lamely added, "I tried to call you to tell you what was going on."

"Ami?" Adam echoed, clearly confused. "Why would she be coming over to the island? I gave her some time off, so there's no reason for her to—"

"Adam," I interrupted. "She called me this morning. She

wanted me to meet her here." He arched an eyebrow, and I continued, "She said she needed to talk to me in person, that it was important. She said she could help me. I think she knows something about what happened to Jimmy."

An indecipherable emotion flared in his expression, but then it was gone. "Maddy," he began slowly. "I know you want answers, especially now. But Ami isn't someone who can help you."

"But Adam—"

"Madeleine," he interrupted. "You know she has her own problems. Leave her out of this."

He had a point, but...still. "OK, but even if you're right, where is she?"

"I don't know." Adam sighed. "Unstable people do unpredictable things. She probably changed her mind and decided not to come over."

He put his arm around my shoulders, and I leaned into him. "Yeah, I guess you're right."

Unfortunately it looked as if I'd gotten my hopes up for nothing. I was so desperate for answers that I'd believed the ramblings of a troubled person. Dejected, I got in my car and followed Adam back to his house. We made a quick stop at my cottage to pick up some clothes. He had suggested, as we'd walked to our respective cars, that I stay at his place. At least for a little while. I guessed he was worried for my safety after J.T.'s actions at the dock. It sounded good to me. Not just because of the J.T. situation, but also because I had no desire to spend another lonely night at the cottage.

After we arrived at his house, Adam made dinner. At one end of a long, ornate table in his impeccably decorated dining room, we sat down—Adam at the head of the table, and I to his left. Apart from a few distracted comments about how good everything tasted—and it really was delicious—we ate in relative silence. Adam seemed preoccupied, and I was lost in my own worried thoughts regarding Jimmy's murder and my unenviable status as the primary suspect.

I reached for my glass of wine and bumped into Adam's

forearm. "Sorry," I mumbled.

His eyes met mine, and I knew he sensed my feeling of hopelessness. "Maddy, everything is going to be fine. You have to trust me on this one."

"How can you be so sure?" I murmured.

Adam covered my hand with his. "The police will find the person who killed Jimmy." He sounded so certain. "And all of this will be over."

"I hope you're right," I muttered.

I didn't know how he did it, living under a veil of suspicion. I'd only experienced it for a little more than twenty-four hours, and I found the burden to be almost unbearable. Adam gave my hand another squeeze, and then we resumed eating. But not a minute later, the doorbell rang, the loud chime insistent. I threw Adam a questioning glance, wondering if he was expecting someone, but he shook his head. When he rose to go answer the door, I did as well. Adam hesitated for a moment and then shrugged.

Together we reached the foyer just as the bell began to ring again. Adam swung the front door open wide, and I could see there were two people on the other side. From my vantage point behind Adam, I saw Max, but his impressive bulk was shielding whoever was next to him. Max began to speak, explaining how he'd been patrolling the ferry dock and noticed someone pacing around in the dark. I thought I heard the name Hensley, so I stepped forward, fully expecting to see Ami. She'd made it over to the island after all.

But no, it wasn't Ami standing next to Max. Instead the person at his side was Sean Hensley. And he did not look happy.

And that's when things started to go from bad to worse.

Chapter 25

With a singular focus, Sean Hensley pushed past Max and rushed into the foyer. "Ward, please," he begged, his face pained, and his voice desperate. "You have to help me. Please! My wife is missing."

"What? Ami is missing?" I exclaimed, though no one seemed to hear me.

An image of J.T.'s scratched arm filled my thoughts. Ami was supposed to have been on that one o'clock ferry, but she never showed. And now, according to her very agitated husband, she was gone. Disappeared. Missing.

I opened my mouth to say something more, but Max and Adam were too preoccupied getting Sean under control to notice. Ami's husband's emotions vacillated between despair and anger at what could have happened to this woman he obviously cared for very deeply, despite her issues.

Sean eventually calmed down enough to put together a coherent timeline of what had happened. "She left the house at around noon," he uttered, dragging a hand down his face. "She was fine though. At least I thought she was." He glanced at me. "Ami said she was coming over here to visit Maddy."

My face grew warm. *Great*, I thought. *Thanks, Ami.*

Max eyed me curiously, and I looked away, feeling guilty for no good reason other than the fact Ami had apparently vanished somewhere on her way to see me. Turning my attention back to Sean, I listened as he explained how he'd waited… and waited…for his wife to return. Hours passed with no sign of Ami. He'd tried her cell phone, but when he was directed straight to voicemail, he realized the phone was off.

"You have the resources, man," Sean pleaded, his eyes focused solely on Adam. "Please help me. Look, I know she has, um, issues" —his voice cracked— "but I love my wife. Please, I have no where else to turn."

"You can file a report with the police," Max gently suggested, while Adam appeared to be assessing the situation with a cool head.

Tears welled in Sean's eyes, and my heart went out to him. He clearly loved Ami.

"I tried the police," he said, turning to Max. "They said I have to wait forty-eight hours. I can't wait. What if, what it…" A tear trailed down his cheek, and in a choked sob, he turned back to Adam and said, "Please, Ward. I know *you* can do something."

Sean's heartfelt pleas must have touched Adam. Or maybe his own feelings for Ami got the best of him. In any case he agreed to help. He promised Sean he'd pull a few strings to get things rolling on the search for Ami. But Adam was adamant that he wished to remain anonymous for obvious reasons. The last thing he needed was to be publicly attached to yet another missing person.

So later that night on the local news—following a report on the search for more clues in the Jimmy Kingston murder that left me cringing—the missing person's report Adam had pulled several strings to have aired as soon as possible was broadcast. Ami Dubois-Hensley's pretty face flashed on the screen, along with her vital stats. Female, late 20s, blonde hair, blue eyes, five foot two…

I watched the report from Adam's bedroom, sitting at the foot of his massive bed. Adam was still downstairs doing who knew what. Surely Max and Sean had left hours ago. I hadn't been in Adam's bedroom since the night we'd spent together in this room, sleeping. I didn't even know if I should be here now, but my bags were by the closet, and he had been the one to bring them up, so I supposed this was where I should be.

The report ended, and I flipped the television off. It was getting late, and I had no clue if Adam was planning on sleeping in here or not. With everything going on, it felt like our relationship had stalled. And I didn't know how to get it back on track. We'd not even been fully intimate yet, even though we'd declared our love.

Adam had been so aggressive before, and I really liked that version of him. I wanted him to be that way again, but ever since my meltdown following the night Julian had stayed, it felt as if Adam was holding back. Did he think I was too fragile? That I wanted space? He couldn't have been more wrong. Because with everything going on, the one thing I craved was to feel even closer to him.

Feeling defeated, I didn't even bother to change into my pajamas. Instead I tugged at the comforter beneath me, cocooning it around me as I scooted back to lie among the sea of pillows. That was me, adrift in Adam's bed. How had things gotten so crazy? Jimmy murdered in cold blood; Ami vanishing without a trace. And I was linked to both.

It was only a matter of time before the police would seek me out to discuss Ami's sudden disappearance. I mean, come on, who had she been on her way to visit? Only the prime suspect in the murder of a local bartender. Not a good position to find oneself in.

I buried my face in a pillow, suppressing a scream of frustration. Choking back a sob, my thoughts turned to the interrogation I'd undergone in Harbourtown. Detective Mitchell didn't seem as if he really believed I was capable of murdering Jimmy. But he surely suspected—correctly—that I was withholding information. On the other hand, Detective Crowley was all set to send me up the river. I imagined him, at this very moment, working overtime to build a case against me. Maybe he liked and respected my dad, but he sure as hell didn't care for me.

I knew the thing my father had said about being honest with the detectives was sound advice, but I was resistant to confessing all I was hiding. Sure I could come clean and tell the detectives everything I'd discovered, thus far, in my own private investigation of Chelsea Hannigan's disappearance. But that would mean I'd have to give up my search for the truth. I'd never find out who was in that photograph. The one Jimmy had ended up dying for. And Adam's name might never be cleared. This case had been in the hands of two local police departments for years, and it still hadn't been solved. So no, I wasn't going to tell the police all I knew. Not quite yet. Not until I had the answer I was so close to discovering.

And as I drifted off to sleep, I prayed that in the meantime no one else would turn up missing…or dead.

The next morning, I woke up fully clothed, still wrapped in my comforter cocoon. From the impression in the pillow next to mine, it was apparent Adam had slept in here with me. I mentally kicked myself for sleeping so soundly. No wonder our physical relationship was stalled. I was just as much to blame—missed opportunities and all that.

Reluctantly emerging from my cocoon, I reached up to the side of the headboard and pushed one of several buttons. The heavy curtains covering the large windows began to pull back, revealing a mass of storm clouds darkening the horizon. The big storm that had been forecasted was on its way, the island blanketed in near darkness.

I snatched up the remote control and turned on the television. The same local news channel was on, and new reports were being broadcast. Ami's white SUV flashed up on the screen. I turned up the volume. Her abandoned vehicle had been found at a small convenience store in Cove Beach. The same place Chelsea had last been seen. *Weird.* But, unlike that case, the vehicle was parked out of the range of the surveillance camera. I wondered if that had been done purposely. But why? Why would Ami park her vehicle out of sight? Or had someone else, knowing the camera's range, parked it there?

But what had happened to Ami? The report made no mention of her stopping in the store to buy anything. So why had she been there? That store wasn't far from the dock, so had she walked to the ferry? Had she still been planning on taking the ferry and meeting up with me? If J.T. were to be believed, he hadn't seen her. Or, had he?

The news update ended, and I flipped the television off. One thing that had changed overnight—despite it still being less than forty-eight hours since Ami's disappearance—was that the police were now involved. The missing person's report on last night's news had ensured it. Sean had Adam to thank for that.

After showering and dressing, I went downstairs. Adam was sitting at the breakfast table, drinking a cup of coffee, and pecking away on a laptop. He wore jeans and a black long-sleeved shirt, so I assumed he was working from home today. I spent an extra minute admiring how good he looked, his hair still wet from his shower and blacker than ever, but then I grabbed some coffee for myself and sat down across from him at the long breakfast bar.

"Have you seen the news reports?" I asked.

Adam looked up from whatever he was working on. "Yeah, I have."

Knowing that Adam had inside sources—such as Max—I asked him if the police knew more than what was being reported. He said no, they knew nothing more. And then, seeing the troubled look on my face, he tried to comfort me by telling me he truly believed Ami would surely turn up soon—alive and well.

In that moment I realized just how much Ami's mental diagnosis tended to color Adam's opinion of her. He saw her as a victim. But not of foul play. No, Adam seemed to view Ami as a victim of her own mind. I heard the pity in his tone and suddenly knew why he'd kept her on as his employee for so many years. Sure she was competent enough to perform her job duties, but it was more than that. Adam felt sorry for her. Maybe even to the point of obligation. Ami probably sensed that. I supposed that was why she had so fervently defended Adam the first day I'd traveled with her over to the island. I just hoped she wasn't in some way taking advantage of Adam's kindness toward her.

Adam closed his laptop and said something about needing

to go make some calls. I wanted to say something to let him know I was ready to move forward with him. I needed him, wanted him, craved him, and I was through with being coddled. So I sat my coffee cup down and said, "You should have woken me last night." I tried to catch his gaze but couldn't. "When you came to bed," I added, stressing the last word.

He eyed me tentatively. "You needed the sleep."

"Don't baby me, Adam," I replied tersely, rising to dump the rest of my coffee into the sink.

He moved toward me, his voice softening. "Maddy."

"Just..." I waved him away, and he released a held breath.

A moment passed, neither of us moving. And then he retreated, departing, I assumed, for the study to make his calls.

Well, that had gone well. Not.

Too restless to concentrate on much of anything, I meandered around the house—making the bed, fluffing the pillows, wandering the long halls. At last I found myself at the closed door to the study. I wanted to talk to Adam, fix things from earlier, so I raised my hand to knock.

But before I had the chance, Adam opened the door. "Maddy," he said, "I was just coming to look for you."

From the look on Adam's face, I knew something was up. When I asked him that very question, he didn't respond directly. Instead he moved aside and asked me to come in. A loud thunderclap reverberated—making me jump—as I stepped across the threshold.

As he sat back down behind his desk, Adam appeared to be less than amused when I laughed at my own skittishness. "Madeleine, why is your cell phone turned off?" he snapped, while leaning back in his chair.

"It's charging," I responded, taking a few steps closer to the desk. "Why?"

"Hoffman has been trying to reach you all morning."

A sick feeling came over me, and I shifted from one foot to the other. "Why? What's going on?"

Adam closed his eyes and was silent for a minute. *Oh, this is going to be bad.*

When he opened his eyes, he said quietly, "The police want to talk to you." He hesitated. "It's about Ami's disappearance."

"What?" I murmured as I sank into the leather chair across from him. "They don't think…?" I couldn't finish my sentence.

Adam raked his fingers through his hair. "Besides Sean, you were the last person to speak with Ami. And the authorities know she was on her way to see you."

"Adam, this can't be happening." I covered my face with my hands.

Before I knew it, Adam was kneeling in front of me. I felt a tug at my hands and intertwined them with his. "Shhh," he soothed, warming my hands in his own. "It's just another formality, nothing to worry about. Hoffman will be here with the detective—"

"They're coming *here*?" I interrupted, just as another low rumble of thunder rolled ominously overhead.

"Yes, but it'll just be Detective Mitchell." Adam eyed me carefully, probably to make sure I fully comprehended that the nicer of the two detectives—Mitchell, not Crowley—would be the one questioning me. I nodded, and he continued, "And remember, Hoffman will be here as well."

Adam hesitated, and I knew there was more. Sure enough, he said, "Maddy, you should know that the Harbour Falls police are now working with the Harbourtown PD on this one."

"'Cause they think it's connected to Jimmy, right?" I stated dully. "They suspect me in both cases. Oh, Adam, this is bad."

"You haven't done anything wrong," he reminded me. "Just let Hoffman do most of the talking. It won't take long. Less than an hour, I'm sure, and then it will be over."

Adam knew the drill with these things. No surprise there, since he'd been through a number of interrogations and questionings of his own over the years.

"So when will they be here?" I asked, suddenly feeling queasy at the prospect of more questions—questions to which I had no real answers. Or rather answers that I couldn't divulge.

Adam tucked a strand of hair behind my ear. "Soon, another hour. Maybe less, since they want to get this wrapped up before the storm hits."

The huge storm that had been in the forecast was promising to deliver a knockout punch by evening. A streak of lightning flashed across the sky, and both Adam and I turned to the window just in time to watch it sizzle into the sea.

Yeah, a storm was brewing, and it was promising to be a big one.

Max drove Detective Mitchell and Elliott Hoffman up to Adam's compound following their arrival to Fade Island. Max took a seat in the foyer, while Adam ushered Hoffman, Mitchell, and me into his study. Detective Mitchell looked unsure when Adam offered his stately desk chair to him, but he sat down, nonetheless, and set up a small recorder after taking out his trusty notepad and pen.

Hoffman and I settled in the seats across from Mitchell, and Adam leaned casually against the wall by the door. The detective seemed about to say something, probably to ask Adam to leave, but held off when their eyes met in a meaningful stare. The implication was clear: Adam may have graciously given up his chair, but the trade-off was that he would be staying for the questioning.

Clearing his throat and focusing his attention back on me, Detective Mitchell said, "I'm sorry to be bothering you again, Miss Fitch, but this has to be done. I promise to keep it short."

I gave him a tight smile and nodded. "Thanks, I appreciate that."

Hoffman shifted in his seat, and Mitchell got down to it, mumbling some preliminaries into his recorder and then asking, "Are you acquainted with a female named Ami Dubois-Hensley?"

"Yes." I didn't wait for Hoffman's go-ahead, since I saw no harm in answering this type of question.

"Would you consider her to be a friend?"

I mulled that one over, but had to say, "Yes."

"How long have you been friends?"

"Since high school," I replied. "I guess that puts it at more than ten years, probably around fourteen years."

Detective Mitchell continued, "Actually, she was your best friend in high school, correct?"

Who told you that? I thought, but instead said, "Yes, she was."

Mitchell scribbled something down, even though the light on the voice recorder indicated I was being taped. "Did you have occasion to speak to Ami Hensley on the phone yesterday?"

"Yes."

"Do you remember what time it was?"

"Um, before noon."

"How did she seem when you spoke to her?"

I glanced at Hoffman, and he nodded. "Um, she seemed normal," I said.

"Mr. Hensley stated that his wife was on her way to visit you here on the island when she disappeared. Is this correct?"

A distracted nod from Hoffman, who appeared preoccupied with taking notes of his own. But I somehow knew he was acutely aware of everything. So I answered, "Yes, that's correct."

"What was the nature of this visit, Miss Fitch?" The detective's voice grew tight, and I knew we were getting down to the heart of the matter. He was hoping to get some kind of lead on this case—catch me up on something, see what I knew.

I opened my mouth and then closed it. I debated whether or not to mention the scratch I'd seen on J.T.'s arm, something I had yet to relay to Adam. I didn't want to make a big deal out of it until I knew if it meant more, so I was ready to let it go. Some part of me wanted to let this play out, get the answers on my own, but then my dad's words came back to me.

I started to speak, but Hoffman silenced me with a light touch to my arm. "Detective Mitchell" he said in his smooth lawyer voice, "my client is not required to answer that question. The context of the visit was, no doubt, personal and not related to the case. Therefore, Ms. Fitch will not be responding to that question at this time."

I nodded in agreement since I had waffled on whether to answer or not. Mitchell conceded with a sigh, "As you wish."

Hoffmann had no idea why Ami had been on her way to visit me, but I supposed he didn't care. In any case I was kind of glad there were no more direct questions for me. Mitchell and my attorney continued to speak, arguing over what kinds of questions were appropriate and what were not. It seemed to go on forever.

I soon tuned out their voices, opting instead to stare out the window and watch the play of lightning across an ever-darkening sky. Ultimately we were at nature's mercy, weren't we? It made me wonder what control we really had. Was it all an illusion? The study felt further and further away as I lost myself in the vivid display until, bringing me back to the here and now, Adam came up from behind me. Touching my shoulder gently, he murmured, "Maddy?"

I glanced around. Detective Mitchell and Hoffman had evidently departed without my even realizing it. "How long have I been sitting here?" I asked.

"Just a few minutes," Adam said. "You looked like you needed some time just to think. Mitchell and Hoffman said good-bye, but it didn't look like you even heard them. Do you want to talk?"

"Not really," I said truthfully, standing. "I just feel so tired."

And I was tired. Tired of being a suspect, tired of police interrogations, tired of not having the right answers. Adam's fingers traced down my cheek to my chin, and then he tilted my head up to meet his gaze. "Why don't you go upstairs, get some rest?"

Our eyes met, and something passed between us. Something unspoken, something unmistakable. "Are you coming up?" I asked, but I was really asking for so much more.

"I'll be there in a few minutes."

"Promise?" I murmured, losing myself in his eyes.

"Promise," he replied.

I made my way to Adam's bedroom in a daze of sorts. With one hand on the bed to balance myself, I kicked off my shoes.

And then I peeled off my jeans, leaving only my panties and long-sleeved tee on before crawling under the covers. I buried myself in the downy comforter, the pile of blankets. I needed to forget, if only for a moment. So I shut everything out, it was easy to do with the storm. Darkness had descended, the winds roared ferociously, and the rain sheeted relentlessly against the windows. The storm had arrived in full force.

Turning to lay on my back, I stared at the ceiling and pulled distractedly at the hem of my sleeve. And then reality came rushing back. So I went over all that had happened while flashes of lightning played like a strobe light against the walls around me. Where was Ami? And who had murdered Jimmy? There had to be a connection. I had that feeling again—like when Julian had arrived on the island—the feeling that someone was pulling strings like a puppet master. But this time, instead of having my ex-boyfriend pay me a visit, this person was making it look like I was involved with Jimmy's murder *and* Ami's disappearance. It was too much of a coincidence. But who would be able to orchestrate such a thing? And why? Had I gotten too close to the truth? Was this person, whomever it was, trying to silence me?

I shuddered just as a huge bolt of lightning lit up the entire room, illuminating Adam standing in the doorway. "Adam," I gasped, sucking in a breath of air. "You scared me."

In a beat he was on the bed, above me, his arms a cage around me. My heart beat wildly, fear morphing to excitement. "Are you afraid now," Adam asked, blue eyes clouded with desire.

"Maybe a little," I replied, my breathing quickening in anticipation.

Adam chuckled darkly while dropping to his elbows. His lips grazed mine, and I responded. Our mouths moved together, slowly at first, lingering and kind of sweet, but soon our kisses grew desperate, hungry. This is what we both needed, what we both wanted.

Finding the hem of his shirt, I fisted my hand in the cotton material, my knuckles skimming his abdomen. Adam sucked in a breath and found my eyes. "It isn't going to be gentle, Madeleine. I've waited too long, we've waited too long."

"I don't want it to be gentle," I rasped.

And I didn't, so I raked my nails up his back to show him how much I wanted it. How hard I wanted it. Adam hissed and yanked the shirt he was wearing over his head, flinging it to the floor. And then his lips crashed into mine in a flurry of hot, wet, frenzied kisses. Somehow my shirt, my bra, my panties, he peeled them off while we kissed like our lives depended on it. I don't know, maybe they did. And then it was Adam's turn—his clothes, discarded in a flash.

We were finally bare, skin to skin. And it felt so good, so right, so different from the night at the cottage. Our kisses slowed, stopped. Our eyes met, our souls now bared as well. Adam's strong hands were everywhere—cupping my breasts, skimming over my hips, tracing up the sensitive insides of my thighs, sliding along my core. *God help me.* He drove me crazy with lust. Had I ever wanted someone like this? I wanted Adam to conquer me, invade me. I wanted Adam to fuck me. I moved with the rhythm he set as his fingers played me like an instrument. And if I thought I could ever want Adam more than this, I realized I was sadly mistaken when he lowered his body and put his mouth on my sex. His lips, his tongue, the things he was doing drove me wild. I raised my hips up to give him more access, and he gripped my ass...hard. "You like this?" he asked smugly, glancing up from between my legs.

I did, oh I did. But all I could do was let out a moan of pleasure. His lips traveled back up my body, until our mouths met once more. My hands trailed down his chest, lower and lower. When I grasped him in my hand, he inhaled sharply, "God, Maddy, that feels good. Don't stop."

I stroked his full length; he was so hard, so heavy, so thick. Desperate to feel him inside of me, I pulled him down to me. He settled between my legs. Lightning flashed, illuminating the room once more. Adam pulled back slightly, his eyes—so, so blue and as stormy as that first night when I'd awoken on his sofa—met mine. No words were necessary. As he'd said, we'd waited long enough. And with no hesitation Adam plunged into me, eliciting a gasp from me. He stilled, burying his head into my neck, "Are you OK?" he murmured against my skin.

"Mm-hmm," I responded.

Words eluding me, my mind clouded with desire. Adam remained still, buried deep inside of me, but unmoving. Not that I didn't savor the invasion, but I could feel him smiling against my neck. He was teasing me. *Damn him.*

"Adam," I huffed, circling my hips, "more."

"What do you want, Maddy?" He chuckled. "Tell me what you want."

Writhing wantonly beneath him, I said, "Just fuck me, Adam. I want to...fuck."

The words sounded erotic as they fell from my lips, and Adam must have though so too. He pulled out almost all the way, very slowly, and then plunged back in, making me cry out in pleasure. Faster, faster, he pumped into me. Harder and harder. He gave me everything I wanted, and more. "Oh my God," I breathed out. He felt so, so, so good.

We soon found a rhythm, moving with desperation, lust, but also with love. With thunder echoing out to sea, Adam and I were one, united in body, united in heart. And when our bodies reached an almost-simultaneous crescendo, for the first time, it felt like we were united in soul.

Chapter 26

While the storm raged through the night and into the next day, Adam and I remained locked away from the world—our current problems forgotten in the darkness of his bedroom. Not surprisingly, electricity had been lost on the island, so we lit candles and placed them all around the bed. The next several hours became a palette of images that blended into one another...

Adam ignites a candle with a flick of flame to wick, bringing it to life. His face as close to perfection as I've ever seen, bathed in the warm glow of candlelight. A playful smile tugs at his lips as he catches my expression of lust. I am ignited as well. And now this gorgeous man's body—a body that hasn't been clothed since yesterday—is above my own...and then behind...and then under me. Again and again—heated skin to heated skin— gliding together on a light sheen of perspiration. Touching, tasting, exploring. The darkness of night never quite goes away as the hours pass. There is just less darkness—a kind of illuminated gray. Until a new black night, this one clear as the storm passes, swallows the gray.

"Maddy," Adam began, clearing his throat. His voice was husky. Though we'd been communicating, it hadn't been with words. I lifted my head from where I was resting on his smooth chest and met his gaze. "I think we should do something special tomorrow. Just the two of us," he continued and then dropped his voice to a mere whisper, "Maybe forget about…things for a while."

Things like me being the prime suspect in Jimmy's murder. And things like the police exploring the possibility that I had played some nefarious role in Ami's disappearance. Yeah, it would be great to forget about those things. Locked away in Adam's bedroom was an excellent way to forget, but we couldn't stay here forever. Or could we? In any case it was sweet Adam was trying to think of ways to keep my mind from getting too caught up in all the unsettling events of the past few days.

"But you have to fly to Boston in the morning," I reminded him, sighing.

Adam was finally closing the deal with the Boston client, which was a relief. It meant his frequent business trips of late would slow down considerably, allowing us more time together.

"Yeah, but I'll be home by late afternoon," Adam reminded me in return, and then he suddenly smiled slyly, blue eyes dancing. "And I know just what we're going to do. We won't even have to leave the island."

"What?" I queried. "Does it involve leaving your bedroom?" I arched an eyebrow. If it involved spending more time here, I was game.

Adam tousled my hair playfully. "Yes, naughty girl, we'll be leaving the bedroom." he said. "But I'm keeping the juicy details secret until tomorrow."

"Adam!" I chastised, swatting lightly at his chest and feigning a pout.

He caught my hand easily and pulled me to him. And just like that, our words were silenced once again.

Thursday night turned into Friday morning, and somewhere during that time frame the electricity was fully restored to the island. Reality was slowly creeping back in. And our brief respite from the troubles of the real world ended completely when Adam left for Boston. Before departing, however, he'd awoken me with a soft kiss. Proclamations of love were uttered from both of our mouths, but his secret surprise for later in the day remained unspoken.

I couldn't sleep after Adam left, so I got up, showered quickly, and dressed for the day. Once I reached the kitchen, I toasted a bagel and glanced out the glass panel windows that ran along the back of the house.

In contrast to the past forty-eight hours, this day was positively sparkling. It was as if the heavy rains had washed away all the darkness. But then I remembered my life was still in turmoil. The Harbour Falls Mystery was no closer to being solved than it had been the day I'd arrived on Fade Island. Jimmy was dead, and according to the morning news, Ami was still missing. Worst of all, I was probably close to being arrested, seeing how I was unfortunately linked to both cases.

The walls were closing in, and time was not on my side. The more days that passed with no new leads, the more likely it was that the police would take me in. Even if I wasn't officially charged with Jimmy's death, I certainly expected to be asked to come in for more questioning. So it was imperative that I find answers. And quickly. As if to underscore my last thought, my cell rang at that very moment.

Without looking at the display screen, I answered with a hesitant hello.

"Maddy." It was my dad, thank goodness. I needed a dose of my father's levelheadedness.

But his tone was grim, so I asked, "What's wrong?"

My father took an audible breath and exhaled slowly. This couldn't be good. "I just got off the phone with Detective Mitchell. He wanted to give me a heads-up…" He trailed off.

"Dad?" My voice trembled. "What kind of a heads-up? What's going on?"

Following another unsteady breath, he began to explain, "Some small-time drug dealer who hangs out at that dive, Billy's, has been running his mouth." —Zeb, I thought— "He was taken in on some kind of parole violation late last night, and they found drugs on him." The mayor coughed, clearly not approving, and then continued, "Anyway he's promising to testify against you in exchange for leniency in his own charges."

I groaned, and my dad added in a strained voice, "Please tell me you don't know this guy, Maddy. He's a drug dealer, for God's sake."

"I met him once," I confessed. But I didn't intend to detail my brief and disconcerting interaction with Zeb to my dad, so I only added, "He was creepy."

My father said nothing. I had no idea what he could be thinking, so I asked quietly, "What did he say about me?"

More throat clearing and then, "He's claiming you were more than, uh, friends with Jimmy Kingston. Claims he saw you there with the bartender a number of times and that you looked rather *close*."

"That's a lie!" I cried out, cursing Zeb. "An outright lie."

I didn't know which was worse, my dad knowing I'd had some sort of interaction with a sleazy drug dealer, or him thinking I'd had something going on with Jimmy. Ugh.

I squeezed my eyes shut, wishing for it all to be a bad dream. I silently wondered if—in addition to saving his own ass—Zeb was getting back at me for not taking him up on his unseemly offer of drugs. I recalled his leering stare when he'd hinted at his "payment plans," and I almost lost my breakfast. Instead I started to cry.

"Maddy," my father soothed, "I know he's lying. This dealer is just looking to get out of trouble, and he thinks he can bargain with testimony against you. He's nothing more than an opportunist scumbag."

Yeah, an opportunist scumbag Detective Crowley was probably salivating over at this very minute. He finally had what he needed to issue an arrest warrant for me. If Zeb were willing to testify that I'd been having some kind of a physical relationship with Jimmy, then the police could claim my motive was possibly one of a lover scorned. Even though the whole idea was ridiculous, that, coupled with the circumstantial evidence, could be enough to convince a jury that I'd killed Jimmy Kingston.

At least my dad was still on my side. If Mayor Fitch ever lost faith in me, I didn't know if I'd have the strength to keep going. But with him (and Adam) believing in me, I knew I had to fight.

And I needed to take action *now*. Answers that could potentially save my ass were not going to come to me while I sat here at Adam's compound. I was going to have to go out and find them. On my own, since Adam wasn't due to return from

Boston until closer to dinnertime.

In that moment I made a decision. If I didn't find anything new by the time Adam got back to Fade Island, then I'd tell him the things I had yet to mention—like my having met this Zeb character on one of my trips to Billy's. And I'd ask for his thoughts regarding the scratch I'd seen on J.T.'s arm. And then I'd go to the police. There were far more things I'd kept from the police, but I trusted Hoffman would keep me from getting into too much trouble. I'd take the "honest" route my father had proposed days ago. Until then, though, I planned to search with renewed intensity.

With the clock ticking on my new self-imposed time limit, I hastily ended the call with my dad. And then I grabbed my jacket and headed out to the Lexus. A crisp blast of wind hit me as I walked across the driveway to my car. Though it was sunny, the November air was icy and brisk. I sat down in the driver's seat and tried Adam's cell. I wanted to get him up to speed on what was happening, but the call went straight to voicemail. No way was I leaving a message detailing the updates—especially the stuff about Zeb—so I hung up.

Tapping the cell to my chin, I pondered the one thing that could potentially blow the lid off this whole mess.

The photograph.

Enough days had passed that it should have arrived. But there had been the storm and, consequently, no ferry service yesterday. No ferry service equaled no mail service. Today, however, the weather was fine, and the ferry would be running on its regular schedule. So I put the Lexus in gear and raced toward town, my focus on reaching the café and getting my hands on the mail.

When I reached my destination, I parked in my usual spot out front and hurried in. I headed toward the coffee bar in the back, glancing around in the hopes of possibly seeing Helena on the premises. I'd not heard much from her since Monday— the day Jimmy had been murdered. And I had yet to apologize for involving her in my explanation to the police for being in Harbourtown. I didn't even know if she was mad. Since that day she'd left only one brief voicemail, asking me how I was holding up. She hadn't sounded angry, but I'd left her a couple of voicemails in return and still had yet to connect with her. I hoped she wasn't avoiding me on account of what had happened in Harbourtown, but I had the sense something was definitely up.

Nate's voice bellowed out, breaking me out of my musings.

"Maddy!" he exclaimed, pulling me into a bear hug once he reached me. Well, at least *he* didn't seem to be upset with me, I thought, as I hugged him in return.

"What about that storm?" Nate asked, stepping back. "You and Adam lose electricity up on that end of the island too?"

"Yeah," I answered, "but it came back on sometime before morning."

He nodded and then shot me an odd look, like maybe he was contemplating saying something of more import. He had to have been aware of my current status as a murder suspect, but I doubted he, or Helena for that matter, really believed I was capable of something like that. Seeing that they were friends with Adam, I suspected they fully comprehended the nature of false accusations. There was so much I wanted to say, and I wanted to start by apologizing for involving Helena.

But when I started to say, "Nate, I'm sorry. If you and Helena—" He cut me off.

"Maddy," he said softly, "whatever it is you're going to say, just know that it can wait. We know you're innocent. Nobody in this café suspects you of anything. Don't lose sight of that."

Tears pricked at the corners of my eyes, and I could only nod in response. I really wished Helena were there to tell me herself, but Nate's words still meant a lot.

"Let's change the subject," Nate said, noticing my watery eyes. "So what brings you to the café today?"

I thought about asking where Helena was and if I could talk to her, but then I remembered my actual reason for being there. So instead I cleared my throat and inquired, "Has the ferry been around with the mail yet?"

Yep, best to get back on task. I'd talk with Helena later. Nate had pretty much confirmed she wasn't mad at me, so I'd just catch up with her next visit.

Nate eyed me curiously, surely puzzled by my sudden urgent interest in postal delivery. "Yeah, it's here," he responded, taking a step back and reaching behind the counter to grab several parcels of mail. "Brody dropped it off a little while ago." Handing me a small bundle of envelopes, he added, "You expecting something important?"

I froze and searched his face for some indication that he somehow knew what I was hoping to find in my small packet of mail. But it appeared Nate was just making conversation.

"Nah," I answered in a controlled voice that belied how I really felt. "Just the usual bills." I held up the bundle, giving him a clear view of the gas bill on the top.

Now that the mail was in my hands, I felt anxious. The photo could be in there, even behind the gas bill I'd showed Nate. But I couldn't check right in front of him, so I made some excuse about needing to get back to Adam's house to talk to Max about something. When Nate shot me another confused look, it dawned on me that I hadn't seen Max all morning. Damn, I wasn't even sure he was on the island today. Had he gone with Adam to Boston? I sure hoped he hadn't, or Nate was really going to wonder about me. But Nate seemed back to normal as we said our farewells.

Once I was back in the Lexus, I paged through the bundle of mail, unable to wait another minute to see if the copy of the photo had arrived.

Bills, junk mail, a magazine, and then...

My pulse quickened as my fingertips grazed over the second envelope from the bottom. A plain white envelope—the same size as the one now sitting in a plastic evidence bag at the Harbourtown police station. This one happened to be addressed to me; Jimmy's childlike printing etched in black ink across the front. But unlike the envelope I'd found at Billy's, this one was *not* empty.

I stared down at the envelope in my trembling hands. And then a burst of paranoia coursed through me when I noticed

Jimmy had printed a return address in the upper-left hand corner on the envelope. A return address for Billy's. *Oh Lord.* I shot a sidelong glance toward the café. Had Nate seen the return address? Why hadn't Jimmy put his home address on the envelope? Or better yet, not written anything at all in the return address area. As far as I was concerned, even the Harbourtown postmark was too much information for this particular piece of mail.

I couldn't help but wonder who else had seen the envelope? Nate said Brody had brought the mail over in the morning, which meant it had been sorted and bundled over at Cove Beach. Had anyone else besides Brody had access to the mail today? Jennifer could have seen it. J.T. could have too. And Helena may have seen it if she'd been in the café earlier. *Crap!*

No matter who had seen it—and hopefully it was none of the above—it could prove to be dangerous for me. Apart from all of those individuals being potential suspects in Chelsea's disappearance—which meant the guilty party would most likely guess what the envelope contained, especially if they'd played a part in Jimmy's demise—it also didn't bode well that I was the recipient of a letter from a guy I was suspected of killing. Yeah, that tidbit might prove to be too tasty to keep to oneself. Surely someone like J.T., or definitely Jennifer, would just love to go to the police and tell them Maddy Fitch was receiving letters from the man she may have murdered. Talk about incriminating.

I was starting to feel a little sick, and I still hadn't even opened the damn thing. But just as I slipped my finger under the flap to tear it open, a rap to my car window made me jump in my seat, the envelope dropping to my lap.

I looked up to see Nate on the other side of the glass. "Everything all right in there?" he asked, his voice muffled coming through the closed car window.

I pressed a button, and the window descended. "I'm fine, thanks," I said, my voice shaky.

Nate looked at me hard. I was sure the color had drained from my face, my eyes wide with the fear of being found out. Without breaking my gaze from Nate, I felt for the envelope, and once I had it, slipped it into a side pocket in my jacket. All the while I smiled, hopefully reassuringly, for Nate's sake.

"OK," he said at last. "I only came out to tell you Helena's back. She saw you sitting out here in your car and wondered if you might want to come back in for a coffee."

So Helena was around after all. Where had she been? At the bungalow? Had she walked right by me? I was parked directly in front of the café, but I'd been so preoccupied I wouldn't have noticed. Oh God, had she seen me staring at the envelope from Jimmy? She could have been watching the whole time.

Damn, I needed to see who was in that picture, and I obviously wasn't going to be able to do that in front of the café. Not now.

"Um, maybe I'll stop back later," I replied. "But I really do need to get back."

Nate mumbled an "OK then," and when he stepped away from the car, I got the hell out of there. Needless to say, I made it back to Adam's place in no time. When I stopped in front of the house, I put the car in park and breathed a sigh of relief. *Safe at last.*

But then I noticed something attached to the front door, a slip of paper fluttering in the breeze. For a moment I watched the lazy movement of the paper, and then, leaving the car idling, I went to check it out.

A thick piece of parchment paper had been taped to the door, a single sentence visible on the front. I peeled the paper from the wood surface. Nine words were written in Adam's neat, concise scrawl.

Home early, meet me down at the lighthouse. Adam.

It seemed odd that he hadn't written more, odd that he hadn't signed it *love, Adam*. I shook my head to dispel my negativity. Surely this was part of Adam's big surprise plan for today. It wasn't his fault he had arrived home early on the day I'd finally received the mail I'd been waiting for. The letter weighing heavy in my pocket dampened the usual excitement I would have felt knowing Adam had something special planned for us. But at this moment, my mind was focused on one thing only—the photo in the envelope.

I couldn't wait any longer to see who was in the picture. Not another minute. I ran back down to the Lexus, wrenched the door open, and sat back down. Pulse racing, mouth dry, I pulled the envelope from my jacket pocket. I flipped it over, tore the flap, pulled out the piece of copy paper, unfolded it...

No no no! It couldn't be.

But the image before me wasn't lying. With my mouth agape, I stared and stared. The envelope—now as empty as the one in evidence—fluttered to the floor.

Oh. My. God.

Finally I blinked. But I continued to stare at the image of the Polaroid photo Jimmy had copied. It depicted exactly what he had claimed it would—an image of a blonde woman clearly making out with Chelsea Hannigan. Maybe it had all been part of a bet, but neither party appeared to be just "goofing around." They both looked like they were into it. Way into it. Well, maybe the blonde more so than Chelsea.

And I knew that blonde. I could deny it all I wanted, but the image showed the truth. The mystery woman was a mystery no longer. The mystery woman had been my best friend in high school. And she was currently missing. Yes, the blonde mystery woman kissing Chelsea Hannigan was none other than Ami Dubois-Hensley. And what did that mean?

Ami had been involved with Chelsea, obviously. Did that mean Ami knew what happened to her? God, had *she* done something to her? But Ami was missing now as well, so maybe she'd known too much. Maybe someone had silenced Ami. Is that why she'd been trying to protect me? Was she afraid that if *I* knew what *she* knew, then I'd be in danger of disappearing too? But what had Ami known?

I couldn't tear my eyes away from the photo and what it depicted. *This* was the reason Jimmy was dead. Why was it so imperative that this picture remain undiscovered?

I shoved the photo back into my jacket pocket and started

toward the lighthouse.

Adam.

How did he fit into all of this? Had he known who was in the photo all along? Was that the reason he'd downplayed its significance? Or would he be just as surprised as I was to find out who was in this picture with Chelsea?

I couldn't imagine Adam keeping Ami on as an employee if he'd know about her and his fiancée. Or was his involvement much more insidious? I was sickened as I imagined all the ways Adam could possibly be a part of this. And if he were, then I'd been played thoroughly...and set up perfectly to take the fall.

As I neared the lighthouse, heavy clouds rolled in, eclipsing the sun. I passed the café, but it was dark inside, the sign on the door flipped to display the "closed" side. Weird, it had been open less than an hour ago. Why was it closed now?

I drove until I reached the end of the road, parking the car close to the edge of the sidewalk where it was only a short walk to the top of the steep, uneven steps that trailed precariously down the side of the cliff. I got out of the car, walked the path I'd traveled with Adam weeks ago. When I reached the edge, I looked down. A fog had rolled in over the dark rocks, engulfing the base of the tall, looming lighthouse in the distance.

Here goes nothing, I thought.

Carefully I began the descent, negotiating my way down the slippery, worn steps. A gust of icy November air cut through my thin jacket, making me shiver. The temperature was dropping, the winds picking up in intensity. When I finally reached the base of the steps, I had to fight the urge to turn around and head back to get a heavier coat. But I forged ahead, knowing that Adam was waiting in the lighthouse.

This may be Adam's surprise, I thought, *but I have a surprise of my own.* Far from forgetting about everything that had happened over the past several days, as had been the plan, we were going to face it.

That's right. I had every intention of showing Adam the photo. In fact, I was banking on his reaction to determine just how much he'd known, and possibly kept from me, all this time.

Resolved, and with surprising dexterity, I navigated the slippery, oily-black surfaces of the rocks, closer and closer to the lighthouse. The dark waves crashed all around me, and through a thin veil of fog, I saw a flickering of golden illumination streaming through the small lighthouse windows. Candles, perhaps?

Adam had promised something special. Maybe he'd managed to set up a romantic dinner in the structure. He could have easily instructed Max to make the necessary preparations while he'd been flying back. Maybe that was why I hadn't seen Max all day?

High tide was coming in, and the waves—now black as a velvet night in the dying light of day—continued to crash over the imposing rocky terrain. It was totally desolate down here. What the hell was I doing? I could be walking right into a trap. What if Adam wasn't even here yet? But then who was waiting in the lighthouse?

I kept on walking, dismissing those crazy thoughts. I reached the sandy path that snaked to the lighthouse entrance. No matter what, I sought the truth. I'd come too far. I was on the cusp of losing a lot. And if my worst fears were realized, meaning the man I loved was involved in all of this, I'd end up losing it all.

I reached the door, and with that thought, I grabbed the cold metal handle and pushed it open. I took a tentative step into the dim, candlelit interior.

The feeling of unease I'd experienced when I'd first visited the lighthouse returned with a vengeance. Something was dreadfully wrong. Every instinct screamed for me to turn back. But I couldn't walk away now. Even if it meant sacrificing my own sense of self-preservation, I was going in.

I breathed in the heavy, salt-tinged air and entered the lighthouse, ready to accept whatever fate had in store for me.

Chapter 27

Stepping into the lighthouse, the first thing I noticed was how many candles were illuminating the interior. Dozens and dozens of them, votives in glass cups placed up and down the winding, iron staircase. The flames flickered rapidly, as if they'd been angered by my intrusion. What struck me most was that there was nothing romantic about *this* setup. All of the candles were black, and the sinister, jaundiced glow they were casting against the pale lighthouse interior was nothing short of eerie.

The heavy, metal door clanged shut behind me with finality, my fate sealed. And just then a person stepped out from behind the staircase, looking not the least bit surprised to see me. I couldn't say the same. Here was the missing person everyone was looking for. And it wasn't Chelsea. No, it was Ami Hensley.

What is she doing here? I thought. Then I feared this was where she was being held captive. But as I glanced around furtively, I realized we were the only two.

"Expecting Adam?" Ami drawled, tossing her long, blonde hair back with a flick of her wrist. She then dipped a hand into the front pocket of her raincoat. The same powder-blue coat she'd worn the day we'd first taken the ferry from Cove Beach to Fade Island. But unlike that time, Ami's stomach was now perfectly flat. No fake-pregnancy bump today.

My mind raced to assess the scene before me. Well, well, well. Ami was not only the mystery blonde in the Polaroid photo with Chelsea, but she was obviously not missing after all. Had we all been duped by a crazy person?

"Ami, I, uh," I stammered, at a loss for verbal coherency, at first. But then I pulled it together. "What are you doing here?

Everyone thinks you're—"

"Missing? Dead?" she finished for me, sounding bored.

"Nope, as you can see, I'm alive and well."

Had she faked her own disappearance? To what end?

"I don't understand," I said, truly confused.

Ami sighed and took another step closer. Now both of her hands were stuffed into the front pockets of her raincoat. *Odd.* But what really gave me pause was how fake her plastered-on smile appeared to be. Instinctively I took a step back as she came closer still. There was something very wrong with her expression.

"What don't you understand, Maddy?" Ami cooed. I didn't answer, and she continued, "In light of recent, shall we say, events, I needed to lay low. See how things played out. Know what I mean?"

I had no idea what she was babbling about. Why would Ami need to "lay low"? And see how *what* played out? One thing I knew for sure was that I didn't care to stick around any longer. I didn't know why Ami—and not Adam—was here at the lighthouse. I had no idea why Ami would fake her own disappearance. But it seemed the longer I stuck around, the more likely this bizarre situation could become volatile. And I didn't want that.

"Look, Ami, I'm leaving. I don't know what you're up to, and to tell you the truth, I don't care. I came down here to meet Adam, but obviously he and I got our signals crossed—"

"You're such a stupid bitch!" Ami shrieked, cutting me off. "Adam didn't leave you the fucking note. *I* did!"

"That can't be right." Dread crept over me. "It was his handwriting."

"Listen up, Maddy, and listen good," Ami said. "You don't work for a man for five years, signing document after document, and not learn his handwriting. I've signed Adam Ward's signature probably more times than he has." At this she laughed maniacally.

Oh God. I'd fallen into Ami's trap. And nobody even knew where I was. Adam certainly wasn't going to come to my rescue. I mentally kicked myself for being so foolish. Why had I not called him to verify he'd written that note? Sure I didn't want to ruin his surprise, but really, was it worth my well-being? And yes, the café had been dark. But nothing had precluded me from dropping by Helena and Nate's bungalow to tell them I was heading down to the lighthouse. Nothing but my own foolhardiness. Not even Max knew I was here because I hadn't searched him out either. I'd been reckless, and now I was going to pay for it.

Panicked, I turned and lunged for the door, my hand grasping for the metal handle. But then I froze when I heard the distinct sound of a gun being cocked echoing in the confines of the lighthouse.

"Turn around," Ami said, her voice icy.

Out of options for now, I obeyed. As I turned to face my captor, I found myself staring down the barrel of a firearm—a .38—aimed directly at me. Behind the gun Ami smiled triumphantly. I thought about making a run for it, but there was no way I was taking that chance. The likelihood of getting shot in such close quarters was high. It didn't matter if Ami could shoot or not. But by the confident way she was holding the .38 with both hands, I was betting she could handle the gun just fine.

"Ami," I whispered. "Just let me go. Please." I wasn't above begging, not at this point.

Her eyes narrowed. "No," she stated, sighing. "You started this with your snooping around. Always asking questions, always wanting answers."

"Please, Ami. I won't ask any more questions, I promise."

She ignored my plea. "You wanted answers. Well, you're finally going to get them."

Sure I'd wanted answers. *But at what cost*, I thought. The temperature in the lighthouse felt like it had dropped several degrees. But maybe it was just the effects of the chill coursing through my body. For the first time since I'd been on the island, I really didn't want any answers. At this point I just wanted one thing—to get out of the lighthouse, alive.

Ami began speaking again, "Like aren't you wondering

how I even got in here, Maddy?"

With the gun she motioned for me to step further away from the door. I moved a few feet to the right, still keeping close to the perimeter and far from the lit candles. God, if a fire started—which could easily happen if even just one of the many candles got knocked over—would Ami let me out? As I watched her eyes flit around the lighthouse, I noted she appeared to be as absolutely crazy as everyone said she was. So no, I feared if there were a fire, she'd leave me here to burn.

"Stop right there," she said, smiling. "Now let's talk. Just like old times."

Ami was enjoying this, I could tell from her expression. I was her captive audience, in every sense of the word. She evidently wanted to talk. So I reassessed the situation. Maybe I could get her to share her story. Why had she pretended to be missing? How did she get in here? What had been going on with her and Chelsea? I had a million questions after all, and if I could keep this crazy girl talking, my penchant for inquisitiveness just might be my way out of this mess.

So I asked, "Fine, tell me. How did you get in here?"

"I bet Adam never mentioned there were once *two* keys to the lighthouse," she said, her voice low and conspiratorial, like she was about to share with me the biggest secret in town.

Good God, maybe she was. Only I feared it was not about a key.

Swallowing hard, I shook my head. "No," I answered. "He didn't."

"Adam had one, of course. But Chelsea had a spare made, so she had one as well."

Yeah, yeah, so her secret lover had given her a key. I'd seen the picture, so I knew Ami and Chelsea had had something going on. My enthusiasm to play along was waning, particularly since the .38 had not wavered. And maybe I shouldn't have uttered the next words, but I did. "Ami, I know all about you and Chelsea. So she gave you a key. Big deal."

The gun shook in Ami's hand, and her cheeks reddened. "That little fuck!" she screamed.

Before I could figure out who the *little fuck* was, cold, hard steel impacted across my cheek. For a fleeting moment, I thought for sure she'd shot me, but then I realized Ami had hit me with the gun. And, fuck, it hurt like hell.

Wiping away at the trickle of blood running down my face, I struggled to stay upright. She'd hit me so hard that the metal had cut into my left cheek, leaving a gash. And though my cheek throbbed, it was my whole head that was ringing.

Ami was pacing, the gun at her side. I shot a glance to the door, but my feet wouldn't move. Terror coursed through my veins, holding me frozen in its grip. When the ringing in my head finally subsided, I realized Ami was not only pacing, she was talking. And what she was saying only served to ratchet my terror level up a notch.

"That little fuck," she repeated. And then she went off. "I should have known he'd have more than one. There were more. I always knew there were more. But I thought they'd been destroyed. I paid that old, perverted bartender for all of the pictures years ago. How do you think he got the money to move to California? And the other morning, I got the final one; the one he must have given to that fucking pervert kid. But there was only *one* in that envelope. I'm sure of it."

Ami continued pacing, and I wiped away blood as it trickled down my cheek. She stopped and aimed the gun at me once again. "He made a copy, didn't he?" she asked, her voice flat.

I nodded weakly, and she mumbled something indistinct about "a plan" and "so that's why," but I couldn't make anything else out. Even so I'd heard enough that my blood ran cold. Ami had stolen the picture out of the envelope at Billy's. Had she also been the person who'd shot Jimmy? I felt a lump forming on my cheek from where she'd hit me with the .38. It wasn't lost on me that it was the same type of firearm used to murder Jimmy.

And suddenly I knew. I was sure she'd done it. "You killed Jimmy," I whispered.

Ami's head shot up. The way she looked at me, I thought for a moment she would hit me again. But then her eyes glazed over, all dreamy, like she was reminiscing. And I guessed she was, as disturbing as it was.

"I didn't really want to shoot him," she said quietly. "I went to Billy's that morning to talk to him. See if any other pictures really were floating around. I had my doubts, but there was just no other explanation for you to keep going back there. I knew he had to have had *so*mething to keep you interested."

"Ami, please—"

She ignored me and rattled on, "And then I saw the look on that kid's face when I walked through the door. I knew then he recognized me from those pictures. But when I saw the envelope on the bar, with an 'M' on the front, I knew what it held."

"So you *killed* him?" I said, shaking my head with disbelief that an act like murder could be so easy for her.

Ami shot me a look of pure hatred. "Don't say it that way," she spat. "It's not like I wanted to kill him. I asked him what was in the envelope, just to be sure. And he immediately lunged for it. There'd be only one reason he'd want to grab that envelope before I did…and…well, somebody had to stop him."

"With a bullet to the head?" I asked, appalled.

Ami didn't hear me because she began to laugh. Or maybe she had heard. In any case it sounded so wrong in light of what she'd just confessed to doing.

Her steely gaze returned to me. "I must say, you showed up that morning at the perfect time." She suppressed a giggle. "Sometimes dumb luck is better than all the planning in the world. I couldn't believe my good fortune. Not only had I gotten to the picture minutes before it would have been in your hands, but then the police suspected *you* of killing the stupid kid." She sighed, a picture of contentment. "It was beyond perfect."

Ami may have been crazy, but she was evil and clever as well. Her tone was cold and calculating, never betraying an ounce of remorse. Not for killing Jimmy. Not for allowing me to take the fall. Not for faking her own disappearance. Nothing.

"Even though the police were focused on you, I had already planned to lay low for a couple of days. Just to be safe. But then

I had an idea,"—another icy smile of wickedness flashed my way— "why not make it so the police suspected you of *two* crimes? So I called you before I took off. I knew you'd take the bait, seeing as you were just soooo curious as to why I'd gone to California."

"Why did you go to LA?" I asked listlessly, since it didn't really matter. Not anymore.

"Contrary to whatever you're thinking, Maddy," she began scornfully, "I'm not *all* bad. I didn't want things to come to this" —she waved the gun around the lighthouse interior— "I really hoped you'd get discouraged. Quit digging around. Go home to a guy who obviously still cared for you." She sighed. "But it didn't work, did it? You just had to fall for Adam. Just like back in high school."

"Shut up," I said, not wanting to hear Adam's name even cross her evil lips.

"Thought you weren't interested anymore, Maddy?" Ami mocked.

"I guess I lied."

"You don't even know him," she scoffed.

"Better than you," I shot back defiantly, but my courage wavered when the gun began to shake in her hand.

"So you think," Ami ground out.

Arguing was probably not a smart move, so I changed the subject. "Let me go, Ami," I pleaded. "It doesn't have to end this way."

"I wish I could." She smiled a sad smile. "But you know too much."

I didn't know why she suddenly looked sad, but I wanted to strike while the iron was hot. Play on her emotions, if that were possible. "Let me go. If not for me, Ami, do it for Sean's sake, he—"

Suddenly she lunged at me. This time I raised my arm to protect my face from the assault. "Shut up!" she screeched as she swung the firearm at me. I ducked, and the gun whooshed through the air. "Don't even say his name, you bitch."

"I'm sorry, I'm sorry," I cried, terrified the gun would discharge with her wild flailing.

Finally Ami backed off, her chest heaving. Her hands shook, but she managed to keep the gun leveled at my chest. "I'm sorry," I whispered once more for good measure.

"I love my husband," she choked. "But *she* was going to ruin it all." Amy took one hand off the gun and wiped at her face, pushed back a swath of hair that had fallen into her face.

"Who?" I asked.

"Chelsea," she replied, her breathing ragged and raw with emotion. "She didn't want me anymore. She was going to tell Sean all about us."

I swallowed hard. Ami was offering up a pretty strong motive. One lover scorned, the other threatening to expose the affair to an unsuspecting spouse. Yeah, my gut was telling me that Ami had played a role in Chelsea's disappearance. The only way to find out was to keep her talking. And her talking bought me more much-needed time. Maybe somebody—Max, Nate, Helena—would see the parked Lexus and come down to investigate. Maybe even Adam would return, wonder where I was, and come save the day. Anything was possible; I had to hold on to that hope.

To keep Ami talking, I asked as gently as I could, "Ami, what happened?"

The Ami I once knew, the girl I'd shared secrets with, that girl met my eyes. If I could reach her, maybe, just maybe, I'd get out of this unscathed. It took everything I had to muster an encouraging smile, but it worked.

Ami began to tell me everything.

She told me how she and Chelsea became friends, even before Adam purchased Fade Island and hired Ami to run Harbour Falls Realtors. She was thrilled that the beautiful Chelsea Hannigan had chosen her as a friend. But Chelsea had other plans. She became intent on seducing Ami. She complained to Ami that Adam had quit sleeping with her years earlier. Ami asked her why she stayed with him, but Chelsea said she'd never let him go. Never. And even though Chelsea claimed to hate Fade Island, many of her trysts with Ami occurred at the lighthouse. When Ami realized Chelsea was using her, she felt shameful that she'd cheated on her husband. And Ami had done so with someone who seemed to just want to get back at Adam for not wanting her anymore.

Shortly before the wedding, Chelsea sought to sever all ties with Ami. She confirmed that their fling had meant nothing to her. It had all been playful experimentation, she'd said. And now that she was getting married, it was time for it to stop. Ami felt slighted; for it seemed Chelsea's words suggested that Ami having been married the whole time meant nothing.

"Chelsea didn't care about things like marriage and fidelity," Ami snorted, echoing Jimmy's words—her victim—without even knowing it. "She just didn't want *me*. She thought she could discard me; move on to the next one."

I wondered if Ami knew Chelsea had been carrying on a fling with J.T. O'Brien as well. Maybe she'd known, and it hadn't mattered to her. Unfortunately I didn't have the luxury of figuring it all out, not with the gun still pointed at me. No, I knew time was wasting. So I stood perfectly still, glancing at the gun. Had she lowered it slightly?

"Ami," I soothed, "I'm sure Chelsea cared about you in her own way."

Ami's pale eyes hardened to an icy blue. "No, she didn't," she countered. "I called her the day of the wedding rehearsal. She had a disposable cell phone she used for our...meetings" —that explained why Ami's number never showed up in Chelsea's phone records— "or sometimes we'd use pay phones. Anyway I asked her not to end it. I asked her to keep seeing me. She laughed at me. She told me she was destroying the cell phone and not to contact her once she was married. Maddy, I begged, but she just laughed."

The emotion in Ami's face was an odd mix of heartbreak and fury. "Ami," I said softly.

But she laughed, the heartbroken moment quickly fading. "Don't pity me, Maddy," she hissed. "After she was done laughing, she threatened to tell Sean everything if I didn't back off. I couldn't take that chance, the chance of ending up with nothing. I asked her to meet me one last time that night. I told her to come down to the lighthouse. I knew she'd show up. And I knew what I had to do when she did."

A sick feeling washed over me anew. "Oh God, Ami, what did you do?" I whispered.

"She came to the lighthouse. It was late, really late. She said she had stopped in Harbour Falls to tell Sean about us but chickened out at the last minute."

That was why Chelsea had been at the bank; Sean and Ami's house was in that neighborhood. It was all falling into place.

Ami continued, "She told me she almost went back to the hotel. She called Adam, but I guess he didn't say what she wanted to hear." Ami swiped at her face, wiping a tear that had fallen. "So she came here to the lighthouse and sealed her fate that night."

I remained silent, fearful. Ami put both hands on the gun once more and aimed it at me. Good God, what had she done to Chelsea? And in this same place.

"I had to get rid of her, permanently," Ami said. It was like she'd read my mind. Her eyes, now disturbingly lifeless, met mine. With a calm voice, she added, "Just like I have to get rid of you, permanently."

Chelsea was dead. And this was it for me. I had to make my move—no matter how dangerous—now or never.

I held my breath and swung, hitting Ami's shoulder. My movement was swift enough to knock the .38 out of her hands. It fell to the floor, skidding across the concrete floor of the lighthouse, out of both our reaches. I tried to make a play for it, but Ami grabbed my hair and yanked me back to her. I elbowed her in the stomach as hard as I could, and she loosened her grasp with a *uuumph* noise.

I hastily judged the distance to the door. The gun was right there—in front of the door. Thoughts raced through my mind: I needed to get to the door. I needed to get to the gun. I needed to get out!

But before I made my move, Ami came at me like a madwoman. I shoved her back with every ounce of strength I could muster, and she flew backwards. A loud cracking noise rang out, and I saw Ami's head hit the metal railing that ran along the winding staircase. The candles shook and flickered madly, but thankfully, none toppled over. Ami, though, crumpled to the ground, knocked out cold.

I turned to make my escape with every intention of fleeing out the door. But the door was already open. *Huh?* What I saw stopped me in my tracks. The person who'd evidently opened the door was blocking my way. And the gun was no longer on the floor. No, it was now in this individual's hands.

The last shred of hope I had dissipated as this person expertly handled the gun, spun the chamber, cocked it once again, pointed it in my direction. At last this unexpected arrival spoke, "You didn't think that a fucking crazy person could pull this off alone, now did you?"

I was too stunned to speak. Ami had had an accomplice all along, and to say I was stunned to see who it was would have been an understatement of epic proportions.

Chapter 28

I slowly edged back toward a still-unconscious Ami. And Jennifer Weston, gun in hand, stepped into the lighthouse, the door behind her sticking on sand and not closing all the way. Through the opening that led to freedom, I could see full darkness had descended on this fateful November late afternoon. Or was it early evening now? I'd lost track of time. I longed to run out into the velvety black night, out to where the waves crashed thunderously against the rocks, beckoning me to safety.

But a psychotic-looking Jennifer stood blocking my way. With a sinister chuckle she repeated the words she'd just uttered, "You didn't think a fucking crazy person could pull all of this off by herself, now did you?"

"You...you're involved in this?" I gasped, finding it hard to fathom that she and Ami had been working together.

I started to say more, but she brandished the gun impatiently, silencing me immediately. "Don't look so surprised, Fitch," she scoffed. "My working with Ami makes perfect sense. After all, as far as I was concerned, Chelsea's number was up the day J.T. fell in love with her."

I couldn't say I was shocked to learn Jennifer had played a role in Chelsea's disappearance. I mean, I had suspected as much the day she wigged out on the ferry. But Jennifer working with Ami in the commission of God knew how many crimes did truly leave me speechless.

Jennifer's glare bore into me, as she spoke in a calm, detached manner. "Chelsea ruined any chance of J.T. ever loving me. I knew he only married me in order to get back at her for getting engaged to Ward. But at the time, I foolishly believed he'd grow to love me." She laughed bitterly, I supposed at this recollection.

"When he told me he wanted a divorce, just weeks after we were married, I knew he'd started seeing her again." She paused. "You know, I refused to divorce him until after she was gone. I even gave him half of the ferry business, so he wouldn't leave this area. But it didn't matter. Nothing I did could stop him from loving that bitch." The last sentence she spat, and I instinctively stepped back.

Jennifer's expression was almost wistful, but her eyes were black. Unfortunately there was no escaping. Even though the door remained partially opened, Jennifer stood between me and freedom, and worse yet, the gun was currently aimed at my heart.

Since it had worked with Ami, it seemed my best chance of survival was to try to keep Jennifer talking. I held on to this fresh glimmer of hope. The more time that passed increased the chance that Nate or Helena would notice my parked car at the top of the cliff steps and come down to investigate. Or maybe Adam would come home and, finding the note, see that his handwriting had been forged and that a trap had been set. Too bad I hadn't realized as much. But I hadn't, so now Adam was one of my only hopes.

With this in mind, I sent up a quick prayer that Ami's forged note wouldn't blow away before Adam got to it, and then I asked Jennifer, "What happened that night?" My words were shaky, but it was my best attempt to stall for time.

Jennifer shot me an amused smile. "You're brave, Fitch, asking me about that night. Either that or you're just plain dumb."

I ignored the insult, hoping I'd not pushed too far. I was about to apologize for good measure, but I stopped when Jennifer mumbled something to herself about it not mattering anymore what I knew. While that certainly chilled my soul, I tried to remain calm and listen as Jennifer focused her attention back to me.

"I was the one who ferried Chelsea over that night to meet with Ami. But what Chelsea didn't know was that Ami and I had planned it all out. I couldn't stand to see that bitch playing with yet another person's feelings..." She trailed off, and I knew she was thinking about how Chelsea had toyed with J.T.'s emotions as well.

I wondered just *how* close she and Ami had become, so I whispered, "So you and Ami?"

Jennifer rolled her eyes. "Not like *that*, Fitch," she spat. "Ami and I are friends, just friends." She paused and narrowed her eyes at me but continued, "Over the years, with her ferrying back and forth, we got to know one another. She told me about her and Chelsea, and as time wore on, I could see she actually cared for the Hannigan slut. But I knew Ami was being used, just like J.T. had been used by Ward's tramp of a fiancée."

I swallowed hard as I imagined a distressed, unstable Ami, confiding in a bitter, angry Jennifer. Little wonder tragedy had ensued. And now I found myself at the culmination of it all.

Jennifer stepped closer to me, her finger lovingly caressing the trigger. "Chelsea suspected nothing," she said, her voice scary soft. "Just like you suspected nothing."

I looked away from her steely, unwavering gaze and down to my trembling hands. "Jennifer...please."

"Please what?" Jennifer yelled. "Let you go? Feel sorry for you? Just face it—you're going to meet the same fate as Chelsea Hannigan. But you should be happy, because you're finally going to get the truth that's eluded you. Isn't that what you've been searching for all this time?"

With my heart hammering in my chest, I nodded weakly. Arguing seemed like a bad plan. Terror engulfed me when I noticed Jennifer's finger twitching on the trigger. *My God, please let me live*, I prayed, all the while thinking it was weird how fear distorted time. Seconds that felt more like stretched-out minutes passed until, finally, Jennifer's finger stilled.

I let out a breath I didn't even realize I'd been holding, and Jennifer continued, her voice back under control. "I waited outside the lighthouse that night, listening. Just like I did tonight." She paused. "Only we didn't have a gun that night. Pity."

Jennifer suddenly seemed unfocused, reminiscing as she

was. I didn't need to hear anymore. I already knew Chelsea had been killed that night, whether they'd had a gun or not. I judged the distance to the door and calculated that if I could get Jennifer to lunge for me, as opposed to shooting me, I might have a chance to get past her. It was a risk, but what choices did I have?

But first I needed to get her off her game.

"You and Ami murdered Chelsea, didn't you?" I said tauntingly, even though I knew this approach could backfire terribly.

Jennifer looked stunned that I'd actually said it out loud, and I took that brief opportunity to make a run for it. Unfortunately Jennifer was faster, and she grabbed me easily, one arm hooking around my neck as she wrenched me back to her with more force than I'd anticipated. I cried out, and Jennifer hissed in my ear, "Shut up! Shut up, or I'll fucking shoot you right here."

She jammed the gun against my temple for emphasis, and knowing she'd follow through on her threat, I quieted. Jennifer tightened her grip until I coughed, and then she relaxed her hold slightly, asking, "You wanna know how Chelsea died?"

"No," I croaked, trying not to sob.

Nobody was going to rescue me. I was going to end up dead, like Chelsea. I wanted to cry over every mistake I'd made that had led me to this. I should have listened to my dad. I should have listened to Adam. I'd gotten in over my head, and my own stubbornness was going to be my end. I didn't care to hear any more about the Harbour Falls Mystery. I'd heard enough answers to the questions I'd once sought. Realizing that I was likely going to pay with my life had a way of killing my last bit of curiosity.

But Jennifer, apparently, was determined that I knew it all before I took that final breath. "Ami tried to strangle Hannigan," she ground out, laughing.

Still trapped in the stranglehold, Jennifer's breath wafted across my face, hot and sticky, her voice harsh in my ear. Some small, incoherent sound escaped my mouth, and Jennifer slid her free hand to my throat. Traitorous tears rolled down my cheeks. *So much for dying with dignity.* Her fingers pressed along the column of my throat, and she whispered, "Ami couldn't finish the job though."

I squeezed my eyes shut, fearful that Jennifer was truly going to strangle the life out of my body. I was sure she—as opposed to Ami—could "finish the job." But thankfully, she moved her hand away and slid her arm back around my neck in a kind of loose chokehold.

"So I stepped in," she resumed, the cold metal at my temple a reminder that Jennifer could shoot me just as easily as strangle me. "I dragged Hannigan out to the water. In her weakened state, she hardly fought. But it still took longer than I thought it would to drown her."

It was all so horrible and cold-blooded: Ami strangling Chelsea to near-death, and then Jennifer stepping in and drowning her to finish the job. "Stop," I groaned. "I don't want to hear any more."

But it was as if Jennifer hadn't even heard me. "After it was done, we dragged her up in the caves,"—Oh my God, the caves!—"left her to rot. And now you're going to join her."

Terrified as I was, I managed to choke out, "You won't get away with it twice."

"Oh, but I will," she said coolly. "Everyone will assume you shot Jimmy, as they do already. And then, when you just disappear, it will look like poor Ward went off the deep end for the second time."

She laughed evilly, and I gasped, "No!"

Jennifer was going to frame Adam. All the years Adam had spent being the prime suspect in Chelsea's disappearance, even still was, it was easy to imagine the police would put him through the same kind of hell once I went missing.

"Come on, Fitch," Jennifer said, pulling me with the arm still wrenched around my neck. "It's time to take a walk up to the caves and finally put an end to this."

In a last-ditch effort to stall her, I asked, "What about Ami?"

Jennifer paused and looked down at Ami's still form. She'd been out for a while so I tried to play on Jennifer's sympathy. "She should see a doctor," I uttered in little more than a whisper, since Jennifer's grip was so damn tight. "She should have woken up by now."

"She'll be fine," Jennifer said. "In fact, this will work out even better. Now, when she shows back up at home, she can claim she hit her head and had amnesia for a few days. Nobody will question it, since they all know she's a little whacked."

Jennifer started pulling me toward the door, but I struggled. "Quit it, or I swear, I'll knock you out before we get to the caves," she warned.

I was torn on whether to take my chances and continue to struggle, or see if I could get away from her once we left the lighthouse. In any case I knew that if Jennifer succeeded in dragging me up to those caves, I'd be done for.

But I didn't have to think about it for long, because, out of the darkness, a familiar voice broke through the noise of our scuffle. "Let her go, Jennifer."

Adam!

I'd never been so happy, and so terrified, all at the same time. I tried like hell to break free but quieted when Jennifer reclaimed her grip, and the gun was once again pressed to my temple. And then I froze completely when I caught sight of Adam in the doorway, his own .38 pointed at Jennifer. But I knew he couldn't shoot her. It was too risky. If he missed, he might hit me. Even if he did succeed in targeting Jennifer, her gun could still discharge, shooting me. And she must have been thinking the same thing.

"You wouldn't dare," Jennifer chided. "If you shoot me, my gun goes off and BAM! Your little girlfriend's brains are all over the ground."

Adam winced at Jennifer's vivid words, but he took a step closer, his gun steady, his eyes never leaving her. "Hold it right there, Ward," Jennifer warned. "Or I will shoot her, I swear. Don't test me."

Adam slowly began to circle the lighthouse interior, his movements shadowing Jennifer's. Jennifer and I were edged closer to the door. I was sure if she got us out that door, Adam would be on her heels. She wouldn't get far. She was going to have to rethink her original plan. If she did shoot me, Adam would surely kill her. She had to know that.

"Give it up," Adam said, echoing this very thing. "Let her go."

Adam took a slow step to his left, and his foot made contact with Ami's arm, peeking out from under the stairway. He glanced down ever so quickly, and Jennifer tensed. But Adam was faster, and his gun swiveled back to Jennifer instantly. "What the fuck is she doing here?" Adam growled, referring to Ami.

Jennifer began to chuckle. "You really never knew, did you?"

"What are you talking about?" he asked.

From his expression it was evident Adam had no clue why Ami was lying unconscious on the floor of the lighthouse. As far as he knew, she was just a harmless, unstable girl who worked for him and had recently gone missing. Hell, he liked her so much that he'd even ensured the missing person's report had gone out early.

Yeah, Adam had not known this tidbit, and in a way I was glad. He hadn't deceived me, and it proved he'd given Ami the benefit of the doubt, even with her mental problems. But now he was about to find out the truth.

"J.T. wasn't the only one your slut-fiancée was fucking around with," Jennifer said, glee in her tone at disseminating this tawdry information. "In fact, your girlfriend here has the photographic evidence. I saw it myself this morning in the mail, and I noticed her car at the café earlier, so I know she has the photo."

So *that* was how she and Ami had known to put their plan in motion, why they'd trapped me here at the lighthouse. As I feared someone had seen the envelope from Jimmy, in this case Jennifer. And knowing I'd end up turning the photo in to the police once I saw who was in it, they knew it was time to act.

Except the one thing puzzling me was that Ami hadn't known Jimmy had made a copy of that lone incriminating picture until I'd told her. Even though Jennifer had seen the mail and figured it out. It was looking more and more like Jennifer had been the mastermind behind this whole thing. She'd obviously kept certain elements of the plan from her own accomplice, even while putting said plan into motion this morning.

I glanced over at Adam. He appeared angrier than ever, having digested Jennifer's words. "What photographic evidence?" he ground out between clenched teeth.

Jennifer nudged the gun against my temple, and I heard Adam growl in response. "Show him, Fitch," she demanded, oblivious to Adam's escalating anger.

Jennifer loosened her grip around my neck. From my jacket pocket, I shakily pulled the folded piece of paper that held the image of Ami kissing Chelsea. Before I had a chance to lift it, Jennifer snatched the paper from my grip, unfolded it, glanced at it with a snort, and tossed it in Adam's direction.

The piece of paper flitted to the floor in front of Adam, and he knelt down slowly to pick it up, his gun remaining trained on Jennifer.

"See, Ami is just as involved in this as I am," Jennifer whined as Adam glanced at the image on the paper. "And now, you know her motive," she added with a snicker.

Adam crumpled the paper in his hand as he rose to his feet. Though he appeared calm, I saw a myriad of emotions in his eyes. Ami Dubois-Hensley had kept her secret so well hidden that not even Adam—the man who seemed to know everything— had uncovered this piece of information. He'd underestimated Ami, as had everyone.

But, then again, how could anyone have known? Ami had admitted to paying off Old Carl, Billy's once-upon-a-time bartender, for all the incriminating photos. And Jimmy had misplaced the only remaining photo, recalling it after I showed up and started asking questions. And threw a little money his way.

Of course, none of it mattered now. We had the evidence to clear Adam once and for all, but Jennifer was determined to get rid of me. Adam might have ruined her original plan to murder me, hide my body in the caves with Chelsea's, and allow Adam to be blamed for another inexplicable disappearance, but

I could tell Jennifer was improvising some alternative plan even as we spoke. And that couldn't be good.

"You and Ami killed Chelsea?" Adam asked quietly.

"No," Jennifer replied, "*You* killed Chelsea."

Adam looked perplexed, but I sensed the panic in Jennifer's voice. She was starting to lose it. She pressed the gun harder into my temple, and I cried out in pain. Adam started toward us, but Jennifer stopped him in his tracks when she yelled, "Hold it right there, Ward, or she'd dead. You can shoot me after, but she'll still be gone."

It was obvious Jennifer wasn't bluffing. Adam must have sensed it because he halted. But I'd never seen a person more furious. If looks could kill, Jennifer would have been a goner.

Oblivious, Jennifer said, "Now take your cell out, Ward. You're gonna call the police and give them a long-overdue confession."

No! This turn in her sordid plan was insidious. I'd rather be dead than allow Adam to take the fall for Chelsea's murder. Of course I'd probably end up dead, regardless. But I could go down fighting.

Adam was removing his cell from the back pocket of his jeans when I cried out, "Don't do it, Adam. Please."

Jennifer hissed in my ear, "Shut up!"

I began to struggle, despite my fear of getting shot. I could hear Adam saying something as I managed to put some space between me and the cold steel of the .38. In response Jennifer wrenched my neck hard, leaving me gasping for breath.

But then, suddenly, a loud shot rang out, deafening me. Jennifer's grip tightened, and I couldn't breathe. But then her hold on me inexplicably loosened. I began to fall, certain that I'd been shot. Jennifer's body fell onto mine, but I felt no pain. *Maybe this is what dying feels like? Painless.*

As I lay drifting in and out, somebody lifted Jennifer's weight from me. I heard voices and then felt someone lifting my head from the ground. "Adam?" I whispered, opening my eyes as I felt his welcome touch.

"Maddy," Adam whispered, "My God, I thought I lost you."

His hands gently ran over the swelling on my cheek where Ami had hit me with the gun, and I winced. I struggled to sit up, and Adam helped me to my feet. "What happened?" I asked, my ears reverberating from the gunshot that had rung out so close to my head.

Before Adam could answer, I saw movement out of the corner of my eye. Max stepped into the lighthouse, smoking gun—literally—in hand. I relaxed back into the warmth of Adam's chest as Max bent down over Jennifer's very still body. "She's dead," he said somberly, releasing his fingers from around her wrist, where I supposed he'd been checking for a pulse.

Max had shot and killed Jennifer Weston. He'd saved me. He'd saved Adam. It was now more obvious than ever why Adam employed him as security here on the island.

"Took you long enough," Adam said in a tone that would have sounded light in other circumstances, but now it just sounded grim. "I was worried I'd pressed the wrong key."

I later found out Adam had somehow managed to call Max from the cell phone that had been in his back pocket. He had Max on autodial, and at some point during the ordeal, he reached back and hit what he'd hoped was the correct key. Thank God it had been the right one. I shuddered, imagining what might have occurred if Max had not arrived or if he had gotten here too late.

Adam held me close to his body, and I looked up at him, hoping my eyes conveyed the emotions no words ever could. "I'm sorry," I said to him, wanting to apologize for having ever mistrusted him.

But just then Ami let out a moan as she began to come to. Max glanced at Adam questioningly. Adam grimaced and said, "She was in on this whole thing. But we finally have the answer to what happened to Chelsea. These two"—he nodded to Jennifer's still body and then to Ami—"killed her."

"And I know where they put her body," I muttered, my voice weak.

Both Adam and Max eyed me, stunned. I told them all Ami and Jennifer had told me, finishing with how they'd dragged

Chelsea up to one of the caves within the cliff face. Even before I'd finished my story, Max was on the phone with the police.

Adam wrapped his arms around me, holding me in a way that showed me he truly realized how closely he had come to losing me. "Let's go outside," he murmured into my ear. "Max can keep an eye on Ami until the police get here."

I glanced over my shoulder; Max was cuffing a disorientated Ami to the metal railing. I'd seen enough, so I allowed Adam to lead me from the lighthouse, out into the welcoming cool air of night.

Under a black velvet sky that I was thankful to be walking beneath, waves crashed all around us. Adam and I walked silently, hand in hand, along the sandy stretch leading down away from the lighthouse, and then Adam stopped, turning me to face him. "Maddy," he began, his voice catching. "I don't know what I would have done had I lost you."

"Adam," I soothed, "you saved me. How did you even know I was here? Did you see the note?"

He nodded. "Yeah, and when I got here, I saw your car at the top of the cliffs. But you're wrong about one thing."

I looked up into his face, beautifully lit by a sliver of moonlight peeking from behind a lone cloud. "What's that?"

Adam took a deep breath, and said, "Actually *you* saved *me*. You've shown me how to trust again. You've shown me how to live, how to love. And I love you, more than you know, Madeleine Fitch."

I stepped toward him, pressing my body to his, soaking in all his warmth and strength and love. "I love you, too, Adam Ward," I replied reverently.

Adam bent down, his lips grazing mine. "It's finally over," he muttered against my mouth.

I caught his bottom lip with my own lips and then kissed him back, slowly and languidly, savoring his taste and the feel of his skin against mine. Breaking away just long enough to speak, I amended his words, "No, Adam. All the bad stuff is over, yes, but for us this is just the beginning. *Our* beginning."

Chapter 29

On a bitter, cold November morning, Chelsea Hannigan's body—or, rather, what remained of it—was recovered from the back of one of the many caves that lay recessed into the jagged cliff face overlooking the lighthouse. Skeletal remains and a few tattered shreds of a once-vibrant sundress were spirited away to the crime labs in Harbour Falls for final analysis. Though there was no doubt from the preliminary tests that were conducted on the scene that the remains were, in fact, those of the woman who'd once been engaged to Adam Ward.

Once the police were finished with both scenes—the cave, and the lighthouse, where Ami and then Jennifer had held me captive—the news of what had happened spread like wildfire, and the media descended onto our usually quiet community.

The story had enough tawdry details, as well as the resolution of a mystery that had haunted the Harbour Falls area for half a decade, to keep the general public hungry for details. Fortunately, since Adam owned Fade Island—and it was, therefore, private property—he was able to keep the news crews and nosy reporters far away from the actual scenes of the crimes. But that didn't mean we'd been left to our own devices over on the island. No, quite the contrary.

My dad, the mayor, had rushed over only hours after the police had arrived on the scene at the lighthouse. My father was so grateful for Adam's intervention that, much to my surprise, he'd grabbed Adam in a manly, awkward way and hugged him. Yeah, actually hugged "that man," Mr. Adam Ward. So I guess you could say miracles do happen.

Following my father's visit, Trina and Walker arrived,

spent a couple of days. Nate and Max also paid many a visit to Adam's compound, where I was still staying. Additionally the phones seemed to ring continuously. There were calls from my best friend and agent, Katie; Adam's parents; my brother, Brent, in Chicago; and many, many more concerned friends and acquaintances. Even Julian had called. But I made sure to take that call in a different room, away from Adam.

Everyone was thankful we'd survived Ami and Jennifer's machinations, and they were all relieved that the Harbour Falls Mystery had finally been solved. So much so that nobody seemed to care that I'd been secretly investigating the mystery all along. I guessed the outcome justified the means.

But among the many visitors and callers there was one notable exception—Helena. I'd yet to hear from her. I found it odd, but her absence was just one of many still unanswered questions that lingered in the days following the lighthouse incident.

Today, however, Adam and I would soon be finding out at least some of those answers. Detective Mitchell was venturing over to the island to bring resolution to many of our case-related queries. The question of why Helena was staying away would have to wait. For now.

Adam's voice brought me back to the here and now when I heard him speaking outside the study with Detective Mitchell. I'd retired to Adam's workspace to look over my own notes regarding the case. I'd long since decided not to write the original novel I'd come here to research and pen. But I had another idea. And I couldn't wait to get Adam's opinion on it.

I folded up my notes and was moving from Adam's big, comfy desk chair to one of the two situated on the opposite side of the desk just as Detective Mitchell and Adam came into the room. Adam motioned for the detective to take the seat next to me, and then he settled into his own chair behind the desk.

Once we were all comfortable, the good detective began to speak. "First, Miss Fitch, I'd like to apologize for any, uh, inconvenience the last couple of weeks may have caused you."

Inconvenience? I'd been accused of murdering Jimmy Kingston and suspected of involvement in what turned out to be the phony disappearance of Ami Dubois-Hensley, so I couldn't help but scoff. But I knew Detective Mitchell's intentions were sincere, so I nodded warily in acceptance of his apology.

"Detective Crowley sends his apologies as well," Mitchell continued. At that I couldn't help but laugh out loud, and he added contritely, "Of course, we both thought it best he not deliver his message in person."

Good call, I thought. I was glad Detective Crowley had remained in Harbourtown, as I sure didn't care to see the man who'd been all set to send me up the river. But to Detective Mitchell, I just nodded.

An uncomfortable silence filled the room, and Adam cleared his throat. "So, Detective, what did you wish to speak with us about today? You said on the phone that you had some information."

"I do," Detective Mitchell said. "I'm sure you'll be happy to hear that Ami Hensley has been extremely cooperative."

Adam and I glanced at one another hopefully. The last thing either of us wanted was a long, drawn-out trial. Now that the mystery was solved, we were anxious to put it behind us. We were ready to move forward. If Ami was willing to confess to all she'd done, our hopes could be realized.

"What does that mean exactly?" I asked, waiting for clarification.

"It means Mrs. Hensley has confessed to everything." Adam and I let out collective breaths. "The planning and attempted murder of Chelsea Hannigan, murdering Jimmy Kingston, assault and battery on you, Miss Fitch." He nodded to me. "She confessed it all. There's more too: kidnapping, obstruction of justice, destruction of evidence. Need I go on?"

Both Adam and I shook our heads, and Mitchell added, "Suffice it to say, Ami is going to be locked up for a very, very long time."

"In jail?" I asked.

Detective Mitchell shifted in his seat. "Actually we've worked out a plea. In exchange for her confession, Ami will be sent to a facility for the criminally insane."

"Willow Point?" I asked timidly.

The detective nodded, and I winced. Willow Point was not much better than prison. Maybe worse if certain stories were to be believed. But Ami would probably receive better treatment for her disorders there than in prison. Or at least I hoped that would be the case. I glanced at Adam to get a gauge on his thoughts, but his expression was unreadable.

Adam ran a hand over his face and quietly asked Detective Mitchell, "What made her decide to plead guilty?"

I wondered as much myself, especially since Ami had guarded her secrets so intently—not to mention very successfully—over the last several years.

"Her husband," Mitchell replied, and then he turned his gaze to Adam. "Sean Hensley said convincing her to plead was his way of saying 'thanks' to you."

Poor Sean Hensley, just another victim in all of this. I couldn't even begin to imagine the torment he must feel at knowing the true depths of Ami's instability. Perhaps he'd wanted to return Adam's favor—helping him when he believed his wife to be missing—but I was sure Sean had his own personal reasons for wanting to avoid a very public trial. In any case I was grateful, and I found myself hoping he could someday pick up the pieces and eventually move on with his life. Sean deserved some kind of happiness after all that had happened.

Detective Mitchell then provided answers to many of the questions Ami's confession had raised.

For example, unbeknownst to me, Jennifer had followed me on my very first visit to Billy's. I hadn't even thought to look for people trailing me that day. Jennifer was also the one who sent Ami to LA, to try to waylay my burgeoning investigation. She had suspected right from the very beginning that I would investigate the Harbour Falls Mystery. After all, my books were murder mysteries. And she worried that unaccounted-for evidence could begin to surface with someone like me digging around. She'd been right to worry.

Detective Mitchell also told us where Ami had holed up

during her faked disappearance. There was a seedy roadside motel named Fowler's that was located on the outskirts of Harbour Falls. It was the kind of place where no questions were asked, and patrons could retain complete anonymity. Jennifer had rented a room there and hid Ami away in the rundown establishment. Thus giving the woman who'd killed Jimmy time to lay low and subsequently appear to have gone missing. And to more easily implicate me, of course.

Detective Mitchell was getting ready to go, when I suddenly remembered that my dad had told me the police had taken a statement from J.T. O'Brien. Mostly to find out what he'd known of Jennifer's involvement in the mystery. So I asked, "What about J.T. O'Brien? Was he involved in any way?"

Detective Mitchell shook his head and surprised me by saying, "No, not at all."

My eyes met Adam's. We'd not been able to find the location where I'd witnessed J.T. burying something over on the east side of the island, even when we'd driven back down with Max yesterday. The recent storms had left the area in shambles. Trees downed everywhere, ruts in the access road turned into gushing torrents. It had been impossible to discern where J.T. had been digging. I'd told Adam I wanted to try again, but he stood firm, insisting that whatever J.T. had been doing, it had nothing to do with the case. Now it appeared he'd been right.

Adam's gaze held mine, and I was sure he wanted to convey that it was time to scrap any further plans to locate that spot.

Well, we'd see about that.

Detective Mitchell, noticing our silent communication, cleared his throat. Adam and I both looked away. "Uh, one more thing you may be interested in hearing." My eyes returned to the detective. "O'Brien admitted himself to an eight-week rehab program over in Bangor. He's pretty broken up about this whole thing, and I guess he wants to start fresh."

Adam had told me he'd heard from his sources—probably Max—that J.T. wasn't taking it particularly well that Chelsea Hannigan had been murdered by his ex-wife. For as much as I was no fan of J.T.'s, I couldn't help but feel a little sorry for him.

After all, Chelsea had influenced the path he'd taken. Unfortunately for him, he had really loved her.

Now that Jennifer was dead, Brody stood to inherit Jennifer's half of the business, so he and J.T. would be the sole owners of the ferry service. If J.T. could finally get help with his addiction, maybe he'd find his way after all. I knew somewhere behind all that vitriol was the kind, gentle J.T. I'd once known and cared for.

I was sure Adam was less concerned with J.T.'s well-being, but he was still thoughtful enough to state, "Maybe O'Brien can finally get sober now that he can put all of this behind him."

I knew he was speaking for my benefit, so I whispered a heartfelt, "Maybe."

Detective Mitchell left shortly thereafter. I sat for a bit longer in the study just thinking. Adam walked the detective to the door, and when he returned, he pulled the chair next to me close and sat down. "You holding up?" he asked, taking my hand in one of his own.

I breathed out. "I think so. It's just been a lot to take in."

"I know," Adam soothed, his thumb caressing the back of my hand. "What can I do to make things better?"

I closed my eyes for a few seconds. "I think...I think I need a break from Fade Island. I don't know. Maybe get away for a few days."

"Are you sure you don't need a break from me?" Adam asked, and though his tone was light, I saw sadness in his expression when I opened my eyes.

"Of course not," I exclaimed, placing my free hand on his cheek and capturing his gaze. "I love you, Adam. I just want to get away for a little while. But not alone. I want us to go somewhere together."

Relief washed over his features, and he said softly, "Wherever you want to go, Maddy, just tell me." A grin formed on his lips. "After all, we have a plane at our disposal...as well as a pilot."

For all of the places I could choose—exotic locales, world-famous cities—there was only one that called to me. A place that was the antithesis of all that was wet and cold, a place far away from this island. "I want to go to Los Angeles," I said.

Adam appeared surprised, so I elaborated. "You can see where I live. You can meet my agent, Katie. She's my best friend out there. I want to share with you what my life is like in California."

"I'd like that," Adam replied, smiling.

"Speaking of meeting important people in our lives," I started. Adam cocked a curious eyebrow, and I continued, "When do I get to meet your parents?"

Back when I'd lived in Harbour Falls, I'd seen Dr. Ward and his elegant wife around town from time to time. But I never really knew them. But now, being involved with their only son, it seemed important to do so.

"I wasn't aware you were all that interested in meeting my parents," Adam replied.

I rolled my eyes. "Of course I want to meet them. After all, they did produce you," I teased.

Now it was Adam's turn to roll his eyes. "Fair enough," he said. "Last I spoke with my dad he said they were in San Francisco. We can fly up there from LA."

I was happy with that, but there was another thing weighing on me. And it had been since the resolution of the mystery. I wondered what was next for us, for our relationship. Where did Adam and I go from here? Though I had an idea for a new book, I wasn't sure *where* I'd be writing it. I had one month left on my lease. But I wanted to stay longer, write my next novel here. Adam, though, hadn't asked me to stay. The thought of leaving Fade Island saddened me beyond words, because I didn't want a long-distance relationship.

I opened my mouth to speak, but the doorbell interrupted. "Expecting someone?" I asked.

"No," Adam replied. "You?"

I shook my head as the buzzer sounded again, this time with insistence. Adam dropped my hand and went to answer the door with me trailing behind.

When Adam opened the door, to my surprise, there stood

Helena. "Oh, Maddy, I feel so bad," she said breathlessly as she rushed in, engulfing me in a hug. "I'm so sorry I haven't been here for you. There's just been so much… Never mind."

"It's fine, Helena," I said. "And you're here now."

Helena stepped back, breaking our embrace, but keeping her hands on my elbows. "Are you OK?" Her blue eyes, looking somewhat troubled, swept my form.

"I'm fine," I replied. "But is everything all right with you?"

"Uh." Her hands dropped to her sides, and she glanced meaningfully to Adam. "There was, uh, something I had to look into over in Harbour Falls." Her eyes darted to Adam's once more, and she added, "Something to do with my mom."

The whole exchange was odd, and I turned toward Adam, but his expression quickly morphed from worried to unreadable. *Okaaay.*

I asked Helena, "You mom's fine though, right?"

She nodded, and the subject was dropped. Everything went back to normal, and we spoke for a while longer.

After she left, Adam and I went upstairs to begin packing for our trip to California. At first he and I discussed only our plans for the trip, but then, as I tossed a pair of jeans into the open, and very overflowing, suitcase on Adam's bed, I ventured, "Did Helena seem a little off to you?"

"She seemed fine," he replied, maybe a little too hastily.

"Why was she looking at you like that?" I asked as I attempted to zip up my too-full suitcase.

Adam gently tugged the zipper from my hand, turning me to face him. "Maddy, you know Helena and her mom have been through a lot. Do you remember her stepdad?"

Of course I did, so I said, "Yes."

"Helena still worries about her mom," Adam continued. "Even though everything's been fine since that man took off."

I recalled how Helena's horrible stepdad—her mom's second husband—had skipped town one day, after years of abusive behavior toward Helena and her mother. Since Adam had been such close friends with Helena, because of Nate, I was sure he'd been privy to even more than what was common knowledge among the Harbour Falls townsfolk. It had probably been worse than everyone imagined.

"I shouldn't have said anything," I said quietly, feeling like I'd somehow intruded.

Adam put his hands on my shoulders. "Hey," he said, "you can ask me anything, you know this, right?" I nodded, but Adam looked sad. "Maddy, there's so much more I want to share with you, but it's not my story to tell."

It made me love Adam even more to see how much he valued his friends. I couldn't help but smile at him. "What?" he said.

"I just love you," I replied, wrapping my arms around him.

"I love you too," he whispered, leaning down to kiss my neck. "So what's next?"

Something about Adam's tone of voice, I knew he was asking something important. *Could he finally be asking about my staying?*

Sucking in a breath, I dared to whispered, "What do you mean?"

Adam straightened, and his eyes met mine. "What's next for us, Madeleine?" he replied, pulling me closer. "Where do we go from here?"

"You tell me," I countered, lowering my gaze.

Time stood still, while I waited for Adam's response.

Quietly he whispered, "I want you to stay. I don't want you to leave the island. Stay for the winter at least."

I nodded, but Adam wasn't finished. "I never told you what my surprise was going to be the day you ended up down at the lighthouse." Adam winced, I supposed at the memory, still fresh, of what I'd endured.

Curious to find out what he'd been planning, I said, "So what was the surprise?"

"You know the room next to my study?" Though I'd never been in it, I nodded. "Well I cleared it out a couple of weeks ago, changed some things around. That night I was going to ask you to help me get it ready…" Adam trailed off.

"Ready for what?" I asked, now more curious than ever.

Adam's eyes, such a clear blue today, met mine. "I wanted you to have a room here all to yourself where you could write. I still do. I know you can write at the cottage, but you should have a spot for when you're up here."

I loved the idea, and I was touched he'd thought of it. I told him as much, and asked, "So what are you asking, Adam?"

"I want you to stay here on the island and write your book. Spend the winter here. We can spend it together, and hopefully I can convince you to stay even longer. Will you stay?"'

My heart soared. "Of course I'll stay."

Adam walked me backward to the bed, where he pushed the suitcase off with one hand. Clothes tumbled out and to the floor, but neither of us gave it much thought. We were too engrossed in one another as we fell onto the downy comforter, quickly tossing our own clothes to join the pile on the floor.

An hour later, as we lay spent in one another's arms, Adam asked, "What are you thinking about?" His hand toyed with my hair as I lay sprawled across his bare body.

"My next book," I replied, lifting my head to rest my chin on his chest.

"Hmm," he mused, eyebrow cocked. "Another mystery, I presume?"

Adam knew I'd decided not to write about the Harbour Falls Mystery, but it appeared he still expected me to pen a mystery of some sort. Crawling up so that my face was inches from his, I ran my hands through the sable locks I loved so much. "No," I answered, "I'm thinking about writing something a little different this time."

"Different?" Adam murmured, brushing my hair back from where it lay draped around us. "Different how?"

"I think I'm done with mysteries for a while," I stated. "I'm going to write a love story instead."

"Oh yeah?" he asked, flipping me easily so I lay beneath him. Above me, he moved his body suggestively against mine. "And what inspired this?"

Breathless, my lips found his, showing him who—not what—had been my inspiration. Within seconds we were one, and as we moved together, I knew that no matter what kind of creative love story I came up with, it was never going to be as amazing as this one right here.

Epilogue

On a snowy afternoon in early December, Adam and I returned from California. We'd stayed longer than expected; hanging out at my house in LA, dinners with Katie and my other friends out there, and just generally sharing with Adam all of my favorite things about Los Angeles. And then we'd traveled up to San Francisco, where we spent Thanksgiving with his parents. Trina and Walker even flew out to meet us, so it turned out to be quite the Ward family holiday.

But now we were back, back on Fade Island. I was too tired to schlep down to the cottage, so I decided to spend the night at Adam's place. In truth, we'd spent so much time together it felt weird to go our separate ways. But go our separate ways we did, because, despite my opting to stay at his place, Adam ended up getting pulled away by business, as usual. Nate had stopped by to tell him he'd missed a lot, so they'd left together to presumably get Adam up to speed.

This was how I found myself curled up in front of a roaring fire in Adam's living room, going through a stack of mail Nate had handed to me before he'd left with Adam. Some of it was mine and some belonged to Adam, so I began the task of separating the pieces into two piles. Not surprisingly, my pile was significantly smaller.

Stifling a yawn, I continued to go through the bills, letters, even a few early Christmas cards. *Adam Ward. Adam Ward, Adam Ward,* the man sure did get a lot of mail. Finally, I reached the final item, a letter, addressed to me. When I noted the return address, despite the heat from the fire, I shivered. It was from Willow Point. And there was only one person I knew who currently resided at Willow Point, Ami.

I fought the urge to toss the envelope into the fire, but curiosity was getting the best of me. Besides, it looked innocuous enough. I couldn't imagine what reason Ami would have for contacting me, especially since the last time I'd seen her she'd been trying to kill me. So yeah, I was a little wary. But at Willow Point Ami was receiving treatment for her mental issues. Maybe this was part of some recovery process. Offer an apology of some sort to help the person move on, that sort of thing. So without further ado, I tore the letter open.

Two photocopied newspaper pages tumbled out. Upon further inspection it appeared both were identical, and both were from the same little-known newspaper in Cambridge, Massachusetts. The one that had published the article detailing Adam's suspicious stock trade from several years earlier that had brought him under the scrutiny of the SEC. In fact, these were exact duplicates of the one I'd found in Adam's desk drawer. *How bizarre.* The only difference was that these were not yellowed, not originals apparently. My heart hammered in my chest. How had Ami found this article? And what would it mean that she had? God, had her ex-lover, Chelsea, told her what Adam had once done—traded on insider info? And why had Ami sent two?

I took a closer look at the two photocopied pages, put them side by side. On first glance, they appeared identical. I scanned each page furtively, awash in a feeling of queasiness. OK, same page, same edition, same date. All the surrounding articles were identical too. But it was the article detailing Adam's stock trade from all those years ago that differed. So they weren't identical after all. One page was an exact copy of the newspaper page I'd found in Adam's desk drawer, the other told quite a different story.

Sure, it detailed the particulars of Adam's fortuitous stock trade. But there was absolutely no mention of any wrongdoing. No words of suspicion, no reference to an SEC investigation. Nothing. In fact, it was actually a rather glowing write-up of Adam. More in line with the kind of thing one might expect from a small publication such as this one. So what the hell did it mean? What was going on here?

I flipped one page over and found a printed note on the back, a personal note from Ami. It read:

Which one is real, Maddy? Did you not wonder why only a tiny newspaper in Cambridge would publish a sensational story involving insider trading, especially if the accused was a wealthy, brilliant MIT student? Would a story so big remain undiscovered? Silly girl! Did you really think Adam would allow you to just happen upon the biggest secret of his life? Put those fine investigative skills back to work. Trouble is brewing. Helena knows something. I suspect Adam does too. And your dear lover's future may depend on you uncovering the real truth. There's just one catch: don't tell Adam anything. Not just yet. Come visit me at Willow Point—I'll give you the next piece of the puzzle. Tick tock, the clock is ticking. Hurry, Madeleine.

See you soon!
—Ami

I stared at the note for ages, the crackling fire filling the silence. Was this some kind of a sick joke? After all, Ami was messed up. But, in my heart, I knew it wasn't.

One of these articles was genuine, and the other was obviously a fake. But if the SEC article was the fake one, meaning Adam had never been under scrutiny, then why had he hid that version in his files in the locked desk drawer? Had he, as Ami seemed to elucidate, *allowed* me to find it? I'd suspected as much at first, but then I concluded the unlocked drawer was Adam's way of letting me uncover what Chelsea had held over his head. Had this not been it? Had he never even been under investigation? Perhaps he had just lucked out in the trade that netted him millions. It would explain why I'd never come across any mention of an SEC investigation. And Ami's words rung true. How could a story so big remain hidden?

But how in the hell did Ami Dubois-Hensley know about all of this? Had she somehow been in on the ruse? Had the article been a decoy? Something to throw me off from discovering the *real* secret Adam held? And did this real secret have something to do with Ami? What did she mean by "trouble is brewing"? And how in the hell did Helena play into all of this? The meaningful glances Adam and Helena had thrown each other's way that day she came over were now looking suspicious.

And if the SEC stuff was all just a smoke screen—one Ami had obviously been in on from the way things were looking—then Adam had never actually told me what Chelsea had been blackmailing him with. And if he'd cooked this up as a diversion, then whatever it was, it had to be something far worse. And that chilled me to the bone. So, yeah, I certainly would be putting my investigative skills back to work. And soon.

In fact one of the first things on my agenda was going to be a visit to my one-time best friend and, more recently, the person who'd attempted to kill me. That was bad. But what was worse was that now I'd have to go to the creepiest place in all of Maine—Willow Point.

Look for another Harbour Falls Mystery—Willow Point—in 2013.

Acknowledgements

It's been a crazy, fun ride getting Harbour Falls ready for publication. Writing the story was only half the battle, one I couldn't have done without the support of family and friends. And lots of Red Bull. Seriously though, I can never thank my parents enough for their encouragement and belief in me. A special acknowledgement goes out to Soul, Biel, Stephie, Lusi, Rosa, Michelle, and so many others for all the encouragement for me to keep writing, especially early on. And a huge shout-out goes to Laura for too many things to list.

Thank you to my Create Space team, especially my editor, Barbara. And a special thanks to Damon at Awesome Book Covers for putting together an amazing cover design. Also over at Awesome Book Layouts, thank you to Benjamin for some very awesome print and e-book layouts, and for being patient with my endless emails and questions.

Finally, to Tom, I couldn't have done it without you. You got me through the rough patches and are always a sounding board for ideas. I appreciate that more than you'll ever know. And here we go again...

About the Author

S.R. Grey is the author of Harbour Falls, first in the Harbour Falls Mystery trilogy. She resides in western Pennsylvania. Grey has both a Bachelor of Science in Business Administration from Robert Morris College, as well as an MBA from Duquesne University. And though she enjoys working in sales and consulting, her true passion lies in writing. Other interests include reading, traveling, running, and cheering for her hometown sports teams.